book of the
little
axe

Also by Lauren Francis-Sharma

'Til the Well Runs Dry

Lauren Francis-Sharma

book of the
little
axe

a novel

Atlantic Monthly Press
New York

FIRST EDITION

Published simultaneously in Canada
Printed in the United States of America

This text was set in 12-pt. Granjon LT
by Alpha Design & Composition of Pittsfield, NH.

First Grove Atlantic hardcover edition: May 2020

Library of Congress Cataloging-in-Publication data is available for this title.

ISBN 978-0-8021-2936-9
eISBN 978-0-8021-4703-5

Atlantic Monthly Press
an imprint of Grove Atlantic
154 West 14th Street
New York, NY 10011

Distributed by Publishers Group West

groveatlantic.com

20 21 22 23   10 9 8 7 6 5 4 3 2 1

To Anand

"A little axe can cut down a big tree."

> —African and Caribbean proverb

"And many strokes, though with a little axe,
Hew down and fell the hardest-timber'd oak."

> —William Shakespeare, *Henry VI,
> Part 3*, Act II, Scene 1

book of the
little
axe

I

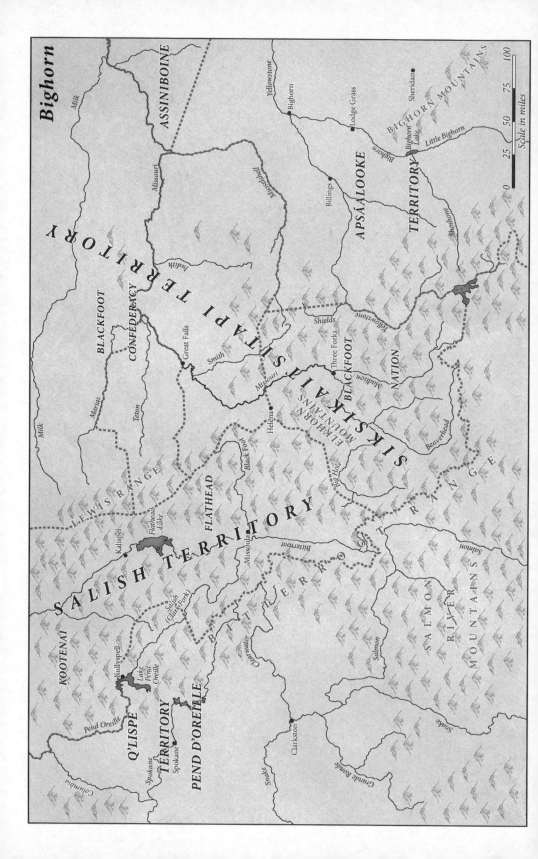

Bighorn

❧

1

1830

Only six of the seven boys saw it. From the branches of a chilled cedar. Through blades of frosty golden grasses. The boys watched its teasing figure stilled in the silver light of that cold winter morning, its horns like serrated half-moons dying at its muscular jaw, the crackling ice echoing over the thrum of the boys' hearts.

The elders had told them to bring back all their horses could carry. But the elders had not meant for the boys to hunt everything. Bighorn sheep were not for the taking. This they were told as small lads, and the boys knew well the warning. They'd heard of men who'd killed sheep on the mountain, knew what those men's fates had been. And so the dilemma for the boys that morning was how to ask and answer the hunter's eternal question: Does one from an abundance breed scarcity?

So upon this land of shining mountains, each waited for the others, listening for quickening breaths of impatience or steady sighs of acquiescence. And from the branches of the cedar, Victor searched below for his friend, Like-Wind, who had been the first to mark the ram. The first to outstretch his solid arms to halt the party's movement, signaling for Victor to climb up between the cedar's limbs for a better look. Once Victor had settled onto a bough, Like-Wind had peered up at him and smiled. Victor knew then that Like-Wind remembered too the story of the boy, a thousand years earlier, taken up onto a ridge of Bighorn by his stepfather and pushed off a steep cliff. The boy's mother mourned, not knowing her son had been rescued and raised by a small flock of bighorn sheep who'd tell the boy, when he became a man, to return to his people and inform them that the collective survival of Apsáalooke and bighorn sheep would thereon be mutually dependent.

"If I live, you live" was what Like-Wind and Victor had decided was the moral of the story. Laughter bubbled inside their noses when they first said this. It was a joke they were certain wouldn't be amusing to their elders.

Now, Victor counted the boys below. There were only five. Their dark squarish heads with sweeping hair, so different from Victor's were almost indistinguishable from one another, but Like-Wind's head, now missing in the count, was different. His head cast a perfect oval. This Victor knew, for he had studied Like-Wind since they were small boys, had watched him grow taller than Victor's reach, observed the muscles in his legs hardening though they'd run the same distances, jumped from the same boulders into the same rivers. As he sat upon the branch, Victor quieted himself, crushing all the wind's words into one long hum, listening for Like-Wind's thick breaths, the sound of a near-man among boys. He found the cragged notes in the tree beside him, where he made out Like-Wind balanced on the edge of a limb, brushing hair from his eye before steadying his arrow. The boys below began moving about, the skins of their moccasins crunching through day-old snow, causing the ram to start. Victor watched as Like-Wind leapt from the tree, his bowed legs like a spider's, carrying him over the white terrain, while the others looked on, their expressions filled with equal parts terror and awe as Like-Wind took aim at the sheep, sized like a bear, that now ran so fast and so hard into the distance it seemed it might run itself into the coming night's sky. But then, it was as if the ram had come upon a mighty boulder, for it stopped upon its cloven hooves, inside a perfect circle of sunlight with rays so comely and brilliant that they shone on the milky fleece of the ram's rump as though gifting the forbidden to Like-Wind.

* * *

Months earlier, alongside the mouth of the canyon, Victor sat with the same six boys to begin his first fast. Below them was the sky, painted sapphire blue, and a sea of red earth not yet covered in frost but at the mercy of low diaphanous clouds that lingered like protective mothers. The rock wall behind them, barbed and looming, protected the boys from an early winter's wind and the rugged peak above them, known as Where They See People, seemed to promise, as it had for genera-tions of boys before, that their visions would soon appear. But several days passed and while the other boys began to see their baaxpée, Victor beheld nothing but bigger sky. He maintained his fast, sweated for additional days, prayed with an earnestness and fervor unmatched, and still Victor's vision did not come. And though this should not have been a source of dishonor, Victor could not be convinced that his humiliation was unfounded.

"Perhaps I had the vision but did not know." Father had laughed with disgrace in his throat, for the other men in the smoke lodge had looked upon them both with quick, sharp glances, reminding them, though it may not have been intended, that they were not Apsáalooke by blood.

"Black-skinned." This was how Father described himself. Half black-skinned, half some unknown tribe, Edward Rose was a revered Apsáalooke war chief who served also as a guide to foreigners. Men who thought themselves explorers, profiteers, compensated Father handsomely to push them beyond the expeditions of Meriwether Lewis and William Clark. And they did so because Edward Rose, though, indeed, black-skinned, had been with the clan most of his life and was nothing short of Apsáalooke.

Victor's mother's birthright could not be so easily explained. Rosa Rendón was of a far different people. A people she'd tried once or twice to explain to Victor in clipped phrases, long before he'd understood he'd need to know of them for his story to be spoken. For Victor, Ma's history began when Father brought her to live with the Apsáalooke after losing his three wives in a horse raid. As it was told, Father's next intended had been chosen—a big-boned widow from a neighboring clan. But before their introduction, Father set off for a yearlong expedition and, to the dismay of the clan's women, returned home with a strange woman, more black-skinned than he, who claimed she was born in the middle of a sea, on a land she called "Trinidad."

It was true that Father and Ma both were and were not Apsáalooke. And Victor could not help but wonder if their origins—if his origins—had anything to do with what he felt was his lack of good fortune.

The boys ran to the sheep that now thrashed against the brittle earth. One arrow in the flank, another in its right leg. As if confused, Lonebull and Fire-Bear looked to Like-Wind who slapped Victor upon his back, congratulating him on their shared kill. Victor smiled, and the boys, who had been ready to praise Like-Wind alone, grinned cautiously, as though both worried about and angry with Victor for believing himself fortunate enough for such a tempting of fate.

"We don't speak of this," Like-Wind warned.

That night, as they ate charred sheep and smoked the pipe with long and heavy drags, the boys agreed they would separate the next morning to meet again on the fourth afternoon beside a cluster of wide-limbed junipers. The one who arrived with the most spoils would be declared the winner.

When Victor woke at dawn, three of the boys were waiting for him to rouse, the creases of sleep still deep on their faces. They told Victor that the kill he'd had with Like-Wind had been a manifestation of Like-Wind's good fortune, not his. That Victor, alone, could never be so lucky. Would never be so lucky again. Like-Wind, overhearing, told the boys that if good fortune could be lost, it could be made again. But the boys laughed and said Victor's good fortune, if ever made, had long ago been unmade.

They had traveled days from camp, down their mountain, and Victor now found himself alone in a region with trees so plentiful there seemed no sky to view. It was the third day and Victor had already taken two stout bucks that he'd hung like meaty nests in a tree. He believed he could win the competition with the buck he sighted now from a large divot where he lay in snow. As he contemplated the shot, he thought over what the boys had told him, thought of how much he'd always wanted the good fortune of which they spoke. He believed he was born unlucky, but he could not have told his friends this, could not have told them how he longed for Like-Wind's physicality, his doting father, his mother's line of chiefs, could not have told them that his Ma had warned him about coveting another's fortune.

As Victor counted the buck's tines—twelve to match each of his years—he wondered whether good fortune could be all the things the boys had said: given, made, unmade.

When Victor had journeyed to sweat the second time, it was against the advice of Father and the akbaalia, both of whom suggested he was not ready. After Victor returned to camp with no report of a vision, Father did not speak again until Victor assured him he'd fasted for more than a week's time, assured him he'd done more than the expected.

"And still no vision?" Father had asked.

Victor had felt the embarrassment of his shortcoming like a brash wave of smoke burning his throat and eyes. He left Father and hurried to deliver the last of the day's water to Ma, who had only just finished dressing his sisters inside the lodge. The little twin girls, happy to see him, clambered about him with their long, pliant limbs while Ma watched Victor from afar. When Ma sent the girls away, she oiled her fingertips with something from a pot kept always beneath the lodge smoke hole, and set Victor down on the mat, kneeling behind him.

"Be still." Ma reached for the bark comb she had fashioned for the bushy hair Victor and his sisters carried like jeweled crowns. She began the part at his hairline, then kneaded the oil onto his scalp, the warmth of it traveling to the base of his neck, her scent a fruit he could not then name, her long dark legs encasing him. "Your time is coming," she had whispered.

Now, as he rooted the bow between his sure hands, his sight firm upon the buck, Victor wondered if Ma might have been correct.

"To properly hunt, one must be unnatural in his arrest, extraordinary in his belay." Ma's father, her Papá, had taught her to catch the prey of her homeland, had taught her to call to them, to bleat, to grunt, and it had been Ma, not Father, to teach Victor that to win at anything one must control all that is within one's control. "Beginning with breath," Ma had said. "Listen for it, capture it, fight to control it; direct Breath, and the heart and mind will follow."

Victor felt his thoughts narrow into the arrow's tip. He saw the buck tumble in his mind's eye long before the bow was emptied. The buck bellowed. Victor issued another arrow, then another, until the buck's figure masked the snow like a great muddy print. It groaned and Victor pitied it, for somehow he already understood this feeling of losing control of one's breath.

All the boys save Like-Wind arrived at the cluster of junipers on the fourth day.

Victor knew he'd have to wait until dusk before the count could begin. They kindled a fire, warmed their lithe bodies at the edges of it, and it was only when the great owl was heard that Victor began to tell the story of his triumphant hunt: seven bears, a talking coyote, four vengeful does, and fawns that bared their teeth. The story was to be funnier and more thrilling than truth, and the boys laughed as he told it, gripping their firm bellies, nodding at him with favor. But Victor had wanted Like-Wind there too, wanted Like-Wind present so that he might feel the heady effect of his victory.

"We will sleep here and wait for him," he told the others.

In the grey light of morning, when Like-Wind still had not come, they returned to camp, expecting to find Like-Wind in the lodge where men went to smoke. They were met at the edge of camp by a troop of girls in quill robes who'd been sent by the women to collect the game. The girls flanked Victor with smiles and praise, their hands reaching out for him, and Victor loved the attention, for it had always been Like-Wind, ropy and powerful and capable of making them laugh, who garnered it.

Father had approached from behind, causing the girls to disperse "Always you with the girls," he said. He wore a fine coat of beaver with a tall, stiff collar framing his face in a way that made him appear more handsome than usual, for his dark skin looked to have its own light and his thick hair rippled like lake waves.

Father's Apsáalooke nickname was Cut Nose, for he had lost the lower half of his left nostril in battle. Yet even with this imperfection, there were few whose figure drew such attention. Father had enough height to share and possessed a chest that burgeoned and arms like oak pillars. As he moved toward Victor's spoils, Victor walked beside him with his own skeletal torso and his own skin, a milky gold like Ma had described her Mamá's skin, and Victor saw nothing of himself in the man.

Father bent down, peeled back the frozen hides, turned over the flanks to find the kill spots. "You lost your whole quiver for just three bucks?"

The girls, still within hearing, covered their mouths and watched Victor's jaw tighten with shame. He swallowed the shame and turned toward the elders who wished to congratulate him, and one elder, Bluegrass, who wished to question Victor on the whereabouts of his son.

Victor, Father, and Bluegrass, along with a dozen others, went off the mountain in search of Like-Wind. They traveled nearly two weeks down to the plains, across Bighorn Lake and along the Shoshone River. When they returned to camp, Victor avoided the other boys, knowing they blamed him for the curse that'd befallen them. He felt the grief rush upon him mighty and terrible, for Victor hadn't known days without Like-Wind. For as long as Victor could recall, the two had eaten beside each other, had left their mothers' warmth to find each other's giggles, and Victor felt the pain of Like-Wind's absence like a grinding in his chest, making him think that control of Breath was an illusion for the heartless.

It was a month after the hunt that the first melt began. Trees sparkled wet with relief, the sky became the color of maple in the early evenings, and the elders were forced to conclude that Like-Wind was lost to them, that he'd met his fate. Like-Wind's mother and sisters mourned in prolonged wails and shaved their heads. When Victor told Ma of his unsparing heartache, of the way dreams of Like-Wind shook him awake at night, Ma told him that his dreams meant there was life there still.

"Just because men say it is so does not mean it is so," she said.

Often, Victor found himself confused by his mother's way of speaking, a spattering of phrases in French, Spanish, and English, sentences that spoke not only of her indifference to linearity but also of her unwillingness to plumb the depths of Apsáalooke words and purposeful Apsáalooke silences. It angered him at times, for it reminded Victor of how he was unable to think or dream or even speak in one tongue, reminded him that he was not of one place and of one people but of many places and of many people he'd never know.

"Maybe Like-Wind paid for my conceit that day." This was not what Victor believed. He believed it had been the forbidden killing that had taken his friend. But he could not tell Ma this.

"Your spirit is not tied to Like-Wind's," Ma said. "You are no more responsible for his absence than an elephant stamping the earth in Africa."

Africa. Elephants. Victor smiled, for it was all he could do with his Ma at times. He wasn't always certain that she understood him so he found it odd that that day he felt comforted by her words. "I only wished to beat him. He was best at everything."

"He wasn't best at being kind."

Ma's words struck Victor as a betrayal, though he knew them to be true.

"Don't humble yourself in victory to make others forget you are victorious."

"You say this because I'm your son."

"Not true."

"Because I'm your *only* son."

She laughed. "I do not—"

Outside, the twins shouted, their delight resounding like chicks at first flight. They peeled back the lodge's flap so Ma and Victor might see their flickering eyes, their four little hands fluttering.

"Like-Wind is here!"

"He's brought something!"

The path through camp was long and winding, lodges lined on both sides for as far as the eye could see, as women cooked at hearths, beat dust from mats, treated nits on the heads of naughty boys with bitter

pulps and seed oils. As Victor hastened alongside his sisters, he worried that Like-Wind might have returned unwell, and felt a nervous
perspiration bubbling at his neck. But as they arrived at the edge of
camp, where the snow still lay quite thick, Victor spied Like-Wind
beneath a yew, still tall, still crimped with muscles, smiling, as the
other warriors surrounded him as though he were victorious and the
women hovered about something Victor could not yet see.

"I see you got lost, eh?" Victor embraced Like-Wind. His damp hair
stuck to Victor's face, and Victor smelled an unfamiliar air upon him.

"Brother, I am never lost." Like-Wind laughed and began telling
Victor his story until Like-Wind's mother, at the center of the women,
called out for him to explain what he'd brought. Like-Wind told them
he believed his vision had meant for him to ride east. That he didn't
know the purpose until he found the girl in a clump of ninebark bushes
peeling off her skin with a whittled branch. He said he assumed that
a Hutanga warrior had crossed paths with the girl, for she had corn
in abundance and the ill-fitting robe she wore, now like a misty web,
had Hutanga paint upon it.

The women quieted, as if saddened by the horrors that lay in the
empty spaces of the girl's story. Then Like-Wind told them of the
whispers he'd heard of wars in the east, tribes forced from their lands.
The women crossed their fists over their hearts, hoping none of it was
true, then Like-Wind's mother told him to carry the sickly girl inside
their lodge. When the women opened the circle, it was only then that
Victor could look upon her.

"What is she?" one of the twins said, picking at the sinew thread
on Victor's leggings.

He paused for a moment, watching the girl's dark hair separate
at her shoulders to show the skin on her back like spackled clay, and
he tried to recall what Ma had called it. "I think she may be a slave."

2

Ma was asked to see about the girl. She picked her special barks and
gathered her dried healing leaves, crushing them with rocks until they

powdered. She told Like-Wind's mother to give the girl nothing else but the medicinal tea. When Ma returned home she stopped at the entrance of the lodge and washed her hands and feet with fresh water. Later, she told Father that "nothing good will come from that girl being here."

After the women wrapped the girl with verbena burn dressing, the girl told the one elder who spoke her tongue that her Shawanwa mother had been taken captive during the Battle of Tippecanoe by a French-speaking warmonger. That when she was born the man moved them west into Arkansaw Territory. For many years her mother planned their escape but remained too affright to leave, until the man, who was also the girl's father, began to take the girl away in the nights. When her mother threatened escape, the man told her mother there was no place he wouldn't uncover them. But still they ran. Until the morning the girl woke to find herself alone in a land she did not know, her mother dead beside her.

The girl spoke Shawanwa, but also a broken English that looped and spiraled like weaving bark. So Like-Wind's sister began teaching her Apsáalooke words: *ishté* for eye, *apé* for nose, *bilé* for water. Static words, though Apsáalooke was a language of movement. The women said the girl was a quick study of words that had no life.

"She's traveled a long way," Father told Ma as they broke fast the following morning. "She's very brave."

Ma nodded, but Victor knew there was something more. When they were alone, he asked her what she thought of the girl and Ma wrinkled her nose as if it had caught a whiff of something sour. "I have little tolerance for people who don't wish to battle their own fright."

Victor did not know what Ma meant, but he had felt, since Like-Wind's return a week earlier, that there had been a difference in the texture of his days, a coarsening he could not yet grasp. He did not understand why Like-Wind had left the way he had. To Victor, it had felt like a small betrayal. Yet there were no words between men that could convey such feelings, so Victor decided to give it time.

Meanwhile, the girl, though made to feel she would be accepted by the women who nursed her, had little idea that many referred to her as "Yellow-Eye," for her skin was quite fair and her ways not Apsáalooke ways. Yellow-Eye, or baashchiile, meaning "one who wishes for everything he sees," was the name the Apsáalooke had given to two of the earliest Europeans they encountered. Victor did not know if the girl wished for anything other than Like-Wind, but to the women of the clan that seemed too much want. The girl was plain, the women said of her, wide-eyed as if in a never-ending state of surprise; her stringy hair lacked elegance, and she had a habit of nibbling at her upper lip, leaving it pink and swollen—a habit the elders suggested might be indicative of a weak mind.

In the weeks that followed her arrival, the girl rarely left Like-Wind's side. With this, Victor and Like-Wind had had little time to catch up their stories. So when Bluegrass asked Victor what Like-Wind had told him about the girl, Victor was unable to answer.

"Circles the Earth with His Toe," Bluegrass said, using the endearment he'd bestowed upon Victor as a child. "I worry about Like-Wind. I need you to learn more about what he intends to do with the girl."

The next night, after the clan was seated around the nightfires, Victor squeezed himself into the space between Like-Wind and the girl. Turning his back to her, Victor found his friendship with Like-Wind unchanged, for Like-Wind laughed his buoyant laugh, and each settled across from the other like wings on opposite sides of a dove. It seemed only seconds after Victor felt the relief of this confirmation that the girl mounted him. She pummeled Victor with heavy fists, which felt like logs jamming into the flesh of his neck and arms, making Victor feel as if he should pound the girl's face into the earth.

"Let off!" Like-Wind pulled the girl away. But she bit at Like-Wind's hand, and while the women who'd once cared for her sat aghast, the girl bared her pink gums and growled.

Later, Ma told Victor that his restraint had been commendable but that he needed to keep his distance from Like-Wind and the girl. "Remember what I said about her fright? Wait until Like-Wind comes to you," Ma said.

It was the next afternoon when Like-Wind asked Victor to walk along a path of still-dormant grasses, away from the stack of lodgepoles the women had begun collecting. When they came to the creek, they pelted rocks as if angry with it, the sheets of ice floating, unconcerned. There, Like-Wind apologized as though he could speak for the stranger among them, tossing his hair over and again, a thing he did only when nervous.

"Brother, she's not well," Like-Wind said. "But she'll mend."

"She's mad! You can't heal madness."

"She lived with many who were captives like her. This fact is shameful to a proud girl." In Like-Wind's earnest expression, Victor was certain Like-Wind had taken a serious severe liking to the girl. "They were beaten and put to work. They all ran away."

Victor knew what Like-Wind wouldn't say. Ma had told Victor long ago that people believed only those with black skin might be undone in this way. Victor understood that many in the tribe believed death to be better than any enslavement by Yellow-Eyes, but Ma had told him that there should be no embarrassment in coming from a people strong enough to battle for life. She told him that choosing to live is not the same as being scared to die. Victor didn't know if he believed in Ma's words. But he knew Like-Wind had never had to twist his mind to make sense of them. Not until then. And it seemed only because of the girl that Like-Wind could now admire the survivor's courage.

"Bluegrass is worried about you."

"My father worries too much," Like-Wind said. "He says the girl is not suitable for life with us, says he will smoke against her if I don't let her alone."

"Bluegrass asked Father and Ma if she could stay with us, in our lodge."

"She would never agree to that," Like-Wind said, as if surprised at the suggestion.

"I think you mean Ma wouldn't agree to that."

Like-Wind's nose flared and Victor knew they'd come to the end of their talk. It had gone nothing like Victor planned. When they returned to camp, they seemed further apart, and Victor thought about the grinding in the chest he'd felt when he believed Like-Wind to be dead. He wanted things back as they were.

"Tomorrow," Victor said, "bring her with us to care for the horses."

The next morning Like-Wind and the girl met Victor in the open fields near Stink Hill. The winds there carried words so they spoke little and instead unhobbled three horses, tethered them, led them to drink. At Like-Wind's urging, Victor showed the girl how to brush the horses, remove their loose hairs, trim fetlocks, and the girl seemed pleased, fawning over the beauty of Victor's favorite mares. Victor thought then that a softening had come over the girl, and he, at once, saw a glimpse of what Like-Wind had seen in her, a gracefulness in her manner that perhaps he'd overlooked.

"Brother, you'll sit with us at the nightfires tonight?" Like-Wind said this when they were back at camp, pulling his hair behind his ears, making his face open before looking to the girl, as if for approval.

That night the three of them sat side by side at the nightfires. Like-Wind and Victor told the girl stories of their hunts, and of the first time they smoked a pipe, when Victor vomited chunks and Like-Wind curled into a ball and sucked his thumb. The girl laughed a charming laugh, and Victor found himself watching her with new eyes, this girl who smelled candied, like fresh honey, her mouth pregnant with words as she struggled in Apsáalooke to tell them of the place she once lived, four moons away, off a soft clay road.

"My mother said we might have to run from my father forever," the girl told them.

Victor did not understand this life the girl described. Not the work, the harsh words, the violence. Not the father who did no fathering. He did not understand, in all the terrains he'd traveled, where there could be a place where one could not run or jump or speak or laugh or bathe or eat without permission, where one's next breath turned on the whim of men predispositioned to find one's breath dispensable.

"Did you see her dead? Your mother?" Victor was not certain why he wanted to know this. But he'd imagined that the story the girl would tell of that moment would be gripping.

The girl leaned back onto both arms. She did not seem to like his question, but he could not swallow it back down. "Like-Wind told me you went to sweat three times."

The girl uttered the words with great satisfaction, and Like-Wind shrugged, for he had told Victor many times that there should be no shame in seeking a quest. Yet Victor wondered, if this were true, why the subject had come up at all between Like-Wind and the girl.

"Is it because you are not Apsáalooke?"

"My father's blood is not Apsáalooke blood, but he is still a chief."

The girl grinned a grin that would not be considered sister to a smile. "You are not your father." She bit her lip, gnawing the thick skin that nested there. "You are nothing like him."

Victor knew Like-Wind had told her this too.

The girl went on. "And why does your mother stare at me so?"

The girl's gaze rested on Ma, who sat plaiting the twins' hair. Victor watched his mother, her dark fingers slithering like snakes in a scorched field, and he felt a new shame. And this new shame swelled like it had its own pride when the girl winced at Ma, who was by then smiling down at the twins.

"She doesn't belong here," the girl said. "And you don't either."

Like-Wind nudged the girl to quiet her while Victor searched the campsite, trying to make sense of her words. The clan had spent the end of fall and all of winter at that camp, Awáassheele Hátchke, at the foot of the Bighorns, near the mouth of Lodge Grass Creek and within view of Red Springs Canyon. There, no fewer than a thousand men and women, boys and girls, had been protected by firm saplings, tall grasses, tribal sentries who stood at night like stout hills, monitoring their lodges constructed of brightly painted pelts and hides and grand lodgepoles that gave company to the heavens. The women made every new campground home, willing the mountains to welcome them, and each night they lit the center of camp where there was always laughter. So much laughter. Victor looked now at the boys who raised a new blaze in honor of the lost warriors and another so that the women could see the dances of their fat-bellied children, and he thought that this place, among these people, was all he'd ever known. If he didn't belong there, where then did he belong?

"What does that mean?" he said to her.

The girl pursed her lips as if to grin again, and it was then that Victor felt a pinch upon his ear, the cartilage in a hot, angry kiss with itself as Ma upraised him with the hooks of her nails and pulled Victor along by the seat of his leggings, her French words plummeting into the stunned silence of the circle: "Ne sois pas bête!"

Overcome by Ma's reaction, Victor did not resist Ma, and she said nothing to explain herself as they made their way through a rich black dark, between serviceberry shrubs whose debris created gruff earthen runners beneath them. When they reached the lodge, Ma lit a torch and, as always, Victor's eyes were drawn to the jagged lines along her hairline, the carved necklace upon her throat like a tributary to deep cracks of tissue across her breasts.

"Why'd you do that?" He straightened his leggings, brushed Ma's finger smudges from his arms, embarrassed, not solely because Apsáalooke did not correct their children in such ways but because Apsáalooke boys Victor's age were no longer taken up by their mothers.

"That girl is Like-Wind's business, not yours."

"We were only talking."

"I saw the way you looked at her," Ma said.

"What way?"

"Like your eyes have teeth."

Father arrived then and reminded Ma that to be among the Apsáalooke is to be as they are. He told Ma that without brothers, without her own family, she must confer the disciplining of Victor to men—uncles like Bluegrass and other ā´sa'kua in the clan—for people must begin to regard Victor as a man.

"Then take him with you on your expedition. Let him see the world like a man should." Ma reminded Father that Victor had learned nearly everything a young warrior was to learn—to run fast and hard, to swim without the need for breath, to track under moonlight, to hunt until his back could carry no more. And that he had completed two of the four required war honors: taken both a weapon and a horse from the enemy.

But for Father, none of this seemed enough. "I leave in the morning. Forty men I'm leading this time. I cannot manage the boy."

"Aah," Ma said. "I'm not to embarrass him because he's a man, but when I ask you to take him, he's a boy, yes?"

Later that evening, after Ma and Father had quarreled about Father's refusal and quarreled again about Ma's insistence on quarreling over his refusal, Ma took the twins to the lodge where the men smoked and asked to speak to Father outside. The twins told Victor later that Ma had requested that Father visit the akbaalia and one of the clan's chiefs. "He is getting confused. The girl is making things complicated for him," Ma told him.

"She is just a girl," Father said.

"Bluegrass does not think so."

"When it comes to Like-Wind, Bluegrass has no mind," Father said.

"I want Victor to go again to sweat."

"You know it is not any chief who decides when he should—"

"There must be someone to speak to."

"They'll tell you the same as before. You know what must be done first."

The twins said Ma paused for some time. "I cannot," she said. "I will not."

"Then there is no reason for me to speak to anyone."

When Father returned inside, Ma and the twins followed. The other men and Victor, who had been smoking the pipe, sat upon their elbows as Father reached for the maps he had stored there, the ink smudged, the hide furrowing. Father began to refold them, pretending Ma and the girls were not there, and Victor imagined then that Father was recalling the risk he'd taken bringing Ma, an outsider, to live with him. Imagined how Father must have wished after all their years together that Ma would better conform.

"I leave early in the morning," Father said.

Ma noticed then the expressions of the other men, as if they meant to suggest that she should let Father alone.

When Father woke the girls the next morning, he wore the Yellow-Eyes' clothing—buckskin trousers with buttons and a loose tunic hidden beneath a fringed and hooded capote. He performed his usual ritual of sweeping the twins into his arms, their four cheeks like hitched wheels, their smothered cries achy to the heart of anyone within hearing. "We'll meet again soon." Father set the girls down and lit an offering, fanning the spectral billows of smoke, sprinkling dirt over water, left to right, to bless his family in his absence.

"Come," he said to Victor, touching the crown of Victor's head, then he moved toward Ma who requested that he bring back a diary and a quill pen. Father told her he liked when she gave him tasks and would do his best, then he touched Ma's face, as she regarded him with anxious eyes, the quarrel from the previous night no longer in view.

"Please mind yourself." Ma thumped his chest. "That man, Glass, plunged into the stream to save his own life. But not you," she teased him.

Ma, of course, was speaking of some years earlier, when Father had been traveling with a Yellow-Eyes named Hugh Glass, and they'd come under attack. Every man in his crew, save Father, retreated, including Glass, who'd plunged into the water, while Father, alone on the shore, covered them against an advancing clan of Cheyenne.

"That was war," Ma said, "so you had to make the enemy cry. But now, you're a guide. There is no honor in dying while leading Yellow-Eyes across this land. You have children here. Remember you are to return."

Father nodded and grinned an uneasy grin before pulling Ma aside. This was all Victor overheard:

"Akbaalia says you must do it first," he whispered. "For the boy."

Ma stared at Father as if to say something she could not speak. They pressed their heads together before Father gathered his belongings and departed from camp.

3

The other women laughed and teased Ma, said she was heartsick that Father had left. That she didn't know her toes from the hairs in her bum. Ma giggled, clapping her cheeks coyly, her eyelashes batting like marauding moths, pretending the worry that had made her mouth a worn horseshoe was because of Father. But Father was gone much of each year, and Victor, though certain that something else was the cause of Ma's worry, did not know the cause was him.

It was nearly a week after Father's departure when Bluegrass sent the girl to live in a lodge across the valley, a half-hour's walk from

Like-Wind. There she would be welcome, would be given work. Bluegrass told Like-Wind he was no longer permitted to see the girl and that he—Bluegrass—had arranged for a two-party delegation to ride east in search of Shawanwa who might claim her. It was only a matter of days after this that the girl found her way back and began seeking out Victor. Victor knew the girl hoped to be in proximity to Like-Wind, but that didn't lessen Victor's elation. He wanted the girl to favor him. It was a fact that both shamed and propelled him. And though perhaps he should have thought better of his pursuits, Victor felt Like-Wind had given this opening to him, for he'd made himself scarce, refusing to complete his chores, skipping their hunts, hiding himself away in his mother's lodge as if in sufferance. When Victor visited him in the mornings, they ate in a cloak of quiet, and afterward, Like-Wind wouldn't accompany Victor to care for the horses or to make arrowheads. So the girl and Victor were left alone and all seemed well between them until one misty morning when they roamed along the edges of a field and noticed horses struggling to find fodder. In the four days prior, rain had come down with such cruelty that some of the earth looked to have been bashed into the muddied pools where it now swirled.

"We'll need to move the horses to higher ground," Victor told the girl.

As they trampled into the morass to tether the horses, the girl stood smiling beside the runtiest of the stallions, and pointed her pinky at its tangled tail.

"Your hair is like this, yes?" she said.

Victor had never thought of his hair as being like that of a horse's. In his hands, his hair felt like the lacy leaf of a maple or the ruche of a spider's web, but if the girl was asking if he had ever wondered why his hair, why his mother's and father's and sisters' hair, was so very different from all in their tribe, the answer, of course, was yes, he had. He'd admired, sometimes even envied, the straighter hair of others, occasionally wishing for the easy flow and the growth that descended. But Ma seemed to know that such desire would come and she'd told him long ago that in the faraway world of their ancestors, straight hair was an anathema. She laughed when she said the word. Said that it meant her people would have wondered what there was to do with such straight hair, would have wondered why it did not have the same powers of stability and dexterity, did not have the ability to captivate light and resist air. And any time Victor questioned why he'd been made so different, Ma would smile with her eyes and touch his hair, and her hands inside his twisty strands, softly grazing his scalp, always made sense to him.

But now, looking at the girl's gnawed lip curl up as she pointed at the tangled, coarse hair of the horse's tail, he could no longer remember the feeling Ma's fingers had offered him. And so he laughed, hoping his feelings of inadequacy did not reek.

It was not long after that the girl asked Victor to walk with her, south alongside the creek, down its shaded path, the claret cliffs in the distance like cones. He had hoped she would offer a declaration of some kind, for those banks were known to be a lover's place. Ma had warned him against "sins of the flesh" when he'd before met other girls there, and Victor remembered laughing at the earnestness with which Ma spoke of unrighteousness, of a man-god named Jesus, but as the girl walked alongside him in her blue robe jingling with elk teeth at the shoulders, appearing graceful and regal and lovely, Victor understood better why Ma had spoken of tempering desires.

They searched for spent arrowheads that afternoon, climbing up the chilled earth, the limbs above them still low from the weight of winter's snow. When they came to the top of the hill overlooking the creek, the girl stopped and stared into the frothing waters.

"When the sun warms the earth, we'll look for arrowheads in the water," he told her. "I've found many at the bottom, between stones."

The girl's eyes widened. "I can't swim."

For Victor, to swim was as natural as to walk. There was joy in water. And at that time of the year, water was everywhere. Trickling down the face of mountains like a profuse sweat, overflowing onto the banks, flooding already muddied soil that seemed to wish for no more. "Then we must teach you."

The girl said nothing more until she asked that they stop and sit in the striped light of the afternoon. Victor reached for a shiny pebble and began showing her how to chip at its skin to create a head. The girl nodded, but her eyes flitted about as if she'd heard something.

"Who's there?" She stood and Victor readied his bow but heard nothing for some time until limbs began to shake and dried leaves snapped, and from behind a thicket of branches came Like-Wind, his large hands outstretched before him as if waiting for a proper welcome.

The girl's face, slightly cracked with worry, tightened until Like-Wind moved forward to embrace her. Like-Wind mouthed "thank you" to Victor and when the two broke from each other, Like-Wind held out the girl as if to inspect her and said to her, "I thought we would now be alone."

The girl turned to Victor as if Victor should've known what to do next. Like-Wind arched his eyebrows and cocked his head, and the girl peered up at Like-Wind and grinned as though the two of them shared some special love language. And Victor heard blood ringing in his ears.

"You don't need that tree here." Victor said this about Like-Wind, speaking in Apsáalooke, the words coming sharp as if from a snake's tongue, before kicking up his leg in a slow arc, pitching dirt onto Like-Wind's thighs, though still surprised when Like-Wind steered a solid punch into the side of his neck.

The girl cried out as if she'd been hit, and Victor looked to her before leveling his head into Like-Wind's midsection, locking them together in a way that feigned a momentous battle, entangling his arms between strands of Like-Wind's hair.

The girl hurried away and Victor broke from Like-Wind, running after her, pulling her into him. "Don't touch me!" she said.

"What did I do?"

"I didn't come here for you," she said.

Like-Wind was behind them now, his breaths heavy and shrill.

"You don't know your place," the girl said. "You think you're the same as them—as us—but you're not."

"Did he tell you to say this?" Victor pointed at Like-Wind.

"He doesn't have to. Look at your mother." The girl said the words as though certain they would feel like icy lances in Victor's heart. But he would not let on that she had hurt him.

"This is the news you carry?" Victor said. "I've told you my mother is from Trinidad."

"She probably escaped from wherever that is."

"Escaped?" he said. "You mean, like you?"

Victor thought of Ma's chest, the scars about which she never spoke, meandering from her neck to her waist like a wild river, and he wondered what the girl had heard about Ma, wondered what he didn't know about his own mother.

"She's making you believe you're free," she said, "but you can't be free."

Victor didn't wish to hear any more from this girl who had only just arrived. He was angry in a way he hadn't been ever before, and so he left them and returned to camp. In the smoke lodge, he found Bluegrass, lying on his back, his eyes open as if he'd been waiting to hear what more he must do to keep the girl from his son.

Victor could not draw the line between confusion and anger. Night after night, he sat alone at the nightfires, biting his nails into flat-top hills, watching the girl, who sat far from him, gnawing at her lip, waiting for the one moment when she would catch Like-Wind's eye. But Like-Wind did not look her way. And he did not look toward Victor either. Not long after Victor told Bluegrass of Like-Wind's meeting with the girl, Bluegrass and the āʹsaʹkua called a meeting with Like-Wind to remind him that he had been chosen by the First Maker. The men told him that one day he would be a great chief of the tribe and that his destiny was predetermined so long as he remained on his path. That path, they'd said, did not include the girl.

Victor knew Like-Wind had only ever wanted the future the elders now promised him. They had both dreamt of growing up to be wise counselors, brave men. The boys had agreed that after taking their first wives, they'd build their lodges side by side. They planned that their children would be the best of friends, that their mothers would grow old together, and that their wives would make meals over the same fire—meals the two would share as they discussed how to maintain all Apsáalooke ways upon Bighorn, how best to hunt, how to raise up their children in a world free from the Europeans who swelled in number each year.

Victor was certain the girl's hopes had been dashed and was not surprised when she sat beside him and told him she was sorry for her words. And Victor was happy.

Each night thereafter, the girl told him more of her life in Arkansaw Territory, told him about living without knowing if a future was promised. "My mother hoped only to be free," she said one night. "And now that I'm free I do not know what else there is to hope for." So Victor told the girl she could share the life he and Like-Wind had planned. In Victor's mind, the girl would be his wife and Like-Wind would choose another, but that evening Victor watched the girl find Like-Wind's eyes across the nightfire circle; eyes that were big and wanting and filled with regret.

Victor was not often one to despair, but over the coming days he felt himself low, with a new rage forming beneath his skin like a slow burn. He felt he was a man with an innocent boy's heart, a boy with a man's wicked desires. As the days passed, Victor worried, but Ma, she worried more. She kept watch over him, setting his favorite stews before him at the far end of the lodge, encouraging the twins to ply him with questions, until one night Ma told him she'd been having unsettling dreams and wished her children close in the night. Father had told Victor long ago that Ma sometimes had terrible dreams, that in her homeland, history had been written and the memories she brought were not pleasant. So, Victor waited until the twins slept before finding a place next to Ma's mat. That night rain fell like pounding fists, the mountain's walls fended off lightning while the torches shook to dim and the lodge grew cold. Ma, half awake, reached out to touch Victor's hair, and as he began to sleep, Victor felt himself loosen, felt a relief he'd forgotten he could feel. And he thought he might lie next to Ma forever, happy.

There was only darkness—a glaring, impenetrable darkness—when he felt his breath stymied. The palm smothered his mouth, the thumb bore down upon his nostrils, and he flailed, bitter and urgent, as he heard the mountain wind rush into the open flap of the lodge, shouting gusts as if pained. Victor was certain he was dreaming, yet he was unable to open his eyes. He smelled the breath of someone he could not name, a warm and pickled air, and through a blur of raindrops, he thought he saw in the light of a torch the salt whites of eyes and an expression, hardened and terrible.

"Now," Ma whispered. "Wake up."

Victor wiped spittle from his mouth and fought to put time between breaths. Ma hovered and her skin smelled of outdoors, sap and dew, the odors of dawn and sleeplessness. He listened for the sounds of war—the earth rattling beneath them, the dogs yowling, a drum thumping—but heard little more than the heavy resting breaths of his sisters, one wrapped within the other like a budding flower.

"It was a dream," he said.

"You too? I suppose I'm not surprised."

"I couldn't see a face."

"We are in for something. And not a good something." Ma dusted her hands as if to wipe away the thought and began to leave before turning back toward Victor. "Give yourself a break from that troublesome girl. And get to the horses early. The rain fell heavy again last night."

As Victor exited the lodge he noted that the aspens were budding and the mountain goats grazing a little lower than expected for that time of the year. It seemed spring had fully arrived. And he felt his tread lighter for it. He ran for the day's water, tended to the horses, and it was late afternoon when Victor found Bluegrass among the other elders, near the foot of Wolf Mountains, drinking chilled water they'd carried from a spring. There, Victor saw wildflowers blooming as plentiful as pine needles in bell-shaped blues and purple whorls and spiky pinks on bright green stems. Bluegrass looked as surprised to see Victor as Victor was to see those early flowers. Victor assured him he'd not come to deliver death news.

"Like-Wind and the girl are not over." Victor said this as if Bluegrass had asked for the news.

Bluegrass tilted his head, for the sunlight dressed the side of his leathered face. "You wish for him to make room for you. Yes?"

Victor wanted the girl. This, he knew, was not a well-kept secret. But as he stood before Bluegrass, Victor did not know his true motive for going to speak to him, save he did not believe things had turned out in the best way.

"What I want for my son, I want for you," Bluegrass said. "Cut Nose is my brother, and he would not like this any more than I." The other men had finished resting, so Bluegrass stood along with them, his stomach less firm than it had once been, falling over his belt like an udder. "Neither of you should be thinking of a future with this girl," he said. "Men who lay claim to her are searching for her. She'll have to go soon."

"How do you know this?"

"How do you know the sun has risen? What kind of question do you ask your ā´sa'ke?" Bluegrass adjusted his bow. "There are enough Apsáalooke girls here. It's insulting that you and Like-Wind fall over this plain girl who is *not* Apsáalooke."

"Ma is not Apsáalooke. But she has been a good wife to Father. You must've told him the same when he brought her to the mountain."

Bluegrass almost smiled. "That was different. Your mother has never been plain." Victor had never heard any of the men speak of Ma in this admiring way. More than once, Ma had been honored for her contributions against their enemies. Though she was not exceptionally strong, she was known to be vicious in battle. Yet this felt different. "And you, Circles the Earth with His Toe, you are not like this girl."

"No? We are both outsiders."

"Young eyes are not yet strong eyes." Bluegrass shook his head, touched the strap that lay upon his chest. "But tomorrow, take her across Little Bighorn and wait by the big chokecherry. I will send Like-Wind. He'll tell her that she is to forget him. He is ready to be done with her. This I know. After you return, we will smoke and I'll tell you some things."

The next morning Victor sent the twins with a message for the girl to meet him. The horses had taken another wicked battering from the heavy rains, and Victor brushed them, led them to drink, inspected the frogs in their hooves, then brought back those to be used for the day's hunt. He hoped to meet the girl before the end of morning, but Ma had other plans.

"I sent the girls to Eagle Foot," she said, referring to the third of Father's three wives. "She will mind the twins. You and I have much to do."

Victor was certain the twins had told Ma he was meeting the girl. This is how, later, he would make sense of the lying. "You've run out of your salve. Martinique has a little cut on her hock. I'll see what I can forage for her," he said.

Ma looked startled. Other than her children, Ma's most cherished possession was her mare, Martinique. No one in the clan owned a horse but Ma. Horses belonged to the collective. But when Father brought Ma to live with him, he asked the elders to make an exception for her, this woman who had traveled across seas and many lands with this beloved horse. Martinique had been named after the place where Ma's mother was born. She was a graceful old gal with a faded black coat and oversized hooves, and she was as steady and as charming as any. Ma would not keep Victor from leaving if it was on Martinique's behalf.

"Is it bad?"

"No, I would tell you." Victor motioned with his hands for her to remain calm. "As soon as I'm finished, I'll find you and we'll go together and fix her up. I'll be quick," Victor said.

Victor hurried to the boulder where he and the girl were to meet. She emerged from behind him, said she'd been there too long. Her eyes were distant.

"I had to finish my work." He told her Like-Wind planned to meet them, that he would take her to him and they rode together across the shallowest part of the river and up the left bank, climbing a rocky path until they came to the chokecherry where Bluegrass said they were to wait. The girl was excited, and though Victor felt guilty, he knew that once Like-Wind had a chance to put her down, he would be there to mend her heart.

"What do you think he will say?" she said.

"I don't know. He sent the message with my sisters. Little girls don't remember such things."

"You should've asked them again." The girl knelt in the soppy earth and when she looked up at him, she began to laugh, the sound like a tongue smacking erupting from her soft mouth as though she were a coyote devouring fresh liver. "Are you scared of me?" she said.

He was, indeed, scared of something within her, but also he wished to feel her lips pressed into his, to have her hips dance atop his fingertips. Nothing felt the way he thought it might feel anymore. Even his thoughts did not feel like his own.

"On dirait que tu es un bébé?" The girl smirked at his surprise. "The King of France used to own the Arkansaw River. French is that river's language." The girl crossed her arms over her bosom and leaned into the tree as if the jagged bark at her back were feathers.

"I speak this language too," Victor said, wondering if the girl knew that he understood, understood she had called him a baby.

"Yes, I heard your mother the day she pulled you away from the fire." The girl pitched clumps of muck from beneath her fingernails toward him, then said, "I was scared when we crossed the river today. The water was loud."

"The rain has made it wild. If it doesn't rain again, it will calm in a few days," he said. "But where we crossed was shallow."

The girl searched the land around them. The clouds bloomed and hung low atop the muddied hills, and small patches of green stood stark against drowsy grasses. "How long will Like-Wind be?"

When she spoke Like-Wind's name, something inside Victor rose up. A wave of remorse, perhaps, for Like-Wind was his closest friend, and Victor knew he should have asked Like-Wind for his blessing, but Victor also knew that to ask a question, one must be prepared for any answer. And Victor wished only for an answer that would clear the path for his desire.

He and the girl moved closer to the river, for the trees were obstructing their view of the valley. It was chilly—a spring kind of chilly—and the skin on the girl's horribly notched back shone more brittle. Victor wondered what kind of beating could break skin in that way. And he wondered if what he felt for her wasn't tied to what he didn't know of her.

"Are we in the correct place?" she said.

Victor took off his moccasins and sat down. He loved the feel of the cold earth between his toes. Loved to listen to Little Bighorn's currents thrash against stodgy parties of boulders before hurrying away. "Yes, of course."

The girl spent the better part of the next two hours surveying the empty banks, searching for the oval crown of Like-Wind's head in breaks between grassy knolls, sighing at the river's grumblings, disappointed in the land's failure to present Like-Wind.

"Did you lie to me?" she said.

The accusation surprised Victor, and it made him nervous though he had no reason to be. Yet he too wondered where Like-Wind could be.

"I know your kind. You are lying," she said. "I want to return to camp. Now."

"My kind?" he said. "I told you he'll come." Victor wanted to wait. He was certain the conversation between Like-Wind and the girl would be short. They need only be patient. "We will wait just a bit longer."

"I don't wish to be here in the darkness with you."

Misunderstanding her meaning, thinking the girl was worried about impending nightfall, Victor said, "I could never get lost here."

"I know why you brought me to be alone with you. Take me back."

Victor was angry now. The accusation, the insinuation, her tone. He wished to punish her, to make her wait until near dusk, so she would know he was not to be her footman.

She began to walk away, while he remained seated, watching her as she moved down the bank's decline. The big sky, rife, looked prepared to drop its clouds, and the river water, having yet to reach spring temperatures, spewed frigid bursts of pellets, its music deafening.

"Don't," he said quietly, not wanting to beg, not wanting her to think he would run behind her again. "Just wait."

Victor thought that maybe the girl could not hear him, for she moved rapidly, her shins and knees now covered in froth. She must have been cold. She turned back toward him and he stood so she could see his mouth form big circles of sound.

"I'll take you back," he said. "The water is deeper here."

"You're lying. You told me it was shallow!"

The water swooshed about the girl's waist now, splashing along her back and rib cage, disturbing her balance enough to trouble Victor. He watched as her eyes bloomed like two mounds of dry dust in wind, as though surprised that the water flushed about her in that way, and she cinched her shoulders as if to keep her arms from falling away. Victor slipped on his moccasins and turned quickly to loose the stallion, but when he looked again toward the river, he saw in the girl's movements, a vile fearfulness, the kind of fearfulness Victor knew too well.

"Come out!" Victor dropped the lead, noticing the whirlpools and ovals forming around her, and knew that one wrong step would send the girl downriver. He hoped the waters would still themselves long enough for him to reach her and prayed that his forward motion would not panic her, and so he smiled a smile so gaping he could have been crying. And when she saw it, the girl outstretched her arms, and those gnawed lips went pouty, and Victor thought for a moment that the girl was laughing. And so he laughed. And he hoped that the laughter would cut a hole in the thick slab of fear crushing his chest as he watched her lose her footing and wobble upon one solid leg. He felt the waters part for him, as if they remembered him; felt the sturdy rocks beneath his feet, and when he reached for her, she fell from his grip, her head slamming into the one boulder that shouldn't have been there, the one that had urged the rushing water to go around it, and Victor saw the girl's eyes close and saw that pouty mouth snarl like the day she bared her gums at him, and her blood made tiny rainbows in the water's froth before the currents carried her away.

Like-Wind had told Victor her name once, but the girl had told Like-Wind never to speak it. That her name was only for her mother's tongue. Victor called it out now. "Under Foot!" And he wondered what kind of mother would give her child a name meant to both implore and dismiss, and he wondered about a father who would allow his son to be known by Victor rather than Circles the Earth with His Toe, and he felt he had been right about the two of them needing each other.

Victor plunged beneath the plane. The mighty force of the currents roiled beneath the surface and Victor saw nothing through the darkened muddied waters. He resurfaced, shivering, panicked, and scrambled out to get a clearer look downriver. He saw the girl's head bubbling along the surface, and he dodged around boulders and trampled over wet, gummy leaves, running faster, his arms pumping, the pea gravel and shale stabbing the soles of his feet. "Hold on!" The girl's arm slammed into what looked to be a boulder bridge—one that perhaps she could grasp until he reached her. He swore he could hear her fighting for her breath, her blood pounding inside his ears, her tears crackling like dry twigs in fire. She went beneath again, until her arm broke the water's surface once more, only to be swallowed again by the currents. Victor threw himself at her, splitting the icy tide ringlets in halves, again and again, until he reached that arm, which revealed itself as a rotted branch.

4

It was nearing sunset, and the ice hung in the air like fine thorns on Victor's still-wet skin. The men searched along the stony banks, halfhearted but undeterred, while the women whispered that the girl had gotten her medicine, that dying had been her fate, and that spilling tears for her would be proof of callowness.

Ma called Victor into the lodge. The other women and children, who had earlier convened, left them alone. Victor and Ma watched each other in the quiet.

"Are you all right?" Ma searched his eyes, but Victor knew how not to let her in. "I've asked Bluegrass to request a meeting for me with the Chiefs' Council."

"For what reason? They didn't call us to sit." Victor had set his moccasins to dry next to the flame Ma had started. He gathered them now. They were damp still, the sinew glistening.

"You must know this isn't yours to carry," she said. "You must hear it from someone other than me."

Outside, the clan's members began moving toward the nightfires. The twins entered the lodge expecting Ma to join them. When they saw Victor, they rushed to him, pressing their cold noses against his, promising him that the First Maker would find the girl.

"Let us go," Ma said.

Victor followed Ma along the dirt path. The newly lit torches were like dull eyes in the light of dusk. Victor did not yet know how he should feel. Whether he should grieve when he believed it possible that the girl had made it to land or whether he should allow himself to remember how he'd let her walk into the water knowing she could not swim.

The twins ran ahead with Eagle Foot, while Ma and Victor waited outside the council tent. Hours passed, and as the night descended, the stars pocked the sky like a plague of silver, and the moon shone as just a sliver of its old self. Victor felt sorrow like a terrible itch, and as he sat on a stone seat, watching Ma pace to the beat of drums that cracked the air like lashing branches, he wondered how he would stand before the council chiefs with their skeptical, rutted brows and explain something he could not.

Of course, Victor should have expected to see Like-Wind. But Victor had given little thought to Like-Wind after returning from the river. And Ma, with her ears to the skin of the council chiefs' tent, did not notice Like-Wind coming from behind them, swinging a wooden club with such force that Victor was thrown from his seat. When Victor scrambled from the dirt, he felt his bones throbbing, the pain so vivid his teeth clenched, and when he turned to see Like-Wind with his hair pulled from his reddened face, Victor thought for the first time that he might very well like to see his best friend dead.

Victor searched for the right stone while Ma shouted, the drums from the nightfires swallowing her words. Victor knew he'd done everything wrong, and yet still he didn't believe he deserved to be punished more. Not then, not when his heart felt heavy. He was tired of having to prove himself worthy, tired of failing to do so. So Victor threw the stone, larger than his own head, at Like-Wind and watched Like-Wind's neck wrench back and blood run into Like-Wind's eyes, watched as Like-Wind swiped the blood away and reached for the knife on his belt, fending off Victor, cutting through the night air, Like-Wind's hair loose again, flapping across his shoulders as the strands painted themselves in blood.

Victor dodged the blade each time it drew closer. At some point he must have come out of his damp moccasins, for his feet were bare as he worked to keep his breath ahead of him. He heard Ma, closer; heard her tell him Like-Wind was his brother. That one must not betray one's brother. He felt in her words incrimination, for all that had gone wrong. He believed she had blamed him before. For the tension between he and Father. For not succeeding at his quest. For loving the girl when it seemed natural he would do so.

Victor reached for Like-Wind's knife. The bone blade pierced Victor's hand as if his skin were made of wet clay, and there was something about the pain that felt relieving. Like-Wind recoiled at the knife dangling from Victor's open palm, and Victor knew then that Like-Wind had never wished for it to go that far.

Bluegrass exited the council tent; the expression upon his face was one of surprise and disappointment. He hadn't heard the commotion from inside. He told Victor to stay put and asked Like-Wind to follow him, lecturing him as he escorted him back to their lodge. Ma ripped the lower half of her tunic, pulled the knife from Victor, and wrapped the hole in Victor's hand. Victor felt the blood soak the cloth, but still he did not feel pain. When Bluegrass returned he glanced at Ma and frowned, and Ma grimaced, for between them there was shared frustration at what their children had undone.

"The council will see me now?" Ma said.

Bluegrass shook his head, as if an explanation was not needed. He told Victor they would make offerings together with Like-Wind the next morning. Ma moved forward, as if ready to implore Bluegrass to return inside and urge the council to reconsider her request, but Victor spoke first:

"You told me to take her there. To wait for Like-Wind," he said to Bluegrass. "He never came."

Bluegrass looked again to Ma, a quizzical expression upon his face, and Ma looked to Victor, surprised to be surprised that she knew none of this.

"Me? I did not tell you to take that girl anywhere. Why would I send Like-Wind to be with her?" Bluegrass shook his head and quickly disappeared into the dark.

When Victor turned to Ma, incredulous, Ma bared her teeth, which shone like polished bone; her chiseled face glowed red in the torchlights. "Didn't I tell you there'd be trouble?"

5

Victor could not sleep. He decided as he lay that he would find Like-Wind in the morning. Tell him he never meant for things to be this way. He would speak to Bluegrass too. Ask him if it was because Ma was present that he had denied saying what clearly he'd said. Victor would make everything right. Or make things as right as they could be. Yet each time he thought of returning to what had been, he remembered the girl. Saw her face so clear in his mind's eye that it felt as though he could touch her—touch her in the way she would never have allowed him to do before, touch her in a careful way that would not cause her to flinch or curl her lip or make him feel that way that he found too hurtful to describe.

Victor closed his eyes and promised himself he would search again for the girl when morning light rose from the sky. Up and down the banks of Little Bighorn River. He would search for her tracks, for evidence of her having clawed her way out of that awful water, for he knew she must have crossed rivers before. She was a hearty girl. Rugged. Father had said so himself, that she was brave. *Brave girls don't die*, he thought. Victor fell asleep with those four words on his dried lips, like a chant, and it seemed only minutes later that Ma woke him, whispering something about needing to take him away.

"Let us go," she said.

He got up from his sleeping robe, and she urged him to quiet his steps. As they walked out beneath night-clouds snarled like wet matted grasses, he saw that Ma had already packed the parfleche and travois with goods and provisions to last them at least twenty days: dried berries, strips of venison and buffalo fat, blankets, an extra robe, a small clay pot. It was colder than previous nights, and Victor's sliced hand felt numb, the fresh bandage damp with new blood.

"Drink this, there's no time to eat." Ma gave him a pouch filled with a warm, bitter root tea he had never before tasted.

"Where are we going?"

It seemed Ma didn't wish to answer, but then said, "Those who eat their own death will eat another's life." She mounted Martinique and held Victor's favorite mare steady for him. "I will explain later," she whispered. "Now it's time to ride."

II

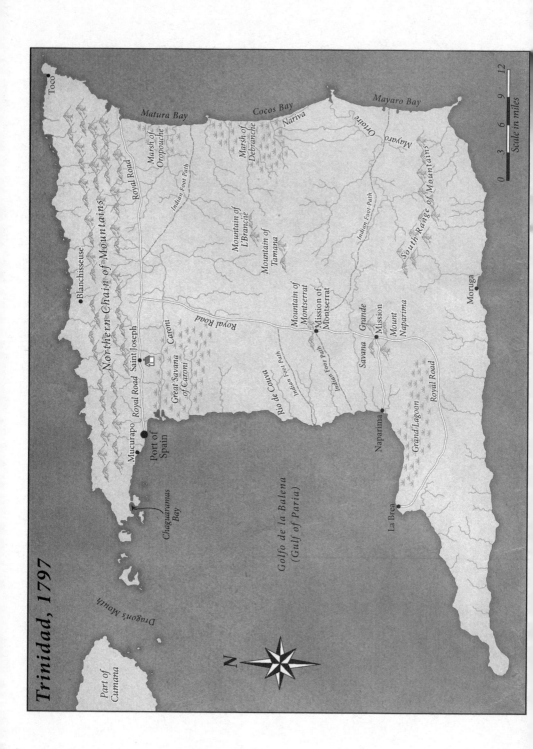

Trinidad, 1797

Part of Cumana

Dragon's Mouth

Golfo de la Balena (Gulf of Paria)

Chaguaramas Bay

Port of Spain

Mucurapo

Royal Road

Saint Joseph

Great Savana of Caroni

Caroni

Royal Road

Northern Chain of Mountains

Blanchisseuse

Toco

Matura Bay

Royal Road

Marsh of Oropouche

Indian Foot Path

Marsh of Debranche

Cocos Bay

Nariva

Mayaro Bay

Mountain of L'Branciie

Mountain of Tamana

Mayaro

Oroise

Indian Foot Path

South Range of Mountains

Mountain of Montserrat

Mission of Montserrat

Savana Grande

Mission

Mount Naparima

Moruga

Rio de Couva

Indian Foot Path

Indian Foot Path

Naparima

Grand Lagoon

Royal Road

La Brea

N

Scale in miles

0   3   6   9   12

Isle of Trinidad

⤙⤚

1

1796

Rosa felt her bonnet's loose ribbons grazing her cheeks seconds before they were used to wring her neck.

Jeremias dragged Rosa to the rear of the stable, the cords tightening until her gulps backed into her ears. She gasped, and the stallion Maravilloso roused, a hoof tapping the stall over and again, until Jeremias let loose the ribbons and shushed the horse, spraying Rosa with his spumy, liquored breath.

"You're always such a bloody mutton-shunter!" Jeremias's words fell heavy from his tongue, the nouns enunciated with teeth. He stood a foot taller than Rosa, but in the darkness, Rosa saw nothing of her brother's pale baby face or the oft-matted sandy-colored curls he'd inherited from Mamá. She felt only the heel of his vexed palm pinning her against the wood.

"Stop or I'll scream!" she said, the words only coarse whispers.

Jeremias quickly removed his hand and propped himself next to her. She heard him swallow and wished to move away but didn't feel she could.

"Scream for what? I did nothing to you," he said. "You want him to hate me, is all."

She had never been fond of her brother. Rosa was told that this sort of ambivalence between siblings was normal, but Rosa did not feel disdain to be normal.

"If you don't want Papá to hate you, why disobey him so much?"

Rosa had heard Papá warn Jeremias that the neighbor, Monsieur DeGannes, was an immoral man. A Frenchman even the French did not want. "What man offers a twelve-year-old boy hot spiced rum?" Papá had said. "Or teaches him how to cheat at poker and insert swears into the cracks of perfectly fine sentences?" Monsieur DeGannes was a powerful man. Papá had told Jeremias that no man became powerful in the West Indies without soiled hands, and so Papá made Jeremias promise to keep his distance and he had monitored Jeremias's whereabouts every day, until Jeremias took to leaving after all were sleeping.

Jeremias never suspected that his nine-year-old sister would trail him into the night.

"I'm happiest with Monsieur DeGannes," he said now.

"Happy?" Papá would have said it in this way—accusatory, judgmental. To diminish Jeremias with that irrational one-worded question made Rosa feel accomplished.

"Monsieur DeGannes is a learned man. He understands the heart of an intellectual."

"Eh-eh, then he could never understand your heart because you are not an intellectual."

"Hush up."

Rosa felt the heat from his skin radiate down and across to her.

"We talk literature and politics—you know that the French voted to end slavery? That there was a slave revolt in Saint-Domingue five years past? Why don't we know such things? Monsieur says the swift end put to the Jacobin-led government might lead to free men becoming slaves. We live in unsteady times, and people like Papá are under a cloak of ignorance and darkness."

Rosa didn't understand one word of what Jeremias had said and was not certain he did either. She happily imagined Jeremias in the morning, his belly quivering, weeping before Papá, trying to explain why he'd been so very disobedient. But now it was well past Rosa's bedtime and she was tired, too tired for Jeremias and DeGannes's big ideas about "Jacobin" people who had no bearing on her life, and even if she had understood, still she could think of little else beyond the bonnet strings that had burned the skin beneath her chin.

As Rosa began to walk away, Jeremias snatched her arm, with a grip she felt deep beneath her young flesh. "What if Papá took away the horses from you, told you you could never again dirty your hands in the soil?"

What Jeremias was asking her to contemplate was not possible, not even imaginable. It was an absurd scenario, so Rosa did not consider it as much as she considered what to tell Papá of this night. All of it? Almost all of it? His absconding, his drunkenness, his violence. What if someone had seen Jeremias creeping home through the fields? That was the scenario Jeremias should have been considering. To some on that Spanish-held island, a Negro like Papá, even a well-regarded, landowning Negro, was still a mucama or, worse, a slave. One error in judgment, one moral lapse by any one of them, risked all Papá had built. Jeremias knew this.

Yet Rosa wished for her bed, and more, she wished for Jeremias to let her loose. She agreed to keep his secret. "But you'll hurt all of us if you keep this up," she said.

2

Jeremias sat before the table, neck loose, eyes befogged, eating jiggly peppered eggs from the spoon Mamá held before him. "We should take him to see someone." Mamá flipped her hand over and back again upon his forehead, reaching for a fever that would never be found. "Every morning he's sick. And you know my dreams—empty fishing nets for three weeks. It's not a good sign, Demas."

"He's just lazy." Papá spoke without glancing up from his plate.

"You mustn't speak of the boy so. He's sitting right here."

"You does want me to call him lazy when he ent here? I have other words for them times." Papá looked to Rosa with that glimmer in his eye, for the joke seemed to be theirs.

Mamá moved aside Jeremias's plate and held him by the waist. "Come, chile, let me help you into the room."

"What room? My room?" Papá set down his spoon, half full of the sweet potato that Eve, Rosa's older sister, had pestled for his breakfast. "If the boy is sick, set him outside. Let the fresh air take him, nah."

"He's sweating from fever, Demas."

"All the more reason not to have him in my room."

"Notre chambre!" Mamá said.

In the Rendón home, the predominant language was Spanish. They spoke French too, of course, and Papá, for business, spoke English, but Spanish was the language they all shared and the language Papá knew best. He spoke it with a uniquely African lilt that Mamá openly disfavored. More than once, Mamá said that Papá's manner of speaking was an unfortunate remnant from Papá's people, who had crossed the Atlantic at the bottom of a slave ship. To Papá's great irritation, Mamá often hurried to correct him when he spoke, for Mamá preferred her Spanish the way she preferred her Martiniquais French—with no sign of "African bastardization." As such, when Demas Rendón wished to pick a fight with his wife, he flooded their house with a coarse, thunderous, African-tinged medley of colloquial Spanish and her beloved French.

"You know how much work is piling up at the blacksmith shop? In the afternoons, after I does put in a long day alone, Jeremias is lookin' quite fine, assez bien. But in the mornin', he's close to death. Pourquoi, Myra?"

Mamá, only half listening, returned to the front room to fold the pallet where Jeremias slept now that Eve had become a woman. She sniffed it, wrinkled her nose as if the odor was surprising somehow, and rolled it into a corner. Rosa watched Papá's eyes trace Mamá's deep-bend curves, her loose ringlets of hair, as if they were roadblocks to sincere anger. By most accounts, Mamá was a lovely woman, though if you were looking to find fault (and most everyone did), it would be with her height. She was taller than Papá, who was a tall man, by an inch, maybe two, and no tall woman could be a "fair lady" even in the opinion of the un-fair.

"What work is he doing, Demas? Half the time you send him home from the shop so you can finish whatever it is you don't wish any of us to see."

Papá's brows collapsed in the space above the bridge of his nose. "What gibberish you speakin' there, Myra?"

"Oh, don't pretend I'm imagining this."

"Speak! Speak your mind since you does have so much to say."

Mamá poured more hot water into Papá's mug. "Shh . . . never mind . . . the boy needs rest."

Papá brought the spoon to his mouth but set it down before it reached his lips. It was as if he found the sweet potatoes suddenly too much like sweet potato. Papá's skin, already the color of moist aged wood, deepened and his face seemed to flatten into sharp corners. "Rosa works like a man. And I does leave for the shop most mornings before the sun comes up, not because I does have some great secret, Myra, but because I have too much to do and that boy doesn't wanta do hard work!" Papá rose from his chair. "You better make sure he gets up from my bed today and finishes his chores."

Mamá watched Papá tug at his braces as he passed the side window, the skin on his hands glazed from decades of burnings. Her expression could not be mistaken for love. She removed his tin mug from the head of the table, placing it inside the dry rinse bowl, and it seemed only then that she remembered it had been Jeremias's job to fetch the day's water. That she would be without enough for the cleaning and cooking.

"'Rosa works like a man,'" Mamá said, mocking Papá. "And to think it is he who insists that you do so! Insists that I let you shirk your duties as a young woman and let you blacken more in the sun, and then he pretends it is my doing?" Mamá looked to Rosa now, her eyes examining her in the way Rosa knew would lead to some critique. "Rosa, don't let your father make you think that the work to be done outside this house is more important than the work to be done *inside* this house."

"Oui, Mamá."

Mamá reached into her apron pocket and removed from it a wooden clothes peg. "Your nose is looking a bit broad again. Put this on and go and help your Papá." Mamá set the peg into Rosa's palm and closed her fingers about it, as if to secure its safekeeping. "Voilà."

Rosa knew if she peeled away Mamá's words to expose the layer beneath them, the sentiment might become gummy like sap and stick to her in a way that would make it her own. So she skimmed only the surface, accepting the differences between herself and Mamá, Jeremias, and Eve, acknowledging that their skin rang yellow and hers brown, their limbs plump and hers gangly. She knew all too well that the peg wouldn't transform her face and knew better that if it could, Mamá would find only more deficiencies.

But Rosa fastened the peg, squeezing her nostrils into a line so that she could no longer smell the morning air. Unable to find her boots, she hurried past the stable, feeling the tickle of the tall java grasses on her calves and the grit of the earth, soft as berry jelly, lodging itself between the web of her toes. She searched for some time before she found Papá at their newest plot of cacao, nestled beneath a row of old banana trees. The pods bore the colors of a tropical-fruit rainbow and gave off a scent of bitter so fragrant, Rosa wished to taste it. Papá, on his knees, measured taproot growth and tested the structure of the soil with the flats of his fingertips. When finally he looked up, he observed her in the same manner he had considered the beans.

"Take that chupid t'ing from your face!" He stood and snatched the peg from her nose. "You need that? Your face is fine. You does like my face?"

"Sí." She rubbed her nose. The mucous unsticking itself made noise in her ears.

"Your face is my face. Is this face not good enough for you?" Papá pointed to his high cheekbones, the very white whites of his eyes, the thinning hair across a high burnished forehead. Rosa thought her Papá handsome. But Rosa wished to be pretty.

With the morning breeze dank on their cheeks, they made their way to the stable to see about the horses. Other than his wife and children, Papá was most proud of the horses he'd raised, bred, bettered. The line of mustangs he shared with Monsieur DeGannes extended thousands of years. They were kind and competitive, with stamina and immense beauty. Papá harnessed the mare Espina, while Rosa slipped on Jeremias's boots and began prepping the stalls. Most days Papá would rope and lead the horses to the clearing to graze, leaving Rosa with plenty of time to muck and clean tacks before he returned on foot. But that day Papá extended his hand toward her. "Hold me properly," he said, pulling her up onto Espina by both arms.

Rosa understood her father best when they rode. As they trotted, she sensed how he lightened his weight so as not to tire Espina, noticed the manner in which he stroked the mare's neck. The way her father loved struck at the core of anyone or anything fortunate enough to be loved by him. He was not diplomatic, never spared truth, but Rosa knew that every task Papá performed lay in service to others.

That day Maravilloso pulled ahead of Espina. The mare flattened her ears to express her outrage and Rosa laughed. Maravilloso was most handsome, moderately muscled with a broad chest of fair depth, paired with a long stride and an exceptional mind that often favored its own opinions. He found a spot beneath the cloudy green shade of a clump of Spanish cedars. While Espina stood off alone, the three others—Iker, the young colt Santiago, and Josefina—idled beside Maravilloso, their lips in motion, their bicolored manes swishing in the warm morning's breeze.

"He has a t'ing for Rosa." Papá laughed as if the thought were delicious. "A real show-off you is, Maravilloso."

Later, in the warm flush of midmorning, Papá and Rosa mucked out the box stalls, replaced the bedding, scrubbed the pails. Rosa was not afraid of work. Papá often said so. Mamá often said the opposite. She was a natural farmer, a talented handler, and, in these ways, an outlier among the Rendón children. Eve and Jeremias often complained about the intensity of the midday heat, about the land too vast, too unruly, about the horses too wild, both of them hoping Papá would permit them to drown themselves in letters and numbers. But for Rosa, there was no existence without that land.

Or at least this was what Rosa believed until the time came when she could not believe this anymore.

3

Eve was the first to notice the dust clouding the road. Demas Rendón had taught his children that when there was an unrecognizable approach, they were to gather and arm.

Mamá instructed Rosa to keep an eye on the covered wagon, a type rarely seen outside rainy season, and urged Eve to ring the bell that hung just over Papá's cane rocking chair. When Mamá returned to the verandah with Jeremias, Rosa and Eve stood ready with weapons drawn, their linen bonnets tilted, the wagon progressing faster than expected.

"Can you tell who's there?"

The haze about the wagon was uncertain of clearing, and Rosa knew if the wagon drew any closer, trouble would be harder to dissuade. She was the next best shot after Papá and Jeremias, so when Rosa aimed a hundred feet ahead of the wagon, spooking its horses for a loss of fifty yards, it was intended only to be a warning.

Jeremias snatched the musket from her.

"It's Byron," Papá said, climbing the stone staircase to join them.

"And Cousin Philippe is with him," Eve added.

Papá met the men at the palm trees. Rosa watched her uncle and father greet each other with a nod. Words had long been inadequate between them. Rosa had often ached to know her uncles and cousins, to know a familial love beyond Mamá, Papá, Eve, and Jeremias, but she knew, long before she understood that that love could not be, that to love them would be to unlove Papá.

Mamá greeted Tío Byron as he and Papá led the wagon to the mouth of the walking path. "Mon frère," she said, and Papá grimaced. He'd told Mamá that he felt it rude when she spoke French with others in his presence. Mamá had cheupsed long and hard, the saliva at her back teeth working to create a hissing sound, before telling Papá she thought it rude that he thought to say it was rude.

"Bonjour." Tío Byron held his sister's face, the grip resolved but gentle. It was an unexpected gesture, for the siblings had been at odds since soon after they'd arrived to Trinidad from Martinique at the end of 1783. For boat passage and a sixteen-acre plot of land, the three brothers, their wives, and Myra, their one sister, all free mulattoes, had sworn allegiance to the Spanish Crown, to Pope Pius VI, and to one another. Let the brothers tell it, and Demas Rendón had come between this last and most important alliance.

"You'll have some tea?" Mamá said.

"Non, it's too hot. But gimme some sorrel. Nobody makes it like you does make it, Myra." Tío Byron, a man of considerable girth, sweating almost wastefully, examined Papá's rocker, outfitted with a feather cushion. He seemed to wish for a seat that Papá did not offer, so instead he remained standing, complimenting Eve, the spitting image of Mamá, on her beauty and remarking on what a big girl Rosa had become. "You nearly got me on le bec," he said to Rosa, pointing to his flushed nose.

"Sí, but if I wished for the nose I would have had it." Rosa responded in Spanish.

Papá smirked, and Mamá swatted Rosa's bamsee.

"Get inside, all of you," Mamá said to the children.

Tío Byron fanned himself with his hat, his creamy skin glistening like damp dough, his thinned hair lying flat with sweat. "I t'ink it's best if Jeremias sets himself right here," he said.

Jeremias's eyes, casting about as if in surprise, were pink-rimmed still. His unbrushed hair reminded Rosa of an untamable mountain ridge. He returned the musket to Rosa and watched as Eve pulled Rosa into the house, seeming to know that his sisters would crouch beneath the windowsill, that they would not miss anything of what was to come.

Papá sat upon his rocker, as if only willing to be a spectator, while more French-spoken pleasantries were exchanged: how healthy Myra looked, how the house kept up even without maidservants, how the grasses grew so green, so very green. Papá chewed a piece of dry salted bark until Tío Byron turned to Jeremias, his oldest nephew: "I understand you've been spending quite a lot of time at the DeGannes property."

From Rosa's vantage point, Papá showed no sign of irritation save he removed the bark from his mouth and set it into his shirt pocket.

"Together, you read books, talk learned man's t'ings, isn't that so? And sometimes it's not just you and DeGannes sitting at le grand table," Tío Byron continued, "sometimes you have a guest. Oui?"

Papá stood now, and Rosa swore she could see the rod in Papá's back, straight and hard. "Say what you sayin', Byron. I must get to the shop to prep the furnace."

"Oh, the island certainly can't do without your services, Demas."

Rosa and Eve ducked again below the sill. Tío Byron did something Rosa thought sounded like scraping the soles of his boots upon the verandah, though she could not be certain. She remembered when Mamá told her how Tío Byron, in Martinique, had earned money playing the fiddle on the verandah for guests of the monsieur who owned the land where they worked. "Your tio earned enough to keep us fed when we arrived here." Mamá had spoken of Tío Byron with such admiration that Rosa had asked if she too could learn to play the fiddle. Mamá told her fiddles were only for boys. Rosa remembered wondering how it was that boys had become so fragile that everything seemed to be set aside for them.

"Myra, when am I gettin' that cup of sorrel? A man needs to quench his thirst. I ridin' here since dawn," Tío Byron said.

Mamá leaned across the threshold to catch Eve only then rising to her feet. "Dépêchez-vous," she whispered.

Rosa, peeking again, saw Tío Byron turn to Jeremias once more. "Sometimes you come all the way to my home and you does pick up Francine so you and she can spend time with DeGannes. Isn't that so?"

Jeremias, with his right shoulder to the window, latched his thumbs about his braces. "I ran into her in town and she saw me carrying a book I'd borrowed from Monsieur. I told her how much I was learnin'. She begged me to bring her along to introduce her to him."

"And sometimes you and she talk about your futures. Isn't that so?"

"There's nothing wrong with that."

"Your future together?"

Papá moved toward Tío Byron, blocking Rosa's view. He stood a few inches shorter than Jeremias now, but Papá's shoulders were more squared, as if he'd been chipped from something more solid. "Byron, what's this you sayin'?"

"Jeremias knows what I'm sayin', oui?"

Papá took a step toward Tío Byron.

"Francine is now with chile. Your Jeremias has made certain promises and I intend to ensure he keeps them."

Papá's shoulders drooped, Rosa was certain of it, but quickly they firmed again, as if remembering those solid roots. Mamá, on the other side of Jeremias, gasped. "Jeremias, is this true?"

"Non. I took her there to talk. We didn't—I didn't make promises."

Eve arrived with two full mugs of the root drink Mamá had boiled so long with cinnamon and cloves that it was now blood-red. She had a practiced smile—Eve did—one that evoked the utmost femininity, but Tío Byron scarcely noticed it as he snatched his and Philippe's share from the tray, downing the contents in seven crude gulps.

"Byron, you washed down your drink so be on your way," Papá said. "We'll be in touch."

"I know you t'ink of yourself as a man of integrity, but I know different." Tío Byron belched. It was deep and long, and Mamá covered her mouth as if she were the one who'd set it forth. "I come to make sure my gyal has the future that garçon here promised."

"He doesn't have a future unless I give him one. And this is not about my boy and Francine," Papá said. "This is about two families. And I'm the head of this family. So I'm askin' you again to take your leave, and I'll say again that we'll be in touch."

"Une famille, Demas. You believe us to be separate. This has always been the problem. It's no wonder your boy t'inks this is all right."

"We'll be in touch."

"What I can't seem to get from Francine is how exactly garçon here convinced her he would make t'ings right."

"Francine is fifteen, Byron! She's practically a woman," Mamá said.

"And Jeremias is a big boy! Look at him!"

Rosa recognized the sound of Papá's footsteps as they crossed the boards. Papá set himself before Jeremias as though he would not permit an assessment of the boy's oversize. Big boys don't have long childhoods, Mamá often said. "Byron, either you're accusing him of somet'ing or you're hoping he'll keep his word. But you can't do both. So, which is it?"

"I'm askin' him to be a proper man."

"You can't ask a boy of twelve years to be a man."

"He snatches my Francine and takes her where he chooses. He's certainly a man."

"He kidnapped her? Is that what you accusing him of now?"

"Even if she went willingly, it didn't give him the right to—"

"I've done nothing!" Jeremias moved beside Papá. He was a small boy again, malleable, compliant, Demas's son, if only for that one moment more. "I didn't do any of that, Papá. It's been weeks since I've last seen her. We had a quarrel and stopped speaking."

"A lovers' quarrel, oui?" Tío Byron said.

Eve and Rosa were now standing at the door, no longer troubled about being seen. Papá held Jeremias's hand, reminding Rosa of the way male frogs kept their tadpoles protected in their mouths. "Walk with Francine next time you come," Papá said to Tío. "I wanta hear this story from that mout' of hers."

"As a matter of fact, I'll bring she now."

Tío Byron and Philippe moved toward the wagon. Mamá, believing them to be departing, started after them, but Papá held her back. The five Rendóns watched Tío Byron instruct Philippe to unveil the cloth-covered wagon. Rosa rose to the tips of her toes, mouth agape, as Tío Byron hoisted Francine from the wooden bed. Her long dark hair, sweaty and creased, was pasted to the gauze swathing her pale neck. Tío Byron lugged her by the arms, tilting her torso so that she might be posed across the lip of the wagon to display her shrouded wrists.

"Come now and talk!" Tío Byron shouted from below. "See what your boy has caused my girl to do to sheself."

4

Mamá was determined to have Sunday afternoon tea upon the verandah. She said she would not have this thing with Francine and Byron put her back in the bed. Mamá had had short bouts of illness for as long as Rosa could remember. Sometimes she'd be without the use of her wrists and knees, bedridden for days, but inevitably, some turn would occur, and slowly she'd return almost to her old self.

Yet even when she felt more fair than ill, Mamá was careful with her cast of mind.

"Come, come, come and take a sit outside," she insisted.

Papá sat quiet in his rocker beneath the bronze bell, his tea in a cup upon the floorboards, too hot for consumption he'd said. Mamá, in the chair beside him, sipping hers, glancing at the front field, its grass blades, sharp and vivid, appearing as if joy had not evaded *them*. Mamá and Papá had not spoken much to each other in the weeks since Tío and Philippe's visit. In the living body of their marriage, silence had always been the keeper of peace, but this time it coursed as though it were sludge, the lees of a sickly matrimony.

Demas Rendón, a child of emancipated Negroes, had lived in the former capital city of San José de Oruña (Saint Joseph) all of his life. He met Myra Robespierre in 1784, when she and Byron came to his newly opened shop to order a hoe. Within weeks of meeting, Myra and Demas were married. Love, an afterthought for both. This fact was no secret in their home.

For Myra, the big man with nary an education was an escape from ill treatment by an oppressive family led by her eldest brother, Byron. For Demas, the tall woman with too much lip for her own good was excellent stock for his future sons. The two were not so much one as like a wheel and axle, they sometimes said, both resolute that one would be useless without the other.

During their first years of marriage, Myra had polished out much of Demas's rutted finish, teaching him to read, offering him lessons on how to defer to others without losing honor, how to not only take pride in his ability to be more than one man, but to see it as an asset rather than a burden. And though Demas resented his wife's maternal tendencies toward him, as well as her particular strain of Martinique haughtiness, he became certain that with her guidance and his natural talents he would break through and achieve a success that at one time in his life had seemed unattainable. Thus by 1790, Demas had earned a reputation as the most masterful and accomplished blacksmith in the Lesser Antilles, affording him the opportunity to purchase seventy-five acres of land upon which he and Mamá grew tidy rows of cacao, bred horses, and eventually built the home where they would raise their family. By plantation owner standards, the Rendón home would be quite small, but with Demas's most excellent carpentry skills, it developed into quite a handsome three-room home, with a French double door, an open gable roof, and jalousie windows, all lightly obscured by a scant row of hedges. From a distance, one could see that the house, upon its raised foundation, offered unobstructed views of the town's verdant hills and boasted twin beveled spires, like periscopes, one on the far left, the other on the right upon a dormer lined in a lace wood trim. It had stone steps that Rosa and Jeremias were required to scrub before Easter each year, ending at a wide verandah that allowed visitors to feast on an interior that would not be outdone by that of a French madame or a Spanish señora, for Mamá had in her possession soup chargers, teacups, eight pieces of silver flatware, a fine six-seat table with rounded corners, and two extra chairs for unexpected guests. But it was the Rendón children, not their home, who were to speak for Demas and Myra's éclat. Eve, Jeremias, and Rosa were to be learned, charming, industrious. Their job was to make Mamá proud and to never embarrass Papá. It was a task the children were not always up to.

"You know what I heard in town?" Eve sat on the top step, promising to wade into her parents' sludgy silence. As the eldest girl, it seemed she carried the special burden of the parental relations, willing when there seemed no way. "I heard Señor Cordoza was at that obeah lady's house last week for quite some time." Señor Cordoza was Papá's occasional trading partner, a European who'd become a family friend of sorts. On occasion, Cordoza visited with Papá, but mostly they saw him at Sunday Mass with his wife and her pet pig that Padre José refused to allow indoors.

"Which obeah lady?" Mamá motioned for Rosa to come to her. "The one with the dead husband in the house?"

Papá shook his head at the nonsense that passed for conversation, while Eve laughed.

"He ate from that woman's pot?! He doesn't know better?" Mamá spread her legs and folded her dress inward to make space for Rosa. From her apron she removed a hairbrush with a shagreen handle. Rosa shook her head as though she had a choice in the matter. Mamá eyed her with incredulity.

"I hear Cordoza had already taken a liking to her before she give him the bois bandé in his tea," Eve said. "Now he's a slobbering lubber when he's with her."

Mamá pulled Rosa's arm and set her down upon the floor of the verandah so she could get a good grasp of Rosa's hair. Rosa did not think of her hair as needing Mamá's intervention, for though it was linty, the strands of her plaits had yet to unravel and were not near downy enough to require redoing. As Mamá began to pull apart the strands, Rosa set her hands atop her head and Mamá rapped her knuckles with the brush. "No," Mamá said to Eve, "that woman must've given him something long before. You've seen her. Only obeah could cause such a thing." Mamá licked her fingers and set the saliva at the tip of Rosa's plait. "Cordoza thinks too much of himself to be with that ugly woman."

"I hear he come from her house wearin' some too-short biddim bim trousers inside out. The seams his wife restitched and the patch in the crotch—there for everybody to see."

Rosa giggled, for Eve had told her she had visited with the obeah woman on occasion, and in return for covering Eve's absences, Eve shared stories she'd heard of scorned African women who took flight in the nights, philandering men, neighbors who hid furry tails.

Papá peered beneath the shadow of his hat brim, expecting Mamá to admonish Eve, but Mamá only chuckled. "Eve, enough." Papá's face was grave, the lines at his eyes webbed.

"Papá, I only tellin' what I does hear."

"Ow!" Rosa cried, crossing her arms over the top of her head. Mamá rapped her wrists this time.

"Myra, this is the kinda talk you encouraging from a young lady?" Papá said.

For a few moments, Mamá said nothing. She brushed Rosa's hair with long, maddened strokes, while Papá seemed to relish the dampening effect he had had on her. Then Mamá rested the brush on Rosa's shoulder. "If men didn't have so many dirty secrets, Eve would have nothing to speak of." Mamá returned the brush to Rosa's hair and ran it across a knot.

"Mamá, it hurts!"

"If you stop fighting, it wouldn't hurt!"

"Oww!" Rosa wailed.

Eve looked to Rosa, then to Mamá. "Let me finish her hair for you," Eve said.

When Mamá dropped the brush on Rosa's thigh, Rosa jumped up from the verandah floor. Her hair had grown and tickled her neck, and she wasn't sure how she felt about its brushed-out length. Rosa pushed the strands from her cheeks and caught Eve looking to Papá now, her eyes brimming with mischief. She had this way about her, as though she could make rose petals from thorns. "You t'ink next time you see Señor Cordoza, you could tell him that Mamá could sew him a pair of trousers with extra buttonholes, so he could just—"

"Eve!"

Jeremias laughed. Snorted, in fact. It was the first time Rosa had heard him laugh in weeks. She didn't realize until then how she'd missed it.

"Was that your belly makin' wind, Jeremias?" Eve said.

The three of them laughed all the more, but Rosa stifled her chuckles, hoping Papá would appreciate her attempt, wondering how she so often found herself trying to please both Mamá and Papá when she knew that pleasing one often displeased the other. As Rosa moved toward Eve, she looked out at the road and saw a rider. The amber light of dusk was upon them, but still, Rosa made out the figure. "I guess you'll be able to tell Señor Cordoza about the trousers sooner than you think."

Papá tugged at his braces, watching the pace and posture at which Cordoza rode. One could tell a lot about what's to come from how a man rode, he often said. And by the looks of the strides, something was amiss.

"Myra, please go and bring out a proper cup of tea for Señor Cordoza, and, Jeremias, bring a chair from inside for him to sit."

Señor Cordoza was a squat, coconut-oiled Spaniard with a goose neck. He had been married twice, both times admittedly for money. The first wife had died in childbirth, and afterward, it was said, he wailed like the baby he lost until his father-in-law gave him a decent enough sum to make the whining stop. The second marriage had landed him in the West Indies, where he found himself keeper of his new father-in-law's hilly property, wishing the second wife and her swine would take the path of the first wife.

Now, he and Papá, hoping to deter eavesdropping, spoke in English, while Mamá reheated water, stirred in the honey, and clinked the spoon against the rims of her teacups. She had brought her special set of egg-blue porcelain cups from Martinique, which had been given to her grandmother by her grandmother's French madame. When Mamá delivered the tea to the verandah, she set the Martinique cups down as if to display them and waited upon the porch to hear the news Señor Cordoza had come to deliver. But Papá, with the flick of his hand, sent her away.

Mamá, angry, returned inside and instructed Jeremias to sit beneath the sill so that she might know all the things Papá would not share with her. Rosa sat beside Jeremias and watched as Señor Cordoza sipped from the cup, inhaled the scent of Mamá's tea, then sipped again though Papá had yet to touch his. Each time Cordoza had come to their home, he'd mentioned how much he admired Mamá's black-rose tea. To Rosa, this compliment seemed always to evince a liking for more than Mamá's brew.

"I've received news that the English will soon arrive," Cordoza said. "This could be very bad for all of us, but most especially for you."

"What specific information have you, Señor?"

"Come, Demas, those French privateers have been blocking the port for weeks! The English merchants can't conduct their business in Port of Spain. How long do you think they'll allow that? And now with Spain at war with them, it is only a matter of time before the English begin attacking the colonies."

"But you can't be sure of this, Señor."

Cordoza sipped again and set his cup atop the saucer. It wobbled, and he waited until it settled before speaking. "After L'Ouverture in Saint-Domingue, it is clear France is weak. Our upper class, particularly the French royalists, are frightened that the instability in Saint-Domingue could spread here. The Saint-Dominguans who escaped have come to tell of their horrors. With such stories of instability, it would not be a surprise if the English were to try and seize French assets and, once in the Caribbean Sea, come to learn how exposed our Governor Chacon has left us."

The 1791 Negro revolt in Saint-Domingue had resulted in a thousand ruined plantations and three thousand Frenchmen with their heads balanced on spikes. The English and Spaniards had taken full advantage of the chaos and joined the fight alongside the enslaved, until in 1793 the new French government abolished slavery so as not to lose complete control of Saint-Domingue. But the isle's fate remained an open question. And as Rosa would learn later, this uncertainty had affected the entire chain of islands.

"If this happens, maybe a year or two at most we will have," Cordoza said.

"The French on this island have no reason for concern," Papá said.

Señor Cordoza rubbed the palms of his hands on the arms of Mamá's kitchen chair. "Ay, there are bands of revolutionaries—French farmers —roaming the streets at night, trying to create a fever-pitch among the coloreds to overthrow Chacon. There is much reason for concern." Cordoza looked to Papá as if he intended to pose a question. "I had imagined with you being a free Negro and Myra being colored that you would've been pulled into their protests."

Papá paused as if considering the best response to what he felt was a clear accusation of treason. "You presume me so naïve that I can be incited by Frenchmen who fare worse than me? Why is it that the moment there's unrest in this country, I can't be a Trinidadian? You Spaniards talk of goin' back home every day you here, but here I am with no home country I can name, and still I can't claim this one? I can only be a Negro and my wife only a colored? Why can't I be Trinidadian too? Trinidad is, after all, where I lay my head, Señor."

"Sí, sí, of course, you are correct. The people who are promoting this conflict do not think of themselves as Trinidadians. They are opportunistic and—"

"And we have nutting on this island to offer any other crown. We are all barely surviving and—"

"You are surviving better than most." Cordoza stared into the well-sanded ceiling of the verandah and looked to Mamá's teacup. "Many of your Spanish neighbors do not own two matching shoes."

"This is true of many neighbors, not just Spaniards, Señor. Look around. Negroes, both free and enslaved, and coloreds and French, all alike, suffer. Relief can only be had when we put away our individual desires and instead work tirelessly to satisfy the needs of the 'we.'"

Indeed, Papá knew of the unfortunate state of his fellow country-men, many living in nothing sturdier than mud huts. He had immense compassion for them, and yet Papá believed in his heart that he had made his own way. He had lost his mother to an abscess in the bowels, his father to a planter's temper, and his only brother had headed south into the brambles when Papá had just begun his apprenticeship. So Papá had created himself in the image of no man he knew.

"What I am saying, Señor, is that as a people, as Trinidadians, we have been forgotten. Perhaps there is a case for self-governance," Papá said.

"What will happen, do you think? Spanish royalists will disappear and French planters will rule? You think you'll be freer if French farmers have a say in the future of this colony? They'll put you all to work for a pittance!"

Papá seldom spoke of being a descendant of one of the first hundred Africans brought to Trinidad. Both his great-grandfather's and grand-father's lives were a far cry from the life Papá lived now. The thought of a fine and proper man like his grandfather, whose face had all but faded from Papá's memory, living such a pained existence rendered Papá's heart sorrowful. "Well, Señor," he said. "The revolutionaries may not know what will come of their actions, but respectfully, I must say it also does not help that the French upper class have invited the English here. They could very well put free coloreds and free Negroes into slavery. I have lived as a free man my entire life. I too fear for my family."

Cordoza crossed his arms over a stomach low set with bulge. He leaned back into Mamá's kitchen chair. "Yes, 'tis true. Chacon has been the worst governor, pandering to the English, ignoring crimes committed in broad daylight. The country is awash with smugglers. They take riches right from under Chacon's nose while we pay taxes to the king and live in squalor. Some of these vagabonds have even found gold, I hear!"

Papá laughed a rueful laugh, his mouth unmoving. "That is just rumor," he said. "There's no gold in Trinidad."

Cordoza firmed his back as if recognizing some vulnerability, perhaps even naïveté in Papá. "Ay, Demas, whether gold is here or not, people come to abuse the land in search of it, and the English will find other uses for this place."

Papá was not flustered by much. Yet with Mamá's recurring dreams of empty fishing nets and Governor Chacon refusing to stamp the records Papá had recently presented for the purchase of additional lands, he had secretly begun to worry.

"They can take the island within days, and with so little of it cultivated and those mad Frenchmen running amok, I'm certain Spain will readily abdicate." Cordoza removed his hat, balancing it upon his left knee; his curvy nose shone with sweat.

Even if Papá believed all of what Cordoza said to be possible, what to do with the information was another question. There was no place in all the world where a man like Demas Rendón could own land, earn a living, raise a family, as he had done on that island. Trinidad was the land of opportunity. The only land of opportunity for a man like him.

"Several of us, your friends, have discussed your options." Cordoza wiped his head and set the hat back upon it. "Of course, you could wait to see what happens, but presuming a new English governor is on the way, we are proposing that you sign over your land and the blacksmith shop, and as your friends, we will keep them until you are able to make proper arrangements. Perhaps we can even help you curry favor." Cordoza reached for Mamá's cup, allowing his thumb to linger over its silver rim. "You can't be sure they will allow Negroes to retain land and businesses, especially prosperous ones. The English have been known to upend such liberal policies in other colonies."

Papá folded his hands before offering the faintest nod to Cordoza. "That is very kind, Señor. An offer that I shall consider."

5

Supper was served beneath a cloud of quiet discontent, a fog of despair that, though they would not know for some time, would seep into their dreams and choke off mirth at its inception. After Papá saw

Señor Cordoza to his horse, Jeremias and Rosa relayed the exchange to Mamá, who warned them not to speak of what they'd overheard. When they were all seated, Eve set down the shell tureen filled with hake and plantains that'd been boiled in coconut milk gravy, and it was perhaps two minutes later that Jeremias said to Papá, "You knew about Saint-Domingue and never told us? Monsieur DeGannes thinks the world order is collapsing and that the last sovereign nation to abolish slavery will be triumphant, if morally bankrupt." Jeremias moved his hands about as if he were a schoolteacher with a pointer. "Under the circumstances, I think Señor Cordoza's offer is a good one."

Mamá grimaced as she reached for Papá's bowl. She served him his food, sliced his fish, and Papá waited until she had returned the spoon beside his dish before addressing Jeremias. "Did I ask for your opinion?"

"Oh, I see," Jeremias said. "With Cordoza, behind back is dog, before face is Mr. Dog."

"Eh-eh, what did I tell you about tu boca?" Mamá said to Jeremias.

Papá spit a delicate white bone into his cupped hand and examined it. "You know about Sandy?"

Mamá shook her head as if to warn Papá. "No, Demas, they don't need to hear this story again."

"Again? I never tell them," Papá said, turning to the children, certain he would remember if he had. "It was November of 1770," Papá began. "The English had come to rule Tobago and the conditions were horrible for the African man. More terrible than anyt'ing we seen here. This man Sandy, they called him, has a name they won't use. He's a big, African-born man, muscled, and rightfully angry to be living like an animal. He convinces his people to take up arms and kill the English. The Africans terrorize them English boys for six weeks, ticking them off one by one, at night in their beds, at their posts, any place they can find them. It's so bad the English must call for help from Grenada, Saint Vincent, and Barbados. The men come from them other islands by the scores, and after some time and after so many dead, they quell the uprising. Then the governor lies. Says only twenty or so Englishmen were injured. That more Africans than Englishmen were killed. But they couldn't lie about Sandy. He up and disappear. They got no head, no body, to prove he's no longer a threat. In fact, the idea of Sandy still haunts them. But we here on this island know the truth. Sandy and a few others crossed the sea into Trinidad. Into Toco. Where men fished out them tired bodies and give them a place to rest, give them a piece of land, and give them a good horse. Now let me tell you . . . they will be ready when the time come again. All this right beneath the Spaniards' noses and within arm's length of them English." Papá set the bone into the back of his mouth, grinding it fine, not taking his eyes off Jeremias until the bone was like dust. He washed it down with water. "This is what we do for ourselves. You t'ink I need a lil weasely man like Cordoza to protect what's mine? You gointa see."

Mamá picked up Papá's bowl, thankful, it seemed, that the Sandy story had been cut short. "And if we hear of you at that DeGannes house again, I'll come with the switch to collect you myself," she said. "Every day the bucket goes in the well, but one day it's gointa stick."

Wheel and axle.

That night, as Jeremias and Eve slept, Rosa, who had been forced to finish plaiting her own hair, overheard her parents. She had been waiting for weeks to learn of the plans they had for Jeremias, but now Rosa regretted being awake, for little else had the effect on Rosa as her parents' quarrels. The tightening of her belly and the quickening of her breaths often took her by surprise. When they were like this, she found herself caught between wanting and not wanting to hear what ugliness they would say to each other.

"So much rope I does give you and now you hangin' me with it?" Papá said to Mamá. "Your family's not getting my land. I'll leave it to one of my girls before I does let Byron have it."

"Demas, I've got nothing to do with why you're upset."

"Tell me you ent know he was with that gal, that . . . that Francine."

"They're cousins," she said. "I didn't think anything of it. Why would I?"

"Because I warned you to keep your family away from my chil'ren."

"The children have no one but us. They're holed up here night and day, year after year. Look at how Jeremias sneaks off to be with that man. Who has power over that boy? Not you. You think I could keep him from his cousin if that's what he wanted?"

"You shoulda seen this comin'."

"Me?"

"Byron has wanted my land and my horses ever since we married, and now he's trying to use my son to get them." Papá slapped something hard against the wall, causing Rosa to start. "I fightin' one too many devils, and one of them devils is you."

6

1797

It was early in the new year when Eve added more to the story of the obeah woman and Señor Cordoza. Cordoza's wife had arrived at the obeah woman's door on Christmas Eve morning. There was a loud quarrel, and the wife drove her way inside to find Cordoza dressed only in stockings. "Here I find you with your package shriveled like a man with no shame! Let her keep you!" The wife shredded his trousers, picked up the scraps from the obeah woman's dusty floor, took them out to the road, and tossed them in a pile of runny dung. The neighbors said she then drove over the shreds with her wagon, as her pet pig bounced atop the wooden bed. The obeah woman, having missed this confrontation in her predictions, had no choice but to remove the pantaloons from the cadaver lying two years on her table so Cordoza would have something to wear in his race home. As he rode off, she ran into the street, yelling at him to "bring back de trousers when de wifey finish wi you!"

Mamá and Jeremias laughed so hard at Eve's recounting that Mamá gripped her stomach as if to keep it from severing. Papá, not finding the story funny at all, rose from his rocker and made his way to the stable with Rosa not far behind him.

"Your mudda is there laughin' it up as if not a t'ing in the world is wrong. She's accusing *me* of not taking seriously this situation with

Jeremias?" Papá spoke roughly, as if he did not remember Rosa was still only a child. "She pushing me too far." He turned to inspect Maravilloso, for the stallion had not been well. "If the English come, this horse might be the only t'ing to keep us from starving. If he is sick, we is sick."

Rosa had never seen her father worried in this way, so she remained by his side until well after Papá discovered the abscess on the stallion's left hind hoof. "I'm happy you're here. I needed another pair of hands." Papá went on to instruct Rosa on how to be mindful of the center, the frog, which had already begun to show signs of heat. He taught her how to distract Maravilloso with a feeding of guineos while soaking his hoof in a bath. "T'ree times a day this has to be freshly bandaged," he said. "He wants to get better and you'll show him how." They snuck malodorous ointments made of coupie and soursop from Mamá's medicine jars—"horse medicine," Papá called it—and he told Rosa it would be her job to keep it evenly applied. He demonstrated how she was to knot the old cloth scraps around Maravilloso's hoof—"Pull it tight, tight, tight"—warning Rosa that the stubborn stallion would likely resist and grow more irritable with each day he was penned. "He could develop colic since he can't be turned out until this heals." Rosa would have to ensure he was fed just the right amount of hay, given enough water to ease his digestion, and kept, until further notice, away from the other horses. "This is the most important job in this family, you understand?"

At day three the abscess burst, and though it was runny and foul smelling, Maravilloso was immensely relieved. Papá was delighted and impressed by Rosa's steady commitment and the following Sunday made a big to-do about her work. "She's an outstanding assistant, a natural!"

Jeremias, looking up at Papá, stabbed at the boiled cassava on his plate; the strings unraveled like thick white thread. Papá had not spoken more than eighteen words to Jeremias in the month since Tío's visit. Jeremias had counted each and complained to Eve that his life was at a standstill while he waited for Papá to act, to react, to do something.

"Rosa is no natural," Jeremias said. "You take the time to teach her, is all."

Papá smiled, and it seemed to Rosa then that Papá might have baited Jeremias.

"You have me at the shop, pounding horseshoes, making nails, and then you send me home before the end of the day to do woman's work." Jeremias's voice grew louder though it shook still. "I should be in the stable. With Maravilloso."

"Now you wish to help?" Rosa didn't know if she meant to burst in but found herself relieved by doing so. "'It's too hot'; 'Papá should send me to the schoolhouse'; 'Who wants to live like this?'" Rosa realized only after she'd begun that she had shifted her voice into a whiny falsetto and lolled her head from side to side like Jeremias was apt to do. "All you ever do is complain!" Rosa took a quick gulp of water—water she, not Jeremias, had carried from the stream that morning. "You're only jealous that—"

"Ferme ta gueule, Rosa!" Jeremias turned to Papá. "You don't believe me about Francine, do you?"

"Now is not the time," Mamá said to Jeremias.

"When is the time? When Tío returns again with Francine and her big belly?"

"Your Papá will speak when he's ready." Mamá said this, though she herself had stopped speaking to Papá for this very reason.

"That's not my child Francine's carrying."

Papá waved his hand to stop Jeremias.

"You see, Mamá, he never believes me," Jeremias said.

Papá closed the same hand into a fleshy knot and put it to his mouth, bouncing it off and onto his lips, as though it were a leather ball. "I have never spoken an ill word of anyone in this world other than that tío of yours," he started. "Your entire life, I let people live as they pleased. The one t'ing I asked was to leave your mudda's bloody family be."

Jeremias pointed his finger. "You never said that. Those words were in your head."

"That is your Papá you're speaking to," Mamá warned.

Wheel and axle.

"Gran hombre is about to have his own family. Let him speak his mind, nah," Papá said.

"I am not having a family."

Papá stood. The table shifted. The world seemed to follow. "How will you prove the chile is not yours?"

"You'll believe a puta over your own son?" Jeremias said.

The quiet became more still. Rosa felt the beat of her own pulse in the bottoms of her feet, could hear air seep into her ears and the scratch of a chick on the roof. She spotted a pearl-colored spider making its way across the table. Its undeterred effort seemed to unstill the quiet in Rosa's head and she suddenly grew angry. She had spent nights in the stable while Jeremias slept and was now tired of his grumbling, his self-pity. All day, every day, he moped and sighed, and she and Eve and Mamá had kept silent in an effort to protect his feelings. But she remembered how much effort it'd taken for Mamá to make Christmas feel special. How Mamá, despite the weight of the situation with Francine, had marked the season with tradition, with revelry and parang music; how her table had been opened to everyone, every inch covered with fresh breads and cakes and Martinique teacups and saucers. And Rosa couldn't stop thinking of that day, early in December, when Tío Byron had come, when Papá held Jeremias's hand even as it became clear what he had done to Francine. The aggravation Jeremias caused was like a darkness that poisoned, that persisted. Rosa was done with it all.

"I saw them," Rosa said. "I saw his lips pressed against hers. I saw his hands."

"Take that back!"

"I told you Papá would be vexed and you told me to hush up, as always." Rosa stared at Papá, who now, for the first time she remembered, looked as if he wished her to be a liar. And suddenly Rosa felt quite sorry. But it was all too late. "They were at the guava tree between our fields and Monsieur DeGannes's. I was setting out Espina. I hadn't seen Francine since long ago and didn't know it was her until I saw the blue birthmark on the shoulder he was kissing."

"We were walking. Only walking!" Jeremias said.

Papá pulled the table toward him, took up his spoon again, and looked down into his plate as if he didn't recognize the food any longer. The spider slithered across his knife. "I will continue to teach you my trade and you can work at my shop for as long as you do as I say. But you will marry Francine and you will build a life outside of my house."

Jeremias shook his head as though this act alone could make Papá change course. "But they're not selling land now. Governor Chacon is holding on to everything. How will I tend to a woman and child with no land?"

"Eh-eh, you should t'ink to get a cage before you catch a bird." Papá reached for Mamá's hand, not so much to comfort as to insist, and the spider made its way down the table's leg.

III

West of Apsáalooke Territory
of North America

∼∼

1

1797

They had been traveling for four days at a creeping pace, the wear of their saddles the only comfort, for the afternoons were cold and the nights colder, and the descent down the mountain and over Bighorn River and into a ridge of pines, while snowflakes fell like prodigious blossoms from well-brewed clouds, proved more precarious than expected.

Victor was brooding. Ma had told him they were going to see a man she once knew. That this man would give them a good story or two and a place to rest. When Victor asked why they had left under the cover of night, Ma told him only that she'd had a dream and in the dream she'd seen Bluegrass with two faces.

On the fourth afternoon they ate a lynx that Victor captured with beaver castoreum as bait. The white flesh made for a tangy roast, and they sat shrouded by a forest roof of pines. After supper, Victor searched the hardened earth—the raccoon trail alongside them and the old cinder gardens—for any sense of who'd passed through before, for any clue that would goad his memory of a time traveled there.

"Have we been here before?"

"Yes, but you wouldn't remember." Ma met his eyes, then looked up as if to check the sky for a more appropriate answer.

Victor hadn't noticed that day's sky until then. The sun was pink with scalloped edges, as if it had decided upon tenderness. Ma and Victor had many times moved beneath that sky, beyond the reach of the Bighorns. In search of food, or higher water, or safety, the chiefs, abiding by their visions, would not hesitate to lead them elsewhere. There had been months, sometimes years before they camped again at a familiar woods, a welcoming ridge—long stretches of time that threatened to make them forget trees that had once sheltered their children and grasses their sick had slept upon, but no matter the passing years, no place was ever forgotten. And as Ma and Victor continued west into what he believed was Siksikaitsitapi territory, Victor was certain he had never before been to this place beneath that tender sky.

"Did you hear me?" Ma looked at Victor oddly now.

"What did you say?"

"That we should try to find sleep now." Ma threw rocks into the flame, reminding Victor of the pebbles that had met his feet as he ran alongside Little Bighorn River, calling out for the girl.

"I wanted her to be my sweetheart," Victor whispered.

"Yes, I know you felt this way." Ma did not look at him. "But that is not what she felt. And you thought so little of yourself that you blinded your own eyes to this truth?"

Victor knew his love had been unrequited, but he had never thought of himself as wanton. "But why did she run? I wouldn't have hurt her."

"What is love to a girl who knows only fear? She knew the kind of fear that likes to dress itself in love's clothing. That girl wasn't right for a world that still hopes for joy. She wasn't right for a boy with a full, loving heart."

Ma leaned forward, rubbing together her work-worn hands over the low flames. She had once told Victor that she had hands like her father's. He looked at them now and thought they were only his mother's hands.

"When I was a child, they brought Africans into town, paraded them around, chained them to one another. Every inch of them was

sorrow. Until then, I didn't know sadness could travel on the wind."
Ma threw another handful of rocks. "I thought, as I watched them
from behind a tree, that maybe it was possible they'd had a good life
before. When I told Papá what I saw, he too looked frightened. I didn't
know anything could frighten Papá, and I had to wonder if that feeling
would ever go away, and how I would keep from passing fright on."

Ma offered Victor a strip of dried buffalo as if she didn't think him
satisfied enough. It was tasteless, but he ate more of it for no reason
other than that Ma wished him to.

"I came all this way and chose to raise you here, praying no one
would make you feel the way that girl made you feel. I wanted to
explain this to the council," she said. "I didn't want them to think you
were dishonorable. They trained you to be a warrior, but they didn't
know that girl was trying to unmake you, that she wanted you to see
yourself through her frightened eyes."

Victor remembered, years earlier, when Ma was big in the belly
with the twins, her ankles like water pouches. It was a cool summer day, when Father arrived after a long expedition, bringing with
him a new wife. He and Ma had discussed it once or twice before,
Father explaining to Ma that another wife would ease her burdens
once she had the new baby. This second wife was kind to Ma, but
Ma seemed to find her prettiness painful. And late in the nights,
when Father left Ma and slept in his new wife's lodge, Victor would
hear Ma weeping. Even as a boy, Victor knew Ma questioned herself
and he remembered feeling sorry for Ma then, remembered feeling
angry that she had passed on to him everything that had made her
question herself.

"This 'unmaking' you speak of had already happened," Victor said.
"Before the girl."

Ma drank from the water bag. Big gulps pretending to be necessary
while she seemed to be thinking of what to say next. "The elders told
me to take you on this journey long before now."

"Why?"

"They thought it would answer questions you have about yourself,"
she said. "I should've listened sooner. Now you carry the burden of
the girl's death."

Victor knew this to be true. He would never again be free of that burden.

"I think she was sent to show me that we are supposed to be here now."

"She didn't die for you," Victor said. "It's arrogant of you to believe this."

"No, I did not mean—"

"I want to return home."

Ma poured a palmful of water over the remaining flames. "Let's rest. We have still many days, maybe even weeks."

"Did you hear me? I am going home."

Victor could not see Ma's eyes in the dark. He thought he heard her catch her breath, but then she said, "Well, go. I can't keep you. You're a man."

"Will you return with me?"

"No. I have things I must do." He heard Ma turn from him and set herself to rest.

2

That night Victor was to keep watch over the mares. Bats fluttered overhead, the wisp of their wings sliced the air, their prey scrambled through the musky leaves that had become his mother's sleeping mat, and Victor dreamt of loose red feathers at the base of a tree—a tree with leaves as thin as moth wings. When Ma stirred him, he was certain he'd been sleeping only for a few moments.

"Ha!" she said to the suggestion.

He tendered a smile and looked up at the sun gathering its strength. Ma gave him more of the bitter drink, told him that on his way back to camp he should sleep at dusk and watch over his horse from the trees when the night drew nigh. All things he knew. Victor swallowed a gulp and returned the pouch to Ma. He picked up his bow and intended to offer his mare a bite of the leftover dried buffalo, except his mare, Black Tail, was not there.

"Where is she?"

Ma hurried alongside Victor, then together, they mounted Martinique to widen their search.

"Did you tether her properly?" Ma asked.

Victor had never not taken proper care of any horse. Ma had taught him that they were to be like his children, and thus he had become a father of horses.

"Of course," he said. "Wasn't Martinique roped?"

Ma clucked her mouth, widened her eyes. "I can't quite remember."

They rode for two hours through the hollows of burnt woodlands, searching, as oily, fat squirrels scurried before them.

"I saw my Mamá last night in a dream but she did not smile," Ma said.

They stopped at a stream for Martinique to drink. Victor remembered the red feathers of his own dream and wondered if both their dreams had not been omens.

"BlackTail is gone," Ma said.

"How will we go home?"

"I am not going home. You'll have to come with me."

"Both of us together on Martinique?"

Victor wished for nothing more but to be back at Little Bighorn River. He thought that he might see what others had not, thought he might find the girl.

"What's true, Ma? What will we do away from camp? Where are we going?"

Ma sighed as though tired of repeating herself and Victor was annoyed at her theatrics, for he didn't feel as if Ma had given him answers to any questions.

"The akbaalia told Father that you've been on the wrong path. That we must right it."

"But why would they let me journey to sweat so many times if they knew this?"

"*You* chose to sweat."

"But what does this have to do with you? A man should find his own way. This is what they teach us."

"I am your mother. There is no way unless I put you on it."

Victor did not know if this was true, though he imagined it was comforting to a woman like Ma to believe she held such power. "Did Father say my vision would come if I do this?"

"Father?" Ma splashed water onto Martinique's legs, before saying, "What I know is that if you do the thing you've always done, the same thing will have been done."

"But no other warrior has been sent from home. Maybe they feel I've brought them shame."

"Likc-Wind was called away and he left you without explanation. This journey is your question and if we continue, you may find the answer," Ma said. "My friend Creadon Rampley will host us while we search."

CREADON RAMPLEY

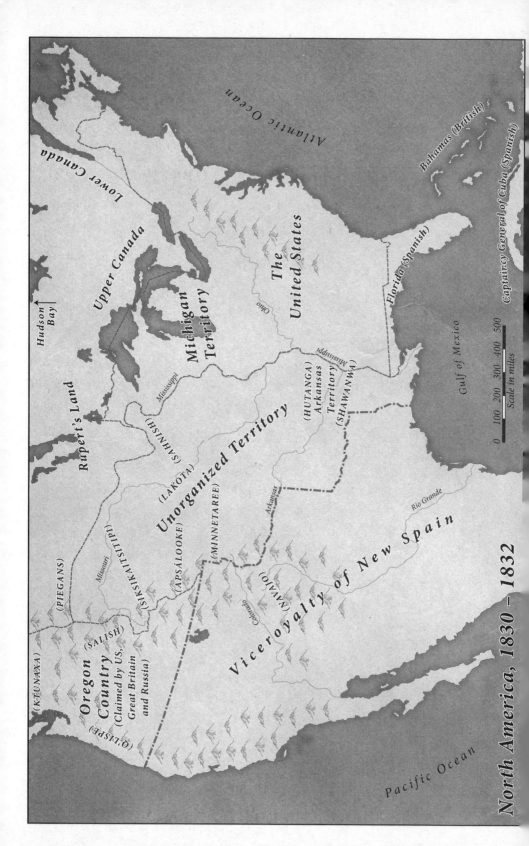

North America, 1830 – 1832

Rupert's Land

~⚬~

Memberings from 1804 to 1807

Sometimes now I feel like an old man. Weak memory. Slow to wake
in the mornin. Thinkin more than workin. Been some years since I
opened this diary. Figured I was gonna fix up these lil notes and fill out
my story so if you ever find this thing you was gonna know everything
that I did from Rupert's Land through to Oregon Country, from New
Spain down into Trinidad. And what I aint tellin is prolly cause it aint
important enough to member.

My mother was Indian from a Plains tribe I think but dont hardly
know. She left or died dependin on who you ask, long fore my memory
was fixed on her. My Pa was Reardon Rampley, born to an Englishman. Aint know his mother. Aint much care for his father. Set out on
his own fore he reached thirteen. I was thirteen myself in 1804, when
Pa died. First heartbreak. Not the last. Not the worst.

Pa was a hard man but he loved me. I suspect most sons think this
about their pas, but being that I was a half-breed, I knowed he aint
have to. Pa was a guide for Hudson's Bay Company. One of their best.
Knowed Rupert's Land better than most, and Hudson's Bay paid him
good to lead a brigade along the Northern Divide. A brigade that turnt
two, sometimes three times more profit than others. A brigade I aint
knowed hated Pa til he was gone.

Mountain life wasnt nothin more than gruelin work, bad weather,
and hard drink. Pa was the boosway, the leader. He made the jour-
neyin easier and an Irishman by the name of Lik Smith made easier

the drinkin. Lik had a recipe for a berry shine that could "peel the skin off a mans toes," Pa used to say. Pa sometimes dry-trembled on molasses during winter and couldnt hardly wait til spring when Lik would find yeast and begin fresh makin. Sometimes itd take up to a month to get it right but after it was, only work gettin done was by the muskeetoes.

There was a fiddle and a deck of cards and the dim light of a fire sometime during that ninth month of 04. I was sleepy but I knowed that Pa, who was losin his eyes cause of snow glare, was gonna need help findin his sleep sack. There was a fist thrown early. Some cussin. And then Lik told me I needed to get Pa fore things got worse. Pa was like that sometimes. Was tellin them what dumb arses they was and how they couldnt walk in a straight line without him then ten seconds after I throwed the blanket over his head he gets to snorin like an old goat.

Seventh mornins was always the same. Camp woke and theyd wait for Pa to rouse then when he didnt, theyd set out in groups of twos and threes to collect skins without him. It was a seventh mornin when Lik told me to stay behind and keep watch over Pa. Lik had a beard that coiled up on his grey-scabbed lips that he was pickin at when he stood over me. "You know how the old coot is when he wakes," he said.

I knowed. Pa was piss-mad most seventh mornins. Stumblin. Shoutin. Sickly. Only times I member Pa scoldin me was on seventh afternoons. "There aint no better guide than me, and every goddamn time I close my eyes, theys thievin right under my own sons nose!" Usually we would set out to find the other men then Pa would take what he swore was less than his fair share and turn all his anger on me. Them whippins wasnt good for nobody. I wasnt a boy to bite back tears. I yowled and howled and made Pa feel downright rotten for punishin me when he shoulda been punishin that thievin brigade of his.

So that mornin, as the day had yet to decide what kind it was gonna be, I made what I thought was a wise choice and followed Lik and two other men off that ridge and down to the Missinipi, leavin Pa to sleep off the drink.

And I seent em too. Hidin half the skins in a nother spot covered by low branches heavy with ice. I hightailed it back to camp. Couldnt wait to see what Pa would do when I told him. Holler or fight. Whatever it was gonna be I was gonna help him. Cept when I got back to camp Pa wasnt there. His pack was rifled. His boots was gone. And there wasnt no sign of him havin eaten. And Pa wouldnt go nowhere without eatin. I straightened up the grounds and waited. Figured he just gone for relief but the minutes crumped into an hour and I got worried. I called out for him and searched all the usual spots then figured I was gonna have to track him.

I started at camp. Found his boot tracks and followed em as they crept along a cliff he warned me never to walk. "This ledge is every bit as shaky as an old pair a tits." I was too scared to glance down. But I was sure he went over. I sat there with my legs danglin, knowin I shoulda never left him. Darkness slid over me like a drunk whore.

In the first year after Pa's death, things changed. I never had no agreement with Hudson's Bay. Only Pa did. So nobody owed me nothin. And the men in our company soon learnt I wasnt no proper guide like Pa was and the money dried up fast. Course they put his death on me and I couldnt much blame em since I sorta figured it was my fault too. I tried not to trouble em. I tried to be as helpful as I could so one day maybe they might let me be a free trapper or maybe even a company man. But the loss of Pa was like a heavy swellin that made me stick out, made me unnatural to men who thought sorrow turnt a man to easy prey.

Bow bender. Ki-yi. Prairie nigger. Them was the names they started usin for me in the second year after Pa died. I was demoted from skin hauler to cook. From cook to water gatherer. From water gatherer to sack minder. They teased me about Pa havin raped my mother. Said she was his slave. Told me she escaped and left me for dead. Said Pa threatened many times to be rid of me but that he was scared them Injun spirits would curse him if he did.

By the start of the third year some of Pa's crew moved west. Others left for North West Company or the new American Fur Company. None of em asked me to come with which was just as well since I couldnt think of leavin Hudson's Bay then no how. I mighta been a lowly servant but I had food enough and aint think I coulda asked for more outta life.

Then somethin changed. We had a free trapper join us for a few months that year. A strappin fella who talked kinda funny. Said he come north from Arkansaw Territory. Said he worked on lands where horses roamed free. He wiggled his fingers when he said the word *free*. "Damn good life it was, cept a man cant bide by laws that has him believe a man who work alongside him aint a man cause his skin is dark. Didnt make no sense to me so I left." He argued with the others but then told em if they hadnt seent it with their own eyes then it wasnt worth his time talkin about it. I aint think much about his thoughts. I sorta reasoned them negras wasnt livin much different than me. But what stayed with me was his tales of warm sun and feral horses. I kinda got my mind stuck on that and couldnt get it unstuck.

It was the end of winter that same year when Lik set his mug near mine. I wasnt yet sixteen. My heart been so lonely them three years that sometimes I thought my chest been pried open and robbed of everything that coulda kept my heart company. Nobody talked to me. Nobody laughed with me. Most times they aint even notice me. When Lik sat, I was just shuttin down the cookin flame and was pilin wood for the evenin fire. Lik stretched out his arm and touched my shoulder and I thought I mighta cried. Touch was a long lost memory.

"Make sure you tie up good." His breath smelled like white tongue and the thistle-root soup I made. "Storms comin and we might not make it back for a few nights. We come back round soon as we can. Keep the pelts dry. Hear?"

I nodded but couldnt think of nothin cept that pulse of current I felt when he touched me. I woulda killed a man to feel again like somebody could see me.

After the men left I nibbled on some leftover "beat meat," we called it—dried, smoked, and pounded buffalo. I collected bowls and buried scraps and piled pine brush so thered be dry spots for the men to sleep on when they got back. By midday the breeze picked up from the northwest. Branches bounced and the sky looked to be bout to vomit.

I tested the wind careful to choose the right spot to tent. I piled extra buffalo pelts to protect the cookin supplies and weapons and pallets of castor gras beaver skins. Since them pelts sold for two, sometimes two dollar fifty a pound, I was keen on safeguardin them. I tied the tents low about knee-high to tree trunks. I didnt forget the drip sticks and I didnt forget the extra storm loops either. I aint forget nothin. But when that wind come back round from the northeast and that snow fell like white ink from a jug, it was too late to reset the tents in the other direction. I battened down and buried my head in my arm. Them pans and mugs rattled then slammed up against twistin bodies of trees. The pelts fought against the rope that held them fastened to one a nother. Cold air ripped clean through me. I wouldnt make it through the night. I felt my lungs tighten and burn so bad that I had to belly-crawl to the pallet and yank three pelts from beneath the knot. I stuffed one down my trousers, wrapped myself with the other two. I slept then woke again. Fought to fix the flappin canvas overhead but still the snow rose inside.

At nightfall the wind died so I built a small fire. Bout an hour later wind started growlin again. It went like that for two days. Took out my flames. Ticked off pelts one by one. Ripped off the canvas over top a me.

When it was all over, wasnt hardly no snow left on the ground. Pelts was flung cross a hundred yards. Some wadded up like snails. Some in trees. I picked up what I could then figured I better put together camp, knowin they was gonna be back soon.

"Tell me you aint untie them pelts." Lik's mouth was hung open. His tongue was the whitest I ever seent it. White-hot, I heard it said once. "There aint no way them knots woulda come undone. Tell me you wasnt stupid enough."

I thought Lik woulda understood.

"Stupid goddamned squaw!" He walked the camp. Kicked over traps and pommel holsters with flintlock pistols inside. "Come tomorrow mornin I want you gone!"

I was nearly a man but cowered like a child. I thought to finish cookin supper but was too shamed to move so I tucked myself into a ball and hoped for night to fall quick. Didnt know where I was gonna go at daybreak. The thought of bein alone scared me. I talked myself outta beggin Lik to change his mind. Told myself I was a decent enough guide. Thought I could lead a slow-runnin brigade. Thought I could go south and tame horses. Them childish thoughts was the only things fightin against the sourness that swished cross my throat.

Night fell and the men drank before settlin. But sleep wasnt no friend of mine. Some minutes after the hoot of a great horned owl, I heard footsteps. Enough drink could cause a whole camp to wake lotsa times a night. But them steps was movin in the wrong direction. I froze. I seent grizzlies, mad ones and couldnt-care-less ones, and there wasnt no way to know which was comin. I held my breath. It all got quiet again. I squinted into the dark but couldnt make nothin out. A squirrel or a fox, maybe? Wasnt none a them.

A hand covered my face. A nother dragged me by the hairs of the fur pelt I was tucked inside of. One or two or maybe three men. Four or five or six heavy hands and one white-tongue puff a air. I caught my breath tween the slits of fingers. They tied my wrists. Tore away at my trousers. Felt like an ice bath. You ever have one of em? I got pleurisy once. Pa had left me at Blood River Post with a man they called Nan who had tits like a chubby girl. Nan was tryna save my life for days. Seemed I was slippin away when he put my four-year-old body into a wood tub a snow. I only member screamin. Felt like a skinnin, burn was so bad. I woke a day or two later to find myself under Pa's coat. Nan had sent a message that Reardon should come back for his son's corpse. Pa had tears in his eyes. He brushed my hair and told me for the first time I was loved. You dont forget them moments and you dont forget the feel of your young flesh rippin at the hands of men.

IV

Siksikaitsitapi Territory
of North America

⁓⁓

1

1830

The camp was still smoldering.

Bodies extended outward in each direction, their charred and waxen faces melted into torsos, and toes and fingers were no more. Children —the littlest ones—were laid atop mothers, knees to their chests, tiny pearls of teeth the only indication of where mouths had once been. Victor wished to leave. The odor was of smoked timber, rotted flesh, but Ma, indifferent to the smell, considered the arrangement of the camp, trying to determine which of the Siksikaitsitapi tribes had perished there.

"A chief succumbed first." Ma determined that the cause had been a plague. She pointed to the carcasses of ten horses next to a chief's death lodge. Their manes, now like burnt grasses, had been clipped. "He must have been a great man to have had so many ponies escort him into the next life," she said. "The remaining horses—there must have been many—might be in a pasture nearby, hobbled no doubt. They might all die off soon."

"I could return home if we had another horse."

"It's been said that this plague can take a man's mount. Many years ago, after the pox came down from the north, tribespeople swore that when they were dying the animals were dying too. Those who lived through it say it was harder to gather food."

The camp had been left in perfect order, as if death had cared to be tidy. Through fluttering ashes, Victor eyed a medicine bundle set atop a pelt-covered rock altar. In its corners sat two red and two black plumes. "Whoever was last here knew enough about horse medicine to believe it could heal them." Victor told Ma he believed that someone had arranged the bodies and burned them. "Let us go."

As they rounded the perimeter, Ma told him the origin of one of the Siksikaitsitapi's horse medicines. She had heard the story from a Siksikaitsitapi captive, whom many in the clan believed Ma had helped escape from camp. The girl had told Ma that a young man named Wolf Eye once had a fiery horse who liked to mix with another man's lot. The other man, angered, told Wolf Eye that his horse should be broken and cut. Wolf Eye told the man he would do so when he was ready. The following week, the man roped Wolf Eye's mare and tied bones to her forelock and about her neck. The man thought he had rid Wolf Eye of his troublesome horse, but that night the mare returned without the bones, again bothering the man's lot. Embarrassed, the man threw the mare down, roached her mane, cut and tied her tail. The man was certain the horse would never return, but the next morning she was there again, her head painted in red and white clay. Wolf Eye knew nothing of this treatment until the night his horse came in a dream and spoke: "Father, tell that man to leave me. If you help me I shall give you great power that you can use all your life." Wolf Eye stood vigil every night, and a year later the horse came again in a dream and offered Wolf Eye the secret horse dance and the healing roots that would be the Siksikaitsitapi tribes' medicine.

"Only stories make one world seem different from the other," Ma said. "And then sometimes you tell the same story and it can make one world seem the same as all the others."

Dusk was near and the sky had taken on a grey hue so that it looked like an enormous trough of dirty water. Victor and Ma were eighteen days tired, having recently gone down into a golden valley then up around peaks that felt heavy with spirits, a feeling with no other name in Yellow-Eyes' languages but *crazy*. It had been difficult travels, but Ma did not wish to stop until they'd journeyed west long enough to forget what they'd seen.

This would not prove easy.

"Do you see them?" Ma nodded at something near a clump of withered gumweed on an icy hill. Victor did not know until then that both he and Ma had been tracking the same moccasin prints: three women, two children. "Must be the last of them." Ma raised her hand, signaling to them that she and Victor wished no trouble, for Apsáalooke and Siksikaitsitapi were often at odds. The women, whose shadowed faces reflected stripes of red and yellow, widened their eyes—eyes that from a distance appeared like dark holes. "Cover your face. It might catch on the wind."

"We must help them," Victor said.

"They're already too close." Ma directed Martinique forward. "If we believe that this sickness had once taken our horses, then perhaps it can take us too."

The children began to cry as they stumbled on the descending path. Ma was unsettled, disquieted in the way one becomes when one witnesses another's pain but cannot assuage it.

"I wish to die—I wish my children to die—in battle, like warriors, not like this," Ma whispered.

"A woman shouldn't wish to die in battle."

"I live in a world with men, Victor, so I fight." Ma directed his eyes to the women upon the hill. "Look at their paint. Red for war, yellow for hope. Sometimes Breath demands that you war to have her."

They rode for several hundred yards before Ma asked Victor to unpack the travois. The children scampered past thickets toward them, their thighs catching on branches, while the women, with knotted hair swinging like bells at their necks, came down the incline on another path, cutting off Martinique at the front. Victor noticed the sharp outline of the women's rib cages, like horns, their hands and fingers twisted, lips parting without sound.

"Lord," Ma uttered, and Victor saw too their bloodied arms and gaunt feet, their skins dripping from their frames. He had thought them women but, in fact, they were girls not much older than himself. Now they pointed to the smaller children and one of them signed to Ma in a hand language Ma did not know.

"What is she saying?"

"They wish us to take the boy and girl," Victor said. "She says they'll all die if we don't."

The three older girls inched closer, while the flat-faced little boy and the very petite little girl stuffed food from the travois into their tiny mouths and began to cough, to choke with pleasure and relief.

"We will find them a horse and take them back to camp," Victor said.

The girls looked to the younger ones now, and Victor saw the girls' eyes, prominent, bursting from their split faces, awaiting Ma's agreement. Ma *click-click*ed from her back teeth. Martinique trotted forward, forcing the girls to uphold their hands to block her.

"What are you doing?" Victor said. "You saw the camp. There's no one left. They are—"

"Sick. Yes, they are sick," Ma said. "We cannot take them."

"How can we leave them? We can't know if they have the sickness."

"No. We cannot," Ma said. "If they are not sick, they will survive on what we've provided and they will find people to take them in."

"I won't do this."

"Leave them your bow and arrow then. You will ensure they eat through spring."

Before leaving camp Victor had fastened his bow to his back. He and Father had made the pair together over many months, with two buffalo horns and a backing of sinew. That was all he had taken of home.

"You cannot give up what you love?"

"I would," Victor said, "but I don't know where we're going, what we'll face."

"Yes, the risk is too great for you too, eh?"

Ma tossed an extra water pouch to the girls, who began to weep. They wiped their faces with the same hands they used to beg Ma to reconsider. Their cries grew wings, becoming long wails as they rushed Martinique, pulling at Ma's moccasins, the skins of the slippers stretching beneath nails sharp like spears, nails that turned more vicious against Victor's calves and shins. Ma kicked out her legs, fought them, but Victor thought only of the girl he'd lost in the river.

Martinique charged with a stuttering step and cleared the girls from the path. Victor heard the girls' cries filled with venom, then a sudden quieting as they began collecting the food.

"This isn't what I've been taught to do," Victor said.

"It is not. They were suffering and I turned them away." Ma reached for her pouch and drank. She offered it to Victor, but he did not drink this time. Instead he searched behind them, inside the shadowed folds of trees, until the girls were no longer in view. "I hope those children will turn east. It is safer for them."

"But we're continuing west?" Victor had never known any Apsáalooke but Father to travel so far in the direction of the sun's sleep.

"Yes, more beautiful and more dangerous." Ma slowed Martinique, looking behind them one last time.

"I heard you say once that Trinidad was also beautiful and dangerous."

"Yes, for different reasons, but still I think every land is this way," Ma said. "Wherever we are, we toil in dirt that we come to think of as beautiful, we defend against hostiles, and we begin again when the earth where we settle does not provide what we need."

They rested for the night under a wide-bottomed larch, the needles clusters of pale green, the soil beneath them moist, and they ate fresh rabbit Victor had hunted that tasted of clover and charred chickweed. Ma rummaged through her sack and took out a pipe. She lit it, took four puffs and offered it to Victor. They had never smoked together, and for the first time on their journey he delighted in being there with her.

The next morning as they rode out from under the larch, Victor searched the morning sky and noticed that nothing was as he expected. Ma, driving Martinique forward, appeared certain, yet something was not right: they were headed northeast.

"You think we're being followed?"

"I don't know, but I don't wish to pretend my restlessness means nothing."

"Lakota?" Victor said. "If we go this way, we'll surely meet them."

"Maybe we will meet Lakota, maybe we will not. What I know is that either way we go we will come upon something or someone," she said. "This is the kind of land that yields."

V

Isle of Trinidad

⁓⁓

1

1797

Jeremias had been gone for a fortnight. Mamá, Eve, and even Rosa had expected Papá to cool, expected that things would settle, that he would collect Jeremias from Tío Byron's, make arrangements for the baby's care, and all would return to normal. Instead, Papá appeared to be forging a new way of living, a way of living without Jeremias. He had begun including Rosa more, soliciting her ideas about the crops, the horses, the designs for an addition to the barn, and all of this had made Rosa feel as if she were finally taking her rightful place in the family. If someone had asked, Rosa wouldn't have said she was happy Jeremias was gone, but she wouldn't have said she was unhappy either.

For Mamá, however, Jeremias's absence was a casualty, a dreadful miscalculation made by God Himself. A God who seemed not to take seriously her threats of spiritual abandonment. Mamá mourned Jeremias like no mourning Rosa had seen for the living, taking to her bed with confounding ailments, speaking often only in utterances and grunts. Yet the time spent in her room had little to do with healing or forbearance. Rather, it was a nasty, diabolical brew in which Mamá steeped her grief and, for good measure, threw in a pinch of resentment and bitterness, that once coalesced, needed only a willing (or unwilling, as the case was) emptor. And Mamá found him at the stable explaining the use of anvils to Rosa.

"I should have never let you send that boy away!" Mamá's skin was sallow and pitted. She shuffled now rather than flounced. Her hair was half pinned; wisps of curls masked her left eye as she fastened a too-short housecoat about her neck.

Papá scanned her from scalp to slippers, expressing without words that it might be best for her to remove herself from his sight.

"What honorable man sends his own boy from his home?" Mamá went on to suggest that bad things would come for Papá if he did not correct this misdeed. "What's sweet in the goat's mouth will be sour in his bamsee," she warned.

Mamá had sometimes joked that Papá's stubby ears made him hard of hearing. Now Rosa wondered if there was not some truth in this, for during Mamá's oration, Papá, despite the steady commotion only inches from his face, had turned to Rosa as though he might continue explaining the hardy hole, the step, the face of that anvil.

"If you don't collect him, Demas, I'll go and get him myself!"

Papá said nothing until Mamá, in a final act of desperation, threw her heavily steeped brew at his face. "At least I know he'll grow to be a proper man under my brother's care." She looked to Rosa now, her eyebrows raised, as if expecting Rosa to add something in solidarity, but Mamá's efforts to induce Jeremias's return felt to Rosa as though they were meant as much to hurt Rosa as they were to soothe Mamá. Rosa couldn't be sure what Jeremias's return would mean for her, so she offered Mamá nothing by way of support.

"Oh, Byron is such a proper man?" Papá said. "This is how you fool yourself, eh? Believing I'm the bad one?" As if to keep his hands under control, Papá petted the horn of the anvil, his calcined fingers gliding along the smooth surface, as though proud of their work. He had fashioned three of the same anvils, one for home, the other two for him and Jeremias to use at the shop. Only hours earlier, he had told Rosa that Jeremias no longer wished to work alongside him, and so the third anvil would be hers to practice upon. "Well, go then, Myra, if you ent want the shelter I provide. Let's see if you remember how Byron let his wife beat you, how they treated you like one of them slaves allyuh had penned up in that yard in Martinique."

Mamá took to her bed again. Papá tried to ignore her groans, hoping they were mere pretense, but worry eventually gripped him and he called for the closest man the island had to a doctor.

The short man with a mustache arrived in a tatty suit of black and white stripes and spoke with a lisp that made his top lip tremble when he issued an *s*. He said Mamá would return to normal in a matter of days. That what Mamá suffered was called "hytherics," brought on by an unfavorable temperament. Papá thought the diagnosis nonsense, said if this were the cause, Mamá should have long ago died from this "hytherics" thing.

"She doesn't sicken like this," Eve said to Rosa after the tatty-suit man's departure. Eve had expressed more worry than usual, for she had been the one tending to Mamá: changing her sodden sheets, watching her knees swell into breadfruits, her fingers fatten like red bananas. Eve had only just finished feeding Mamá on a chilly Sunday afternoon when, returning to the front room, she said to Rosa, "Why don't you tell him? He listens to you. Convince Papá that Jeremias should be brought back home. Mamá will rally if he returns."

Rosa ripped a corner of bread, still warm beneath cheesecloth. It tasted like bark. Like the color white. Eve's coconut bread didn't even smell like coconut. Rosa missed Mamá's cooking. "Jeremias should've listened to Papá. He should've been more loyal."

"You're lecturing on loyalty? You remember it was you who turned Papá against him." Eve slid the loaf away from Rosa as if it were a prize, setting it on the windowsill as she searched for Papá, due any moment for lunch. "You're such a chile."

Rosa did not respond but felt if she could, she might've told Eve that she did not feel like a child when she had undertaken all of Jeremias's tasks with no complaints, wondering every day, when she was tired and cramping, if maybe childhood was only for compliant girls with practiced smiles. But Rosa knew she would never win that debate against Eve, so instead Rosa peeked through the window and when she spotted Papá moving swiftly toward the house, his braces dangling at his hips, his arms at a full swing, a light whistle in the cloud of air before him, she thought if her childhood had had a face, it would be the loving face of her Papá.

2

Papá lifted Rosa to the lowest limb and remained watchful until she climbed inside the wooden lookout that he and Jeremias had built some years earlier. In an hour, at dawn, the tree limbs overhead would create striations of sunlight and the damp floor of the forest would begin to coarsen. But for now it was dark and cool, Rosa's moon-lit shadow making a long, ghostly figure on the muddied ground beneath them. Rosa settled into the hunting stand that reminded her of an enormous picnic basket. A bed of soft grasses dulled the creaking made by her adjusting body. She touched the horizontal slats that rose above her and peeked through the gaps large enough for a musket's perch and an arrow's sling. Papá sat across from her as she imagined he'd done with Jeremias. It had been a month since they'd seen Jeremias, and Papá had not spoken of him. Now, Rosa watched as Papá unpacked the supplies they would need for the day: water, sacks, a woolen blanket. With no rutting season in the trop-ics, Papá had scouted the area, the day prior, and found deer rubs, their droppings near the stream that Rosa could hear gurgling from their perch. "They're the hardest deer in the world to hunt," he said. "Brace yourself for a long day."

During the hours they waited, Papá taught Rosa how to strategize her shots, reminding her that broadside was the goal, the aim four or so inches behind the shoulder, and demanding that there be no head shots, no heart shots; imparting the importance of patience, persis-tence, and "Breath," he said. "Listen for it, capture it, fight to control it; direct Breath, and the heart and mind, and all your actions will follow its slow and steady lead."

Papá taught her a call, short and urgent, that he said should rise from the chest in a breathy vibrato. "With your young voice, the doe bleat will work best." Rosa practiced it again and again, with Papá correcting. "Suave," he said. "Now a bit louder."

The sun was on the backside of morning when the trees opened like hand fans to the sky. Some, Rosa noted, had browned into golden crisps as though they'd been fried, while the soft spikes of wild red bottlebrush blooms twitched like pony tails in the kind lift of the breeze. Rosa had eaten only two golden apples and a zaboca, for Papá had rationed their provisions, but now her hunger swelled into fatigue, and her body began to slacken.

"You wanta story to go along with that sleep?" Papá pulled the blanket onto her legs and moved himself closer, not seeming to care whether she wished to hear a story or not. "There was a man, Papa Bois, an old man he was, who could wrestle the fiercest snakes and who kept tarantulas next to his pillow. Papa Bois loved teaching chil'ren about the marvelous birds of Trinidad, and when the chil'ren working in the fields grew tired, he'd take them up on his shoulders and let them suck sugarcane while he did his work and theirs. After he died, he became a great legend of the forest," Papá said. "People believe now that he protects the trees and the animals and turns people into swine when they treat the eart' poorly." Papá touched her bonnet. "Your Mamá likes knowing that there is a hairy ole man carrying a bamboo horn who'll come and turn me into a wild hog if I misbehave." Papá moved her head to his chest. "Take some rest so Papa Bois can come and give you sugarcane."

Rosa heard his sighs beneath his breath, plentiful, bottomless, as though it was Papá who most needed rest.

When Papá nudged her awake, the late-afternoon sun had already sliced through branches and landed on the paler insides of Papá's hands, making it seem to Rosa's sleep-heavy eyes as if he were carrying a ball of light meant to direct her sight to a buck and three does.

"Your calls worked," Papá whispered, before smiling the smile he saved only for her.

They felled three of the four that afternoon. Rosa clipped the lung of one with her arrow, and Papá finished the two others.

Along the three miles home, Rosa practiced her bleating, happy to make Papá smile. "You're quite a bit of fun," he said, his face soft around the cheeks.

"Oh, you fill me eyes!" Rosa batted her lashes as she looked up into Papá's lovely face. He laughed the kind of laugh that threatened to grow bigger inside him, inside her. She loved that kind of laughter.

"Bueno. Try this one, Quite a Bit of Fun." He tried several times to teach her the buck grunt. Some of her attempts were too shrill, others had too much pulsation. "Your voice isn't old enough yet," he said. "Your Mamá can do a good one."

They were nearing home, the last bend of the grassy path within a hundred yards, and the mention of Mamá made Rosa dread their return. The sludgy silence between her parents felt like a slow, unrelenting suffocation. The day out with Papá had offered relief, but Rosa was familiar with the long-suffering nature of her parents' quarrels. "Will you stay vexed with Mamá forever?"

"Does that worry you?"

She wondered why elders thought their burdens mattered only to them. "It makes you sad," she said, only then realizing she did not have the power to keep Papá happy. "I don't like for you to be this way."

"Mamá needs hearts, livers, and a good brocket deer broth to heal. She'll get better now that we have this." Papá gestured toward the sacks they dragged behind them.

"You did this for her?"

"You hunt them and then you hunt for them." Papá looked to Rosa, who must have appeared confused. "Love has no quarrel. Love sits high, like we sat today, watching anger and disappointment from afar," he said. "Of course, this love t'ing is a burden too. A very big one." He laughed. "Once it lights, the torch is carried forever, even when wrongs are committed, even when your heart aches because it is so open. How to love and not break is a question that won't be answered in my lifetime, for sure."

Perhaps he and Mamá were more than just wheel and axle.

"You'll understand all this better one day," he said.

"No, I won't. I'm never loving anyone but you."

3

Payments had been made for the fattening and slaughtering of pigs; thirty and five white-feather fowls born in January would not see the rainy season; holds had been placed on the neighbors' extra ground provisions; the aging of cheese had been rushed. And two of the brocket deer Papá had smoked at the backside of the stable were to be brought to Tío Byron's.

Padre José of the Cathedral of Saint Joseph wished to set a date for the wedding sometime after he returned in May from Venezuela, across the Golfo de la Ballena. Tío Byron, however, contended that the delay would cause great troubles for the traveling families, who had already been told the wedding would occur before Easter.

"A fast marriage has plenty teeth," Padre José reportedly said.

Nonetheless, he agreed to delay his travels and set the wedding for the sixth of February 1797, believing it to be the most auspicious date for the young couple.

Mamá and Eve prepared for weeks. They sewed dresses with false sleeves, fitted Rosa twice for a frock with piping she swore she would never don. They made tamarind balls, black cake, chow, and toolum thick and sticky with molasses. Mamá and Eve were molding coconut bread into heart shapes the afternoon Monsieur DeGannes met Rosa at the bend in the riding path that abutted his land.

Monsieur sat hunched on a frisky horse and held forth something Rosa could not make out until she stopped beside him.

"Good afternoon, Monsieur," she said.

"Would you be kind enough to offer these to Jeremias as a gift from me? I'd like for him to study the binding."

Rosa accepted the books and set them inside her saddlebag.

"Demas and Myra must be delighted at the upcoming nuptials. I'm sorry I cannot attend."

The few times Rosa had spoken to Monsieur, he'd been warm, often speaking longer than she wished. Now Rosa offered him a half smile so as not to encourage him to chat longer.

"They are a fine couple," Monsieur said before riding off.

When Rosa arrived home, she removed her work gloves and extended the three leather-bound books to Mamá. "Monsieur DeGannes gave me these for Jeremias."

Mamá wiped her hands along her apron and looked through the window at Papá, who stood sanding the backsides of new chairs. She had been on the mend since Padre set the wedding date, her skin again dewy, though her eyes remained like old yolks.

Mamá passed the books to Eve. "Go and hide these somewhere."

Mamá and Eve seemed now—maybe it had been forever—to have their own language, a woman's language Rosa did not share. There were eye flits and mouth intimations, sighs and nods and humphs that seemed to capture every necessary feeling and expression between women. Rosa remembered the day in the barn when Mamá had come to quarrel with Papá. How Mamá had sought her support and how Rosa had refused her with silence, the one act of that woman's language Rosa knew, the one act that now kept her on the outside of it.

"I can hide them," Rosa offered.

Mamá shook her head as if Rosa could not be considered for such a task.

"He sent his regrets," Rosa added. "Said he wouldn't be able to make it to the wedding."

"I'm certain," Mamá said, and Eve clucked her tongue behind her.

"Can I send my regrets too? Like Papá and Monsieur DeGannes?"

Mamá glared as though she knew how much pleasure Rosa had taken in speaking those words. "Who said Papá's not going to that wedding?"

Rosa knew better than to say it was Papá himself, but still Eve scowled at her while Mamá made her way outside.

It was a breezy day. Clouds hung like dirty parasols in the sky. The gnats, fighting against the wind, were less obtrusive than in the weeks prior, though the flies swarmed every blooming poinsettia and wild orchid bush Mamá had ever planted. The greens—the many greens of Trinidad—were most vivid as they shook in the breeze, displaying their fairer undersides, while Mamá marched to their wild rhythms toward an unsuspecting Papá who hummed and sanded as dust from the purpleheart collected in the coily waves of his beard.

Mamá began her recitation with her hands upon her hips. It seemed to Rosa that she was always in this defiant pose, and Rosa wondered if life for a wife and mother wasn't a never-ending quest to be seen and heard. A life hardly noted between hands-upon-hips moments.

"Demas, you will not bring more shame upon this family."

The patch of dirt beneath Papá had become a small dune, and with every six strokes against the grain, he ground the tip of his right boot into it.

"Jeremias will not be able to make a living for his wife and child if people believe this an unholy marriage. You will lose business, and he will never be able to earn the respect of others. The only reason we have what we have is because people know you to be an honorable man." Mamá often went too long. Four sentences when one would do. "You must attend this wedding. You must do what's best for our son."

Papá sanded and blew, sanded and blew. He seemed to remember, though it appeared Mamá did not, that silence was the beating heart of their marriage.

"Demas, are you hearing me?"

"You gointa tell them I'm ill."

"No. I'll not lie."

"You want me to tell them she's already with child? How will your priest-man feel about that?" Papá wiped the sawdust from his nose with his calloused hands. They were large, his hands—the hands of a man who had been born into labor.

"Demas." Mamá said his name softly now.

"Don't Demas me." He cheupsed, and it appeared he was suddenly struck by the absurdity of this all. "You can lie to a holy man about somet'ing as sacred as a chile, you can pretend that two first cousins marrying is sanctioned by their parents, you can close your eyes to your brudda owning people who look no different than his own mudda, but you cannot tell another lie? Your family spent the last fourteen years lying. Telling anybody who'd listen that I stole their special Martinique cacao beans and made riches from them. That I owe them everyt'ing I does have, that I'd be nada if it wasn't for them. You ent know what it does to a man to see his only son in such a predicament with them kinda people."

Papá looked to Rosa and Eve. His rhetoric softened, if only a little. "You and I both have been on our knees in prayer, hoping the boy would turn out all right. That all our work wouldn't be wasted. He wished to read books, yes, let's give him books. He wished not to toil in the heat, then no, let's let him get a bit bigger before we put such demands on him. His whole life, we tiptoed around our needs so he could have his desires, and this is what he go and do?"

"I don't know that he's done it," Mamá said.

"But you not arguing that point with your brudda, eh? You'll see your son be eaten up because you scared of your own family. What kinda mudda are you?"

Mamá removed her apron and set it down into the grass like a woman who thought she needed to unwoman herself for a man's fight. "What kind of mother am I? I'm the sort who consoles a boy whose Papá won't mind him. The sort who tries but fails every time to explain your indifference toward him. Rosa, you give all your words to. Eve and Jeremias and I must fight for what little is left. Must I remind you that Rosa is not un garçon? She will blossom soon enough into a girl whose body will turn on her, make her into a woman who will have to marry and leave you and this place. What and who will you have then?"

Papá dusted his hands. His marked dune was now crushed. Rosa felt much the same. "I'm making chairs for your family so they can sit and watch my son's life be destroyed by one of their own. I t'ink it's suficiente."

4

The guests said Francine was a most angelic bride. The not-so-white lace dress covered her neck, framing her fetching face, the long gloves revealing a touch of warm-colored skin at her elbows. "Plump and blushing," the children whispered, pleased with the pageantry, though many of the adults in the front pews had been certain Francine did not recite the Lord's Prayer at the outset of the ceremony and even more certain she hadn't once looked toward Jeremias. Such musings were largely confirmed when Padre José stopped his recitation of Corinthians 13, leaned into Francine with his bushy white beard, and said, "Why the long face?"

The women and men who were not already sleeping sat forward, gasps locked in their gullets. All the babies were quieted.

Tío Byron was half raised from his corner seat in the front pew, sweating like a jooked piglet, his new white hat resting upon his wife's thighs. "You know how young people are these days!" He turned and winked at the crowd, the guests laughed, and Padre continued.

After the ceremony, Rosa overheard Mamá speaking to Tío Byron. "Why would Padre ask such a thing unless he was suspicious?" They directed Tío Byron's new girl—a dark-skinned gal with one cockeye and one sad eye—on how to prep the flatware for guests who were waiting to be served lunch in Tío Byron's yard.

"It's done. It can't be undone now." Tío Byron said this of the marriage as if he were speaking of burnt cake.

Despite the fetid heat, it was a most picturesque day: leaves aflutter, bird feathers in blurs of red and white and black, grasses glossy like emeralds dipped in hot wax. Chairs and tables from every near and dear neighbor had been lent for Francine's mother to adorn with tablecloths in a dye of sapphire blue. Children wore their Palm Sunday pinks and played beneath the row of palm trees that shaded the front of the five-acre plot. Tío Byron's home had been in a state of unfinish since Francine's birth. Half the house remained a hard-packed dung, while the other half had been refurbished with timber that looked to have been freshly painted in a sunny eggshell white. The one change remarked upon by everyone, however, was the replacement of the house's wooden three-step staircase which was a not-so-exact replica of the Rendón stone steps. There, Jeremias now stood in a new coat, the measurements of which were perfect across his barrel chest. Jeremias smiled generously at the guests who bestowed compliments upon his fair bride, as if he'd earned Francine by way of a righteous courtship, allowing his gleeful expression to fade only for Eve, who brought him a mug of pain-bush juice to cool his sweat.

The wedding feast seemed endless, compensation perhaps for Francine's "long face." There were bowls of downy rice and boiled plantains; callaloo bush bathed in coconut milk, fresh ginger, and cracked crab; pickled pork souse in a sea of lemony cucumbers; slices of roast pork, sizzling hot off the spit; tender pigeon peas seasoned with salt and garlic; roast corn so sweet and juicy one would have thought it laced with sugar water; pitchers of lime juice adorned with cane sticks meant to be chewed and sucked until wrung of their sweet serum.

Padre José, in a white cassock, ate at a round table with Francine's parents and the newlyweds. To Tío Byron's great irritation, the cock-eye/sad-eye girl offered Padre the thickest cut of charred pork atop a bed of roasted onions, and Padre ate such pork with his white tab collar jouncing at the base of his perspiring neck, while openly admiring the beauty of the Robespierre family, their skins, he said, like a blend of alabaster and copper, their hazel eyes wide, their curled lashes long like baby fingers, their dimples deep like the sea, and their mouths bursting with teeth white like lilies. It was remarked more than once that Francine, who was as fair-skinned as Jeremias, could have been Myra's daughter and that her babies might turn out to be the whitest of the family yet. Francine's mother, a runtish redbone with a weak chin and chubby hands, took offense to such comments, only to be reminded that Myra was her husband's sister (or cousin, if Padre was within hearing distance, for Padre disfavored marriages between first cousins), and thus it only made sense that the children would favor the Robespierres.

"Yes, but Myra ent the one who push that gyal out for eighteen hours," she said.

"You should be happy your chil'ren take after their fadda."

Trinidadians didn't believe in truth veiling.

Of course, stories of long labors and commentary about parental fatigue quieted Mamá long enough for her to spot Papá holding court with a drink she was certain he'd procured from some ragged neighbor determined to turn a sanctimonious occasion into a drunken fête.

"At least he waited until after the rites," Eve whispered to Mamá.

Rosa knew Mamá and Eve had spent the better part of the week worried Papá would not show. He had told Rosa he would be sure to attend, if only to keep Rosa company, but within minutes of Mamá carving the roast pork atop his plate, Papá had taken refuge with his drink, while everyone pretended not to notice the groom's father sulking beneath a chenet tree.

Now, Rosa was left alone to bear the brunt of being her father's child.

"How old is this one?" The woman asking of Rosa's age had only just ceased complaining about the conditions of the road from Port of Spain. This woman, Madame Bernadette, held a special reputation among the colored women on the island for being the loudest and most bold-faced, which in Trinidad was saying a great deal. She was a sizeable woman with flamingo-pink gums longer than her teeth.

"Nine years. Almost ten." Mamá looked to Madame Bernadette as if to seek approval of Rosa.

"Humph, she favors Demas, eh. Goat doh make sheep. Skinny like him, but so bozal." Madame Bernadette used this word that could have connoted "unlearned" or "raw" or even "stupid," but Rosa knew Madame Bernadette meant to suggest that she—Rosa—was "savage," for the term had come to be used by the Spaniards solely to describe the undesirableness of Africans. "With that dark-dark skin," Madame Bernadette continued, "it's possible to find her in de night out on dat big piece of land allyuh have?"

Several of the women and girls giggled. Rosa felt the heat rise inside her, easy-footed, like it could melt her into nothing, and so she smiled, for she knew no better way to conceal how she felt. She herself had wondered if the color of her skin made her more visible or less, for it seemed to have both those powers.

"She's definitely her father's child," Mamá said, as if resigned to this indisputable fact.

"Demas still not lettin' you take on any help? With all dat house and land, you should have t'ree, four maids. This lil darkie you does have here must be tired to de bone."

"We all work hard," Mamá said.

"That big gyal you have over there"—the woman nodded toward Eve, as she fanned herself, uselessly—"how many years she does have?"

"Eleven. She'll have one more year soon," Mamá said. "There are ten months between she and Jeremias." Mamá covered her mouth, seeming to remember only then how very young Jeremias was on this, his wedding day.

"Now *she* will be easy easy to marry off." Madame Bernadette bit into an ear of corn. Juice squirted upon her dress and she rolled her eyes as if the cob were to blame for it. "She become a woman yet? I have a nephew who would take a real good liking to she when de time come. But she gointa have to move to San Fernando cuz he ent movin' this close to town, for sure. He a bush boy."

Mamá rubbed perspiration from her neck, and Rosa noticed that her fingers were again swollen.

"He's Monsieur Benoit's son," Madame Bernadette added.

"The cocoa estate owner, Benoit?" one of the other women said.

"Yes, well . . . he's one of his sons." Madame Bernadette seemed to be struggling to find the right words. "Benoit sees about him. Doesn't deny the boy is his. He's a fine boy."

Eve, overhearing, smiled politely. Rich planter's son or not, Rosa knew "bush boys" were not to Eve's liking. Much like Jeremias, Eve wished for a life of intellectual pursuit, she wished for a man who might one day take her away from their stifling little island, a man who could recite Voltaire and who might refer to her as "the goddess everywhere so much admired," she'd once joked. Indeed, Rosa knew whenever Eve was ready, she would have her pick of boys who were *not* from the bush.

"But this one here will give you plenty problems." Madame Bernadette moved toward Rosa as she sucked a remnant of husk from her teeth. The long hissing rang in Rosa's ears like a circling gnat that she wished to smack down. "Dirt under she fingernails, skin like mud-cakes, and dat cheveaux tac-tac with hair knots like knuckles." Using her thumb and forefinger, Madame Bernadette pulled at a clump of hair at the back of Rosa's neck, causing Rosa to wince. The woman then twirled the tuft and released it as if to see how it might perform. "She not ugly, no, but she doesn't try to pretty sheself. You must make her downplay la mauvais."

Mamá nodded, and Rosa felt the embarrassment flush her chest then her face like a mad rash. If she could've found her words, she would've said she had no interest at all in prickly dresses with piping, no interest in massaging her hair with coconut oil or picking out grit from beneath her nails only to have it reappear within hours. Whom would she be trying to impress? There had never been a boy or a girl, a woman or a man (save for Papá), to offer her anything but a scowl. Even on that day, when she had prettied herself in precisely the way Mamá wished, not one soul thought to set their eyes upon her in the admiring way they had set their eyes upon Eve and Mamá.

"Go and call Papá to come and toast with Tío Byron," Mamá said mercifully to her.

Rosa sprinted toward her father, taking only a small interest in the lone rider she noticed in the distance. A latecomer, she thought, as she skipped over two children tumbling like wild dogs in the grasses. When Rosa reached Papá, he remained with his back turned, staring up into a vivid silver-blue sky, as if he were counting sparrows. Playfully, she reached for his cup. He turned toward her in a start, wiped his face, and she felt she could not reconcile the sickening feeling in her belly with what she knew could not be true.

"Were you crying?" she said.

"Sweating. The blasted drink is just too strong."

She took his cup and sipped from it. Guava juice. It had turned a bit rancid, but strong it was not. Rosa took Papá's hand, moist from tears, and found that her hand was too small to fully cover his. She offered him a moment before guiding him toward Tío Byron, who stood clapping beneath a new cowbell, one much the same as Papá's.

"You don't have to say anything if you don't want to," she whispered.

Papá's face was still damp, the lines upon it grainy. He had broken his promise "never to set foot in that house again." "A man with broken promises is never again a man who does not break promises," he often said. As Papá walked toward Tío, the crowd erupted into applause, surprising Rosa, for she would not have guessed that the rift between her father and the Robespierres had become a matter of public concern.

Tío Byron panted, pushing out big words like *proper man* and *destiny* and *reconciliation* into a pocket of thick air that seemed to be roasting all those guests who'd moved in closer to look at the flaring of Papá's nostrils and the hardening of his jaw.

Rosa watched Papá closely as Mamá reached for his hand. Mamá smiled as if she appreciated what the performance had taken from Papá. When Rosa saw that Papá had accepted Mamá's comforting, she turned her attention to the man who'd been riding, now hitching his fly-bitten horse to a tree at the front. The man's face, half shadowed by his wide-brimmed hat, was a broken oval of whiteness against a sea of shiny black, brown, and copper skins. His hands trembled as he waited for Tío Byron to release Papá from an embrace. When the guests turned to scrutinize the man, he nodded first to Tío Byron, then raised his hand to Papá in an expression of apology. He placed his hat to his chest, and Rosa was relieved to see that it was only Señor Cordoza. But Papá moved through the crowd as if more alarmed that the face was a familiar one.

"Demas, Byron, everyone," Señor Cordoza said, "they've come."

5

Papá wouldn't allow the torchlights. They were gathered at the table—the four of them—listening to the cannons and arquebuses explode in darkness. The ground felt less fixed beneath them, as if the island, under the force of the English general Abercromby's eighteen battleships, was at risk of tumbling into the Caribbean Sea. What would they do, where would they go, if the English demanded their departure, if the English demanded their freedom? Mamá said she was tired and that she wished to find her bed, but Papá held her close, insisted they stay together. Eve asked if she could search for the biscuit tin. None of them had eaten much; the reception had been cut short, and the guests had retreated to their homes, had packed their belongings, and waited, as the Rendóns, to learn the outcome of the invasion.

Eve doled out one and a half of the stale biscuits to each of them. Rather than satiate, the small offering had the effect of sickening already anxious stomachs.

"Was that your belly? Tell it only one biscuit." Eve said this to Papá and they all chuckled. It was a great relief to laugh, and Rosa was reminded then that Jeremias was not there, might never be there again.

"Do you think they'll attack inland?" Mamá said, slicing their smiles at the knees.

In the months before the wedding, the English had completed the conquering of all but one French-held island. They pivoted then to Spanish possessions. There had been reports of raids, savagery, small and deadly insurrections, few signs of peace. Trinidad, it was said, was particularly attractive to the English, for it was fertile and sat within short distance of the most vital continent, South America. It was presumed the Spanish would fight to the death for the island.

Papá rose to open the front door. There was one torch lit for each rider on horseback, two for every wagon. Since sundown, members of the upper class had been filing along the dirt road from town, their belongings in tow, their pace mad with terror. Papá said he was willing to open their home to a family or two, for Papá understood the uncertainty, the many questions that hung like flaxen webs in the air: If the English succeeded, what would become of the Spanish lands, the Spanish churches, the Spanish-held slaves? What would become of free coloreds and Negroes like them? Señor Cordoza had told Papá at the wedding party that Governor Chacon had failed to fortify the port and that there were already loud cries of betrayal from French farmers.

"But the English . . . nothing good has ever been spoken of the English," Mamá said. Another boom was heard in the distance. "They don't even like themselves."

Then Mamá asked Papá to tell them a story, and Papá told what he knew about their little island. He spoke of the cultivation of it by the Caribs and the Arawaks, specifically the Lokonos and Taínos, and about how those peoples had fostered the growth of corn, tobacco, cassava, peanuts, cotton; how they had been the island's only inhabitants until the arrival on July 31, 1498, of a sickly-looking man, leading a ragged crew of others. The twenty-four Taínos, who had been gliding across waters inside slim canoes, did not know what to make of the men they found sleeping in tall grasses. The Taínos saw the emaciated company of men as no threat, for the men were crying for assistance, for sustenance. The Taínos shared their food, showed them the island's beauty, taught them the name they'd given themselves, which would matter little when the crew's leader, Colón, became healthy again and would go on to brand the people of the island as "Amerindians" and rename their island, *Lëre*, Land of the Hummingbird, to "La Isla de la Trinidad," proclaiming their bodies and their land property of the Spanish Crown.

Rosa recalled only bits of this story from past tellings, but she remembered Papá speaking of the small wars fought for a hundred years afterward. How the Spanish had come for riches—gold and silver—and how the Arawaks and Caribs resisted month after month, year after year, ship after ship, until finally the diseases the Europeans brought had weakened the natives' defenses to such an extent that the export, intentional displacement, and subsequent enslavement of most of the remaining first people of Trinidad had been simple to execute.

By the mid-1500s, operating with native enslaved labor, the new Spanish settlers had cultivated a well-refined tobacco strain, Papá told them. In an effort to purchase it, the English began trading Africans to the Spanish settlers, while the French offered them textiles. The King of Spain, wishing to protect the gold he expected to find, attempted but failed to cut off the island's trading routes. He would learn not long after, that Trinidad was, in fact, gold barren, and it would not be until cocoa was discovered in 1618 that Spain's interest in the island piqued once more.

"Of course, for cocoa to be profitable, more workers than ever were needed." Papá nodded as if the story might have turned in a way that could have saved the Europeans from their inexpungable immoral stain. "Africans were brought to the island, but fewer Spaniards were willing to relocate to the tropics to manage the cultivation of cocoa that no one knew for sure would flourish. So the Crown turned to

French farmers on surrounding islands—some free coloreds, most Catholic—and by last year's count, there were close to twenty thousand people in Trinidad: a bit over two thousand Europeans, one thousand 'Amerindians,' ten thousand Negro slaves, and forty-five hundred free persons of color, including those like Mamá, born elsewhere, and Negroes like me, born or made free in Trinidad.

"We are never again of one soil." Papá reached for the torch and kneaded his hands above the flames. "So we find ways to stretch the world so there's room for us."

It was some minutes after two o'clock in the morning when a final and thunderous explosion was heard. Papá blew out the flame and rose to open the door. He said he could see nothing in the distance, but Rosa did not believe him, for she could hear his breaths, quickening and fiery.

At dawn they learned that as a small crowd looked on, the Spanish had put up no fight at all. The four ships Chacon had ordered to protect the territory against the English fleet had been torched by Chacon's own commander, and many of the soldiers who had been aboard fled into the bush.

6

1802

Placards were nailed to the trunks of the fattest trees on the corners of each dirt road in Port of Spain, in Saint Joseph, all along the coastal towns. They read:

THE COLONY OF TRINIDAD HAVING, BY VIRTUE OF A CAPITULATION CONCLUDED ON BETWEEN HIS EXCELLENCY DON CHACON, LATE GOVERNOR FOR HIS CATHOLIC MAJESTY, AND OURSELVES, BECOME SUBJECT TO THE CROWN OF GREAT BRITAIN.

Subject to the Crown of Great Britain. The words themselves meant little to the island's citizens, but not long after the Capitulation Treaty was signed on Valsayn Estate, life began changing for the Rendóns. And it was not for the better.

The English declared English the official language of Trinidad, and though the country would remain under Spanish law until further notice, in practice, all trade was to be conducted in English, all documentation requiring enforcement needed English translations, and all non-English anything or anyone would be treated as unsavory until otherwise noted.

By the first day of March, male inhabitants were required to swear an oath of allegiance to the English Crown. Failure to do so would warrant deportation to a colony more suited to his loyalties.

During the first few months of English ascendancy and immediately after taking his oath, Papá began spending his days at the new government's offices, hoping to guard against the deleterious effects of the English arrival. Finally, he was taken into a small office with one desk surrounded by loose stone walls and told he would have to wait for a census to be taken before he could declare his holdings and before he could declare himself a free man.

As time passed, Papá worried more. He began requiring a reporting of every family member's whereabouts. He told Eve that he would place her best dresses in a wooden box in the barn loft beside the muskets he had refused to turn in to the authorities. He asked Mamá not to ever again bring out the Martinique saucers and cups, not even for longtime friends. And when the influx of the Englishmen began in earnest the year of 1802, Papá planted more silver-thatched palms alongside the road not only to obscure the view of their home but also to obscure their view of a changing world.

The most notable and perhaps most distressing change in Papá, however, was that though Papá had never been a superstitious man and had often argued with Mamá about her visits to the obeah woman, he had suddenly begun taking note of certain bleak correlations: within a day of Mamá waking from her last dream of empty fishing nets, Byron had come to demand that Jeremias marry Francine; within hours of crossing the cursed threshold of the Robespierre property, the English arrived at the Dragon's Mouth; and in July 1802, as Papá worked an iron pipe in the furnace, he noticed, to his chagrin, a potoo, the ugliest and unluckiest bird in the entire Southern Hemisphere, with its sickly, raspy song, perched on the windowsill of his smith shop.

Papá's shop was situated at the end of a yet-to-be-named road overlooking a shallow tepid-water stream. On the backside of the three-walled store, set inside a rocky hill, Papá had built a stone furnace. Many had wondered how a lone blacksmith could afford such an elaborate establishment, but Papá never felt he owed anyone an explanation. Without shame, he fired the furnace once per week, and when Jeremias stopped working alongside him, Papá fired it more frequently, sometimes for a continuous forty-eight hours, sleeping in two-hour intervals on a thin pallet in the corner, then rising to finish the next order and the next. As more Englishmen arrived, the demand grew for axes, shovels, cooking tools. And though the quality of his work was largely admired, Papá told Rosa, who by then was fifteen years, that he felt as if he were trying to keep a young man's pace with old man's boots.

It was before midnight on a Sunday when Papá sat upon a wobbly stool across from the furnace. A breeze blew in from the east. It was a soft, tickly kind of breeze, the kind that could lull a tired man into a deep baby sleep. When Papá woke, he wiped his eyes only to realize that the sun had risen long before, and that that ugly bird, with its oversized grey head and bulging yellow-rimmed eyes, still remained across from him.

He remembered then that potoos swallowed their prey whole. "Shoo!" he said.

The bird flew off in the precise moment Papá remembered his furnace. Panicked, he doggedly attempted to relight it, but his efforts were useless. By the time the Englishwoman Mrs. Teller arrived beneath an unseasonably warm grey woolen hat to collect the pots needed to equip her kitchen, Papá's only choice was to ask for more time. He promised that the handles (for this was the only part missing on each) would be finished by the end of the day, but Mrs. Teller would not hear of it.

The constable arrived within the hour. He browsed Papá's tools with a seedy admiration, fingering the extra kitchen knives and massaging the nails Papá kept in the same biscuit tin from which the Rendóns ate the night the English invaded the island.

"Demas is the name?" The constable said Papá's name as if it should rhyme with *erase* rather than *toss*. "Can you read?"

"Spanish, sir, yes."

"So you can't read."

"I read Spanish words, sir."

"Do you? Do you? You never read the Bible."

"Yessir, I have. In Spanish." Papá said this, though he now knew the constable was not interested in his answers.

"Certainly you heard o' Tubal-Cain?" the constable said in his very heavy English accent. "Descendant of Cain? Cain who spawned a lower caste of beast on earth?" The constable lifted an axe from a hook in the wall. The felling axe served as a model for Papá's clients to describe the customized elements of their orders. It was a shining example of the superiority of his work, with its tapered head and perfect weight distribution. The constable stroked the flat side of the blade, clasped the curved handle. "He was a blacksmiff too. Very strong. Very wicked."

"He was also a chemist, sir."

The constable bit down upon his tongue; his jaw jutted back and forth. He walked with the axe to the furnace and wiggled his fingers over the cooled coals. "You'll soon leave off sayin' that, 'cause it's a fact that blacksmiffs make weapons of war. And you could be charged wif breaching the peace." The constable held the axe against the furnace wall for some time before returning to the counter where Papá braced himself and hoped the constable might set the axe upon its proper nail, demand that he pay a fine and be done with him.

But Papá also knew hope to be a distraction for the hopeless.

"And if blacksmiffs are on the wrong side o' the war"—the constable gripped the axe as if he saw before him a cadaverous tree—"then thems be the enemy." He brought the axe down with such great force that it took Papá's thumb as if it were a single hair in a virulent tidal wave.

Papá never spoke of the pain. The English took most of his tools, leaving him with only nine fingers and remnants of a business he'd built over twenty years. Before leaving, the constable had placed next to

Papá's bloodied hand a calfskin scroll from which Papá could make no sense. He warned Papá that the new governor, Picton, would be reviewing all assets held and taxes unpaid by coloreds and Negroes in the coming months.

7

1803

It took six months for the Rendóns to begin again. They had been forced to sell two fine-haired colts sired by Maravilloso and made smaller the horse stalls to ensure room enough in the stable for what little remained of Papá's supplies. Papá didn't know what the English would do next. With the cruelty of Spanish laws at their disposal, the English were impugning people for the most minor crimes. Beheadings, brandings, mutilations were becoming the norm. Papá knew that in every country they'd overtaken, the English goal was to whip up enough fear so that the order created from it would serve their ultimate intention of ensuring the greatest financial benefits to the homeland. Many of Papá's customers feared the repercussions of continuing to patronize his business, so Papá had to set out to the sugar mills, cotton mills, coffee mills, distilleries to hire himself out. What he learned at these places was that raw goods would soon be hit with a heavy tax and that the English intended to turn all the inhabitants of Trinidad into purchasers of English manufactured goods. All sugarcane would be processed on the island, shipped to England, and returned to the island for sale. This would be true for every crop, and the English intended to twist the arms of the small farmers first.

Papá, of course, was no longer himself. Rosa was certain that even if he wished to be, that that self could never again be found. He never complained, for he was not a complaining sort, but anger swelled within him, like mist, clipping sentences, impeding joy.

Mamá, too, had grown weary, sickly with listlessness and a need for vengeance that none had seen prior. When news of the constable's raid spread and people became convinced that the Rendón family was near its end, Mamá's friends stopped calling. Men she passed along the road no longer tipped their hats, and workingwomen who'd once respected her avoided her eyes. Mamá wished for her neighbors to grow angry alongside her, for the English had taken from all of them—they had taken the pride of their merchant community and unsettled one of its most upstanding families. But none felt the losses as deeply as Mamá, and many mornings Mamá could not rise. And on those mornings Eve took charge, ticking off from a list of directives, until one day, at the start of the New Year, Mamá dressed herself, pinched her cheeks to a full blush, and told Papá that Jeremias was coming for lunch.

"He's bringing the boy," she said. "Please dig up a few carrots for the breadfruit stew and pick a tomato, even if it's not fully ripe."

"I'm gointa meet with Cordoza. I can't be sure I'll return in time to eat."

"You will," Mamá said.

"The carrots are too young."

"I need them before you go."

Rosa had not seen Jeremias since the night after the constable's raid, when he'd come offering little Pierre as a balm for Papá's quiet fury. After, Jeremias would only drop off the boy, who by then was five years, leaving before forced to initiate a conversation with any-one but Mamá. Pierre's visits, however, soothed everyone, but most especially Rosa, who looked forward to taking Pierre to sit upon the great horses. After Mamá would give him his bowl of dessert crème, Pierre, with his excitement growing, would wipe his dirtied face and call out for Rosa by the name he'd invented when he was too young to know better. "Rotha!" he would shout. Rosa loved Pierre's thin voice, loved the way he reached out to her as if nothing could satiate him more. He had taken her place as the youngest in the family, and she had dubbed Pierre the new Quite a Bit of Fun.

The afternoon Jeremias came, lunch was light and unsatisfying, though no one dared speak on it. And the talk about the table was as stiff and insipid as the bland stew of green plantains they'd eaten. After, Papá and Jeremias, who had yet to exchange a word, sucked stalks of sugarcane, while Pierre, with one long-tongued lick, consumed the single spoon of dessert crème that Mamá, with great shame, had offered him.

"Rotha!" Pierre called out, but Jeremias pinned the boy down at the hips.

Pierre, who had a slighter build than any child on either side of the family, squirmed beneath his father's grip. "Non! I want to go!"

"But why not?" Mamá said to Jeremias. "He loves to ride with Rosa."

The boy, now sulking, climbed atop Rosa's lap like a Quite a Bit of Fun boy was apt to do when heartbroken.

"It's not good to have a tired child near horses," Jeremias said. "He hasn't slept well for a few nights." Jeremias gave the boy a stern glance, then rose from his seat while Rosa worked not to show her disappointment. "The stew is good, Mamá."

Jeremias scraped the pot's remains into his bowl. Leftovers had always been for Papá, but Mamá said nothing to discourage Jeremias, who ate what was left while standing, glancing at Pierre's hair that lay flat and shiny like wet fawn fur.

"Papá, Monsieur DeGannes told me he has been hoping to speak with you," Jeremias said. "He says he has some business to discuss."

Mamá looked to Papá, her eyes in a squint of query. "Since when have you had business with DeGannes?"

Papá glanced up from his near-empty bowl, an expression of too-tired-to-talk upon his face. "The man knows I'm right here. He can find me if he wants."

"That doesn't answer the question," Mamá said.

"DeGannes may be lazy but the man knows people, and I need the people he knows to know me, Myra." Papá sighed as if to let Mamá know he was growing impatient. "But now is not the time for this, is it? You have a guest."

"Your son is not a guest." Mamá turned to Jeremias, as if she needed to mop up the mess of his feelings. "Next time, bring Francine. We are family. You and she are both welcome."

"Merci, Mamá. I know," Jeremias said. "Francine has been quite ill."

"Did you give her the tea I gave you? People come all the way from town for my tea," Mamá said. "I gave you enough for the whole nine months. Has she been drinking it? She shouldn't be sick for this long.

The baby's coming in what? Two, three months? She should be feeling better soon."

"The baby's gone." Jeremias watched Rosa and Pierre mash carrots into the tabletop. "We buried it yesterday."

"Eh-eh? You buried *it*? You buried *what* yesterday?" Mamá roped her apron hem between her fingers.

"The baby. Une fille."

"The child is dead? Did you christen her? Was Padre José present? You're just now telling me this? *After* lunch? Un jour plus tard?"

Papá sat quiet, his arms folded before the empty bowl, as his stomach grumbled. Like Mamá, he too had lost a great deal of weight. His hair grew now like tarnished silver.

"Mamá, forgive me." Jeremias set his bowl down and knelt before Mamá, his hands clasped between her knees. "Francine had to push the child out. And we just couldn't keep it there. It was making Francine so upset. Still, she can't keep from bawling."

Mamá concealed her eyes with one hand and stroked her son's cheek with the other. She could forgive Jeremias, even for burying the child without proper rites, but Mamá could never forgive Francine for not doing everything possible to keep that baby. "If only Francine had taken the tea," Mamá would say later. Mamá never told Jeremias that the tea was intended to lift the curse that Mamá swore was upon that marriage.

Eve took Jeremias's hand and led him back to his chair. She sat beside him while Rosa distracted Pierre, flicking another carrot toward him.

"Things are very hard," Jeremias said.

Papá stared at Mamá, as if seeking her permission to speak. "For everybody," Papá said.

"Ever since those English arrived . . . ," Mamá added. "They are a blight on this country. The roads are better, yes, but I can feel evil on the wind. Do you remember when they first came? How those soldiers left that Negro woman and her child for dead? They received only a few lashes for that crime. But they found the woman's stolen goods in their barracks. The Spaniards would've taken their heads!"

"I thought bookbinding would be profitable," Jeremias said. "But the English are not interested in books."

"They are not learned people," Mamá said.

"Many cannot read, even those who come with titles."

"I can read!" Pierre said.

"Just because they English, you t'ink they educated? Listenin' to that fool, DeGannes. He introduced you to the bookbinding fella? You really t'ink there's a need for a second bookbinder on an island full of illiterates?" Papá rubbed the top of his head, then inspected his hands as if he hoped to find something more than perspiration. "Eh-eh, you expected what outcome?"

"I expected I'd have money to raise a family." Jeremias paused as if he'd never thought of his dilemma in this way. "Almost six years I'm married and still depending on Tío Byron."

"If you spit up in the air, it must fall on you," Papá said. "You made the choice to leave the shop."

"You lost the shop, Papá. How would my position be any different if I had stayed?"

"You would have a trade."

"I have a trade. Just not one which you approve."

"Just not one that allows you to support your family, which is no trade at all. You does always make unwise choices." Papá glimpsed at Pierre, seeming, suddenly, to regret his words.

"Sí, you are right." Jeremias pushed back his chair and stretched out his legs like floating logs beneath the table. Rosa remembered the first time she saw him do this. How it seemed that overnight Jeremias had grown taller than Papá. Bigger than anyone she knew. Now he was svelte, a man with half-moons beneath his eyes who always looked as if he felt cheated. "I'm not certain that baby was mine."

Mamá was still wiping her tears from the news of the dead baby when she began to shake her head, almost violently. That was the sort of talk no longer permitted at her table, in her house; that was the sort of talk that had already caused the ruination of a family and the death of little Cheri (God would open the gates of heaven if a name was chosen, so Mamá had chosen "Cheri").

"Pierre, can you run and get Mémé an egg from the coop?" she said.

Pierre leapt from Rosa and ran toward the back of the house. Papá waited until the boy was out of sight before he began speaking again.

"You bringin' me this story of dead babies and infidelity so I can pity you? Now you wish for me to let you come home? You ent t'ink I know Byron is catchin' hell? Heat does be in Byron's tail." Papá sneered. "Byron thought that whitish skin of his would make him special? He's a Negro now, eh? Them English don't care about allyuh French blood. Not when Byron can't pay the governor his taxes. He put you up to comin' here, sí? You playin' the jackass. Manipulative people . . . all your mudda's family is the same."

"I didn't come for him," Jeremias said. "I came por trabajo. I'm willing to work."

"You kick down the ladder you was climbin' and now you wanta put it up again?" Papá scoffed at him. "The English want people to buy, not earn a livin'. And if you work, you better work for them or they gointa try to starve you." Papá reminded Jeremias that the English had begun taxing every import and export at 3 percent, not as much as in other countries, Papá said, but too much for an island with an economy just barely on its feet. "They want me to feed England before I does feed my own family." Papá placed one finger upon his head. "If this land isn't run properly, we will lose it. They wanta force small farmers like me into forfeiture so they can put their mills on our land, put us to work in their dirty factories, and have us eating goddamn breadfruit day and night."

"Demas, please don't take the Lord's name in vain," Mamá said.

"Even if I wanted to give you a place here, this land now belongs to Rosa. She's worked it. It's the food she grows that feeds us, and them horses are being kept alive by she alone."

"But I'm the eldest and your son," Jeremias said.

"Entonces?" Papá said.

"By law, this land conveys to me."

"Sí? You t'ink I didn't study up before now? You t'ink you and DeGannes the only two gente de libros on this island? I does read too." Papá moved his bowl next to the now empty pot. "A man like me does prepare. That's what men do, Jeremias. Life doesn't happen to a prepared man. You shoulda been learnin' this when you was under this roof instead of lazying around waitin' for my land to drop into your lap."

"They won't let Rosa own land." Jeremias did not look at Rosa when he spoke her name. When Rosa thought of it, she could not quite remember if he'd ever looked at her straight on. "We don't even know if they'll let *us* own land and we're men."

"She will marry."

"Who will Rosa marry?"

They all knew that what Jeremias wished to say was "who will marry Rosa?" Rosa saw that Papá hurt for her. She didn't want him to. She felt she could bear it.

"There've been inquiries. As many for Rosa as for Eve. I've delayed, because Eve is the eldest girl, but she's too damn choosy," Papá said. "So I shall not delay with Rosa any longer."

CREADON RAMPLEY

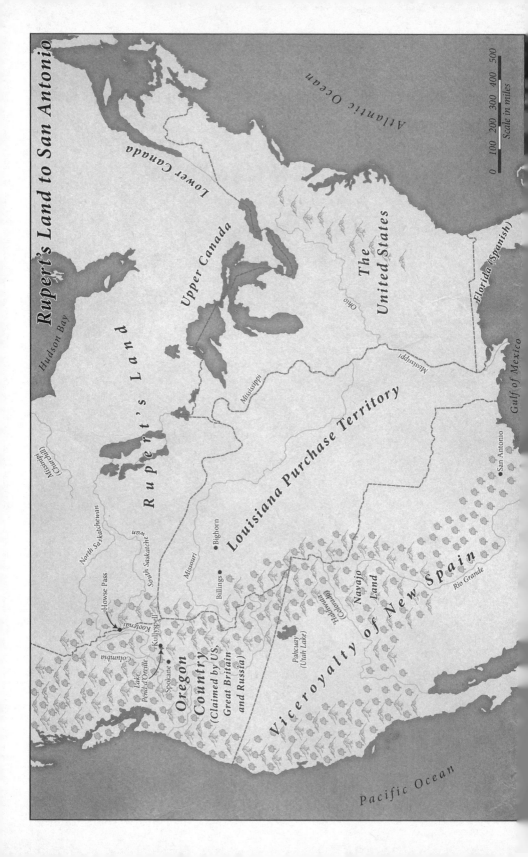

Leavin Rupert's Land

❧

Somewhere about 1807 to 1808

I was as free as I knew free to be. I walked for a year or maybe more, comin outta Rupert's Land then west over the Rockies where I aint knowed much of the time if I was goin or comin.

I wasnt far from the Columbia River when I caught some rabbits and heard that wailin child. A hand muffled the cry and when I heard a man say, "Dead man walkin," I stopped right where I was.

The man with the rifle was David Thompson. A rugged lil fella with a scar cross his nose and dark hair sheared into a tipped bowl. He once worked for Hudson's Bay and thought himself to be a great man of maps and geography and astronomy.

Thompson's youngest child had got sick. He was a slight boy whose name I cant hardly member. When I got there theyd been camped for some days in a place them Piegans called "dead life," where at that time of year mountain goats had to feed high and salmon beached on gravel banks.

Thompson was with his three children, his wife and six men. Theyd been ploddin their way toward the Kootenai River cause Thompson had been hired by North West Company to scout land and build tradin posts. His guide had died clutchin his chest and tween the men left there wasnt one decent hunter since theyd slayed a horse and was makin ready a second when I showed with my rabbits.

It was twilight when I started a fire and roasted my catch. Two of the children fell asleep bout as soon as that rabbit touched their lips.

The wife, a good-lookin Métis with crowded teeth was holdin the sickly one in the crook of her arm, blowin cool air onto his farhead while Thompson fed himself the biggest cut a my meat.

Thompson chewed and watched me real good til finally he said, "Do you have a compass or are you more adrift than I?" Seemed like he wanted both to be true. Told me he lost his compass but had a sextant and a telescope and a thermometer and parallel glasses "all made by Dollond," he said, like I knowed what the hell any of that was. I didnt tell him I aint never had no compass and that I wasnt headin no place particular that I needed to find but I figured he could tell that already.

⌒⌒

Somehow, the next day I ended up guidin Thompson and his crew onto a hard-to-find trail that somebody would later call "Howse Pass" (after a nother David). Course, if I had knowed then that you could name a piece a dirt after yourself just cause you put your boot on it then the whole damn land mighta been called "Rampleyville."

But I guess that aint the point.

While we walked, Thompson watched the world like somebody seein it for the first time. Made me think that maybe the world could be somethin to behold rather than somethin to overcome. At nights Thompson wrote in a diary like if he told it what he saw in just the right way then his words might could change into the very thing they described. He had a diary for the sky and one for the earth and a nother I wasnt sure bout til I asked him one afternoon.

"Do you know how to write?" he said.

"I aint good at it, sir. My Pa taught me a lil. Aint got much use for it out here."

"Appears to me like you may have a little Injun blood. Is that true, Rampley?"

I shook my head. I wasnt sure how I felt bout hearin it much less claimin it.

He went on. "It is a dangerous thing, keeping a diary. Some things a man would like to say should not be said. Yet there are things a man needs to say—things a man needs to set down somewhere to remember and be remembered."

"So you set that all down in there?" I pointed to his book with its beaten skin. "All your thinkin on them pages, just there for anybody to read?"

"Not for anybody. For the right somebody." Thompson had a way of speakin like he was gonna always know more than me. "A story can die on a man's lips. It is best we do not take what we have learned with us."

I knowed then that Thompson had written his whole story in that book. And it was about that time when I asked him if maybe he had a diary to spare so I could start writin mine. I was prolly eighteen by then and didnt think I was ever gonna be a great man but in my mind I hoped one day to have a somebody who might find himself in my story.

There wasnt much time to write. Most days we walked thirty miles or more. Thompson spent lotsa time measurin distances tween riverbeds and ridges and notin plants I aint never seent. I aint knowed if I had a job or not but I come to know how long to wait when he stopped and when to get us goin again. I also come to know that the writer of a history aint have to tell nothin that might make his ownself look bad.

It was midafternoon when I spotted two Piegans trailin us from the east. We was draggin beneath the weight of Thompson's supplies when they stopped to watch us tween cedars. Thompson had us get into a defensive position, stomachs on the ground, weapons raised. I aint never expect to die in no hostility and Im sure it aint no surprise to you that I aint die in one that day. But it aint cause we was smart!

"Maybe we should see what they want," I said.

We was on our bellies for two hours while them Piegans just watched us like we was a ripe batch a ninnies. I didnt usually offer no opinions. Most times if I thought somethin I figured somebody else thought it too and I stay quiet. But Thompson was runnin scared and I knowed for sure Indians aint never attack from that kinda position.

"And you've lived for how many years among the Piegans?"

"None sir."

"And you know them to be peaceful because all Indians are peaceful?"

"No sir."

The other men chuckled.

"We are traders not black robes," Thompson said.

Thompson went between awe and disdain of Indian ways. In this he wasnt no different from all the other men I knowed. Writin in his lil diary bout how different their beliefs and customs and dress was aint come without judgment. And it aint come without him bein frightened that his own way of lookin at the world might could be undone by knowin theirs.

"You rather keep your face in the dirt than listen to good advice?" I said.

"If the advice was good, Id listen." I thought he was done but then he said, "You are not my sauveur, Rampley. I saved *you* from wandering like a Jew in the desert. You have no drive, no history, and until you decide to walk away from this job I have bestowed upon you, I shall need you to button that mouth of yours."

I aint gonna lie. I was humiliated. But Thompson musta thought I was right about the Piegans since we got up off our stomachs soon after. Them Piegans gathered themselves too. Took to followin us with maybe a hundred yards tween while the children pissed their togs with fear.

But we made it to Kootenai House.

Thompson and his men had built the Kootenai House post a year earlier. It was comfortable and most important, it was well fortified. When we got there the Piegans set themselves in the open plain cross from the front door. Close enough that I could see that the five Piegans had weapons for a dozen men—lances, spears, foot-long knives, two buffalo hide shields per man. We unloaded Thompson's boat, skins, and traps into a double-door storage house at the back and kept the ten-guns and all our lead and powder with us. This ended up being wise since by next mornin the five Piegans had swelled to three dozen.

Thompson was pink with jitters. We took turns keepin watch and riskin our hides to set out horses. Fore then I aint never slept indoors and I felt downright trapped. I was lookin out the side window every hour hopin them Piegans would just be gone so I could take in a proper breath. We ate small rations, shared dried berries and my strips of smoked buffalo but wasnt none a us ever full. The wife took the one cot for the children but the two eldest growed more restless each day, while the sickly one kept grabbin at the wife's bosom like he membered somethin tasty been there once.

"We have only a day's water left," the wife whispered to Thompson at the start of the second week.

"What would you like me to do? Offer you in exchange for water?" he said.

She mighta been used to his tongue but I wasnt. I sorta always figured if I was lucky enough to have a woman love me that I might like to be gentle with her in a way that the world aint want me to be with nobody else. "The lake is just outside the window." I pointed to the backside of the post. "We could tie them brass kettles to ropes and dip em at night. Waters high nough now. Wont stay that way."

Thompson planned for us to wait them out but by the end of our third week we had our fill of water but aint have nothin left to eat. And the camp of Piegans outside had only got bigger. Each night they lit their fires and played their drums and sung at the top of their voices til almost dawn. Couldnt none of us sleep! Their plan to flush us out worked.

"I need you to go out and present these to them." Thompson put tobacco pipes and red porphyry in my hands.

I turnt the gifts over. "Is this what they come for, sir?"

When I kept questionin him Thompson asked me if I was a coward. So I stopped houndin him and figured I was just gonna do what he asked since a man like me needed to hear the breeze with its proper voice and needed to see sunlight hit leaves.

⤙⤚

The Piegans took a long hard look at my nose, my dark hair, and the sunlight inside my skin and started tryin out different tongues til we found a common language in French. They told me Thompson and North West Company brung their enemies too close. That Thompson had armed the Kootenais with weapons that the Piegans thought would be used against em. And they didnt believe it was no mistake. They wanted us to burn the post. They told me if we didnt, they would. I gave em Thompson's paltry gifts and told em we was leavin soon. They understood that to mean they could do what they wanted after we left.

When I got back inside and told Thompson they was leavin, he took a long drag on his pipe and said, "Thats how its done. Carrot and stick."

I wanted to give *him* a goddamn stick.

By late afternoon we had already killed and eaten fresh loon and with our bellies full we took a sit outdoors. It smelled like sweetgrass out there and the sun was burstin through some clouds like it was plannin a full-on fight. Thompson sat far off from us so he could catch up his lil diary. The other men pulled their hats over their faces and slept. The two eldest children played while the wife was strugglin with the sickly one, offerin him fresh berries to calm him. I watched her from afar not sure what I was feelin. I seent Pa and the others at the tradin camps with their chests puffed and trousers bustin, hopin to empty out into women who wore grins like they had pebbles on their back teeth. Lik Smith told Pa once that Pa needed to break me in but I member Pa tellin Lik that for a boy's first time he oughta be wanted. That thats what separated a real man from a beast.

The wife caught me watchin her. She brushed hair from her eye like she was givin me a better look fore her cheeks turnt pink like fat blossoms. I looked away but wondered what she was thinkin when she seent me. If she thought me easy on the eye. If she felt the ache I sometimes felt when I looked at her. I wanted to know what it was like to be wanted.

The older boy threw a stone hittin Thompson's girl square on the face. She leapt at him. And I thought to laugh but the wife seemed real upset. She left the sickly one and dashed into the grasses toward the lake. Thompson looked up only for a minute while the wife was givin em a good talkin to. She wiped the girls bloody chin with the hem of her skirt. I was thinkin about what life woulda been like had I a sister and a proper mother who woulda made us take care with each other. I missed Pa. Missed him in the same bad way I had the day they said they found his boots but not a body to pull off that ledge. "He picked a helluva place to throw himself," I member Lik sayin. It stayed in my mind that maybe Lik thought Pa hadnt stumbled.

The sickly one started to cry. He was always cryin so I aint paid him no mind til the cry become like shrieks. Shrieks like I aint never heard. He was followin his mother into them tall, fine country grasses, and I could see the stalks, gold and dry, swayin like mad and his left foot shakin in the air. I couldnt make no sense of it til I stood up to get a proper look.

A full-grown mountain lion was draggin the lil fella off! Half his head was clutched in them jaws. I seent where the cat was headed and ran to cut it off. By then the wife was on the other side of the cat, pushin the other two children behind her. The cat paused and the lil fella stopped cryin like maybe he was already dead cept I noticed the seat of his trousers was wet and his lil fist still wobblin. I hadnt carried my weapon and felt nekked in front of that beast. Its eyes was set on mine and I knowed by the look of em that there wasnt gonna be no talkin tween us, so I picked up a stick.

"David!" the wife cried out. Thompson prolly still had his head in that goddamn diary and I dont know if he saw what was happenin or not but I knowed for sure he aint take up no weapon. I heard the lil boy whimper like he was losin his breath. The cat clenched its jaw and blood ran along its soft tan coat, sleek and bright.

I lunged. The cat bowed back only to find the wife primed for the same fight as me. I couldnt see how that boy had any breath left but I sorta figured he deserved to take a nother if he could. I rammed the stick into the cat's right eye and when the cat shook, its grip loosed and I smacked it round the nose and ears and fought with it til the sickly one fell out. When I pushed the boy to his mother I knowed then what the cat had seent in him, and I knowed the boy wouldnt never recover from what his father aint do for him. I knowed this even as I watched the wife and Thompson pull at his legs and drag him to them like he was important, like he was a net a live fish meant to save a starvin village. The boy give off one last yowl and the cat ran off, knowin good as me that a nother boy like him was always gonna come.

Course, everything changed after that. Thompson aint much speak to me, and both me and him noticed how the wife aint look at him no more when she spoke to me. About a week after, Thompson said the sickly one needed time to heal and we was gonna leave the wife and children behind at Kootenai House for a short time.

Thompson worked us hard to make up the lost days. Rain come down most nights which made for bad walkin in the mornins. By the end of our first fortnight we finished the last of our food and was two days hungry. I hadnt even spotted a squirrel for a kill. Then one afternoon we come cross the remains of an antelope. An eagle had took most of it but there was some flesh left.

"This is our best hope to eat this week." Thompson said we should set the carcass to boil. But I aint agree. A man dont eat after no vultures.

I wasnt never hungrier than the night I watched em eat that antelope. I ate gooseberries—tiny, sour, hard-as-stones gooseberries—while Thompson looked at me like I was the sour gooseberry. By mornin, they was all sick as the dickens. Bent over bushes. Sittin atop bushes. Cryin into bushes. And it felt damn good to be right. While I waited the two days for their runny arses to be done, I hunted and collected enough provisions to last us a solid week. The day we started up again, the geese flapped beneath low clouds and we was surrounded by mountains standin atop a ground that was level and moist and we seent a doe red deer in the distance nibblin at brightly colored Indian lettuce on the shoreline of a most beautiful lake. Thompson looked at that deer and grinned.

"Sir, we got enough food," I said.

At first, the doe aint seem to notice she was shot. She was on a low point of gravel considerin mud hens off in the distance. Then her eyes got real wide and Thompson's man moved toward her, chopped her head clean off. Whoop. I coulda sworn I felt the breeze come off that neck. Pa told me I wasnt never supposed to kill more than I needed so when that headless doe rose to her feet, mad like anybody woulda been if theyd lost their head, I took it to be a sign that good things wasnt comin for us. I tell you I aint never seent nothin like it. She danced and pranced and wagged and Thompson kept inchin back tryna figure how long til she dropped.

"Sepanee," I said, memberin a word Pa had taught me. Pa had said *sepanee* meant "strong life," like the spirit aint wanna be taken.

When Thompson raised his rifle to finish her, it just bout pissed me off. I lowered the butt of it only to have him throw his elbow into my jaw. I wasnt no fighter but I could fight good enough. I swiped the damn rifle and knocked it to the ground. Thompson scrambled for it. Pointed it at me. But it jammed. Jammed. Like somethin was favorin me. Like my spirit aint wanna be taken. I looked to the shoreline where the doe finally bled out and with blood salty on my tongue, I said, "Sepanee."

Thompson's face was tight and his grip loose on the useless weapon. "Redskin," I was almost sure he said.

We crossed the wide lake on our makeshift boat and found a few families of Lake Indians who helped us tow our goods. It seemed we found ourselves a summer camp. An annual gatherin of Indian families. They was smart-lookin Indians too with oval faces and skin I thought mighta been like my mother's. They gave us pike and berries and Thompson's man, the one who took the head off that doe, laughed while he ate the offerin sayin that maybe eatin the "strong life deer" had brung us to the perfect place for a new trading post.

At the point extendin into what one of Thompson's men called "Lake Pend d'Oreille" tween Hope and Clark's Fork stations, near the mouth of Saleesh River and across from a lone island the Kalispel called Memaloose, we got to diggin. One day after a supper of cold fish soup Thompson pulled me off to the side. "Youll have to be going after we finish here," he said.

I half expected it.

For the next few weeks I took down trees, notched posts, mixed mud and clay to seal the roof. We built "Kullyspell" along with a fine storehouse over a few short months. When we was done I went to Thompson to collect my pay.

"You caused me to lose three days," he said. "Youve had a good run. Be on your way."

"Three days?"

"Took us through badlands," he said.

I done nothin of the sort but there wasnt no law to call. Differences between men was bridged by death or love, sometimes both. While Thompson, smug as he was, sat on a stump and flipped through pages of his lil diary, I dragged logs into the Kullyspell House and set em in the front room on the floor. I heard one man say somethin to Thompson just as I closed the door and set down the latch.

"Rampley, what the hell are you doing?"

Thompson was bangin the door. But inside the fire was warm and startin to spread like a shiny waggin tail. Thompson and his men kicked and pounded but we made that door solid and the only way they was gettin in was to break the weaker window boards, which I reckoned theyd do soon as they smelled smoke. Imma be honest and say I wasnt sure I wanted to get out. I had no place to go. No people. No land. I closed my eyes and leaned up against the mantel of the cold fireplace and wondered if this was what my Pa felt the mornin he left me. Like there wasnt enough in his world to fill him up. I waited for the flames to catch the ragged hem of my trousers and coulda sworn I seent a pack of horses in that fire—horses with rounded rumps and low-set tails—runnin like they was comin to save me.

Kullyspell,
Territory Unclaimed by Europeans

1809

Kullyspell Post didnt burn to the ground. Thompson's men was dousin the flames when I kicked out the boards on the back window and set about runnin for my life. After leavin Kootenai River Valley I set off southwest into Missouri and Indian Territories then after a year or so of hard livin I found myself in the New Spain province of Tejas. I had heard that the war in the east had turnt livestock into a real money-maker. Soldiers needed feedin, needed boots and belts, and their government was payin so to meet demand, private ranchers in Tejas hired cowhands to fight back both the natives and the wilderness. By the time I got to the west of Tejas at the end of 1809, one war was all but dead but there was a new war startin and now a grassy piece a land and a few cows could make a poor man into a rich one.

I aint never seent land like that land in Tejas. In San Antonio there was hills and springs, and the dirt was light colored and shallow like it was all a bed of silt. The San Antonio River was fresh, never frozen like the rivers I'd knowed. To the east there was Rosillo and Salado

Creeks, Martinez and Cibolo Creeks, and to the south was open plains of sandy soil. Almost everywhere I looked, wildflowers was as plentiful as ripples in a lake and fat-trunked trees grew like rounded hills. There was bristly hogs and deer and jeweled turkeys runnin wild alongside forestin squirrels and rabbits. And the streams overflowed with plump fish. In Tejas, a man could walk miles believin earth was his gift, could walk miles believin he was whole. I thought maybe my luck was bout to change.

I met Stephen before I met Alexander and Gregory. Three men who come to Tejas cause the United States of America didnt feed the mouths or souls of poor boys. Stephen, a good-lookin fella with smooth skin, was takin a siesta the afternoon I come up on him. I was watchin the big house for some days thinkin how I might like to ask for work, and I followed Stephen to where I knowed he'd be alone. He woke mad. Grabbin his musket. Glared til I proved myself like him, tellin my story not much different than his. He introduced me to Gregory and Alexander then took me to his boss, Meleanos, who was in for the week from what Stephen told me was a real fancy house in San Antonio. Stephen also told me that two hundred years earlier the Spanish Crown had asked Spanish presidial soldiers in the Canary Islands to settle in New Spain with their families. When the peace settlement between the Apaches and the Spanish was ratified, the Meleanos family began makin real money.

Marqués Meleanos didnt bother shakin my hand. He asked me if I could work hard. I told him yes and he clapped me on the back and told me that in New Spain, keepin my scalp was gonna be a full-time occupation.

New Spain

1810

"I hear Meleanos is comin for a visit," Stephen said. "Arrivin today."

Alexander sat up. We shared a cabin—Stephen, me, Gregory, and Alexander. There was other men on the ranch too. Lots. But we was split up like how Meleanos had his land split. We was on our first break when Stephen come in and leant himself up against the door. The housekeep who worked at the main house was sweet on him. He had just come from seein her and was chewin a piece a fresh bread she give him.

"When Meleanos comes from San Antonio trouble always gotta follow him," Alexander said.

"Naw, he come just to check on things and take a quick ride out with us." Stephen swallowed the last of the bread.

"You forget about Kent?" Alexander was speakin about a fella who left off soon fore I got there. "Didnt even get to pack up." Alexander turnt to me and said, "Meleanos caught him rummagin through garbage. Said Kent was markin like a dog and Meleanos told him he was gonna chop off his dick. What kinda man dont wonder why his workhand gotta go through rubbish?" He turnt to Stephen. "You member what he said to him? 'The only pijo that should mark near this house is mine.'"

"I hope a cock inside that housekeep dont count as a mark!" Stephen shoved his hand into his britches. "Whew! Pijo still here. Be hard to chop this big ole bastard off!"

Alexander didnt laugh with us. Took himself too damn serious was what it was. He was in charge of all the ranch horses but worked hard only when somebody was lookin. "Everything aint a goddamn joke," Alexander said.

"There aint nothin to worry about. Aint no crops dead, aint no cattle missin, and aint nothin we could do about it no how. He cant fire all us," Stephen said. "It'll just be you, Alex."

Alexander cocked his middle nail at Stephen and we kept at our chores til late afternoon when the groundskeep come to fetch us.

We was wearin our best shirts when we made our way the three miles to the main house. Shirts and boots Meleanos give all his workers. The housekeep come to the door. She had a square body and hair that grazed her fleshy waist. She was brown colored but not Indian. At least not like the Indians I seent. Her eyes was narrow like the edge of a knife blade. Stephen winked at her. Somethin about that surprised me. Maybe cause it was so quiet and almost polite-like. Her right cheek shook under the skin.

We walked through the house. My pulse flickered, hopin I could get a full-belly lunch or maybe a Dutch oven biscuit and a proper cup a coffee. Sometimes I felt like I was a sideshow animal livin out there, eatin when I was told and not when I was hungry.

We found ourselves waitin in a room lit with lanterns, so Stephen filled the time with stories. Told us Marqués Meleanos was the grandson of one of the first fifteen families to leave the Canary Islands. That when they got to New Spain they built the Church of San Fernando. He said the Meleanos family was like royalty.

When Marqués Meleanos finally walked into the parlor, he smelled like a fine cherry cigar. A nother man with a reedy nose and wide head walked behind him, alongside a thin boy.

"Thank you for coming." Meleanos pointed at the boy to pour drinks then ordered the boy to sit at the desk while the four of us drank, thirstily, our faces wrinklin after the odd and spicy taste we aint have no name for.

"I have brought my sons here with me." Meleanos nodded at the boy and I took it that he was one of em. "They will ride out with us in the mornings." Meleanos took a nother swig. "My wife has not been well. Now that our house in San Antonio is quiet, we are hoping she will recover."

"We wish her a long life." Alexander lifted his glass.

Meleanos thanked him then went on. "I have had news that the missions have continued to confiscate cattle."

Stephen had told me that the missions and private ranchers was always at odds. The missions believed that since they brung all the livestock to New Spain that they owned all their progeny (that means babies) and each time the ranchers fled from the Indians, the missions took back everything. But then in 1794, the Crown gave big chunks of mission land to the heirs of them first Canary Islanders and put all them folks in competition with each other.

"How is the branding proceeding?" he asked.

"When you fired Kent, Señor, you aint never tell us who should keep at his work," Gregory said.

Meleanos closed his eyes and his face got all tight. "You understand the laws. If there is no brand, the missions can claim any livestock I own."

"Señor, we thought you hired Rampley here to do that work," Alexander said.

Meleanos and the reedy-nosed man looked at me. I shrugged and Meleanos waved his small lil hand like to shoo me away.

"Señor Vokel will be in charge from this point forward. He has come to us from one of the missions, now closed after that miserable Apache attack. I expect that you will give him your attention and respect," he said. "Be ready to ride out in the morning."

⌒⌒

"Christ, if I gotta take the lil muck-thrower on my horse again!" Alexander threw the damp rag to the ground. Meleanos had ordered us to wash every day. Said his boys shouldnt have to smell outside on us but I aint never seent Alexander move to water on his own so I knowed he was gonna be angriest of us all. "And he pinches his goddamn nose too. I wish the lil sorner would fall off!"

We laughed but Alexander didnt find nothin funny.

"That lady friend of yourn," he said to Stephen. "Tellin them boys that men aint supposed to smell like men."

"She likes the way I smell." Stephen raised his eyebrows teasingly.

Meleanos, Vokel, Teodoro, who looked to be his oldest boy, Raul, who looked to be the youngest, and Pietro, the one who poured the drinks, arrived round dawn. We rode cross fields and up a bluff then down the other side. Grasshoppers was plentiful. Some clung to our stirrups and brittle locust skins got crushed under hooves. We smelled mesquite coals on the wind and suspected travelers layin low but Meleanos said not to bother with em. So instead we checked the soil and noted spots where the earth was weak. Vokel complained about broke fencin while Gregory marked cows ready to calf. After we took count of the livestock, the boys said they was hungry. I caught em two squirrels and a rabbit and Alexander called me a show-off but I wasnt really showin off til later, when under a midafternoon sky, I taught Teodoro how to skin em with a pared branch.

"Pietro, Raul, go stand near your hermano and learn from the mountain goat."

Everyone but me and the boy Pietro laughed.

"Pietro! Atención!" his father shouted.

Stephen cut in before Pietro moved closer. "Keep your distance from that one," Stephen said.

❧❧

By the time a boy reaches eighteen he thinks he knows somethin about the world. Even if he aint been farther than he can spit. But when I got to New Spain I felt I didnt know nothin. How did them Canary Islanders learn to grow beans, oats, melons, and chiles all in the same square plots? How do you get horses to do what you want? I wanted to know about people too. There was Irish people, English, French, even one or two negras, and all them tribes I knowed along the Northern Divide and in the plains was different from the tribes down south where they had Numunuu and Niukonska and Lipan. And there was Spaniards too. And lotsa men like me who aint know or aint wanna say who their people was. And what I learned was that everybody was suspicious of the other and that there was a certain kinda mistreatment for almost every kinda people. Course, people pretended they aint know that, pretended they aint see a lot, and it was this lyin kinda blindness that kept me from losin my mind at the way people behaved. So when I seent Pietro sittin next to Gregory under a cottonwood, I aint sure I wanted to admit that it left me uneasy. It woulda been too much trouble to tell somebody I seent them together whisperin, and that the boy was smilin a hard kinda smile. And that the questions in my mind all just landed like wind-blown leaves at the pit of my belly.

❧❧

It was the boy who come to me a few months later. I was writin in this diary mindin my own business when he come up spittin mad, talkin to me about how I needed to stop watchin them. Sure, maybe I watched them a few times, I told him. He wanted to know what I saw, wanted to know why I was there, why Id come to Texas. I knew he wouldnt understand nothin about no rafter-hipped mustangs, the ones I believed had crossed flames in Kullyspell to save me. But I told him anyway. "I was followin horses."

"That's Alexander's work. But I will make Father give you work with the horses," he said.

⌒⌒

"When you get what you want, sometimes all you want is more." Gregory said this to me after learnin that Vokel had took horse chores from Alexander and give em to me.

I told Gregory that where I come from more wasnt bad. He scooped a handful of nuts and put it to his mouth.

"Meleanos is leavin soon. He got a friend prospectin in Spanish West India," he said. "Writes to Meleanos bout gold as plentiful as the sea in this place called Trinidad." He stumbled over the word then said it again. "Treen-ee-dad," he said. "Writes bout how rich he got from all that gold. Meleanos is from the Canary Islands and knows a lil somethin about sugar and figures he could make a livin even if he dont find gold. He hired Vokel hopin he could leave. But then his wife got sick." Gregory snorted like he knowed somethin else about the wife.

"You know this from the boy?" I said.

He stared at me oddly then said, "I wanna go there."

"To that place? To Trin-i-dad?"

"Wouldnt you?"

I aint knowed what to say cause I aint knowed nothin about that place that seemed too unreachable and too hazy for my mind to hold on to it.

⌒⌒

First, the cattle went missin.

Fifty-seven. We searched day and night, splittin the acreage into sixths only to confirm early the next mornin that they was really gone.

Stealin that much cattle wasnt easy and Meleanos was pissed.

Gregory and Alexander got questioned first. After that Stephen got took for half a day. When Stephen come back he said to me, "If you got the guts you best leave now."

I aint need more than one warnin. I started packin like I was goin somewhere then Vokel and the groundskeep come and asked me to follow em.

⌒⌒

The slaughterhouse was way down at the edge of the property. It had big wood doors that was flung open and all I could see along the walls was heads of cattle on hooks with droopy eyes and a sea of white spit where there shoulda been lips.

"Is this where you put it on me?" I said.

The bile was risin in my throat and up into my brain like in a rain-logged cave. I looked through them big doors and spotted some hip-high Texas dandelions on the other side, and I thought that maybe havin them in my sight with them long, thin stems and wide yellow faces wouldnt be the worst a person could see takin his last breath. So when Vokel started askin what I done with them fifty-seven cattle, I was relaxed. I looked up on the walls round me and seent the blood-stained napes of the brothers and sisters of them missin bosses and I just started laughin. Laughed like a ball of funny done exploded inside me and this made Vokel so piss-angry that him and the groundskeep pushed me out to the other side of the slaughterhouse and marched me over them choice dandelions, where we come up on a mighty big hole, fresh dug, wide enough to hold a man or two my size and deep enough that not a soul would hear me if I chose to scream or even laugh from inside it.

Vokel asked me again, "Who took the cattle?" He had his hand on my back and I thought I could feel them damn cattle eyes still lookin at me and I thought what a thing that I was the next one fittin to lose my neck and that thought too brung up more laughter. The groundskeep pushed me forward and I seent that the hole wasnt six feet but eight and instead of feelin worried, I aint feel none of the right feelins and I thought maybe I was losin myself, like maybe I come all that way to find out that at the end you dont feel nothin good, and sometimes nothin at all, and that I aint have no memory outstandin enough and solid enough to make peace with feelin nothin. And there was just somethin real pitiful about alla that.

"Someone must go in that hole." It was Meleanos comin up from behind. His face was hard like a man who woulda been fine with puttin somebody like me in a grave and coverin him up.

And I dont know that I understood anything about what was happenin til the groundskeep turnt me around and I seent Alexander and

Gregory and Stephen and a wagonload of men up near the slaughterhouse doors lookin over that field of dandelions with their breaths heavy like theyd been runnin to get there to watch me die.

And then they pushed me in.

The fall was long and I hit the ground hard. It felt like I couldnt move my neck so my face was just stuck in that dirt and I smelt manure in the soil that rained down on my back. The rocks they was shovelin felt sharp on my skin and I heard their grunts like they was movin fast to get the job done with. Then I heard the boy arguin with Vokel. Couldnt hear the exact words he said to make Meleanos stop everything.

"We will return here if we do not find my cattle," Meleanos said, lookin down at me.

⌒⌒

Meleanos wasnt goin back to San Antonio til he found them thieves. He started workin shifts. Him and Vokel patrolled from just fore sunup to just fore lunch, me and Stephen from after lunch to near sundown, and Gregory and Alexander took the shift after supper ended to right fore sunup. I swore I was gonna leave every day after the count was made but there was somethin holdin me back like maybe I needed to make myself innocent again, like maybe if I ran and was caught, I wouldnt even have my innocence no more.

It was the sixth mornin of the week and I knew the head count was gonna be the same. One week of round-the-clock shifts and somebody was gonna have to pay soon. All that week Meleanos had gave Gregory and Alexander an extra hour sleep in the mornin so I was surprised to wake and see Alexander headin out just after sunup.

"Where you goin?" My voice was still soaked with night.

Gregory shot up and looked at Alexander hard, got himself dressed quick.

"To the house," Alexander said. "Gonna see about the count."

Gregory followed Alexander out and I aint think nothin of it til an hour later.

I had already got up and washed my face, ate the last of the cornbread and took a sip of the homemade grouse when I heard the knock.

The housekeep's face was flushed and wet. She shoved me aside and ran to the cot where Stephen was. "My God! Esteban! Stephen!"

Stephen woke and asked her to slow down. To talk in English.

"Someone come in the house while we are sleeping, looking—"

"When?"

"Last night, I think. After Señor found the missing cattle."

"They found the missing cattle? Where?"

"You are not listening good! Señor was out for very long this morning and the boy wakes early. He likes to walk about. His father does not like this, has told him to stay inside, but the boy does not listen." She took Stephen's hands like she was gonna pull him, like she needed to show him everything she seent. "He must have scared the robber."

"Did he say that? Did he say who it was?"

I watched them go back and forth, hopin I was wrong.

"Esteban, you are not understand . . . Pietro es muerto. He is dead!" she said. "His throat is cut." She began weepin. "Alexander is with Señor, filling his head with lies. And a father in grief has no ears, no eyes."

"Wha-what does Alexander know?" Stephen said.

"Alexander said the boy spent every morning with Gregory." She was shakin her head like she couldnt believe the words herself. "He is telling Señor that Gregory used Pietro for information about Señor's money and business. That he was with the boy the way of man and wife."

"He told Señor this?"

"I heard Señor say that all of you must pay. That there is no one with clean hands. They will come." She stood and fixed her dress and wiped her eyes. "Señor will not bother with the law." She turnt to me and then said to both a us, "You must go. Ahora!"

VI

Salish Territory
of North America

❧

1

1830

Spring with her warm, soft hand seemed to be knocking at the door of the valleys. It had been thirty-two days of travel when Ma and Victor tied Martinique to search for young wild plums. They made their way back to the pitch camp, their packs full, and there, two coyote pups waited alongside the path.

Ma pelted them with pits and they scattered but quickly returned.

"You didn't have coyotes in Trinidad?" Victor said, noting Ma's irritation.

Ma shook her head and surveyed the low hills. "Their mother is close by," she said.

Victor was certain Ma knew coyotes would not harm them. "If you didn't have coyotes, then you didn't have Old Man Coyote stories."

Ma inched back toward aspens that grew amid green-eyed buttercups as the mother coyote appeared, moving slowly toward her pups with one silver eye fixed on Ma. Her white throat appeared soft, while the rest of her showed thick and craggy, hinting of stone grey and pulpy orange. Her tail swept the insides of her hind legs like a pulsing heart.

"We have Anansi," Ma whispered.

Victor remembered then that Ma had told him that Anansi stories were from Africa. Ma's father had told her Anansi the Spider, like Old Man Coyote, was to remind children of their cleverness and wisdom when they were told they possessed neither.

Victor remembered the night when Ma told him the first Anansi story. A small boy, he had decided that he too wished to be clever, and he had set his head upon Ma's fleshy stomach and asked her to tell the story again and again so he could feel the words as she spoke them. "Anansi went to the queen," she said, "and the queen told him that White Snake was the cleverest and that all clever stories would be named for White Snake unless Anansi could find a way to deliver White Snake to her. Of course, Anansi needed a plan and soon devised one. Anansi knew White Snake loved chicken, so he set a trap with a fat, delicious hen. But before Anansi could catch him, White Snake slithered across the hen's back, over its head, and onto the path before it and swallowed the chicken whole." Victor had giggled then, for Ma had smacked her lips in the telling. "Anansi tried and tried again, until one day he struck up a conversation with White Snake. He told White Snake that the queen believed Black Snake to be the longest snake in Trinidad. 'I tried to tell her,' Anansi said, 'and I wagered on you too. Can you come with me to the queen's so we can prove her wrong?'" Ma had shaken her head, and Victor had laughed, for he'd wanted White Snake to say yes. "White Snake was certain he was the longest snake in the land and thought the queen deserved to know the truth. 'I will take you quickly.' Anansi told White Snake to lie down and stretch himself as long as he could, and White Snake didn't see what could go wrong with this plan, so he set himself down and Anansi tied him to a heavy stick and gently carried him to the queen. When they arrived, the queen sprung up with delight and laughed! White Snake was so ashamed! That day the queen declared that all stories of cleverness would henceforth be called 'Anansi Stories,' for Anansi had been cunning enough to get the wisest to lie himself down."

Victor smiled, remembering how much he loved when Ma told that story.

"Do you think Father is cunning?"   .

Ma frowned, and together they watched the pups trail their mother along the path. Victor thought Ma's silence meant that she wished for him to swallow back down his question, reinforcing his feeling that Ma had always preferred Father over him.

"This man we're going to see . . ."

"Creadon Rampley."

"Did you meet him through Father?"

"The other way around."

"You met Father through him?"

Victor could hardly believe he'd not known this before.

"Funny," Ma said, "I was with Creadon the first time I saw a coyote."

Ma told him that she and Señor Rampley had been cutting away from New Spain, heading north. It'd been over a half year of travel. A half year away from her home, and still she was heartsick, thinking of her family, thinking of the day they'd parted and all that had gone wrong. This new world she'd come to was vast, its threats plentiful, and it seemed she could not find her legs, for she shuddered at the smallest unexplained sound, grew nauseated at the sight of the unrecognized, her breaths, quick and unformed, left her always dizzy with fear.

Ma told Victor about the first time she'd seen something called "turkeys" and how, in Campeche, she saw her first armadillo split open atop a rock smoky with heat. She spoke of the Americas as a peculiar and frightening place where one could travel months without seeing another human, and how every day she wished to return home and find life as it was. But after some time, Ma said she began to understand that this could never be, and so she wished, instead, to find this new land less strange, wished to believe that she could one day forget all she'd left behind.

Señor Rampley rode always a pace or two ahead of her, though Ma had been the stronger rider. "Maybe two or three months more." Señor Rampley said this as if she'd queried him. And it seemed for a moment that he would say something about where they were headed, but then Rosa noticed he'd set his sights across a field to the north. "A coyote." He pointed to balding turf beneath the canopy of a lone canyon maple tree, where there looked to be a dog. "I could fill your ears with stories 'bout them things."

Rosa stared at the dog's narrow face and angular eyes, its ears like cones, and knew she would never like this creature. "I don't know if I would like to hear them."

"Nothin' to be scared for."

"Any animal that watches me like that cannot be a friend."

"He ain't watchin' you," Señor Rampley said. "He's watchin' that."

The covered wagon had two stripped wheels. It was dust covered and its base rippled as though it had once been floating in water. Rosa assumed it had been abandoned. They'd passed at least a dozen such wagons since leaving Mexico. Señor Rampley had said there weren't enough wheelwrights in the world to fix all the brokenness they'd seen. All had been emptied, some even half torched, but for some reason Rampley and the coyote refused to turn away from this one.

"Listen," he whispered.

Rosa heard a sound she could not place—something human. "We should stop."

"Naw, we ain't stopping."

They passed the wagon and Rosa slowed, staring up into the tops of aspens and down into the white bear grass, as if to find the sound again. Rampley had galloped ahead when a man came running onto the road, rubbing kicked-up dust from his eyes. His hair was scattered like sunbaked pine needles, his shirt opened to a dark, hairy navel. "Help! A baby!"

Señor Rampley glanced back at Rosa.

"Only foals," she said, answering his silent question.

She turned now to face the man, removing her hat and exposing her perky hairs. The man balked. Rosa had seen unkind reactions to her presence before, but this felt rabid, felt personal. The man returned to the wagon, his fists tightly balled.

"Let's go now. We don't go where we ain't wanted," Señor Rampley said.

"He can't speak for her." Rosa dismounted. "Monsieur! Mister!" Rosa overheard the man telling someone he'd thought wrong, that no one was there to help. "Señor!"

Señor Rampley called out behind Rosa, his words fighting against his teeth.

"Wallace, who is that?" The woman's voice was weighty, scratchy, feverish.

Rosa was now at the backside of the wagon. "Can I help you, madame?"

The man pinched the heavy cloth flaps to keep Rosa from entering. "We don't need no help."

There was a long pause before the woman asked Rosa to come inside.

The air was stiff and clammy and breathtaking. The woman was upon her backside, her soiled dress tucked beneath her chin, her brown-haired legs splayed, the rags beneath her soaked and darkened with blood, her pubic hair matted with sweat, pulsing with life.

Though everything inside Rosa wished to flee, Rosa moved forward. She was with Papá now, home in the stable. Papá would have led the restless mare out from the stall, into the open, atop long grasses, beneath sunlight and inside a slight breeze, if one cared to blow. He would have reminded Rosa to wrap the mare's tail, not too tight, and would have told Rosa to stand out of the way, for the mare knew best how to bring her baby into the world.

"Do you have water, sir?"

The man stood, glaring, fists still in balls, and Rosa determined he was useless. She ripped the lower half of her skirt, wiped the woman with it, urged her not to push.

Mares have distinct signs of foaling. Weeks beforehand Rosa and Papá would have prepared, and as the day neared, the mare would have grown irritable and restless, her tail would have swished or stiffened, and when this began, unless there was a significant problem, the foal would be birthed within an hour. The man, Wallace, told Rampley that he and his woman had been on the side of that road for six hours, that she swore she'd felt the baby's head but told Wallace she'd pushed it back inside.

"You must get on all fours," Rosa said to the woman. "He's got to find his way out."

"He?" the man said.

The woman, Beverly, was brave and cooperative, and the boy, an hour or so later, was rose colored and wailing. Beverly thanked Rosa and asked Wallace to find the lavender water she'd packed in her satchel. "You're on your way back to your missus, I suppose? She sure taught you to speak proper. You can give her this lavender water for the good work you done."

Señor Rampley had tried to prepare Rosa. Told her she would need to make herself small in that land. Unseen. But Rosa hadn't been raised to be unseen and wouldn't understand until much later that what Señor Rampley felt he needed to do was protect Rosa from Rosa. He'd wished for Rosa to do nothing to cause another to balk at her, nothing to make anyone know that there might be thought or memory or feeling or even breath in Rosa's body, a body they should never be able to see. It was as if, in that place, Rosa had been given the most extraordinary power to control another, if she were only to sacrifice control of herself. So Rosa, not yet grasping all that he'd asked of her, nodded at the woman, smiled to say thank you, and a short time later, Señor Rampley was urging her to ride through the night as if she'd still not done it all right. "We need 'bout as much distance between us and them as we can get."

But Rosa was tired and wished to rest and eat and rinse her soiled clothing, and when they stopped, the same coyote watched them from downstream, and before the next evening, the tight-fisted man, Wallace, had found them. He was hatless, riding a weak mare, and begging Señor Rampley to return Rosa to his wife. Something "real bad" was happening, he said.

"We can't turn back," Señor Rampley told him.

"But you got to."

"We ain't got to."

The man wept. His tears seemed to be of no consequence to Señor Rampley. "Have you no heart?" she whispered to Señor Rampley.

"You don't understand," he said.

"I got nobody. I left them alone," Wallace said.

"You shouldn't have taken your eyes off your woman," Señor Rampley told him.

When they entered the wagon, Beverly was already stiff. The child to her bosom had been dragged by a predator to the middle of the wagon bed and mauled. Wallace vomited, and the flies dashed to his production, moving away from the baby's open neck. Wallace turned to Rosa with his finger wagging, and Rosa reminded him that she was not a midwife. Rosa told him she didn't know the reason a seemingly healthy woman and her baby would die, but—

"But you just stood there! Let the baby come out by hisself! I ain't never heard a no midwife just watchin'," the man screamed. "Beverly ain't no mare!"

Rosa believed it was best not to speak or move or breathe any more than she had.

Señor Rampley appeared calm and yet Rosa felt an unquieting within him, like a spider skittering across the tabletop. "Sorry for your loss. You got somebody we can send a post to when we get to the next town?"

"You gonna leave me? Who're you to this gal anyway?" Wallace closed the wagon as if Beverly and his dead baby boy were now too precious for them to look upon.

Señor Rampley unholstered his pistol. Rosa had seen him provoked like this twice before and knew that for Rampley, a gesture toward violence meant he was no longer simply contemplating violence. Wallace, saying nothing more, glared at them, and though tears stained his weathered face and filled his eyes, everything about him told of a barely governable rage.

2

The coyote pups and their mother were now following Victor and Ma.

"They must want more seeds pelted at them." Ma pressed Martinique as they climbed out of a thicket of spruce and conifers on a windless morning. The birds flew high as Martinique descended into parched winding foothills. Eventually, they found themselves beside a freshet.

"We should stop and drink," Victor said.

While they filled their pouches, the pups dabbled in the water beside them.

"You never told me that story."

"The story of Creadon Rampley?"

"I always thought you came here with Father. Why would you lie?"

"Lie?" Ma seemed angry now. "I'm certain I told you. You must've forgotten. Just like you forget now that I am your mother."

Ma and Victor settled that night onto a patch of dirt beneath ponderosa pines. They ate the last of their smoked fish. The night was cold and the path before them long overgrown, and in the distance the sky brightened as if lit by a thousand torches. The rain would come. The coyotes took cover, though they watched Ma still.

"I'm sorry," Victor said. "About what I said before."

Ma lay flat against the earth, eyes closed. "You're not sorry. You can't be sorry when everything's been said." Then Ma, as if to avoid speaking further into the trouble that lay between them, told Victor the tale of the first coyote.

Certainly, they both understood such stories were to be told only after the last storm of fall or before the first lightning of spring, but Victor knew before Ma began that everything would be different about that year.

"Different tribes have different stories about how we came to be." Ma moved herself closer to the fire, tossing a twig into the flames. "The Old Man, the First Maker, used to spend time with his some-times friend, sometimes enemy, Coyote. There were no people in the world, no animals, save a few buffalo, and when Coyote went off by himself, the Old Man became very lonely. One day, the Old Man found clay and shaped bones from it and baked the bones in a fire. He took what he thought was the best of the batch, tied them together with buffalo sinews and smoothed them with fat. He then blew smoke into their eyes, noses, mouths, and soon after, the clay dolls came to life as men. The Old Man and the new men sat by the fire and smoked, all very content. When Coyote returned, he wished to know why the Old Man had tossed good bones aside. When the Old Man told him he thought them no good, Coyote convinced him that with Coyote's cleverness, they could make something much better than those lazy creatures the Old Man had made. They set to work and Coyote made changes to the original design, and when the Old Man blew into the eyes, noses, and mouths, the new figures came to life as women. The women began to talk to one another and brought joy to the Old Man and all the other men." Ma nodded as if satisfied. "It is said even now that when men are together, they sit and smoke and stare into the fire, and the women, when together, will talk important matters that men don't know keep the world intact." Ma beheld the coyote and her pups, their eyes closed, their furs glowing by the light of her fire.

3

That night as Ma slept and Victor kept watch over Martinique, it felt like the sky's fire had pestled itself into his chest. He thought of home, his sisters, all that he believed lost to him, and felt his thoughts like a rope, its strands swollen and tangled, and Victor wondered if this was what the girl had felt when she'd run into that cool, sharp river water.

"Wake up, Victor." Ma was kneeling over him, shaking his shoulder. "You mustn't cry in your sleep like so." She seemed sore, like she'd seen something she hadn't wished to see.

Victor rubbed his eyes, startled, before realizing Ma was upset with him. "Then when, Ma? When can I feel what I'm feeling?"

Victor thought of the coyotes, now gone, as Ma sat down, her knees to her chest, staring at him over the dying fire, in a way she'd done only when she thought he did not notice.

"Something feels wrong. I need to get back home," he said.

"Your home is with me."

"What does that mean?" The way Ma spoke was never plain, the words always masks.

"What do you think a mother does, Victor? What do you think I am?"

"A mother."

"Not a mother, *your* mother. Your mother who drips the world into your mouth like milk from a teat. Making sure the host is healthy, making sure you don't get too much or too little. How does that host get fed, Victor? I bring her grain; I fatten her up. You want the whole world? When you see how big and ugly it is, you'll wish for me to break it into pieces and feed it to you so you don't choke."

Victor felt heavy and tight and angry. "You said the girl was unmaking me, but you unmade me first."

"Enough." Ma stood and the last of the blaze shone on her legs, her face vanished into shadows.

"This is not Trinidad," he said to her. "I am not a little boy in knickers, eating tea sandwiches or whatever it is you dream about that place no one has ever heard of."

Ma doused the last of the embers with water and settled back onto her mat. "You're a child."

"A child? Then it'll be a child returning home in the morning."

4

In the days before their disagreement, they had alighted upon the Missouri River path. Its woodlands were thick with brambles and brush and fat rattlesnakes. They'd had to detour, for Shields River was bloated and impassable at each end, and mud had cascaded down the sides of the Elkhorns, trapping them from the east and from the west until rain mercifully washed away the sludge. All this they had managed with aplomb, and yet it was upon Victor's return to his sleeping mat after relieving himself that he stumbled, like a small boy, onto a coiling, clawing branch that held on to his flesh, ripping it, as though starved.

"Victor?"

He bit back the pain and assured Ma all was well. But Victor couldn't return to sleep, and at daybreak, his leg—from ankle to hip—bulged with fever. He wrapped the wound and wished not to have Ma mother him, prideful and too embarrassed to need her.

But his fever raged. Victor slept and woke and saw the girl in his dreams reaching for a fat spider. "Under Foot?" he called to her, but she wouldn't answer. "Under Foot?" Then he saw Ma beside a hearth, resting on a rock and pointing at pin dots of lightning. Dots with brown babies that crawled across Ma's face.

"Sickness has but one intention," Ma muttered.

A breeze blew, sprinkling ice onto his cheeks as Ma propped her musket against a tree trunk. She scooped up his leg and set it under her armpit. The leg was plump and shiny, and Ma didn't seem to like it. She wanted to hurt it. For being so shiny.

"What are you doing?" Victor thrashed and pushed Ma back into her musket, which tipped and slithered inside a brittle clump of leaves. Ma gripped his leg again as if it was a growing threat. "No! Ma, just tell it not to shine!"

Ma choked it. With her clay pot. Told it to quiet down.

It was early the next morning and still Ma suctioned Victor's leg, leaving a trail of bruised ovals atop the shiny. By dusk, the shiny dulled and Victor's head regained its weight, and when he could think clearly again, Ma shoved a cut of sheepskin into his mouth and sliced open his thigh until the blood stood raised and stiff like tomato seeds forced to applaud her.

She lifted his head to the pouch filled with another bitter tea. Her eyes were shadowed, and she slouched like an empty, twisted sack before him. "Drink up," she said.

"Is this your Mamá's tea?"

"No, I don't have what I need for my mother's tea."

"Why don't you ever talk much about your home?"

"Because children use your words against you. Like *tea sandwiches* and *knickers*."

Victor grinned, but he knew he'd hurt her.

"The way you spoke to me—I would never have spoken to my Mamá like that," she said.

"I am sorry. I am." Victor watched her expression, trying to discern if she was open to another question, but could not be certain. "Why did you leave home?" he asked.

Ma wiped the lip of the pouch with a worn hemp cloth and placed her hand across his forehead, flipping it over, hoping, it seemed, that at least one side of her hand would register the relief she desperately sought. "I left because there could be no more dignity. Without dignity, living becomes unworthy of life." She avoided his eyes, placing the cloth back onto her waist, storing the pouch in the sack she would forget later to haul into the branches of a tree.

The smoke from the fire still billowed as the sun broke through like a gorged udder. It was the fourth day of their delay. Victor had been awake for some time, watching Ma's lips move in her sleep as though in prayerful recitation. She woke panicked, smothered the ember chicks, checked him for fever. "We may have to stay here one more night."

They had left to eat only a small bit of wild rice, and Ma, who never wished to be without at least one day's supply of food, was growing concerned. That morning, Victor told her she could hunt, that he would be fine, and though Ma, at first, hesitated, she decided, after surveying the area, that it was best to leave while the world still felt quiet beneath them.

Victor slept and dreamt, awakening on occasion to slap critters licking sweat from his collarbone. When Martinique first began to stir, Victor did not open his eyes, but the old gal was persistent, and finally when Victor sat upright, he saw that Martinique, who stood some distance from him, had pinned her ears and held her head cocked at some sound.

"I'm listening now," he whispered to her.

Dead branches bit at the earth. Their teeth clacked. Victor's bow and arrow lay in a sack upon Martinique. He wouldn't be able to reach them in time.

Clack-clack.

Victor had heard stories of close calls with bears. There'd always been a great deal of laughter over how foolish men became when face-to-face with a two-leggings: screaming fools, running fools, crying fools. Victor didn't wish to be a fool.

He had told Ma that he thought it was a bad idea to cut through those woodlands. But she had convinced him it was best. Now Victor peered up into the grandfather fir's canopy. Its branches were colossal spider's legs, with sharp angles and plunging slopes. This is what

Ma must have noticed when she chose it to shelter them during their delay. *Climb it.* He thought this as he pushed himself up from a ground blooming cream-colored mushrooms. Martinique's ears twitched like parchment fans in the wind. Maybe Ma had changed her mind, he thought. Victor listened for the lilting rhythm of Ma's stride, upright on her toes, the walk of a farmgirl who knew of the sea. But it was not Ma coming.

Victor climbed as high as his leg would permit, hoping the raining needles wouldn't give him away. How could he be injured now? What god served this upon him? A woodpecker flew off, while down below Martinique watched two men in dust-colored shirts and loose trousers ride toward her atop inferior mongrels. They stopped beside her, beneath the tree adjacent Victor's, and chatted softly in French. Victor watched as they kicked at the still-warm firepit and rummaged through Ma's pack, stuffing everything of value into theirs.

"Look." They spoke to another man in the distance. One of the men—a puckered-skinned one—lifted Victor's pouch, held it out to the third man, who now moved toward them. "Bilé." They laughed. "Isn't that how you people say water?"

Bilé. It was an Apsáalooke word.

The third man inspected the pouch. Victor gaped at the top of his oval-shaped head and found the way that the dark hair snaked like a winding river familiar, the broad shoulders so well-known that he was certain of their next motion. Victor felt his heart din, heard the acute thrum in his ears, and knew he wouldn't be able to blink away the tears that scorched his throat. Like-Wind picked up Victor's pouch, dusting the soil from it, sniffing it as though it might speak to him. "You said she was a dark Negress and the boy the color of a mulatto?" the puckered-skinned one said to Like-Wind.

Victor searched for reticence in Like-Wind's stance, hoped to see him tousle his hair, but there were no clear signs. "Le cheval de la mère. Près." Victor had taught him those French words. *Horse. Mother. Near.* And now Like-Wind spoke them with a sureness, like a chief in making.

Like-Wind reached for Martinique's lead, but Martinique became stiff-backed, planting her feet, ears flapping, for Martinique knew she was not to be separated from Ma. Ma had never allowed Martinique to be set out to pasture at nights. She kept her close always, made sure to send her off when raiders attacked, certain Martinique would find her way home. Like-Wind understood the relationship between Ma and Martinique, understood it because Victor had shared everything with him. He'd tracked them by following Martinique's unique prints, her hooves trimmed in the particular way Ma had taught Victor to do.

"There's only one horse here," the puckered-skinned one said. "We ain't stupid. You want us back at your mountain?"

"Two horses," Like-Wind said. "You do not see." Like-Wind must've known there were not two sets of fresh prints, but Victor now could be certain Like-Wind had led those men there.

The Yellow-Eyes remounted. "Let's finish. No use waiting."

Victor remembered when Father had decided that Victor showed no promise on the hunts, when he told Ma that Victor was "a poor marksman with no instincts for the kill." Years before Victor was born, an Apsáalooke man and woman had been ambushed by Minnetarees, and when Apsáalooke warriors gave chase, the Minnetarees sheltered themselves. Father, who had been leading the charge, told his men, "If you are afraid, let me borrow your shields," and with their shields, he rushed alone into the Minnetaree den. He told Ma later that the only way he could get his men not to run away was to call them "delicate." This was what Father called Victor that last time he took him out. Delicate. And Victor had begun to believe it about himself, embarrassed each time Bluegrass and the other uncles returned boasting of the progress made by all the young warriors but him. So Ma took Victor out alone. She analyzed his errors, corrected them, reminded Victor of the importance of patience and persistence. "A too-speedy horse falls down just before the finish line. Take your time and wait out your prey," she would say. It was Ma who taught him to climb high and to wait. It was Ma who taught him the doe bleat, the buck grunt. "Suave, louder, harder," she'd say.

Victor was in that grandfather tree, an excellent huntsman, an excellent climber, a man still being made, safe and unseen, because of Ma. He was sorry he'd made her think otherwise.

Victor wet his lips and held his breath before releasing a soft vibration. He felt it rising from a sprouting seed in his stomach. The bleat soared over the pines, over the detection of the men below, and if the First Maker was with them, he hoped to wherever Ma stood. Let her run. Run away fast.

The men conferred for several minutes before Like-Wind mounted Martinique. The old mare pitched him and the Frenchmen laughed, but both Victor and Like-Wind knew the mare had behaved as such because she had spotted Ma.

Victor followed Martinique's eyes to a thicket of tree trunks and vines. He narrowed his scope to make out Ma's red-painted fringed buckskin tunic and moose hair leggings. She had two bloodstained rabbits strung on a vine rope across her shoulders: one just slightly bigger than a bunny, calm faced as if sleeping; the other, stout, with its eyes sprung open. Ma's chest rose and fell as if she'd been running. The tip of her bow dangled by her waist. There were only two arrows remaining in her quiver. He hoped she would turn and run, but instead Ma searched the earth behind the men, looked toward the base of the tree where she'd left her musket. Even if she could see it hidden among the leaves, Victor knew she would never get past those men—men who had their own rifles raised, men who gaped, men who commanded her to set down the bow and arrows and her string of rabbits whose muted colors matched the sky above them.

"I'll be damned," the puckered-skinned one said. "It sure is a Negress redskin." He turned to his friend, laughing. "I ain't got that girl and her momma, but he'll give me top dollar for this one, don't you think? Be good if we can find her lil bastard."

Victor had felt that something terrible would come. He'd tempted fate and now was on this journey he didn't understand, wondering when he might go home again. He watched Ma as they inspected her. He didn't wish to see her as they did. He told himself that his Ma was exquisite, splendid, different from them, yes, but not what he saw clouding their eyes. Father had once told Ma that she was like "volcanic obsidian, iridescent, luminous, smooth, like all the earth's foes had drawn a truce to make her." Victor recalled Ma, laughing, saying that Father had never seen volcanic obsidian, and yet the tender way

Father had looked at her mellowed Ma, as though his words had been a salve for a great gaping wound.

And Ma *was* beautiful. Her hair stood tall, sometimes defying gravity and sometimes not; her lips were fleshy and full like a spring bloom; and she was thoughtful, charitable, fiercely loyal. It shamed Victor that he could only now see this about her.

They grunted as they stripped her. Profound prehistoric grunts. Like men whose goal was to be drowned in exhilaration. They pulled at her tunic until the pelt bled, powdering their peculiar rawhide boots with fleecy fuzz. They tossed Ma between them, back and forth, forth and back, and Ma looked to be swept inside the currents of a mad bloated river or like a child's favorite toy molested by some vile god's fingertips. One of her breasts had thwarted the disrobing, while the other seemed to resist resistance, instead loosening itself, flailing, wilting like a leaf deprived of sun and water, much the same as Ma, who did not fight, who did not shout, who did not punch or scratch or grab. As Victor watched Ma, it seemed Breath had taken its leave of her. The puckered-skinned Frenchman held Ma by the arms and spit onto her chest; a wad of foamy white slaver coursed its way down to her belly button, and he kneaded some of the spume atop her breast and up onto her naked shoulder with his leaden thumb. Exhilaration. Ma's eyes flitted to the treetops. Treetops masking a limp, impotent, sunless sky. Treetops masking a limp, impotent, hopeless son. Victor wondered if she knew he was there hiding, unable or unwilling to do something, witnessing, as he had witnessed the girl.

Like-Wind, below, hid his face behind the thick black strands of his hair as the two Frenchmen mounted Ma like studs. Victor didn't know his friend to be a cowardly man, didn't know himself to be that kind of man either.

"If I live, you live." Victor wished to remind Like-Wind of their pact. Wished to tell Like-Wind that he would rather die than watch his mother suffer.

Victor released the breath he'd been holding and fell away from that limp, impotent, sunless sky that sat broad and heavy upon his shoulders. He heard his own perfectly fine bones shatter when he landed atop the second Frenchman, heard the breath whisk out of the man before the man's neck snapped, before the mongrel horses ran off.

The pruned Frenchman, pressed into Ma, turned to see what had happened, offering Ma the narrowest chance to throw him off. Victor lay certain he would never feel anything as excruciating as that pain, yet he hoped with everything in him that Ma had escaped.

Minutes later—perhaps only seconds—Victor heard the explosion of iron igniting.

Like-Wind's body thumped like a rotted sapling, his hair splayed like a drenched spring bloom. Ma was blowing into the priming pan for another shot when prune-face stumbled over his own pack, begging Ma, his hands in an uproar about his head. "S'il vous plait, s'il vous plait!"

Ma had forced Victor to learn that curious language. "French," she told him, "must be spoken in the mornings." It was the language that reminded her of her Mamá, she'd said.

"I wished only for you to leave us alone, nous laisser seuls," Ma said.

Ma loosed her grip on the musket, as if undecided about what to do next. Victor tried to call out to her, but the pain was everywhere, deeper than everywhere. He felt lost. Like-Wind was dead, his chest open like a peeled and pulpy fruit. He had been Victor's friend, the boy by whom Victor measured himself, and Victor didn't know yet how to feel, so he turned again to observe the Frenchman, who now served up a half grin to Ma, as though suddenly she'd become more human, for she spoke his language, their common language, and it seemed he believed this made them one people.

"I'll leave you and le garçon." The man studied Victor, then squinted, further scrutinizing Victor's face, and seemed comforted by what he saw, for suddenly he began inching again toward Ma. Ma's remaining clothes were ravaged, her arms and face scraped, the skin on her rib cage peeled and wisped. Ma's musket was now lowered, and she held her body again like an empty, twisted sack. And it seemed by her expression, terrible and deadened, that Breath needed to be wary of an absconding. The man took small steps, looking to Victor, then to Ma, surveying the carnage—his dead friend and Like-Wind, his guide—relieved, it seemed, that he'd survived this woman's wrath.

"Ma." Victor didn't know how he'd found his voice. Maybe he understood that Breath needed affirmation, maybe *he* needed affirmation. "Ma," he whispered again.

Ma glanced up as if from a dream to find the man closing in on her.

"Je vais partir." The man again said he'd leave and made the turn toward Like-Wind's horse, and Ma could have let him go.

"Le musket ne comprend pas français," Ma said.

Like-Wind's horse unloosed itself at the sound of the musket's issue. Victor was surprised by the precision of death's trouncing as he surveyed the three bodies before him and thought how death was both remarkable and yet so ordinary. Much the same as its forbear, Breath. He watched as Ma searched the perimeter before reclaiming her goods and packing away the Frenchmen's valuables—powder, traps, steel knives, and a hatchet.

"I'm sorry," Victor whispered.

He didn't think he said enough, had ever said enough, but also he didn't know what more he could say.

"You see? A little axe can cut down a big tree." Ma touched Victor's nose with her fingertip. "But your work is to reach up—reach up always for Breath. She is now your mother."

VII

Isle of Trinidad

⌒⌒

1

1803

What Rosa would learn much too late and what Papá did not say the afternoon Jeremias came with Pierre, was that his meeting with Señor Cordoza had been far less than pleasurable.

Cordoza, now living as a new bachelor of sorts, invited Papá to ride out with him to inspect a swath of land that his father-in-law, still in Spain, promised to purchase for Cordoza, if Cordoza put an end to his relationship with the obeah woman.

Señor Cordoza told Papá that that would not be so easy, and yet he was in excellent spirits that day, sitting upon one of Maravilloso's colts that Papá had had to sell, wearing new trousers and boots that looked to be of supple leather. Papá had heard that after Cordoza pledged his oath of allegiance to the Crown, he turned over to the authorities two Spaniards for publicly expressing discomfort with English rule. The two men, who had once been his friends, were expelled from the island within days and shipped to Venezuela, and the English demonstrated their earnest appreciation by allowing Cordoza first rights to purchase the men's land. Cordoza promptly bought and sold such parcels for a handsome profit.

"Ay, it seems tables turn quite suddenly on this strange island we inhabit here," he said. Then Señor Cordoza told Papá the news of the

Cathedral of Saint Joseph's impending restoration and also that the English had found a new way to thwart the abolitionists.

"They are now bringing slaves under the guise of domestic service. As if one man needs fifty house servants! They bring them in scores, one to sweep, another to clip nose hairs, two footmen for each child, and when the Englishmen don't have offspring, they write on the papers that a servant must attend to each hunting dog. They must think they're Barbadians!"

Cordoza went on to say that once the English extinguished this current path with the Africans, which had already roused the abolitionists to the brink of war, they planned next to import "servants" from the East Indies. "Hindustans," he said. "They'll tell the coolies that here in Trinidad their caste will mean nothing, that after a few years of light labor, they will have land and even a new name if they desire, and this, the landowners hope, will quiet the abolitionists and open all the free labor any Englishman could need for years, since, of course, there'll be no written agreement with those Hindustan illiterates."

Cordoza then told Papá that what he would say next was not a prediction but a fact: "The English have been here six years. They are readying themselves, looking for well-placed, well-established land to set up more plantations for sugar. Your property, Demas, is on a very short and distinguished list."

Papá would return home and tell Mamá that he no longer knew what to believe, no longer knew whom to trust in this new life of theirs.

2

"He's arriving at two and still you're not dressed?"

Rosa had not wished to be found. She was in the stable, wearing Jeremias's old trousers, preparing her horse, for she had planned not to return home until evening. The young man they expected that afternoon was Madame Bernadette's nephew, and Rosa had no interest in meeting him.

In the preceding weeks there had been a flurry of communication between Madame Bernadette and Rosa's parents. Madame Bernadette had told Mamá and Papá that her nephew would have been far more keen if he were coming to meet Eve but said, "Rosa will do for now." In anticipation of the meeting, the nephew had asked a schoolteacher from his village to write, on his behalf, two letters of introduction: one to Demas and the other to Rosa, telling of his interests—fishing, carpentry, farming—and wishing to hear more of hers. Rosa never read the letter. "Chupidness," she called it. So Mamá and Eve responded in her stead. They wrote of Rosa's industriousness, of her brilliance with the horses, of her desire always to learn.

"Nutting of her beauty?" she'd overheard Papá asking Mamá.

"It's best if we do not build her up too much," Mamá had said. "I know Bernadette has given the boy an earful. He needs a wife who can work hard. That's what Rosa can offer him."

"She is pretty. You know this, sí?"

Rosa knew Mamá did not see her in this way. As she listened to her parents, she could not recall a moment when her mother regarded her face as though to admire it rather than critique it. "Demas, I know how the world sees Rosa. It will do her no good to be told she is lovely here and to be shocked when people do not respond to her in the same way they respond to girls like Eve. Not being prepared for the cruelty of the world can crush a child."

Can crush a child. Had crushed a child.

"Madame Bernadette said he is a prompt young man." Papá pretended now not to take note of Rosa's displeasure. This was what he would do until just after lunchtime, when Rosa would make it so he could not do so any longer. "Your Mamá will die of embarrassment if you don't put on a proper dress." Papá's trousers were pressed, and the vest he wore was fashioned out of something familiar that Rosa could not then place. "Your mudda is expecting you to help with lunch. No man will wish to marry you if you can't prove you's a good cook."

Rosa remembered Jeremias saying once that he believed he was born in the wrong era, too late along the spectrum of human development to take pleasure in the things he loved most. But as Rosa reflected upon his words, she could not imagine an era when she would not have suffered the same fate or worse. She sometimes felt she'd been born not at the wrong time so much as in the wrong body or with the wrong mind for her body.

"Listen to yourself, eh? I have only sixteen years. I have no interest in this at all." Rosa unlaced the saddle and Papá removed it from Maravilloso.

"And what about your mudda?" Papá said.

Rosa knew what Papá was doing. Mamá had been fighting some or another ailment nearly every day since the English arrived. She was not a frail woman, but she seemed to carry the collective weight of the family's strain. She had been Papá's consoler and strategist, had been persistent in her assurances to Eve that they would marry her well and had gone as far as to issue a call to all the gentlewomen she knew on Eve's behalf; she worried always about Jeremias, how he would make do with so little, all while watching the country to which she'd chosen to immigrate become less and less worthy of the risk she'd taken. The strain of living in Trinidad, Mamá had said, was sometimes too much to bear. The English were growing more fearful of being outnumbered by the same Africans they were illegally importing, and the continual enforcement of arcane Spanish laws bordered on the absurd. And so the thought of Rosa marrying, the thought of a proper wedding to plan, of more grandchildren, had not only lifted Mamá's spirits but also lifted the veil that had befallen their home. Was Rosa willing to undo that sweet bit of goodness?

"T'ings change, Rosa, and I know this is hard for you to understand, but your brudda was right . . . we could lose everyt'ing. It is not fair, but this is the way it is, until it is not."

None of this was supposed to happen. Jeremias swore to Eve that Papá would not be permitted to sell the land. He told Eve he had discussed it all with Monsieur DeGannes, who had assured him that Papá could not bypass both English and Spanish primogeniture laws. But Jeremias did not know that Papá had already conferred with men who also knew about such laws. Men who'd told Papá about something called "common recovery" under English law.

"Ay, the English find a way around everyt'ing," Papá had said.

Unbeknownst to Jeremias, Papá could ask a good friend to bring a suit against him in court. The good friend would claim he had a right to Papá's land. The court would request that Papá bring a vouchee—someone who would swear the land title belonged to Papá—but when required to come before a judge, Papá and his vouchee would purposely miss the appointment and the good friend would win the case by default. This would cause the land to revert to "fee simple," thereby removing all of Jeremias's rights. The good friend would accept a few sterling for his troubles and simply deed the land back to whomever Papá wished to have it deeded.

"A man has the right to do as he wishes with his own land," Papá had told Mamá.

Now Papá hung the saddle on the rack. "Go inside and get ready," he told Rosa. "If this works out, maybe we can keep Maravilloso."

Rosa saw this sham probability for what it was. In the weeks prior, Papá had begun declaring that Maravilloso would need to be sold. The drought had once again ruined some of the cacao crop and money was short. Rosa's pleas not to sell Maravilloso had fallen on deaf ears, so why should now be different?

The young man arrived promptly with his uncle, Madame Bernadette's eldest brother. The uncle was a hunched man with eyes milky like pearls. He called out before opening the gate. "Rendón! We come!"

Papá met them at the palms while Rosa watched from the window, the insides of her belly swimming. Papá seemed certain that once he married off Rosa to the boy and deeded the land to him, that Monsieur Benoit, who had been allying himself well with the landholding Englishmen, would pay off anyone who attempted to take the land from his son, even if he *was* a bastard. It was an arrangement Papá believed would please everyone, except, of course, Rosa.

As Papá escorted the two men inside, Rosa heard the uncle mention the peculiar sidelong glances he'd been receiving from the newly arrived Englishmen and the additional questioning by constables. Papá told him that after they got through talking about Rosa and the boy, they'd discuss "all dem Englishmen's nasty ways."

Then Papá brought the men to stand before the table, which was well appointed with a white lace cloth and a red bougainvillea centerpiece. Eve had set the table for five before leaving. Most Sundays Eve attended noon Mass, but with the church under repair, she was instead sent to lunch with a friend, for it was presumed she would have been a great distraction. Before she departed, however, Eve had fixed Rosa's hair into a ball that sat like a tight floating fist and had helped Mamá prepare coconut pone. Eve had also grated fresh ginger into the top of a jar that held eight servings of ginger beer, peeled potatoes, sliced carrots, collected figs, chopped onions, and cleaned the fish. The only thing left for Rosa to do was to add water, salt, a dash of pepper sauce, and drop the fish into the pot at precisely the right time to avoid its overcooking. And, oh yes, of course, Eve told Rosa that she would also be required to smile.

"Take the apron away from your clothes," Mamá whispered, patting down the flyaway strands of Rosa's hair.

Rosa shoved the apron beneath the table as Mamá took the old man's hand, greeting him as if they were long-ago friends. Mamá brought the young man to stand before Rosa, rolling her *R*, introducing him as Lamec, her French accent perfect for the name's rigid ending.

Lamec bowed, his eyes surveying Rosa's as if to seek her approval. Rosa was surprised by this, surprised he had not grimaced or sneered. She suspected that the allure of the land and the sweet neighs of her ponies in the stable made him look kindlier upon her.

"Pleasure," she said, curtseying, as Mamá had required her to do.

Lamec had soft-looking hands (not exactly farmer's hands) and thread-thin lips and smelled of bastille soap. He was not an ugly boy, though he looked nothing as Rosa expected. His aunt was a heavy woman with a red-tinted face bookended by dimples. He, on the other hand, was wiry, his complexion like tea with half milk, and one could not be certain when taking in his features if his father was, indeed, a full Frenchman, for Lamec had a strong, wide nose—a nose Rosa knew would not have been good enough for Mamá if he were meeting Eve.

"Sit, sit, s'il vous plait." Mamá showed Lamec to his seat at the table. Rosa's seat. And offered him a cup of ginger beer and a few slices of ripe mango, while Rosa went to the back of the house to tend to the soup.

Rosa hated fish broth. No one had asked what she wanted for lunch. If they had, fish broth wouldn't have been it. She hated the too-large potatoes, how long it took the carrots to cool in her spoon; she hated green figs and the fish eyes that every other Rendón sucked with fervor. She hated that hot soup could be served on the mug-giest day of the year and hated that this boy-man, Lamec, was in her house, in her chair, making ready to eat soup he believed she'd cooked especially for him.

"La-mec," she said, mocking her mother's French accent.

Rosa opened two full jars of Mamá's homemade pepper sauce—a spoonful of which made grown men wager on who would perspire most—and poured the contents of both jars into the pot, hitting the containers on their bottoms to be certain it was all added.

As she brought in the bowls atop a large wooden tray, Rosa over-heard her father preparing their guests for a most spectacular meal. Lamec rose to help her. Mamá looked on, impressed at the young man's act of benevolence. Rosa could only think what a boar Lamec would be when he overtook their land and took up permanent residence in her chair, pining to sniff Eve's undergarments and bossing Mamá as though he actually owned the blasted place.

Rosa doled out the broth, placing spoons next to each bowl, and poured more ginger beer for Lamec and his toothless uncle. (No won-der Madame Bernadette had told them to prepare soup!) Rosa took Eve's seat across from Lamec, and he watched her as she sat, watched her as she sipped from her cup, watched her as she listened to Papá who would not stop speaking of the tour of the property they would take after lunch, of how critical Rosa had been to the maintenance of the land, of how much Rosa knew of horses. And Rosa was certain Papá would have continued except Mamá reminded Papá then that the soup before them was growing cold.

"Oh, sí! A comer, coma, por favor!" Papá said.

Rosa sipped from the cup again and glanced at Lamec over its rim. He sniffed the contents of the bowl, his eyes narrowing before taking up his spoon. But it was Lamec's pearly-eyed uncle who slurped first. "Oui, it is—" the old man began to speak, but his words were cut by a violent cough.

Mamá, Papá, and Lamec reached for the cups of ginger beer that offered little relief. Mamá cusped her throat with one hand and patted the old man's back with the other, but it was Papá and Lamec who jumped to their feet when the old man began to clutch his chest.

Rosa ran for water. Her hands trembled as she searched for the pail. What had she done? She brought the bucket to the table, dumped out the cups of ginger beer onto the floor, then poured water for the old man, whose pearl eyes had burst into red spiders. He tried to catch air between gulps, but his breathing grew more rapid and the cough more determined. Mamá and Papá were bejeweled with sweat, their tongues hanging for relief, their eyes awash in fear and shame.

Lamec knelt before his uncle, urging him to "drink up, drink up," telling him all would be well. The young man's own eyes rained tears. He seemed to be a kind boy who, Rosa now believed, had only wanted to please his family by coming to that house to meet her.

It took nearly a half hour before the old man was well enough to stand. Papá steadied him at the elbow as they walked toward the wagon. Mamá whispered a most heartfelt apology with her hand to her bosom, swearing that nothing like that would ever happen again.

Lamec steadied his uncle on the seat before dismounting to face Rosa. "I am sorry this was not what you hoped it would be." Rosa did not wish to meet his eyes. "But you could have said so," he said.

Rosa was certain they both knew this to be an untruth. But to say that a girl's words mattered was far easier than to examine why they did not.

Mamá took to her bed immediately upon their departure. And Rosa would not see her for a week. Papá waited a fortnight for Rosa to tell him that it had been an amateur culinary mistake. When she did not, he found another way to make her feel regret.

"The horse must go," he said.

An Englishman arrived a week after Papá advertised the sale. The man was tall and pudgy with a crabby mustache and he wished to negotiate.

"Sorry, sir, my father is out on a job at the mill," Rosa said.

The man climbed down off a striking buckskin mare and drew his pipe from his breast pocket, pushing down the tobacco into the bowl, as if he intended to smoke it, but did not. "Rendón? Is that a Spaniard's name?"

"Yessir, it is."

"But you speak English quite well?"

"My father knew—knows how, sir, so when you—when the English—come, I set about learning it."

"That's very industrious." The man held the pipe away from his mouth and stretched his neck to see past the right side of the house. "I do find this land quite nice."

"My father's price for the horse is one hundred, sir. We have two gentlemen coming tomorrow to look at him."

It seemed he whistled as an expression of both surprise and doubt. "Tell me, how did your father come to this number?"

"Sir, you haven't as yet seen the horse."

"'Tis not necessary to know the number's quite high."

"The going rate for a stallion like we have is two hundred, sir."

"Who said?"

"The men who are coming tomorrow to buy, sir." Rosa looked over her shoulder as if to suggest she had other obligations. "If you'll excuse me, sir, I must get back to the stable. I'll tell Papá you called."

"Now don't you be burstin' out angry," the man said. "I'd like to see him."

"Papá?"

"The horse."

Rosa looked toward the house, wondering if Eve or Mamá was aware they had a visitor. The stable had always been a place Papá would permit only certain men. But now, much had changed. Each day they were shorter on food. The goods they had once sold to merchants from Portugal, Spain, France, were now required to be sold only to London merchants, for the English had blocked all foreign trade. Under the Navigation Act, Papá had called it, there was no profit to be made and no bargains to be had. He had laughed a melancholy laugh and said they "were trapped between England and the English."

"You can bring your mare to the back and tie her up there, if you wish," Rosa said, perusing the man's horse again. "She's very pretty, sir."

"And old and in heat, which makes her insufferable!"

Rosa noticed the thick discharge sliding down the mare's hind leg. It was a healthy bit. "Yes, she seems quite a handful. And looks tired."

The stable had been hand hewn by Papá with wood pegs, mortise and tenon joinery. It was built to house six horses in six spacious stalls. It contained a well-organized tack room and a loft overhead for hay storage. Few in Trinidad had a stable like this. The man whistled again as he took in the extent of it.

"Every horse we've sold—and we rarely sell our horses—has been of the finest on this island, sir, and probably in South America too."

Rosa opened and closed the gate of Maravilloso's stall, going inside to speak to him, shifting to the Spanish she hoped the Englishman would not understand. She told Maravilloso he would soon be leaving their home. She had wished to delay it, for she loved Maravilloso, but now Rosa knew her only power lay in choosing where his new home would be.

"Is this him?" The man said this as though unimpressed. But Rosa observed the Englishman's eyes as they followed Maravilloso's long and tapered backside, his marvelous leg conformation and balanced silhouette, the dark blood chestnut of his coat. Each time someone new was introduced to Maravilloso, Rosa saw the horse with fresh eyes. And he was stunning.

"One hundred is a bargain, sir," she said.

The man chuckled, perhaps at her boldness, perhaps at the undeniability. "Why, I didn't expect him to be this," he said.

Rosa could see the man's appreciation for what he beheld. The man had a pleasant, almost rascally way about him and looked to be the sort who would not take up the whip easily. She questioned him about where in England he hailed; whether he was married, had children; how he'd come to know horses; whether his father was a horseman, or perhaps his grandfather; what he knew about the line of his own mare. He indulged her, answered well, though not always perfectly. He wasn't a man of considerable means but was already well connected on the island. "Sir, how much do you have?"

Mr. Abbott glanced up from the horse. "A bit less than half."

"Would you throw in your mare?"

"Bless thy simplicity! My mare and less than half the price?" He shook his head. "Little girl, I don't wish for your father to hate you on account of this."

"If I can keep her for a week, get a good look at her, then we can agree to this, sir?"

"No man leaves his horse. That's absurd!"

"I've a mare that isn't as lovely but also isn't as old, sir. You can take her for the week."

"It's unheard of."

"If my father returns and I've not had time to learn her and convince him to sell at that 'unheard of' price, then there will be no deal, sir."

"If he comes now I'll discuss it with him."

"With only half the asking price and an old mare?" Rosa shrugged and feigned relief. "Very well. I imagine, sir, you know best."

The Englishman, a Mr. Abbott, looked to his mare once more. She had a light film of perspiration on her legs. He let off a most ostentatious sigh. "Well . . . as you've said, she is quite tired. I'll permit her to stay so she can rest, but if I change my mind—"

"Just return and you can have her any time, sir. She will be here."

"I suppose you know what you're doing?"

Rosa held out her hand as she had seen Papá do many times.

A few hours after lunch, Papá still had not returned from work. When Eve heard the wagon approaching, she angrily set Papá's now cold lunch onto the table only to realize that it was, in fact, Monsieur DeGannes who'd arrived. Eve accompanied Monsieur to the stable, where Rosa was chastising Maravilloso for his obstinance. Eve pulled Rosa aside and told her she had her hands full with preparing supper, that she needed Rosa to keep Monsieur busy.

"What is he doing here?" Rosa whispered.

Eve shrugged, and Monsieur greeted Rosa with a tight grin as if his thoughts were elsewhere. Rosa was reminded of the deference Papá had always shown Monsieur, though Papá thought Monsieur to be far less than a distinguished gentleman.

"You have no idea how dangerous an overly ambitious, unexceptional man can be," Papá once said of Monsieur. "But no matter what I speak of in this house, you mustn't cross him, you understand?"

Rosa turned to Monsieur now. He seemed shorter somehow, and Rosa thought perhaps she had grown, for they were almost eye to eye.

"I hear your père has set quite a price for the stallion." Monsieur browsed the stable as if he believed it would not be only Maravilloso for sale. "If he doesn't receive an offer, I would be happy to take le cheval for a fairer price."

Rosa took note of the way Monsieur examined the now-smaller stalls and Papá's tools, which were taking up space in the back corner of the stable. "This is not all he has remaining of his shop, is it?" Monsieur seemed alarmed.

"Oui, Monsieur. I thought you would have known. They took everything from Papá. He is only just now beginning to buy the materials to make his tools again."

"But there must be more." Monsieur perused the perimeter again, with a frantic determination, looking askew at their one remaining piglet sleeping in a pen. "Demas said there would only be a small delay."

"A delay for what, Monsieur?"

Monsieur DeGannes inspected all the corners of the stable. He searched behind bales of hay, beneath tacks, inside barrels, then began to ascend the steps of the loft ladder.

"Monsieur!" Rosa called out after him. "If you could wait until Papá returns. I do not think—"

"Aah!" Monsieur held up something round connected to another round something but Rosa could not make out the items from where she stood. Monsieur DeGannes picked up another something much like the first something and put them together so that the clinking of iron against iron pealed like dull chimes. "It is not very much but it seems he has been working." Relieved, Monsieur dropped the findings and climbed down, his movements careful but spry. He took Rosa's hand in his and squeezed it as if pleased with her. "Please tell Demas I must speak with him very soon."

As Monsieur began to leave, Rosa heard Papá's wagon, his tools sliding across the bed as though Papá had been in too much of a rush to properly secure them. A few moments later, it sounded as if Papá was running toward them.

"Monsieur." Papá breathed heavily. "I thought we were to meet at your house."

"It is no problem that I am here, oui?" Monsieur DeGannes set his hands under his braces, stretching them forward, letting them snap against his chest. "You've kept the land quite well, considering."

"Only God knows how long I can hold on to it," Papá said.

"I've told you before to come talk to me. That friend of yours, Cordoza, likes to stir you up. He's hoping you will sell to him. He's told everyone this."

Rosa noticed how the lump in Papá's throat hardened.

"But, Demas, on another matter, tell me you have more than what I have seen there." Monsieur nodded toward the hayloft, and Papá uttered a sigh that growled in his chest like a shovel threatening to harvest all the air from him. "I can't delay any further. Tell me you can still meet our obligations." Monsieur DeGannes seemed almost to be pleading with Papá when Papá suddenly noticed Rosa there behind him.

"Come," Papá said to him. "Let us discuss this outside."

Rosa watched the two men walk toward the mouth of the riding path, their hands and arms like windmills before each other. Papá appeared shamefaced, and until that moment, Rosa did not believe that her father could have had any appreciable secrets, that any one of them, save Jeremias, had ever had any appreciable secrets. As Rosa climbed the ladder to the loft, she remembered how extraordinary Jeremias's behavior had seemed to her back so many years ago, how outraged she had been at his lies, how she had been the one to out his meetings with Francine, his late-night visits with DeGannes, all his drunkenness, and she wondered now what kind of willful blindness, how much willful silence, was required to keep up the appearance of any one family.

Rosa stumbled over Eve's dress box. She felt the unrooted surface tremulous beneath her and set herself upon her knees, as though she'd be less likely to die from a fall if she were kneeling. She remembered that when the English had first come, Papá had told Eve he would need to hide away her valuables, her two bits of jewelry and finer dresses. Rosa wondered now, as she looked below at the horses and the wide expanse of the stable doors, what Papá had been thinking. He had to have known that if the English came they would look first to the hayloft. Rosa realized then that she'd never once climbed that ladder, that it had always been Papá who deposited and retrieved the bales.

Rosa found the items Monsieur DeGannes had discovered and held them beneath the weak sunlight. They looked to be ugly bracelets, thick and heavy, tethered to replicas of themselves by a fat, flat bridge. She turned one set over in her hand and felt something slip between her fingers. "Oh yes, wonderful," she grumbled, "I must now find a needle in a haystack." She gently patted around in the near darkness, hearing the straw crackle, feeling the thick sharpness of the stalks unyielding at her fingertips, until finally she felt the thing, small and pointed. It was a key the length of a grown man's thumb. Rosa reached again for the bracelets and again held them out past the floor of the loft to catch sunlight. In the middle of the fat, flat bridge was a keyhole. A bracelet, two bracelets, welded together, requiring a key to open the rings? She felt she should have known this thing, felt that if she thought long enough she'd remember Papá speaking of it, but Rosa realized, as she uncovered two, three, four, almost two dozen pairs buried deep in the hay, that maybe she would never remember, because maybe, indeed, Papá had had an appreciable secret after all.

During that next week Papá did not once look Rosa in the eye and did not once set out the horses with her. He told Rosa he had too much business at the mills, meetings at the clerk's office, and that he needed to see about Mamá, who was again sick.

The doctor came thrice that week and each time prescribed tonics for increased energy. He told Papá that women Mamá's age sometimes tired, swelled, ached. That "pain is part of being a woman." Papá was dissatisfied with that answer but the doctor said to call him again if Mamá did not improve within a week or two.

Mr. Abbott arrived seven days to the hour of his previous visit. Papá was chopping wood at the front, constructing a rocker for Mamá that he planned to place beside his. Mamá had told him she didn't wish for a rocker, but Papá had said he hoped to view the night sky with her seated beside him. Rosa heard Papá greet the man. She'd been meaning to tell Papá, to explain what she'd done. The men exchanged words, and it was not long before Papá came into the stable, his teeth skinned, his face pulsating with ire like a chunk of liver in flames.

"Come." Papá snatched Rosa by the arm. He'd never before done this. She found herself pushing back tears.

"I had to sell him to someone who'd care for him." Rosa wedged her fingers beneath her father's, for he was pinching her skin.

"You put me in a position of having to sell my stallion for less than half what I can get for him! What have you done to us? You're too old for such stunts!" Papá released her arm and gave it a small shove. "Imagine if I tell this Abbott fella that the deal is off. He'll have Governor Hislop's men here within a day and them English will do me again like they did before. I got nutting left for them to take, Rosa!"

Rosa did not often think of *before*, but now she was reminded that Papá had never stopped thinking of *before*.

"But I'm getting this mare in exchange." Rosa nodded toward the Englishman's horse and Papá considered the mare for only a moment before sneering as if he'd smelled bad fish.

"This prune?" Papá said.

"She's more than—"

"Silly gyal! No te enseñe nada?" Papá was shouting now, spittle forming at the corners of his mouth. It was not only the horse; it seemed to Rosa to be everything: the absence of Jeremias, the *before*, Lamec's proposal, Mamá's incapacity. And it seemed Rosa had had her hand in all of it.

"Papá, you don't understand. I have—"

"Shush and let me t'ink!"

Papá left the stable with the Englishman's mare on a lead. Rosa heard Papá offer to return Mr. Abbott's horse, explaining to Mr. Abbott that Rosa had no right to strike the bargain. "The next foal we have will be yours for half the price you've offered for Maravilloso."

"She and I shook on it," Mr. Abbott said.

"I'm the owner, sir, not this chile," Papá said.

"You people are really something. You're quite forgetting your place." Mr. Abbott took out his pipe, wiped the bowl. "If I'd offered her the full amount, you'd have accepted it, yes?"

Papá, forced to concede, brought Maravilloso to Mr. Abbott.

That night, while Papá sat brooding, Rosa again climbed the steps to the loft. She found only Eve's dresses stored in a wooden box.

3

Mamá recovered, relapsed, then recovered again. She'd had Eve traipsing about the bush, picking roots for a bush bath, boiling what was left for teas and soups, crystallizing some into jellies and crèmes. Mamá was fond of saying that she had more than once "fixed herself up" and "done what that crop of unlicensed doctors on the island could not."

While still ill, Mamá had wielded her Catholic sword of guilt to remind Jeremias of the penance he'd have to proffer for not coming to visit his sick mother. As such, Jeremias began attending Sunday lunches again. And Mamá had demanded that he bring his entire family.

"Mamá, you're looking much better." Jeremias said this each time he arrived, whether true or not. He complimented Mamá, always, on the food, spoke with her about the latest cliff-hangers in the magazines and part issues he'd borrowed from Monsieur DeGannes, while Francine, with her "long face," sat always with Pierre on her lap, refusing to eat what was tendered, seeming to regard her lack of hunger as a hindrance to adult conversation.

After lunch one Sunday, as the sword-sharp grass began to wilt under the sun, Mamá suggested they take tea outside. Mamá and Papá sat on their rockers, Eve and Jeremias along the dusty rail of the verandah, while Rosa and Francine shared the top step with Pierre. The ladies hand-fanned warm air while Papá told the story of Jeremias as a young boy, temporarily blinded by a colony of stinging wasps, finding his way home without sight. Pierre was captivated, glancing back and forth between his grandfather and father with large, glowing eyes.

After Papá's story, Eve brought them up on local gossip—the woman flogged by her newly married son for speaking out of turn to his wife and the obeah man who had thus managed, with cucumbers and a candle, to rid an old man with a half dozen children of his young wife's lover.

"I hear Monsieur DeGannes found himself a dog-faced English-woman to marry," Eve finished.

"That's not polite," Mamá said.

"I hear the same," Jeremias said.

"That she's dog faced?" Mamá laughed.

"Non, that he's getting married." Jeremias looked to Francine, as if to apologize for not mentioning it sooner. "If he marries this woman, he's deemed English. Fit to do as he wishes. Putting together old English money and new French money is bloody brilliant business."

"It's all the same dirty business, all the same slave money," Eve mumbled.

Mamá glared at Eve. "People don't make love on a hungry belly," she said before turning again to Jeremias. "Has DeGannes met her as yet or is this all prearranged?"

"The arrangements were made in England, but she's arrived and is staying with family friends until they can get a 'real man of God to perform the ceremony, not a demagogue like Padre José,' she was heard saying."

"Oh yes, we are all devil worshippers here, aren't we? You should see how those Protestants stare when we go to Mass!" Mamá set her hand on her stomach as if to soothe it. She adjusted the top of her dress, which had slackened since her illness. "Sounds like she'll keep him on his toes. I should send holy water for him just in case." She chuckled. "But I guess every bread does have its piece of cheese. I imagine he's very sad living there all alone."

"He does just fine." Francine hadn't spoken at all until that moment. Not even a proper "dog" or "cat" or "good day" had fallen from her lips. But now she was taking issue with what Mamá supposed was a reasonable assumption? Mamá did not appreciate back chat.

"Oui, that's right," Mamá said. "I quite forgot that you know him much better than I."

Eve and Rosa looked to Mamá whose eyes were steadfast on Francine.

"How could you forget?" Francine said. "I heard you mention it only last week to Daddy when you paid us a visit."

Mamá glanced at Papá. His expression bordered on pleasant, and Rosa knew that Papá would never give Francine the satisfaction of knowing she'd caused a rift between he and Mamá. But Rosa also knew that later would come with an angry face.

"Rosa, come and help me with the tea and sweets." Mamá followed Rosa into the house, taking deep breaths before bracing herself on the edge of the table. She talked to her pain, coaxed it back beneath the thin veil where it was to wait. "You believe what that—what that girl just said to me? What a bad mind she has!"

Rosa nodded, finally able to offer Mamá the solidarity she often sought from Eve. "She's never happy to be here. Jeremias forces her to come."

"I'm her tante! She must remember to show me respect, oui?"

"Oui, Mamá."

"I don't bite . . . do I?" Mamá offered a half smile. "Well, maybe I'll bite her!" Mamá checked the teapot for warmth before setting it on the tray. "She's gonna have to stay for as long as I want. Jeremias won't leave until I'm ready to let them go." Mamá placed the coconut roll, covered in dried white flakes, next to the pot. She let out another long sigh. "It'd be nice to have that fiddle now, eh?"

Rosa had pouted for months after Mamá told her girls were not to play.

"It would be perfect to listen to while the sun sets," Mamá added.

Rosa sliced and arranged the coconut roll upon the platter, while Mamá stood quiet, studying her, before saying, "I know you think I'm very hard on you, Rosa. Maybe even that I don't always do right by you."

"What silliness are you talking, Mamá?" This was the response Rosa knew Mamá expected, even if it was not an honest one.

"It's true, I don't always know how to love you the way it seems you wish to be loved, but when you know somebody loves you, even if they're not doing it the way you wish, you must try to meet them halfway. Tu comprends?"

Rosa did not understand. Mamá wanted her to work harder for love? How much was she to give to this endeavor? And what if the person she wished to love her knew how she wished to be loved but simply refused to do it in that way? Was that forgivable? Those were the questions Rosa would have asked Mamá if she had not been in the wrong body or had the wrong mind for her body. Another era would have made no difference, for it seemed no mother in the span of humanity could accept responsibility for inflicting harm on her child when she believed her intent was honorable.

"I know, Mamá," Rosa said.

To Rosa, it felt as if Mamá had always been stingy with her love. Had Rosa not been in that wrong body, she would have been able to tell Mamá that hiding her love away made Rosa feel dirty, made Rosa wish to snatch it from wherever she could find it.

"Mamá, they'll soon wonder how long it takes to put a few pieces of coconut roll on a plate."

"You mean that evil one will wonder if she has me weeping inside here," Mamá said. "That little sorcière, messing with me, is putting her head on the chopping block."

Mamá smoothed Rosa's hair before opening the door for Rosa to pass with the tray.

Tea had long ended when Francine brought the plates to the back of the house. Rosa could not remember ever being alone with Francine, and as such, she had never before noticed the tone of Francine's voice—airy, as if practiced—and had never before noticed the scar across Francine's neck from so many years earlier.

"Did you make your sista and mudda do all this cooking by themselves?"

"Make them?"

"Your mudda is sick, you know." Francine threw the food scraps into the yard. This angered Rosa, for she had always picked her way through anything offered to the animals.

"She's better now," Rosa said.

"For true?" Francine said this as if she, in her right body, knew things wrong-body girls like Rosa did not. "Eve had very much liked

my cousin on my mudda's side. They were hoping to be married."
Francine kicked the scraps toward the chicks as if she could sense
Rosa's irritation but did not care.

"What cousin?"

"It doesn't matter."

"Does Papá know this?"

"Fathers shouldn't know everyt'ing about their girls."

"Papá wouldn't like it."

"She was gointa do it anyway." Francine crossed her arms, letting
them rest upon the small bulge beneath her breasts. "But then your
mudda was ill. Again. And Eve broke off the engagement. Now he's
promised to anudda because Eve told him you would never step in to
help your mudda, told him that she had to stay to tend to your parents and you."

"Nobody has to tend to me."

Francine pulled hair from her face; it was thin and loose with its
waves. "Eve will get fat soon, like your brudda. No one will want her
then."

"Jeremias isn't fat." Rosa didn't know if she thought her brother fat
or not, but felt it wasn't Francine's place to call him so.

"You're not the one with that nasty belly crushing you at nights like
a big hanging moon, so of course you wouldn't t'ink so." Francine
watched Rosa with eyes that dared Rosa to contest her truth or chal-
lenge her decorum. Her head was cocked like a painting that'd been
nudged off-center. "You'll never win this, you know. Your fadda will
eventually forgive Jeremias," she said. "Or just feel sorry for him."

"I'm not trying to win anything."

"You can dig holes in the ground and fix a sick horse, but you can't
even make a cook-up?" Francine shook her head and Rosa imagined
that Francine had already judged both Rosa's ragged bonda poule hem
and her frizzy hair that never tired enough to fall.

"I cook," Rosa said. "I'd be happy to make fish broth for you."

As Francine walked ahead of Rosa, Rosa thought back to the long
Sunday afternoons Eve would disappear. How Eve would tell Mamá
and Papá she was going into town for Mass and lunch with a friend,

leaving a disgruntled Rosa to put out their Sunday lunch. She thought of the many times Eve's face had been wet with tears, how Rosa had assumed it was because of Mamá's recurring sickness. Rosa felt heavy inside.

As Rosa made her way back to the verandah, she noticed Papá in the grass with Pierre, lifting him to the darkening sky, making the boy laugh until a long line of saliva fell from his lips. Mamá, seated in her feather-padded rocker, was reading papers Jeremias had given her, and she had a slight grin upon her face as if the words were naughty. Rosa took a place against the rail and Francine took Papá's seat beside Mamá.

"Jeremias, go and bring the extra chair from inside for your wife," Mamá said.

"I'm happy here," Francine said.

Papá held Pierre as if ready to toss him again. He looked to Mamá and shook his head.

"Demas made that chair for himself," Mamá said to Francine.

"Myra," Papá said. "It's all right."

"Eve is bringing you another tea. Come and take it in your chair," Mamá said to Papá.

"Myra," Papá said again. "Take it easy."

Francine stood, lacing her fingers across her stomach. "Pierre, come and say good night to Tante Rosa and Tante Eve."

Papá brought Pierre onto the verandah, setting him down before Francine. Rosa remembered the day Tío Byron had pulled Francine from the bed of his wagon. Papá had walked to the cart and Francine had reared back like a wild animal until Papá reached for her. She moaned as she held Papá's hand. Later, Papá told Mamá that Francine had whispered to him that she was sorry.

Now Pierre began to cry. Papá wiped his tears and whispered words Rosa could not hear.

"You're a kind man," Francine said to Papá.

Rosa perceived something in Papá's countenance that she did not wish to see. It was only an instant, in one beat of a butterfly's wings, that Rosa in her wrong body caught something in Papá's expression that spoke to feeling so desperate for attention that one would snatch it from wherever one could find it.

Jeremias reached for Pierre and nudged him toward Mamá for a goodbye peck.

"Yes, give your Mémé a kiss and don't forget your tantes," Francine said to Pierre. "And I shall give your Pépé a kiss."

Francine moved toward Papá and placed her hands on Papá's cheeks, pulling him into her in one quick and certain motion for a tender kiss upon the lips. It was the sort of kiss Rosa had never seen shared between Mamá and Papá. The sort of kiss that made Rosa's insides tingle.

"It's nice to do that again, isn't it?" Francine said, in that practiced, airy voice of hers. Papá nudged Francine away, his face twisted as if he'd been dropped into the middle of some strange woodlands and was unsure what to do with his eyes, his hands, his lips. Dirty. He felt dirty. Rosa was certain of this and she was reminded of Papá's countenance the day Monsieur DeGannes had come, the shamefaced expression that suggested to Rosa that her father had had private thoughts, private doings, that could upset everything she thought she knew of him. Now Papá glanced at Mamá, whose head was cocked ever so slightly toward incredulous, and it seemed he would speak, but he did not.

"Good night, Mémé! Good night, Pépé!" Pierre ran ahead of his father, who was now yanking the boy's grinning mother down the staircase of the verandah.

Jeremias did not come for Sunday lunch again and no one dared to make mention of it.

Both Papá and Mamá had wished to be angry, had wished to ask and answer questions of each other, but silence was peace, and Rosa was beginning to understand that perhaps for every marriage this must be both true and necessary.

And perhaps too this was true for fathers and daughters, for Rosa found herself avoiding Papá, feeling guilty for having seen his underbelly, the dark, hairy, unsightly pit of desperation so much like her own.

4

Papá stroked the Englishman's horse. It was a Monday morning and he should have been on a smith job. "How long have you known?" he said.

"From the very first days. I fed her well, have not worked her too hard."

Papá squeezed the mare's mane at the ridge of her neck, attempting to calm her quivering. "Why didn't you tell me? There's milk already running down her hind legs."

Rosa knew Papá was pleased. It had been hard to keep it from him, and still Rosa was not sure why she had. She thought back to Francine's words about fathers and daughters and wondered if there was not, in fact, a natural chasm that developed.

"I assume it was Maravilloso?"

"Sí."

"This is why you kept them together?" Papá threw up his hands. "It was a big risk."

"She's smart. I knew he would like her."

Papá smiled. It was the first time in many years she could remember Papá smiling the smile he had once saved only for her. "Sí. It's hard not to like a smart gyal."

5

The mare began foaling the same week Mamá fell ill for the final time. Mamá had been crying, for the pain had fleshed itself out and now spilled over like back fat from a too-small corset. Papá, like a man half his age, shuttled himself between Rosa, who was aiding the mare, and Mamá. When Mamá's shrieks grew loud enough to hear from the stable, Papá dispatched Eve to Monsieur DeGannes's with a request that DeGannes go and fetch the doctor.

Papá gave Rosa instructions she was not certain she would remember. Her mind was on Mamá, who had, in recent days, eaten only a spoonful of rice here and there, vomiting much of it through the night.

When the doctor came a few weeks earlier, he'd stayed for only a short time before calling Papá out to the verandah, where they whispered over each other—Papá's whisper more like a hard stutter.

"The doctor said you'll rally, just as before," Papá had told Mamá when he returned inside.

They had all found comfort in Papá's words, for they had seen Mamá revert nearly back to her old self many times before. But now it all felt different. Mamá was not a woman to shout and carry on. The pain must have been severe, like waves determined to crash or tree roots that extended deeper and farther than the canopy of its branches. Rosa wished, yet did not wish, to be with Mamá. Rosa felt to be stingy with her love was a necessity now, for not to be so meant feeling everything. And Rosa did not wish to feel everything. So Rosa comforted the mare and prayed too for her mother's comfort; prayed for the continuation of Sunday lunches (even if it included Jeremias and Francine); prayed for Mamá's nagging about her hair, her too-wide nose; prayed for Mamá to recover, even as imperfect and disappointing as Mamá could be at times. And maybe if Rosa were being honest with herself, she would have known that the feeling of despair she felt was not only at the thought of losing Mamá, but also at the thought of losing the one thing she was certain made them still a family. Rosa knew she would never share a language with Mamá as Eve did, nor share a life-building with Mamá as Papá had; she would never garner Mamá's attention like Jeremias; but she and Mamá had had all the in-betweens. And in any family there were plenty of in-betweens. Rosa was beginning to understand what Mamá meant about meeting someone you love halfway, about looking for love in the places you were most likely to find it—at the pot in the yard (though you may hate the pot) or beneath rough hands brushing out your tangled hair (though you may hate the brush)—and she thought that perhaps Mamá had not been stingy with her love so much as giving Rosa love in the best way she knew how.

When the doctor arrived, Papá sent Eve to retrieve Rosa. Eve's face was a nautical map of dried tears. "Go and see her," Eve said.

"I cannot leave the mare."

"Rosa," Eve whispered. "I will look after the horse."

The walk to the house seemed longer than any Rosa had taken before. She observed all the worn sideboards, the twigs scattered across the earth like veins, the dried leaves suffocating patches of grass. There was Fat-Gyal-Hen pecking her own dear chick; tomatoes now splitting, too ripe on the vine; a sun that was suddenly too bloody weak to fight a batch of fluffy clouds.

The doctor's closed bag was atop the table in front of Mamá's chair, posed, as if needless. Mamá's groans were so deep, so sullen, that it seemed on the other side of that curtain not to be her mother at all. And so Rosa peeked inside, expecting, hoping, to find someone other than her Mamá and what she found was a pocket of air clogged with the heat of a fiery body that seemed to wish to rid itself of a calabash stomach, a belly so swollen it looked much the same as the belly on Mr. Abbott's mare.

Mamá lay atop the sheet. The same sheet Eve hung on the line on Saturday mornings, the same sheet Rosa heard rustling beneath Mamá and Papá when they believed she slept. It was such a small thing to dwell on—this sheet—yet it seemed that its life was intertwined with the life atop it. As Mamá writhed, so too did the sheet; as Mamá stilled, so too did the sheet. Rosa trained her eye on this sheet as Papá urged her to inch closer to Mamá, demanded that she sit in his seat at the foot of the bed, where the sheet snaked between Mamá's waxen feet, beneath her plump toes, around her swollen ankles, connected to legs so thin they could not possibly bear the weight of her real mother—her mother, taller and stronger than any woman Rosa knew; their mother who fussed and worried and cooked and shoved boiled cassava into Rosa's growing body, willing Rosa to become someone worthy of all the trouble.

The room felt too quiet. Rosa wished for words, any words, for it seemed without them that the three onlookers—she, the doctor, Papá—anticipated something. It was as if the silence suggested an expectation of performance. And words, perhaps, could keep such a performance at bay.

"La cheval is foaling, Mamá," Rosa whispered. "It'll be the best one yet."

Mamá pursed her lips and sucked in a threadbare breath. Like it was worth safekeeping. It seemed a world of effort for her to perform this feat and even more for Mamá to whisper that one word—one word that spoke for all the many she hadn't before spoken: "Nom?"

Tears burned the corners of Rosa's eyes, falling like soldiers single-filing their way around her clenched jaw. Mamá was meeting her half-way. Maybe Mamá always knew that Rosa felt like herself in Jeremias's trousers, knew to let her roam and discover and dig that land as often as she needed, knew not to force her to marry, knew that what Rosa most needed was to feel the blood of that land, pulsating around her. Maybe Mamá knew it all.

Rosa touched the sheet, tugged on it so Mamá would know she was a part of the very thing that was working to keep her held together. "Martinique," Rosa said. "If it's a girl, the pony's name will be Martinique."

Mamá pushed forth a smile. A full, toothy, fanciful smile. As if she was so pleased that it could take that threadbare breath away.

Then Eve's voice came in through the window, sharp and shrill, slicing Mamá's smile like a cutlass through cane. "She's down! It's comin'!"

6

1804 to 1811

Mamá's death felt like a curse. "The Curse of Seven," Rosa thought to name it.

On the last Saturday of every month, Padre José sat upon Mamá's rocking chair and read verses of the Bible to Papá. After every reci-tation, Papá would say to Padre, "What is this t'ing you call religion that refuses to offer hope unless I excuse your god for the infliction of suffering?" Then Papá would ask to see Padre's Bible and draw his attention to certain passages:

"And there shall arise after them seven years of famine; and all the plenty shall be forgotten; and the famine shall consume the land" (Genesis).

"They shall burn them with fire for seven years" (Ezekiel).

And Padre, who thought it his duty to console even the faithless, would shrug, request Papá's patience, and reaffirm what the obeah woman had also told Eve after Mamá's passing—that there would be a long period of mourning ahead for the Rendón family.

1804: A proposal of marriage to Eve was rescinded within seven days of its issuance. The boy's godfather came on a Saturday to meet with Papá. He told Papá that the family had simply changed their minds. When Padre José arrived for his Bible reading, moments after the godfather had sipped from Mamá's teacup, Papá told Padre that his Bible would not be needed since he, Papá, planned on "cussin' up de place." Papá did not bother to wait for Padre's departure before he took the cup from the godfather's lips, called him a lying bastard, and shouted out behind him, "Eve will find better than your nincompoop boy!"

1805: More than half of Papá's cacao crop burned under severe drought conditions. The sales for the remaining half were most underwhelming, and Papá had almost missed paying the levies on the land.

1806: While cooling horses in the river, Rosa was bitten by a coral snake. Its venom caused her to sleep for thirty-seven days. When she woke she told Eve she had seen Mamá in a dream wearing a lime-green frock, holding forth a baby boy, demanding that she wake.

1807: The country was on the verge of bankruptcy, and though the pressure that had been building around the seizure of Papá's land was temporarily relieved, the mold infection in Rosa's garden proved to be damning for the family's reprieve. The hens had eaten some of the moldy crop and became so ill that they produced only a half dozen and one eggs in a span of forty-two days. For the family, there remained only corn.

1808: Most of Port of Spain burned to the ground. Rebuilding efforts were thwarted by a plot hatched by slaves to kill every Englishman on the island. Jeremias's second son, François, was born then, two months too early, almost dying on the night the monsoon-like rains began flooding roads, breaking fencing, ripping away part of the Rendón stable's sideboards, and entrapping them for thirty-five days so that the sale of their small crop of cacao had to be postponed for eighty-seven days until the next ship from England docked at port.

1809: Eve's next intended, a boy from a landowning family that had agreed to put his land together with Rendón land and save both families from potential ruin, fell ill with fever. To his family's great joy, his mother's half sister nursed the boy back to health, but when he recovered, the two ran off together. Papá had a worse name than "bastards" for that family.

1810: Near the end of that year, when the cacao crops were robust again and it seemed Papá had remade the earth with his own hands, and the rain gently rained and the mangoes grew fat and fragrant, and the vegetable roots sprawled like branches beneath the earth, and the tomatoes fell to the ground like sacks, and the horses grew muscles like river boulders and the stream waters swayed like babies in hammocks, the governor's men came for Papá's land. They placed a placard at the gate, just next to the palm trees, noting that Papá had seventy days to pay back taxes. Papá swore he'd already paid but, to his shame, could produce no receipt, which did not surprise Cordoza, for he'd told Papá this had been the governor's plan all along. When Papá's financial vulnerability became local gossip, seven Frenchmen began a bidding war. They asserted that after a winner was declared, Papá must sell to their highest bidder. Papá did not take kindly to the men's assertions, and so he began a regular nighttime vigil alongside his musket, which ended on the sixty-third consecutive day, Christmas morning, when Eve found Papá facedown on the verandah, weak with exhaustion.

1811: Jeremias met Eve at the New Year's Day market. He told her he'd heard from Monsieur DeGannes that Papá had gone with his hat in hand to ask Monsieur for a loan. Monsieur told Jeremias that he had hesitated to proffer the loan to Papá, for Papá was already indebted to him for a sizeable sum due to a loss of future income. When Jeremias asked what Monsieur meant by "loss of future income," Monsieur said nothing more. Jeremias told Eve that he heard later, from a reliable source, that Papá had gone straight from Monsieur's to the clerk's office and, with water in his eyes, set down DeGannes's money on the desk and watched the clerk write on his receipt: *Recovery suspended for an additional 365 days*.

* * *

It was Saturday, December 28, 1811, when Padre José declared the Rendóns' mourning period ended. Papá, sitting upon his rocker, his arms crossed, having finished Eve's weak tea, looked him in the eyes and told Padre that he could find his way to a hot and smoky hell and could take his blasted false pronouncements with him. And when the obeah woman came and told Eve that the worst was over for now but that Papá would fall ill and that a stranger would come to help him, Papá became so vexed, he told the woman that he wanted every red cent Mamá had ever given her returned, and when she could not scrape up the money from the little cotton purse she carried, he set her upon her ragged heels and told her to find her way back to whatever mud shack she had crawled from.

Yet, it had been earlier in that month of December when Papá admitted to Rosa that he had begun to feel something that could only be described as a numbing relief. "I feel breath filling my lungs all the way up again," he told her. And he had pointed to the crown of his head to show Rosa that some, though not all of the silver that had come to be in his hair, had begun turning black again, and Rosa herself could see that Papá's chest had firmed once more and that his shoulders seemed to remember their solid roots, and she believed that though Papá knew wheels needed axles and axles needed wheels, he was beginning to understand that one could make progress with one's own two feet and one's own two hands alongside one's still-broken heart.

CREADON RAMPLEY

Isle of Trinidad

~⁓~

1810

I went to the island cause Gregory swore it promised gold.

When the boat docked at the quay in Puerto d'España, the December night sky was cast in a black that had such a shine to it that it looked like every light in the world had been eaten by it. And it left the earth so shadowed that I couldnt hardly see my hands. So I set myself down on the first thing I bumped into. A stone mule. And slept off my sea legs, wakin the next mornin under a sun so brutal, I couldnt hardly imagine how much more heat daylight could hold.

I went three days hungry til I stole a dull machete from a scorched field and filled my belly with mangoes and coconut meat and blue plums that sprouted like dandelions in that place. I butchered my way through the thickest, most brambly bush I ever seent, from Naparima to Moruga, from Mayaro to Toco, panning the waters of the Caroni, Couva, Nariva, and Ortoire rivers, casin banks, clefts, rifts of hillsides—any place I thought I could find a few of them yellow nuggets.

After a rain, sometimes I had to wait two, three hours for my clothes to prune on sun-hot rocks—wetness in the tropics could kill a man. At dusk, ocelots followed me til I took to treetops and all cross that land lived snakes so vile that when I slept I swore I was gonna wake to my own chokin.

I walked that island for over a year searchin for any glint a gold. Months in loneliness. Months thinkin about a long-ago past—my time in New Spain and them murderin that poor boy, my split with Stephen in Mexico—months thinkin about a future I aint have no shape for.

It was just fore rainy season when I first noticed them dead birds. Every mornin lined up round me with their glassy black eyes unseein in the sunlight. Damn Indians, I knowed it was. I caught them lurkin once. They wasnt exactly the same kinda Indians from Missouri Territory or Oregon Country or even New Spain but they wasnt much different. They had skin like crisp leaves and bright black hair, and they moved quiet as hummingbirds, light and brisk, and had tilted kinda eyes. I figured all they wanted was to frighten me off and I chuckled at the thought. Not cause I couldnt be frightened but cause I prolly could count the days on one hand when I aint been.

"A scared man is a dead man," Pa would say. I used to think Pa meant that bein scared could get a man killed but now I think he meant that bein scared made a man hard and hardness made joy impossible so you might as well be dead.

Look, I aint no believer in the sayin that if you know everything bout a man you understand a man. Sometimes knowin everything bout a man can make you hate a man and that aint really no kinda understandin, is it? Well . . . maybe . . . but anyhow, I aint think them Indians was gonna kill me but it sure seemed to me that they knowed somethin about the kinda frights I didnt wanna member, the kinda frights I aint think I could ever overcome.

Pa had told Lik Smith not to let that fella join our brigade. The new fella seemed to come outta nowhere claimin somebody from Hudson's Bay sent him to meet us. Pa questioned him and sure enough he had the right names, the right titles for people Pa knew but he aint have no letter. And Pa said he needed a "letter of appointment." *Appointment.* The other men laughed at that word. But Pa told Lik that without that letter he aint want no extra split on the money. The other men put it to a vote sayin they could use a nother hand, so Pa went ahead and led the crew, and the new fella fit in just fine. Til he didnt.

There was lil things at first. One time the new fella questioned Lik and Lik told him to just follow orders and then Lik's water pouch had a slit in it. A nother day, the new fella aint like that his meat was tough and the next mornin the man who cooked supper couldnt find his boots. Then a nother time after the new fella complained about his pack bein too heavy, he "forgot" some skins and cost the crew twenty whole dollars. All this went on with nobody able to much prove none of it was malicious til the day come when he challenged Pa.

I musta been eight years. They was playin cards and Pa, pie-eyed, told the new fella to shut his trap and "be a good bloke fore I beat my fist into your face." It was late. And it was Pa bein Pa. But I seent the look in that fella's eyes. Eyes shaped like talons. I stayed woke and watched over Pa all night, listenin for that fella with a lump the size of a fist in my throat.

But he aint make his move til the next mornin.

It was cool and I was down by the river, sleepy as the dickens. When I splashed my face, water trickled into my belly button and made me feel sickly. Tryna pay it no mind, I looked up and saw a hawk soar up into the clouds. Big wide wings it had. I smiled and wished I could fly like that. Felt like if I thought about it real hard, it might could happen and I member feelin joy at that idea. Real joy til I turnt to the bank and seent the new fella standin there. He had a narrow purple-veined face and ice eyes and ivy ears that jutted outta his head like his head was too hot. Comin outta the water, hopin to pass him, I slid to the left but he moved to block me. I slid to the right and he did the same. Pa was still sleepin off his drinks so I reckoned I was gonna have to stay in the water all mornin or approach the fella straight on.

"Mornin," I said to him with my back set straight. Fore then I aint never had a solid reason to fear a man. That aint to say I aint never been scared but til that mornin I was scared only in the silly way children got scared.

The man movin toward me was gonna change all that. He bared his gums. Them ivy ears inched up and his narrow talon eyes looked like they was sprayin ice-blue balls. He come at me hard, fists pummelin, soundin like wet pelts beatin a rock. I member lookin down and seein his white knuckles redden and that red movin into my belly button up onto my winter-pale chest like some horrid rash. I dont know why I tried to keep standin. The force of some of them blows lifted me into the air and after the last, I let myself fall into one big reddened ball with the shadow of that circlin hawk promisin to cool the back of my thumpin, sweaty neck.

I didnt tell Pa bout none a this cause everything bout that fella told me it could get worse. Two days passed and sleep hadnt reached me again. One early evenin I was sittin fore the fire still feelin the soreness from his blows and tired from a hard day of climbin when the new fella started watchin me. We was at the start of supper when hungry eatin usually kept things real quiet so nobody noticed but me. And my hands just started shakin. I tried to stop em but when I brung the mug a hot soup to my lips, my hand shook so hard I dropped the whole damn thing down my neck and chest. I yowled and Pa tore open my clothin, lifted my vest, tryna keep the soup from peelin away at my young skin. He cleaned me with his bare hands and noticed the purple bruises pockin me from my pits to my waist. The other men turned away like they aint wanna know the story behind them marks. Pa's chest heaved and he stared into my eyes for a real long time searchin for an answer. He had this look on his face like he was a seventh-mornin kinda angry but he was as sober as I knowed him to be. And he knowed. And Pa aint said a word to me fore he turnt to that fella. Priebus. Yeah, that was what Pa said.

"Priebus. You put your hands on this boy?"

Priebus was bout as cool as toes without cover. "Sure didnt."

Pa turnt to the others. "You want me to question every man in this goddamn brigade?"

Fright and dont-give-a-shit travel fast among men. Pa reminded em of the way things was fore Priebus come. How he warned em that Priebus was trouble. How Priebus had caused more of a head-ache than his worth. Pa told the men they was being taken for fools by a swindler who had more comin. More comin if they aint take care of him now.

It was that easy.

That easy to unchain em like animals who tasted somethin once and longed for it again. Violence is like that—a lusty girl who touches every dark chink in a man with all-knowin, all-seekin, all-willin fin-gertips, promisin to free him from fear.

Priebus was a man like the rest but in any man you can find differ-ence enough to justify a punishin violence.

They went at him with fists. Fists and heels and elbows and knees on flesh and bones and teeth and pillowed ribs. I stood back not knowin how I felt that Priebus was gettin it worse than he give it to me. The skin on my stomach was wet and sticky with broth and sweat. I watched his ivy ear get smashed into dirt and that narrow face of his bloated like it thought more flesh was the answer. After what felt like a forever beatin, Pa dragged him toward a thick-veined ponderosa, pulled his arms round it, and with hemp cord, tied his wrists to the trunk.

I seent the fella in the cracks tween the men. He had a smushed face that shoulda summoned mercy. But my Pa couldnt find mercy in the dark marshes of humiliation. It seemed Pa was most riled cause of my two-day silence, the surprise of it, how it made him look weak. He was the one man Hudson's Bay paid never to be caught not knowin. So how couldnt he know about his boy? What else had Violence done to his son with her lusty fingers? I watched the other men now. They aint have no desire to protect me, only a need to reorder the world so they couldnt be accused of weakness by the one man who held power over em. They broke Priebus cause if they didnt then it meant they seent themselves in him. In his crushed eyes. In his ribs that wouldnt member their pillowed places no more. They broke him cause they could. Cause Pa told them to. Cause I let Priebus pummel my chest and silently swallowed them bruises like berries and they never wanted to be like me—the bitch of Violence.

"Come here, boy," Pa called to me.

The men parted. Their heavy wheezin wasnt no different than when the gripes hit camp. Theyd just finished pushin out the worst of em and it was nasty but relievin. Pa made me lift the left side of Priebus. He was heavy like a pile a wet fur and smelled sweet and foul like the first minutes of meat over a spit. Lik had already fashioned the noose. He done it quick like he done it plenty before. It was a narrow loop, and me and Pa had to flatten them ivy ears against that bloated head to get it on. A head that was just as hot as I thought itd be. Sweet and foul smellin and hot. I wanted to run. But Pa was waitin and watchin and demandin. *What had Violence done to her bitch?* he seemed to be wonderin.

"You know why we did this, dont you?" Pa whispered this to me but he aint want no answer. One man threw the rope over the branch of that cryin tree, and me and Pa yanked it like we was haulin a stack of skins over a ridge. Cept furs dont gurgle up yellow bile and their fingers dont wiggle and their ivy ears dont sprout fresh blood.

The dead birds lay on their backs surroundin me. I moved em closer and saw on their breasts the place on each where somebody had plucked out the arrow. Their lil bodies was almost weightless, bones so soft it woulda took only a pinch to crush em. I put em back in their places along the circle and sat crossed-legged in the middle while them island Indians watched me. The fear was in me. Fear wasnt ever lettin me alone. And them Indians seemed to know it. And Pa knowed it too. He just wanted me to understand how to get some relief from it.

1812

At the risk of soundin mad, Imma tell you I mighta walked a nother year lookin for gold, if I aint run into Mr. Abbott in Saint Joseph. You see, I couldnt let myself believe that travelin cross treacherous seas and livin months in that miserable jungle without findin gold could be right. I went there to discover somethin, become somethin. David Thompson told me once that I aint have no drive and with all my heart, I aint want him to be right.

Mr. Abbott's top hat stuck out against a backdrop of turf roads and mud-shack fronts. I come out from the bush in search of a town but found instead a barely there village. The guard on my machete had shorn clean off and I needed help, so I sidled up next to his horse and asked if he knew a blacksmith. He got all giggly when he heard my accent, whistled, pointed down at my leather chaparajos then grinned with teeth black as crow plumes.

"The Union, you dont say? Isnt there a war raging now?"

I aint never been to the part of North America people called the Union but tryna explain the bigness of them territories beyond it woulda been like tryna explain a mountain to a blind man. So I nodded then reached cross his stallion (the nicest I seent) and offered him my hand.

"Rampley? Quite a good English name!" Then he winced like he seent somethin that wasnt quite so English. "Dont tell me youve come for gold?" He laughed. "Each year this wicked island murders a half dozen men from that Union who didnt ought to come. Men reeled in by the tall tales of mates who rather hope youll arrive with money to aid them in their continued miseries. Oh! To hear them!"

He laughed harder, and I thought that was exactly what somebody woulda said if they aint want prospectors on their island.

"You dont believe me?" Mr. Abbott climbed off the stallion and dusted his clothes and pointed to the road. "Tell me, do you think this place would look so terribly bedraggled if there were secret riches in the rivers? Wouldnt you suppose youd have run into others during the—" He took off his hat and pushed it into my chest. "Tell me, how long have you been here?"

"I suppose eighteen months or so, sir."

He fanned the hat at me like a spinster with a parasol. "What the devil! You jest, no?" he said. "Eighteen months and not one piece of gold and youre dragging your arse back into the perilous forest to fight off that crazy lot of Amerindians? God bless you! And for what? Indeed, you must wish to die!"

I aint want no lecture. I just wanted a blacksmith. I thought to tell him I found minor deposits but there was somethin about him that made me not wanna be dishonest.

Abbott leaned over and with breath like the most wicked belly wind, he whispered, "Some of them prey on human flesh, you know. When the desire to eat their mothers falls upon them, theyre sent into the wild with the hopes that the gods will do battle against those evil spirits." He licked the corners of his mouth. "But of course, this is not before theyve chewed on the bones of lost men like you." He looked me in the eye and I aint knowed what to make of what he said til he chuckled. "All right, then." He slapped me on the back. "Youll not be convinced. But all that gold wont disappear in one night. You ought to come home with me, have a drink—"

"I dont drink, sir. Trying not to no more, sir."

"Long sad story Im sure to grow quite bored with," he said. "Well then, let me recommend you a pail of water to bathe? Then to make an end of it, I can direct you at dawn to the best blacksmith on the island, a darkie no less."

It was kind of him, so I agreed. "And where can I find a stallion like this?"

The horse had beautiful sheathin.

"You might not believe I got him from the same darkie youll meet tomorrow," he said. "But given that youve found no gold and have not a sixpence, I imagine the only thing youll get on with is the two tired feet youll walk there on."

That evenin Abbott warned me that my time in Trinidad might be short-lived. That the country hadnt met its possibilities and given the Crown's mismanagement, might never. He told me that many had been close to starvin for thirty years and that the best talents on the island had left in search of real prosperity.

The next mornin, I hurried along a macadam road wonderin what I got myself into til I spied the blacksmith's home through some trees. As I neared, I wondered if Abbott aint mislead me, cause I aint never knowed a colored man with any somethin to his name. But the house was just what Abbott said it would be. Double doors. Two spires. Wood trim. And a rockin chair (two) under a bell on the front porch. The place wasnt big and looked to have fallen on hard times but there wasnt no mistakin that it was once a damn fine piece a house.

I walked halfway down the dirt path fore she left the porch. I took off my hat and let her have a look at the hair I cut without a lookin glass and at my vaquero cowhide boots that Señor Meleanos had gave me. There was suspicion in her eyes as she set her sight on me but there was somethin else too. Somethin in the brightness of her glance and in her barely there smile like maybe she was expectin me all along.

VIII

Kullyspell, Oregon Country

⮰⮱

1

1830

Ma disappeared inside a dwelling of cedar logs. A "post," she called this structure that sat south of the western trail they'd traveled up alongside the Clark Fork River, past mountains specked with trees and brush and grasses in blinding colors of gold and bronze, sage and evergreen, like a display of fall squashes. To the west, across a lake as vast as Victor imagined the ocean, stood seven snow-covered peaks that disappeared behind another hill that curved to the north, resembling the chimney on the post now before him. A bearded man lay on the face of the peak to the east, a round tip next to this one, and just across from the post sat a green mountain like a sweeping butterfly.

Ma called the area Kullyspell.

It was late afternoon when Ma helped Victor cross the splintered plank at the threshold. She sat him on a stool next to the door, between four solid, riveted walls. The place smelled of pine needles and the bitterness of burnt rosemary and cured skins. Crisscrossing pine slabs boarded two windows, one north facing, the other west facing. Across from him, propped against a raised and flushed fireplace inlaid with stone, sat a small square table, which Victor presumed would have to be moved before the fire was kindled. Atop this table was a coverless Spanish Bible, appearing as if someone had not so much neglected it as thrown it. Upon a plank shelf to his right were three cups, three plates, and one wooden spoon with a curved handle. The floors, fashioned from cedar split logs, round side down, were smooth, save for three large boles that lay blackened and jagged, as if a fire had once nearly razed the place.

Ma returned outside to Martinique. She, with the last of their water, wiped down the tired mare while Victor watched through the open door as Ma's chest heaved in a sigh like a great wind. He felt he should call to her, comfort her in some way, but knew that doing so would make him feel things both violent and useless.

When Ma reentered, she escorted Victor through the first room where lay a second room. Ma set him upon a thing she called a "bed," large enough for two adults and two children, which sank beneath him like a nest of plumes. Next to him, Ma slid aside a hemp curtain, revealing four shelves bearing hides, hemp sheets, and two cedar bark baskets. She removed a pot from the top shelf—an odd-looking thing with flanges like turkey wings—and placed it beside the bed. It was clear then that she'd been there before.

"Are we finally where we need to be?" he whispered.

Ma examined Victor, patting his flesh with feathery fingertips. He had several broken ribs, she said, and a shattered leg. She bound him with strips of cloth that looked permanently stained with another's blood.

"Do you think we will be safe here?"

Ma looked to Victor as if to say, *Are we ever safe?* and if Victor did not know better, he might have said Ma was aquiver, might have said she was thinking of what could have been, what might still be, for Victor himself had not stopped thinking about any of those things.

When he woke it was nightfall. Ma had removed the boards and thrown open the window. A cool, rich breeze whispered over them, and Victor found the moon in the middle of the window's square, as though someone had plugged a wall around it. Next to him, Ma slept on the ladder-back chair; the light of a dying candle shone on the skin of her jowls that fell slack toward her ears, the fine bones in her hands stitched together like too-tight tunnels. Victor watched her for some time, wondering if she could still smell her Frenchman the way he smelled his, wondering if she thought of Like-Wind the way he did.

Many nights after that first night, Victor lay awake considering all that had happened. He had wanted to question Ma about so many things—Was Like-Wind sent by the elders? Could the girl have survived? Where was the man they were to meet?—but had refrained because he wished his silence to be her balm. Wished his silence to be *his* balm.

One night, a week or so after they'd arrived, Victor reached for the candlestick, determined to relieve himself in private. On their first day there, Ma had taught him how to use the chamber pot, and though he had twisted his face with disgust, declaring outdoors to be the proper place for such things, he'd since grown fond of the contraption, happy not to have to drag his shattered body into a darkness whose shadows he had yet to meet. Until then, however, Victor had relieved himself only with Ma's assistance, but that evening he couldn't wait long enough for Ma to wake and clear her eyes.

The pain was wicked as he contorted himself to avoid mess making. As he began sliding the pot back beneath the bed, he knocked over his water pouch and, in his effort to retrieve it, lost his balance and planted his right hand squarely in his urine. Disgusted but a tad amused, Victor thought of Like-Wind, who would have never stopped laughing had he been there; Like-Wind, who would've balled his knees into his chest and clutched his chuckling belly. And Victor began to cry. For no matter the memory of Like-Wind—and most were good—there would always be Like-Wind alone on that sooty earth with his young chest split open. Victor had asked Ma before they left those woodlands if she could wrap Like-Wind in hide, set him upright into the branches of that majestic fir. But Ma said she didn't know what to make of Like-Wind keeping company with those men, and she told Victor that if she set Like-Wind in the arms of that tree and if his body was ever found, Bluegrass would know for certain that Apsáalooke had killed his son.

Victor rinsed his hand and cast the light about the floor, hoping to see how much spillage he'd caused. Ma would have words for him in the morning, he knew. For now, however, she remained asleep, her left foot beneath the right, her legs pinched together like a flower's bloom on a chilled night, and as Victor drew back the candle, he noticed something—a shadow of a thing—beneath the bed. He bent toward it, raised the candle, tilting it left and right to get the light just so. What Victor discovered, suspended by a crispy vine rope, was a diary.

2

It was Creadon Rampley's diary.

Victor read the pages as if it were his first taste of sweet. When the candle died and Ma didn't wake, he read by the dawn's light. He read slowly, the man's poor handwriting—English words about Creadon's father and his meeting with David Thompson. Who was this man? How did Ma come to know him?

Ma woke, as she often did, in a start, bolting upright, eyes glazed and terrified. Victor slipped the book beneath his shoulder before her eyes cleared. He didn't want to share it, not yet; didn't want to be told not to read it, not yet.

"How long have I been sleeping? Let me help you with the chamber pot. I'm sure—"

"I managed." Victor forced a yawn. "Can I rest longer?"

Ma straightened her shoulders, pushed out her chest. Her tunic was stained, her hair littered with tiny chips of wood, making Victor feel shamed, for there was proof before him that since they'd arrived, Ma had been thinking only of him.

"I found a well," she said. "It won't take me long to get water."

He wondered why anyone needed a well with a lake only steps from the post. "You didn't know there was a well?" he asked instead.

Ma squinted as if the question were nonsensical, then took up the chamber pot and left.

The wooden door crackled like a dying fire and Victor began to read again. He continued each day when Ma went for water or food or air, and each night when Ma slept in the chair beside him. As Ma waited the many weeks for Victor to heal, he thwarted such healing by living for nights, straining his eyes to make sense of the smudged words—words in an English Ma had taught him to speak and to read over many nights by the light of a torch—letters in a fading ink that seemed to be holding on just long enough for Victor to taste and feel and breathe them. During those weeks, Creadon lived in Victor's head, in his heart. Creadon's adventures became Victor's adventures; his fears, Victor's fears; his story, part of Victor's story.

CREADON RAMPLEY

Isle of Trinidad

❦

1812

She was goddamn lovely. Lovely in that way you cant grasp the moment you see it. Cause you aint seent nothin like it.

She met me fore I could make it to the front door. She spoke Spanish and I understood much of what she said. Her name was Eve Rendón and if I was lost she could help me find my way. I smiled and she blushed, thinkin I aint understand her, then lifted her finger like to ask me to wait.

"My Papá," she said.

I prolly wasnt supposed to but I followed her. I barely noticed the windin path I walked down or the handsome stable she walked into just as she started speakin real fast in French to someone I couldnt see. "Where is Papá? How long will he be gone?"

"Non!" I figured that was the voice of a brother.

Eve looked shamefaced when she peeked out from the barn. She held her hands steady in the air, like to tell me to wait then I heard her and the boy firin off. Voices risin. A long sigh. Somethin slammin. Then she come back out, leadin a strange-lookin girl dressed like a strange-lookin boy toward me.

"Sir, I am Eve's sister. Is my Papá expecting you?" The girl who maybe I should call a woman cause I found out later she was twenty-five and Eve was twenty-seven, spoke to me in a near perfect English, lookin me over like she seent better.

I shoulda told em then and there that I spoke French just fine. All Hudson's Bay trappers did. But I was too busy tryna make sensa how them two coulda been sisters. They looked so different.

"Mr. Abbott called me," I said in English. "I mean, Mr. Abbott sent me."

The woman smirked at my misspeak.

"My machete." I pointed to the broke handle in my pack. "I need a blacksmith."

The woman translated for Eve who looked embarrassed that she hadnt already reasoned out why I was there.

"Papá will return soon, sir," the woman said. "Please wait."

Their father was a tall, lean-muscled man with an open face. He had burnt hands, one with only four fingers, and dark eyes that looked like they was memberin every pain they seent. After I told him I couldnt pay him nothin but a word a thanks, he made himself clear. "I cannot help you, sir." His English landed not so good as the woman's but good enough for me to understand no.

I followed him back round the stable tryna explain how I got to the island. Told him how I aint asked nothin from nobody since I got there. Seemed like he figured I aint know nobody who could hurt him cause then he turned and talked to me like I wasnt no decent man. "Then what will you do?" He was holdin a bundle of hay in his arms like he was fittin to throw it at me. "Tell me. Once I fix this cutlass of yours, what will you do? Hack away at the trees, rape the land of its soil to find a few specks of yellow dust? Why again should I offer you this charity?"

I wasnt so much embarrassed as cross. To be spoke to like a child by an African in English? "I dont much like your tone," I said.

"I am certain Mr. Abbott did not tell you that I am a man without pride. I am sorry if my tone offended you, sir, but youve come to my home requesting much and offering nutting." He tipped his hat. "I must get back to work."

"I can work," I said suddenly. "Here. For you."

He set down one bundle and moved to a nother, pickin em up between long breaths. "You plenty desperate to find this gold, eh? Well, we dont need your help here."

I took the bundle and refused to take no for an answer. I had nothin else. No other way.

"Sir, if you please." He pulled the hay from me.

"I insulted you. Imma find a nother way to fix my cutlass. But lemme do this."

He let me work. And truth is I felt good about it too. He seemed like a good man, which come clear when I seent the way him and his two daughters was together. This way of bein where it seemed each was a piece of a whole. They moved their hands the same, the two girls smiled the same, him and Eve even frowned the same. They was real people. A real family.

At lunchtime, Demas Rendón led me up to the timber-frame house and in through a double door. There was true to life furnishins inside! I aint knowed what it would take to dream that one day I might have a home with puncheon floorin and a sturdy roof of logs lined with animal pelts. My dreams wasnt that big. There was unlit candles against the walls like they was happy waitin for dark, and a basin of water near the table where me and Demas washed our faces and hands fore takin a sit.

Demas sat at the head and I sat next to him, cross from Eve, who was seated beside the woman whose name I learnt was Rosa. Eve put down the plate for Demas first, then the rest of ours. Cool water was in my cup and I drank it thirstily then stabbed my fork into the glistenin roast fowl about the size of my fist fore realizin the three of em had paused for grace to a God I hadnt given no thought to.

"And dear God, bless the strangers among us," Eve added.

That Eve Rendón was somethin special! She had thoughts on Europe and South America, on abolitionists and the Union. She aint knowed English but she peppered me with so many questions that I finished only half my plate by the time her father leant back in his chair, satisfied.

"She wishes to know about your family." Demas was translatin for Eve. "Your mudda and fadda, any bruddas and sistas?"

"My Pa raised me but I aint got nobody left," I said, dippin somethin they called breadfruit into a tangy brown sauce that made my farhead sweat.

"Your mother was not English, sir, was she?" That Rosa had a sharp way about her. Like she was made a corners and was tryna catch my lies on em.

The afternoon sun streamed in like it was mad at somethin, hittin the side of my face where Rosa had her eyes set. "Naw she wasnt."

"Indian?"

I nodded though I aint sure why then and not ever before. Suddenly Rosa seemed to be lookin at me with new eyes.

"I aint knowed my mother," I said.

"But you call yourself English?"

Demas shook his head and tapped Eve who then elbowed Rosa.

"Was your mother a slave? An Indian slave?" Rosa said.

Demas glared at Rosa then said to me, "My apologies. Rosa is only curious. She and Eve lost their mudda eight years now."

Been the same since I lost Pa.

It got quiet then. The kinda quiet that made me feel shame for havin caused it. "Señora Eve, this was about the most delicious meal I ever ate." I said this though I was still hungry. "Thank you much."

Eve smiled then Demas said, "If we ever invite you for Rosa's cooking," he chuckled, "you'll know we wish for you never to return."

Rosa laughed like the joke had legs that could walk cross lifetimes. She tossed her bonnet at her father, who caught it with his four-fingered hand, and when he chuckled even more, her face lit up the whole place.

Lunch was long over and after helpin Demas fix a crushed gatepost, I readied myself to leave. I aint knowed where I was goin. I only knowed that if I made it there I could survive on the way to someplace else.

"Stay for tea," Demas said.

Birds twilled and the sunlight spiraled down tween branches as we set up on the porch. Demas told me a lil about Trinidad. That it was a Crown colony and that that meant everything was controlled in England. That bekre negres, coloreds, like his wife's family, made up most of the free people on the island. That that wasnt true on other English-held islands. And that was a major reason England aint want no self-governin in Trinidad. He told me that cause there wasnt as many slaves, Trinidad aint turn profits like Barbados or Jamaica or Antigua and that, at least for now, wealthy planters on them other islands didnt want Trinidad as competition cause the land there was virgin and fertile and they knowed theyd be outdone.

"A man can make his way here if he is willing to work," Demas said.

"Papá t'inks work can change everyt'ing." Eve laughed. "Work and your foot will heal. Work and a husband will soon come. Work and youll live to be old."

"It is true!" Demas laughed then said to me, "You have stories, Señor Rampley?"

It was a test though I aint knowed it then. Him and Eve was on the rockers under a cowbell and Rosa, payin me no mind, sat on the steps slurpin up a tea-soaked biscuit.

I started with Pa, leavin out the parts bout his drunkenness and foul-mouthed ways in favor of how funny and clever he was. Then I told em bout meetin David Thompson. "It was summer but there was still icicles in the lakes and whirlpools in the river." Demas said my words to Eve in Spanish and I watched her brow furrow. "But the most prettiest thing youll ever see is when the ice on a lake freezes over and the vapor makes ice flowers. Some small like pearls. And when the sun shines on em, they get so bright with the colors of a rainbow, they can actually blind a man. Blind him, for real.

"We built a nice place—Kullyspell, we called it. Most beautiful place I ever seent. A different kinda beauty than here." I stared over quaverin treetops past the Rendón land to a sky of orange and rose. Looked like the horizon was berry stained. "Seems your own homeland always feels better in your heart even if the beauty is bout the same as where you standin." I thought about the lands I seent fore arrivin there. Creamy snows, grasses in shades of green and tan and red, trees whose trunks was interrupted only by sky. There shoulda been more words to describe what I seent in my lifetime. And maybe there was. But I aint have em. "I never wanted the kinda life where you couldnt stay long enough to learn it. But then again, maybe there aint never enough time to learn life."

I was feelin like a cheat for not tellin how I broke with Thompson, how Id up and run from Meleanos. "I was in New Spain, workin for a man who looked to have everything and still wanted more." I watched Demas and wondered if maybe I was speakin to and bout the same kinda man. "But I figure every man's gotta have ambitions."

Demas looked like he was decidin whether to be offended. He uncrossed his legs and leaned over his knees. "True. A man must not be idle. But his ambitions should not be to the detriment of those he should be loving." He said this like he knowed I needed him to make himself different from all the other men I met. Eve and Rosa looked to be proud to have that man as their father. I wondered what it might be like to have somebody be proud to claim me. "And what about the rest of your family?"

"I aint got people to claim, really. My Pa told me that my mother was Crow Indian. Apsáalooke."

"Apsáalooke?" Rosa said.

"Means 'Children of the Long-Beaked Bird,'" I said, though I still aint sure that was true. "Some say the long-beaked bird wasnt a crow but some kinda water bird that dove into the sea, pulled up a plant from the bottom and made the earth. The bird made a whole world for himself." I gulped the last bit a my tea. "That dont seem much different from this world you and your girls looked to have made here."

IX

Kullyspell, Oregon Country

~~

1

1830

One step, two steps, three steps. Each afternoon, Ma forced Victor out of bed and made him walk the plank floor. It had been twelve weeks since they'd arrived at Kullyspell, and the sun seemed more often to find shelter behind trees, for winter was coming. They would need to make new clothes, gather food, ensure there was enough fat for light. Ma told him she'd need his help to get through it.

During their fourth week, Ma had fashioned a brace and an under-pinning to help Victor walk. He had set it aside, complained that it rubbed his skin raw so Ma had lifted him, his legs stretching longer than hers, until she buckled beneath him, forcing her to prop him against the threshold to catch her breath. "You want to die out there?" Her eyes had bulged, the lines in her neck, strained. "Is that what you want?"

Victor did not know what he wanted.

During their fifth week at the post, Victor had reached the part of Creadon's diary where Creadon had been nearly buried alive. He stopped before he knew whether they had found the cattle. At first Victor believed he'd paused because he wished to savor the story, to live with it as long as he could, but soon Victor realized that he'd grown restless with it, angry with it, for he felt, as he read the words, that Creadon had been teasing him, his diary holding out a world Victor would never know, places and people and a time that were not accessible to him.

It was the beginning of the twelfth week in the cabin when Ma clasped her hands, exasperated. "You don't want to get better? Must I always push you, carry you, cover you? I'm tired too, Victor. Your legs are still attached to your body. Look down and see them. They still work."

"I'm not ready."

"What is ready?" Ma said. "Without pain? Is that what you mean?" She shook her head, then narrowed her eyes. "You will never live without pain again. That fact has nothing to do with your legs."

One step, two steps, three steps.

Victor couldn't make it to step four. Not to the fireplace they'd begun to need as the nights grew cooler. Not to the plank on the other side of the door. His hip bones throbbed, the friction inside his knees could have kindled fire, and the drag of his legs was as if lodgepoles had been tied to his ankles. Victor wished to tell Ma about his pain. He wanted to tell her that he thought of Like-Wind every day; tell her what he'd discovered from Creadon's diary, the knowing and all its unpleasantness—how he was now frightened that there were more people in the world who looked at him the way the girl had looked at him, and how frustrating and infuriating it would be if this proved true. But a warrior could not speak such brittle words, and even if he could, Ma would not hear them. She wanted only for Victor to take steps. But to where? And to what end?

2

Victor could not see the whites of Ma's eyes. She had shut the window, and only fine traces of a blue morning light fought off the cabin's darkness. The air felt moist, hectic, reluctant to cool. Sweat bubbled like an upwelling at the top of his head. It was her thumb and her index finger pressed into the supple sides of his neck. Her other hand lay over his mouth. His right wrist had been tied with red hemp stems hooked to the window shutter. Victor set the palm of his left hand onto her head, nudging her away. Some pressure released and he gulped air, only to have her fight off his blind hand and veer back stronger. She planted her fingers like poles in the open prairie of his neck. Poles bearing flags of victory. As he writhed beneath her, he remembered that Ma had told him she was tired, angry that he would not stand on his own. Step four. That was all she'd wanted. She would rid herself of him, get back to his sisters and to Father. She would tell them Victor died bravely, fighting off Like-Wind and the evil Frenchmen. It would be a story for the ages.

Except Victor didn't want that to be his story.

He clawed at her face, catching tiny pellets of skin under the beds of his nails, earning himself another gulp of air. She fought back harder, grunting, then threw the hemp blanket onto his face, holding down the edges with her hands. Victor drove fists into the sides of her face, knowing all the contours of her, even in that darkness.

Victor sat now against the interior wall, the acrid taste of bile in his throat, his neck as sore as if it'd been feasted upon, his thoughts still unclear hours after Ma must have untied him. He watched a silver spider thread the corner of what looked to be a rectangular web. Victor didn't know how long he'd been sitting there, how long since Ma had left him, but he guessed nearly a half day, for the sun had weakened and the shadows grown tall.

Step five. Victor opened the door of the post and rediscovered the world. The crisp *chur-chur* of the bluebird; the sky pocked white, as the high gale of wind swirled the tops of the ponderosas and rickety aspens that grew uphill. Stumbling along, it wasn't altogether clear where he was. Q'lispe or Ktunaxa territory. Grasses and mats of creeping juniper grew like wild hairs atop chestnut-grey soil until meeting stout shrubs that seemed to have agreed not to encroach. As he walked farther, Victor hoped to see the top of Ma's head or the windlass of a well, but he saw nothing but an old log storehouse before a backdrop of unfamiliar wilderness and a lake that rippled as though hungry.

Victor closed his eyes and listened to the trees that spoke differently there. They called to him, told him to brace himself against them, and he took cautious steps as they steadied him, nudged him to the next of them, until he came to the well.

Victor peered into its mouth and imagined the water, still and waiting and cold. He shouldn't have been frightened, but fright can only be reasoned with if one has never been frightened. The ground surrounding the well was moist and infirm, as though the hole had been backfilled with loose soil. It was a grave lying in wait, he thought. He limped around it, and on the other side, found Ma's buckets. The water inside was not yet sun warmed.

"Ma?" Victor spoke down into the well. When he raised his eyes, he saw a dead bird, partially covered by caked birch leaves on the ground near his foot. Yellow breasted and horribly delicate, its neck snapped and its little black eyes jutted like pumiced stones, as though it'd been shocked to find itself in such a state. Victor sat in the earth beside it and heard the hawk bellow overhead. He thought it a sign but didn't know of what, and so he rose to his feet, wound his way between silver-leafed black cottonwoods and the creamy trunks of paper birches and searched.

"Ma?" He was not so much calling her to come as he was asking her to reveal herself.

And so she did.

Still shrouded by trees, Victor watched Ma in the earth, clawing her fingernails like hooks, revealing the reddened clay beneath the topsoil. Under the shadows of a cluster of blue-needled spruces, Ma grunted, punched, bit her lip as if to restrain a gruesome cry, folded herself like a heavy sheet of skin, her hair standing as if each strand were shouting to the First Maker. Victor had never heard a moan that he could feel beneath his feet.

3

When she spotted him, he was near the well, pretending he'd been waiting there all along. Ma, with her musket, moccasins, and a spear that held two wide-eyed trout, chastised him for having left the post.

"What were you thinking?" She gripped his face and peered at his neck. "Look at you. You're a mess. Did you stumble?" She handed him the musket and the fish, and she took up the bucket. "All of a sudden you can walk and you decide to come all the way behind God's back to hurt yourself?"

Upon their return, she insisted that Victor set himself down on a high stump next to the pot. She placed the coverless Spanish Bible onto his lap as though he needed a better god. She worked in such a way that seemed a plea for silence, feeding the fire whenever she thought Victor cold, scaling and gutting fish, gathering red clover and wild carrots for a fish broth, a specialty of hers that had always delighted Father though Apsáalooke did not regularly eat fish. "My ocean woman," Father would say, clapping his hands as the broth dribbled down his chin.

Ma searched inside the bowl of a wide leaf for hyssop and dill for the pot.

"I'm feeling better now." Victor set the Bible on the ground, drawing Ma's attention to it, though she said nothing.

"I can see."

"This morning . . . why did you do that? Would you have killed me?"

Ma flitted her eyes as if to make light of his words, then grinned. "I want to kill you all the time."

"This morning, before you disappeared, you were fighting me." Victor said, noticing, suddenly, that Ma had no visible wounds.

Her face folded into itself. "I left you sleeping. I went to catch fish."

Victor wondered now if he had dreamt it all and if he had, wondered what kind of meaning was in a dream of a mother trying to murder her only son. "You never tell me about home."

"I am certain your sisters are fine."

"Not that home," he said. "Trinidad."

She stirred the broth with the long wooden spoon. The smoke sweated her cheeks. "What more is there to tell? Shadows fall the same there."

Ma dipped a bowl into the hot soup, then wiped the outside of it on her skirt. Victor followed with his bowl and, together, they sat and ate in the quiet of dusk.

The next morning Victor expected he would find Ma gone again. He stretched for the diary, felt ready for it once more until Ma cleared her throat from the chair. Victor offered her a nervous grin and took in her months-tired eyes.

"My father wished for me to marry," she started. "He invited a young man to come for Sunday lunch."

Victor sat up, forgetting the diary. "You didn't like him?"

"I didn't know him. Papá made me cook for him and his uncle," she said. "I made broth."

Victor smiled, for he too liked the fish broth.

"I almost killed the boy's uncle," she said. "I put so much pepper sauce in the broth that his heart stopped." Ma wiped the corners of her eyes, then wiped her mouth, before Victor realized that she was laughing. Really laughing. "Papá was so upset."

Victor laughed too, though he'd never tasted this pepper thing she spoke of. "What was he like?"

"The boy?"

"No, your Papá."

"You would love that man. And if he were here with us, he would love you, Victor, in a way that any love coming after it would seem not worth the trouble." She scooted to the edge of the chair and crossed her feet. "He was magnificent, strong and confounding, always confounding. I like to think his love for us took him by surprise. There were so many things I didn't know. So many things I wish I could've asked. Why? So many whys. He was a hard worker, a protector, but why wasn't that enough?" Ma seemed to think carefully of what more she would say. "In the face of all the conflict on our little island, my Papá did everything he could to keep us together, to keep us from harm. What more could I have asked?"

"Then why did you leave?"

Perhaps she wouldn't tell Victor everything, for he had asked for the end rather than the beginning. Ma rose from the chair, and

Victor thought she would set out for more lake water and wander about the shore as she had often done, leaving him there with his thoughts, but instead Ma lay beside him, settling into the feather bed, and Victor could smell her morning-washed skin and her breath sweet with ripe berries, and he thought then that there must be no greater comfort in all the many worlds than a mother's body wrapped about yours.

X

Isle of Trinidad

❧❧

1

1812

Demas Rendón was nothing if not polite and he would never have sent Creadon Rampley off into the darkness. That first evening, Papá asked Creadon Rampley if he would like to stay. And the next day, after Creadon Rampley helped Papá reorganize his workspace, helped Papá groom the horses, helped Papá loose dirt for his new water well, helped Papá with everything Papá could not do alone, Papá asked him to stay for another lunch, for another tea, and finally Papá offered him the muggy hayloft, alongside Eve's dresses, for as long as Creadon Rampley wished to work.

Creadon Rampley was a stranger, a prospector, a wanderer. To Rosa, a man with too much purpose and a man with no purpose were equally dangerous, and Creadon Rampley seemed both. Yet he also seemed to be doing everything right, even while Rosa was certain everything was wrong.

One early morning while alone in the shop, Rosa believed she'd uncovered the truth. "He's after Eve," Rosa said to Papá.

"He is a nice, respectful young man. Eve could do worse," Papá said.

Rosa blushed with surprise.

"This is why Eve takes to him. He's been places she's not been, done t'ings none of us have. He's unafraid. Men like this are being made no more."

"Unafraid? He's fearful of everything. You can't see that, Papá?"

"And yet he still rises each day," he said. "That is not fear, that is la valentía."

Papá turned from Rosa and walked to the grindstone which he'd had to build to replace what he'd lost in the raid, along with smaller, more efficient instruments including a three-legged forge that burned wood at its base. Without proper roof ventilation, Papá had had to perform much of his smithing near the door.

"But he's not one of us."

"In his heart, sí, he is. Here, he is beginning to learn this about himself." The muscles between Papá's shoulders jumped like small fishes as he pushed the grindstone from the stable wall.

"He is learning nothing but to be in my way," Rosa said.

Papá turned so that Rosa could now see a sliver of his face. He appeared slightly bemused by her frustration. "Your mudda has sent us help. The t'ree of us couldn't do this all alone."

Once more, he leaned into the grindstone set within a heavy four-legged stand. It moved, albeit begrudgingly, and though Papá did not ask for assistance and might not, in his chipped-from-something-solid way, have wished for it, Rosa leaned alongside him and helped reposition it from the wall to the middle of the floor where it could freely turn. He breathed heavily and Rosa felt saddened that the space that he had had to carve from the stable for his work was so regrettably small, that it required him to move tools and equipment several times a day.

"Even if it is not in the form we wished"—he fanned his face with the brim of his hat—"my prayers were answered."

Rosa was disappointed, and yet she could not deny that in the weeks since Creadon Rampley's arrival, the list of things to be done each day was cut to a third by noon. Señor Rampley was methodical and strong, did not prattle as he worked, and spoke only to ask what more he could do. He knew carpentry, hunted so well they often ate fresh meat at lunch, was a walking compass (never once had he been turned around) and masterful fisherman (could catch them with his bare hands!), and wielded a cutlass like a caner. Like Rosa, he was of the outdoors.

"Tomorrow, I wish for you to take Señor Rampley out with the team," Papá said.

"That's my job. I set them out, you and I bring them in together."

"Not tomorrow." Papá placed the blade of a ploughshare against the grindstone and waited for Rosa to take her leave.

Rosa woke an hour earlier than usual. She hoped Creadon Rampley would still be resting, but when she arrived at the stable, he was there with that strange stupid smile wearing those silly wide-legged trousers, alongside the horses that he had already roped. Rosa recalled the day he'd arrived, when Eve had told Rosa how much she liked those trousers, how striking they were on a man with such powerful form. Now, the strong-legged man with the ridiculous trousers and that dumb grin waited for Rosa with saddle in hand. He reached for her seat, as if to assist, but she shook her head.

"Mornin'," he said.

Rosa mounted, made sure the two horses she led were secure on the line, then looked down at him. "What do you know about mustangs, Señor Rampley?"

His eyes were filled with anticipation. "I know they're horses."

"They're not horses, Señor. What you call a horse would be closer to a dog." Rosa wished to tell him that her mustangs were not what most considered "mustangs," that her mustangs were true to the meaning of mustang. They could survive on less feed than a human child for weeks, they were good in a stall, good in pasture, didn't stumble when the soil was rocky, didn't slow on a march uphill, and would not colic quickly when thirsty. But Rosa believed her efforts to elucidate would all be wasted, for she was certain Creadon Rampley would not be there long.

They began along the trail with Creadon Rampley a head's length behind her leading two horses on one lead. It was a morning like all others during dry season, holding the promise of a blue sky and a mocking breeze. Rosa rode with confidence and vigor. The sun's break felt like the slow, warm rise of an irrepressible yearning, quickening the beat of Rosa's pulse, her blood pumping as she rode harder, the bop and sway of the fillies reading like the elegant necklines of choice women, the stallions' manes blowing like the carved hairs of the wildest Arawak boys. As she came upon a shallow woodlands, Rosa dipped beneath low-hanging branches as if she had created the swerves of that land—land that before long would disappear at the foot of three hills, one larger than the hill before it, wooded and shaded and pitted at its base with seeds and rotted fruits. And over those hills, new land would snake to the left and to the right until becoming a clearing that dove into the mouth of the stream where Rosa would take the horses to fill their bellies.

Rosa was aware as she rounded the last bend that it was there where usually she spoke aloud the words she'd never spoken to Mamá—telling her she loved her, that she wished she'd allowed Mamá to brush her hair without complaint. But that morning, Rosa spoke no words to Mamá. She listened, instead, to the thud of the horses' footfalls, predetermined by their round, dense hooves, and watched their long strides make the brown-tipped grasses genuflect before her. And Rosa felt that perhaps this was not morning at all. Perhaps this was the end of mornings or the end of something she couldn't quite name.

Creadon Rampley had fallen back. As Rosa cast her eyes behind her and watched him slump in the heat, Rosa remembered how Eve had behaved the first evening he sat for a meal. "Dios mío!" Eve later exclaimed. "Jolie comme une fille"—pretty like a girl, she had said—"but so much a man!" As they lay in bed, Eve had remarked on Señor Rampley's strong square brow and thick eyebrows; his dense, sinuous hair in a long-steeped luminous black that shimmered sorrel; his cheekbones, high set; his chin like an arrowhead, the dimple in it like a split for hafting, the projectile point directing the eye to full pouty lips that seemed to make his skin glow bronzer. Eve saw in him a loveliness Rosa did not believe she would ever see.

Over the coming months, Señor Rampley continued to join Rosa on her morning turn-outs. Sometimes they led the horses on foot; other times they rode out on two and returned on one, and Rosa's resistance eventually gave way, and she began to appreciate Señor Rampley's helpfulness, resent less his presence, such that now when they ate their meals she found herself leaning in as he spoke, surprised by how important he made her feel.

Then one afternoon, an unexpected rainfall forced the four of them to take an early lunch. Señor Rampley, soaked through to his knickers, brought in wild yams. He had been excited to gift them to Eve. But Eve had responded most ungraciously. Flustered over having to give over the house to a meal before she was ready, Eve quietly complained to Papá that Señor Rampley might expect the ñames to be offered for that day's lunch. Papá assured her that no such thing would be presumed, but still Eve fretted.

The three of them felt Eve's displeasure thickset in the air. They sat quietly eating saltfish buljol, sipping pawpaw juice that Eve had steeped in sunlight. Papá finished his mug of juice first and looked to Eve to pour more. After she refilled it, he drank again. "Tomorrow morning Señor Rampley will go alone with the team," he said.

Rosa drew a chunk of tomato from her mouth. "What do you mean?"

"He has learned a great deal," Papá said. "Let's see if he can do it alone now."

"Of course he can do it. I taught him everything."

"Sí, and now you will learn from Eve." Papá shoveled a large spoonful of the buljol into his mouth, then spoke again only after he had chewed it all and sipped again from his cup. "Eve needs help in the house. There is wash pilin' up, t'ree meals to be cooked a day, a floor that requires scrubbing." His words sounded as if they'd been placed upon his tongue by someone named Eve. "It is time. One day you gointa marry and have chil'ren, and your mudda will turn over in her grave if I don't make you learn what you need to know."

"Papá, no!" Rosa leaned forward as if to press all her energies against Papá's will. "I can help Eve in the nights. I'll do the wash, the cleaning, but don't take the horses. Don't, Papá."

"Basta."

Rosa noted the tone. It was as if Papá had analyzed all the merits of her impending arguments. "No, it is not enough!"

"Rosa." Eve looked to Señor Rampley as if to apologize for her insolent little sister.

Rosa stood, pushed her plate to the middle of the table, spilling the oily mixture of fish, tomatoes, onions. She felt her breath with the sharp sweetness of undigested peppers and took note of Creadon Rampley's hanging head and melancholy eyes, appearing as if tragedy had struck him. "This was your plan all along, wasn't it? You make me teach you and then you take what's mine." Rosa turned again to Papá, refusing to wait for Señor Rampley's response, for the life they seemed to take for sport was very much her life. "You're so blind, Papá, you can't see his plan?"

"Watch yourself, Rosa," Papá said.

"You spend years keeping this place close to your chest, sending your only son away, fearing what's yours might wind up with Mamá's family or the governor, and then this . . . this tonto comes and you just give it away?"

"Rosa," Eve said again. "You're a big woman. Behave!"

"Don't 'Rosa'! Everyone is always saying 'Rosa'! You two don't even know this man. Did you know he came here because he was running away from a murder?"

Papá turned to Creadon Rampley. "Is this true?"

"Yes. Yes, it is." Señor Rampley sat forward in his chair, his fingers locked, as he looked Papá in the eye. "But since Rosa got this from readin' my diary, I reckon she can tell you it wasn't me who murdered that boy."

"You went tru the man's t'ings, Rosa? I ent raise you like this," Papá said.

This was not where she wished to be. Patience, persistence, wait out your prey. Papá had taught her this. "All I'm asking is not to allow him to do this to us. He's filled your head with these thoughts about what men should do and what women should do. I know men like him."

Papá pinched his lips and shook his head. "No, you don't know men like him." Papá closed his eyes as though he wished the words he would speak next were not true. "But when you come to learn men, you will understand that you is not one of them."

2

Rosa mourned. Perhaps the Curse of Seven had been extended, she thought. And yet this particular grief was felt by no one else. They now treated her as if it should be in her nature to find joy in mending men's trousers, in sweeping plumes, in making soap from ashes. In tediousness.

The Rendón meals were seasoned with Rosa's tears. And Eve appeared to take great satisfaction in eating them. Eve chided Rosa for every misstep, for not putting forth the same effort she said Rosa would have extended with the horses or the swine or the calves. She invoked Mamá's name to shame Rosa into pickling vegetables and squeezing the life juice out of fruits, invoked Mamá's memory to guilt Rosa for not wishing to be a second-tier mucama in her own home. Rosa was to kill babies she'd fed since birth, clean them, salt them, stuff them. And if that were not punishment enough, Eve demanded that Rosa serve. Serve Papá. Serve Creadon Rampley. Pour their water and ginger beer, dish out their food, carve her babies before them, while listening to them discuss *her* horses, *her* barn, *her* land.

To lose your life while still living it is to know no greater sorrow.

Rosa was in a prison of Creadon Rampley's making.

Oh, if they could only see that man for who he was!

Eve flirted with him as if he were Henry VIII and she, Anne Boleyn. She chatted incessantly about him. About the stories he told of buffalo herds, deep white snow, rugged cliffs, frozen mountains. "Bueno y hermoso!" Eve would say, and she'd remark on how much Papá valued Señor Rampley, how happy Papá was that Señor had given up his prospecting dreams.

And Creadon Rampley . . . shameless! "How is Eve? Please tell her good mornin' for me." He no longer sought Rosa's opinion of the horses, of the feed, of the condition of the soil. He wanted Rosa to be only their go-between, the keeper of their silly love secrets.

"You know she doesn't favor you." Rosa said this to Señor Rampley while he inspected the hay for mold, performing the task as though Rosa hadn't been the one to teach him. *Oh, how men can erase!* Rosa thought. "She's nice to you only because Papá tells her to be."

Señor Rampley grinned, though the muscles in his face quivered. Before Rosa turned on her heel, she noticed the lines deepen across his forehead. That night at tea, Señor Rampley sat quietly, observing Eve as if for any signs of repulsion or repudiation. Eve offered none, of course, but still, it gave Rosa the smallest bit of joy.

The blacksmithing work picked up again. Papá spent more time now manufacturing rifles, wagon parts, horseshoes, screws. The customers —the English, the French, the Spaniards—flocked to the property from morning 'til late afternoon, ogling the acreage as well as Eve, who often greeted the men at the gate and directed them to the area behind the stable, where Señor Rampley and Papá had built a larger workspace.

When Rosa found time alone with Papá, often she pressed him to release her from the clutches of domestic bondage. Papá told her more than once that she knew nothing at all about bondage and was disappointed she would say so. But Rosa could not hear such an admonishment and would point out to him how Señor Rampley had been improperly attending to the needs of an expectant Martinique, and mishandling significant tasks at the stable—bringing in the horses too soon, not sweeping the barn vigorously enough. And more often than not, Papá listened and took her suggestions back to Señor Rampley, who'd correct course, making Papá all the more pleased with him.

It was after lunch on a Sunday when Rosa left Eve and Señor Rampley on the verandah to whisper silly sweet nothings to each other. Papá was at the stable, finishing work due in the morning. When Rosa arrived, she found him with his back to the door, his head dangling from his neck like a too-heavy weight.

"You can't keep me forever doing this. I'm not Eve. I won't die trapped."

Papá didn't turn to face her. It was as if he wished to spare her the embarrassment. "Watch how you speak to me," he said. "And Eve does not feel trapped."

Rosa took a breath to remind herself that it was, indeed, Papá before her. And that though she was a big woman now, there *was* a proper way to speak to her father. "How do you know, Papá?" she said. "Did you ever ask Eve or Mamá what it was like to live this life? To be bound to living between four walls. To have others demand drink and food and cheer and comfort, ceaselessly. Do you know what it is to deny oneself all pleasures? I never asked them. It is miserable."

Papá turned the lathe with a metal rod in hand, twirling it, searching for ruts in its surface. "And you t'ink to be a man is easy?" He set the rod on the worktable. A table with a foot treadle carved with the initials "D.R." that Señor Rampley had built for him. "To know that if you should fall, you will bring down others—others you love more than life? That there are men waiting outside your gates to ravage and seduce all that is yours? That there is no one to trust with your fears? That to trust even in God is to be weak?"

The rod rolled to the edge of the table and Rosa waited for it to plunge, but it remained poised, as if Señor Rampley had foreseen that very moment. Rosa thought then of all she'd not foreseen—Papá's losses, his clandestine dealings, the many ways Papá had tried and failed to protect what was theirs.

"You couldn't know how that can build up inside a man."

"Then we should both be free to choose."

"Choose? You wish for the right to choose when men will never have a choice?" Papá rubbed his hands together and wiped them on his work apron. "No man can live outside of manhood, what the world t'inks manhood should be. You t'ink if a man cannot remove himself from beneath his own burden he'd be so generous as to help a woman?" He picked up the rod again. "But I am your Papá. And I'm the one who let you believe you could choose." He shook his head, as if still surprised that he had ever thought of Rosa as anything other than the woman figure before him. "So, lemme give you somet'ing important to do. You can help Martinique when she's ready to foal. And beneath your mudda's side of the bed, there's a stack of books that that man sent for Jeremias. I want them returned to him. Take the ride there, catch your breath, and when you come back, I never wanta hear you complain about this life I been killin' myself to give you."

3

The wife was, indeed, ugly. And bad-tempered too. As was her baby.

When Rosa arrived, a housemaid about the same age as Rosa was seated upon a worn, armless chair, under the shade of a saman, nursing a waxen-colored infant. Rosa removed the books from her sack and set them into the grass beside the maid until she stamped her foot to suggest that that was not the proper place for them and, in doing so, caused the baby to unlatch. Rosa felt herself sickened by the yellow-tinted milk trickling from the maid's swollen nipple. The maid sighed with frustration, offered the baby the other breast, but it would not be assuaged, its bawling growing more feverish as Rosa knocked upon the house door.

Monsieur's wife was called by another housemaid. The very English-looking woman glared at Rosa as though she'd never seen anything like her. Rosa had never been able to explain what it was to be the tangible embodiment of a tale, of a legend, of fear. But she knew it when she saw it, for it was always in the set of the jaw.

"And who might you be?" The woman clutched her collar as if chilly, but Rosa had seen this gesture before, this pinching at the neck, as if to reinforce her own propriety and suggest Rosa's impropriety.

Rosa remembered years earlier, when Mamá decided it was time for her to accompany Jeremias and Eve to the schoolhouse. Mamá had wanted Rosa away from the horses, wanted her "to learn to write letters," wished to give her some refinement. Rosa was the youngest pupil in the schoolhouse. The one who knew the least. And "the blackest one too," Señora Cecilia, the teacher, once reminded her. Señora Cecilia would clutch the buttons at the top of her blouse and recoil from Rosa any time a smidge of anything could be seen on Rosa's little face. The same smidge that might have melded into the lighter skins of the other children, but against Rosa's lambent dark brown, gleamed.

One day the students had eaten zabocas for lunch. Rosa had been given a morsel of a too-ripe one, the pulp of it grey and mushy. A boy, Manuel, who called the zabocas "avocados," argued that the smidge of zaboca on Rosa's face was, in fact, a blob of snot. He laughed at Rosa.

Then the other children laughed, alongside Jeremias and Eve and Señora Cecilia. Rosa did not weep until she returned home. When she told Mamá she didn't wish to go back to the schoolhouse, Mamá told her that "fear has no place in my home" and sent her to sleep on the verandah for the night. By morning, Rosa's skin was pocked red from a night of hosting mosquitoes. Her face was swollen and tight, and Mamá held her and said, "You're uglier than you were yesterday. This will happen to everyone. Go to that schoolhouse this morning and if that devil-boy says one word about you, you bounce him, you understand? Cuff his ears and make sure he's on the ground when you tell him that your Mamá said you could do so."

Rosa stood tall now, looked down at the square-hipped English-woman, resisting what the woman's eyes spoke of Rosa. "I am calling on Monsieur." Rosa said the words first in Spanish, then in French, then in a well-formed English, as though she did not know which tongue the woman spoke. Rosa quite enjoyed the surprise on the woman's face, so Rosa continued in Spanish. "If he is unable to greet me, please tell him that my father, Demas Rendón, has returned his books and gives his most sincere thanks." Rosa offered the books to the woman who pretended she understood what Rosa had said.

"He is out with the horses." And the woman closed the door.

Rosa found Monsieur DeGannes behind the stable that Papá had helped him build. Jeremias, as a lad, had accompanied Papá many days during that year of construction. Jeremias would come home excited that Monsieur DeGannes had paid him some mind. Now, as Rosa looked upon Monsieur she could not remember if his hair had always been speckled with white. He was flushed with sweat, taking an axe to wood, his lips parched, his linen shirt unbuttoned. Rosa had never known Monsieur to be a hard worker, but much had changed since the English had arrived. She wondered, as Monsieur kicked the splinters aside, what work Papá had done for him, wondered if Papá had repaid all the money.

"Aah . . . I have not seen your face in some time." Monsieur DeGannes set down the axe Papá had gifted to him and reached for his hat. "Your brother speaks of you often." He walked forward to greet her. Rosa did not remember his smallish teeth or his dark, thick lashes. And now his French pealed with an accent of English he must have been required to speak at home.

"I didn't know he still called on you, Monsieur."

"Oh, we are good friends. He and mademoiselle have paid me visits. Less so now that I have come to the long, dark channels of le mariage." Monsieur laughed, and Rosa supposed she should have joined him, for he seemed disappointed that she had not.

"If I had known, I would have left these for Jeremias to return to you." Rosa held up the books. "My Papá offers his thanks for lending them to Jeremias."

"We both know that is not true." Monsieur reached for the books and in doing so, his thumb grazed the back of Rosa's hand. Rosa went rigid and he watched her for a moment before browsing through the titles, smiling at some, frowning at others.

"Have you read these?" Monsieur said, examining the first three volumes of the encyclopédie.

Rosa shook her head.

"Your brother borrowed these for your mother," he said. "She was a different woman, impressive even." Monsieur nodded. "You have her ways."

Rosa didn't like that Monsieur had watched her mother. That he had formed an opinion and offered it as if it could be the only one of Mamá.

"If you would like, I can teach you to read," he said.

"Merci, Monsieur, but I can read."

"No, I do not mean *that* reading. I mean the reading your brother enjoys. That your mother enjoyed. Where you read for relevancy and knowledge." Monsieur held the books at their bindings and crossed his arm over his chest. It seemed the pose of a younger man, a nervous younger man, and Rosa remembered then how Jeremias would speak about Monsieur as if he were a god, how he'd come home with intellectual musings about the "noble savage." Jeremias told Papá that this was the idea that the more primitive a man, the more virtuous and childlike. Monsieur had told Jeremias that he, in fact, was the noble savage, and that Jeremias must work tirelessly to "propound his Caucasian blood." Monsieur had quoted some man, Buffon, who believed that all other races could return to their "predegeneration Caucasoid form" with the correct environmental controls, that it would only require effort. Papá thought it was a joke since Buffon sounded so much like *buffoon*, but soon after Papá grew incensed, lecturing Jeremias on the virtues of a history not written in Europe's texts, a history that would be unveiled to Europeans when they no longer wished to be the benefactors of its suppression.

Rosa wondered if this was the kind of relevancy Monsieur wished to discuss.

"You might find that you will like such an engagement," Monsieur went on. "I know I would like to know you better. I can teach you a great deal."

Rosa felt something beneath his words, as if they were searching for something more than an answer, and it seemed to Rosa that Mamá had been right: Monsieur was a lonely man. But Rosa was certain that no marriage could change that shade of loneliness. And neither could books. For Monsieur seemed a man who could never be filled up, who would always seek more or less or other, but would always seek, seek, seek.

"Merci, but Papá keeps me very busy."

"Oui, it's been hard for him. I hope you know I've always done my best for your family."

"Oui, merci," Rosa said, though she was not sure of all the reasons she should have been thanking Monsieur.

"I do not see you riding anymore. I used to watch you in the mornings."

Rosa felt the lump in her throat tighten. She did not wish to, but Rosa liked knowing that Monsieur had watched her. That someone had watched her. And there seemed in the exchange between them the makings of a transaction, the terms of which Rosa did not know and yet felt it was unseemly, like finding droppings in your last bit of porridge but being told to finish it for it may be your last meal.

"Good day, Monsieur." Rosa thought leaving was best and turned toward the house to retrieve her horse, then turned back to him again. "And congratulations on your firstborn."

Monsieur stroked the back cover of one of the books, his pale hand striped with fine scratches that were like narrow trails of red clay. Then

Monsieur tapped the book twice with his index finger, as if he wished to mark the end of something. "Oui, my firstborn. Merci, Rosa."

4

June 1813

It was Sunday and the sky was purpling when Jeremias and Francine arrived. They were collecting their youngest boy, François, who had been visiting Papá for the day. Francine remained in the wagon with her usual petulant "long face." She had taken to wearing only white. White dresses, white hats, white stockings on skeletal legs like veiny streaks of white lightning. When Jeremias climbed down from the bench, Francine removed her white glove and pointed a thin almost-white finger toward him, warning him not to be long.

Rosa roused François from his nap. Through the window, she spied Jeremias walking down the path toward the stable, then stopping to crane his neck, as if to search for Papá, but turning back as though he thought better of it.

As Rosa set the still-sleeping child into his arms, Jeremias whispered, "How long is that man staying?"

Rosa couldn't recall if Jeremias had spoken directly to her since Mamá's passing, but he spoke now as if there'd been no time at all between this time and the last. It was the sort of farce Rosa now understood was a necessity for any family to persist.

"He's been here too long already," Rosa said.

"Hard to no longer be the favorite, eh?"

"I was never the favorite in this family. Besides, that man is not family."

"He will be."

Rosa followed Jeremias to the wagon. She watched as he lifted François so that Francine could take the child. Francine grabbed the boy, kissed his pouty lips, and did not acknowledge Rosa, even as Jeremias spoke to Rosa once more.

"Eve tells me she's spoken to Papá."

"Pourquoi?"

"To discuss a marriage."

"Papá wouldn't."

"Yes. He would." Jeremias grinned. "Your padre would do anything not to lose this piece of land. Monsieur will eventually stop loaning him money, so he must do something."

Rosa felt as if she were betraying Papá by allowing Jeremias to speak of him so. She didn't know if Papá had continued to borrow money, didn't know if Jeremias spoke the truth, but Rosa was desperate to vent to someone who might see the injustice of all that had taken place since Creadon Rampley's arrival. "Señor Rampley is no good for us," she said.

"Oh, he seems very good for everyone but you. Look at this place." Jeremias moved his chin to guide Rosa's eyes to the new fence, the new roof, the barn addition. "It's never looked better. The pigs and chicks are fat, the fillies and the new colt you have there are all healthy and first rate. Eve will have twenty-eight years next month. She's old." Jeremias walked to the driver's side, leaving Rosa to wonder if he had deliberately or only carelessly reminded her that her twenty-six years rendered her in nearly the same position as Eve. "Papá must be very pleased with himself."

There had been no time to speak on a wedding. Before that evening descended, the clouds arrived over the Northern Range, and for the following weeks, the rainy season puffed out its broad chest and its winds took off roofs, felled trees, scattered fruits as though they were tulip petals. Mud slid from hills like scorched cacao, burying arrogant men and their disagreeable horses. Water rose to the underbellies of sows, and industry slowed as all attention turned to saving what remained.

By day, the four of them—Eve, Papá, Señor Rampley, Rosa— worked harder and smarter than ever. Bagging, reinforcing, patching. The ferocity of the rain had forced teatime from the verandah to the supper table. It felt quite perfunctory—a few sips to warm the blood, a bite or two of a biscuit, and off to bed. Each night before turning in, Papá offered Señor Rampley the same warm sleeping mat on the floor, but Señor Rampley always refused.

Those nights during rainy season offered the only respite from the constant harassment of an overrunning sky. Sleep, when it came, felt deep and tender, as if the world were being peacefully restored. Papá always slept first, his snoring more a comfort now than a nuisance. Eve, beneath Mamá's quilt, read by candlelight, fighting off the chills she was unable to shake at that time each year. The sound of raindrops, like blunted fists to a wall, assailed Rosa's ears, and sometimes she would lie awake, sticky and hot, waiting for the rain to slow so she could throw open the window. It was a Saturday night when after doing so she noticed the flicker of a lantern outside. Rosa cupped her hands over her eyes to sharpen her view. Fat, slow raindrops distorted and blurred the figure holding forth the lantern, but Rosa did not need to see clearly to know who it was.

Creadon Rampley, who should have been asleep, was instead walking about, and Rosa was certain he was up to no good.

Rosa strained to focus on the bobbing light that moved toward the stable. She thought for a moment that maybe her suspicions were unfounded, but nonetheless, searched for her boots. She'd warned Papá, told him there was something quite wrong about Señor Rampley.

"You don't sit on de river bed and talk de river bad," Papá had said. "It's your envy clouding your judgment."

"What envy? What can he do that I cannot? Only your rules are in my way, not my abilities," Rosa had argued.

Papá had smirked as if he knew more than she of her envy. Now, Papá would learn to heed her warnings.

A funneled stream of rain fell from the roof atop Rosa's bonneted head. The cold shot through her skin, the wet gown sticking to her like lard. She tossed her bonnet into the mud, wiped her face across her sleeve and by memory, moved through darkness.

Papá and Señor Rampley had laid planks at the beginning of the rainy season, but now, she could not find them. When she reached the barn, she peeked through the transom. The light from the lantern had vanished and she thought for a moment that perhaps Papá had been right—envy could have indeed clouded her judgment—until she heard the horses moving about, most disturbed.

"Quién está ahí?" Señor Rampley's near-perfect Spanish surprised her. And she hadn't expected him to have so quickly climbed up the narrow ladder and into the hayloft. Yet there he knelt, holding a lantern before him, casting the light wide onto the ground below. "Who's there?" The rain roared over his calls, but beneath it Rosa heard Martinique and Espina stirring.

Rosa backed away. Her chest thumped with nerves; her saturated nightie seemed to be growing longer, for she stumbled over one of the elusive planks. Rosa didn't know why she felt panicked but knew she didn't wish to be seen by Señor Rampley. The darkness played tricks on her memory, yet she was certain she was almost to the coop when her forward movement was choked by the unexpected explosion of a musket rifle through the roof of the stable.

The horses reared up, their hooves striking the boards of the stalls sounding like small detonations, and Rosa caught clipped phrases of raised voices while she darted to the house and collected, just inside the door, Papá's old firearm.

As Rosa walked again toward the stable, Papá met her on the path, a lantern swinging inside his left hand, and she perceived in his eyes that he did not know what to make of it all. "Get back to the house!" Papá threw open the stable doors as Eve shouted from the window for Rosa to "come back inside at once!"

Señor Rampley had reloaded. His hair was clumpy, damp, his feet, pale and veiny against the muck of the stable floor. Papá held up the light and Rosa wished she hadn't noticed the tremor in his hand.

"You t'ink you gointa come in the night and take my horses?"

"Demas, we not interested in talkin'." It was Tío Byron. And Jeremias. They held Martinique and her new colt, Carlos, by their leads.

"Oh, you's a bad john now, eh? No talkin', just takin'?" Papá said.

"My sista had a right to this land and to these horses. You grew my family's beans and never once thought to pay us." Tío Byron's face was shrouded beneath the soggy brim of his hat. The same white hat he'd worn to Jeremias and Francine's wedding. Rosa had not seen him since that day. He was thinner now, his shoulders more rounded, and he seemed to have long forgotten the truce he had proposed before all the wedding guests.

"It was Myra's cacao. There was no need to give anyone anyt'ing." Papá was steady now, angry even. "And this is not about Myra. This is about you losing everyt'ing because you ent earn your land. They giveth and they does taketh away."

"A woman t'irteen years younger than her husband dies as soon as you feel threatened by her reconciliation with her family?" Tío Byron said.

"Everyone in this country is suffering, Byron. It gives you no right—"

"I'm here to help this boy claim what's rightfully his." Tío Byron nodded to Jeremias.

"When Jeremias left to marry your gyal, he give up his right to what's mine."

"You gave me no choice," Jeremias said.

"The choice was not mine to give, son."

Tío Byron stepped forward, squeezing tight Martinique's lead. He shushed the mare, calmed her, and she responded.

"You plowin' right tru me? Is that what you t'ink?" Papá put up his hands, and to Jeremias, he said, "Is this what you learnin' from these heathens?"

"You cast your own boy aside and I'm the heathen?" Tío Byron moved forward again, lifting the heavy brim from his face, curling it until it stiffened at the ledge of his forehead. Tío's jaw was knotted; his eyes, the same hazel of Mamá's, were widened as if in the midst of some delirium. Jeremias took Martinique's lead from Tío and appeared as uncompromising as his uncle. As Rosa recalled the vindictive nature of her brother, she raised her musket, the barrel not quite centered on Jeremias but angled enough that she could clip him, only to then realize that it was not Jeremias but rather Tío Byron who posed the most substantial threat to Papá.

There was a great vibration as if thunder had abandoned the sky for Papá's stable. Water sprayed as those big bodies clashed—two men of tight flesh and fiery blood had become one wellspring of rage. Rosa watched with horror the collision of indignant masses, underpinned by fists and might and will. Papá caught Tío Byron on the chin with a four-fingered right, then on his brow with a tight-fisted left. Tío's head jerked back and back again as though it might loosen from his shoulders, and Jeremias shuddered, dropping the leads as if preparing himself, and Rosa felt certain that Jeremias would put an end to all this, that he would gather Tío and they would depart in a cloud of shame. Martinique stepped back as though she wished to give Jeremias space to do so, and Jeremias, with a more expansive view, watched as Tío swiped at the shiny blood dripping from his brow. Between the two, a quick glance was had, and Jeremias lurched forward, his chest widening, his lips like Papá's, curled into iron shavings, the sweat on his mustache shimmering in the light of the lantern. His hands found their places a foot apart from each other, arched like half-moons, poised for attack. Rosa knew then that Jeremias would fight his own father. On his father's land. To protect his uncle. And so she raised the musket to the line parallel to Jeremias's heart. "Broadside," Papá had taught her. "Hit the target." Rosa would do it, she said of herself, as if herself were another. And that other self knew Jeremias would die on his father's land, bleed into his father's soil, and that other self thought that maybe it would be as it should have always been.

"Jeremias," Rosa whispered.

Jeremias turned to her, and it was as if he could see the same future—Papá grieving, laying himself atop his only son—for Jeremias suddenly threw his hands into the air as a gesture of surrender, or perhaps earnest query, and Rosa heard behind her the whoosh of fists on air and the soft hammering that working hands made against flesh, and she turned, expecting Tío would be in a similar pose of surrender, but instead it was Papá, convulsing as if he'd been set ablaze. He had fallen. And both the earth and his shadow shook.

"Step back." Señor Rampley raised his rifle at Tío Byron who seemed poised to pounce atop Papá. Tío reached for his hat but it was now gone, and the skin over his right eye appeared cracked like sappy bark. Rosa could not help but notice how much Tío and Jeremias resembled each other then, how they looked to be father and son, their faces puffy and red. "My next shot aint gonna be a warning." Señor Rampley repeated his words in French. "La prochaine fois ça va pas être un tir d'avertissement."

"This isn't your business." Jeremias said this to Señor Rampley but glanced at Papá while he spoke. Papá was attempting to raise himself from the sludge, seemingly unable to bear his own weight. Jeremias did not move to help his father, and Rosa felt disgusted by this until she herself averted her eyes as Papá's foot slid away beneath him.

The rain slowed and Rosa heard Tío Byron's wagon recede into the night. Señor Rampley exhaled, as if he had been acting against his very nature, and Rosa was suddenly embarrassed to find herself before him, dressed in her nightclothes, her hair wet and afluff, her face and hand smeared with mud. Papá was upon one knee now, bracing himself to rise, holding his chest as if to steady himself, seeming to catch his breath . . . until Breath ran away from him.

Señor Rampley lunged to catch Papá as he fell forward, but he was too late. Papá landed upon his chin. His teeth snapped shut.

5

1813–1814

The doctor did not open his bag. "He needs rest. Stricken by apoplexy."

"How can you be certain he will be the same again?" Eve asked.

"He will not," the doctor said.

That morning, Eve began gathering roots and leaves and herbs. She forced Papá to drink Mamá's bitter teas. She rubbed Papá down with ointments and asked Rosa to baby a pot of liniment that Eve applied to his chest each night before putting Papá to bed. Over days, weeks, months, Eve helped Papá form words again—French in the mornings, for this was when he used to talk over the day's plans with Mamá, and Spanish when he wished to discuss horses or crops or Pierre and François. Eve exercised Papá's chipped-from-something-solid legs, his arms; forced him to sit upright when taking his meals; commanded that he move his ankles and toes, use his nine fingers to grip. And at nights, Eve sometimes moved to Rosa's side of the bed, and when she found Rosa's heartbeat, Eve cried. A big sister beaten back into childhood under the moonlight by grief and fatigue.

"Tomorrow, we will be past now," Rosa often whispered to Eve.

And then one night Eve replied with, "Maybe we can look past tomorrow."

Rosa did not understand Eve's meaning until the morning, when Eve asked Rosa to bring two fresh eggs from Fat-Gyal-Hen's cage.

"Mamá just did this for fun," Rosa cautioned.

Eve cracked the first egg carefully, allowing the loose white to fall over its shell and into a bowl. She set the bowl on the sill and handed Rosa the shell that still held its bright orange yolk, which Eve would later use for a cake. "You do the next one."

Rosa cracked the egg just as Eve had done and set her bowl next to Eve's.

"Let's hope for a strong sun so that at noon we can take the reading." Eve was more excited than Rosa had seen her in some time.

Just before noon, Rosa heard Eve calling her from the rear door. When she arrived, the house was fragrant with the odors of boiled callaloo and fried plantains. Eve hurried to the sill and brought the bowls to the table where Rosa waited. Rosa remembered Mamá doing this only once before, when Rosa was very young, and she recalled how her insides had churned when Mamá looked up from the bowl, her color blanched, and told Rosa and Eve that she thought she would die before she grew old. When Rosa began to cry, Mamá laughed and told Rosa it was only a joke, that "Mamá would never leave her babies."

"You called me away from my work for this?" Rosa said.

"Shh . . . ," Eve said, "let me concentrate on the pictures."

Eve stood for some time looking into her bowl, her eyes searching, tight and watering, until finally she looked up at Rosa, disappointed. "Mine didn't take." Rosa, though relieved, felt sorry for her. "Let's look at yours." Again, Eve's eyes tightened, but it took only a few moments until they alighted upon something she urged Rosa to view. "Look there." Eve pointed, and Rosa shifted the bowl to the left and right but saw nothing save egg whites.

"Right there." Eve pointed with more urgency. "You see it? The ship."

Yes, Rosa could see the sails of a ship, but it also resembled a school of fish, wild tulips, a heavy cloth sack.

"Get ready for an adventure!" Eve laughed for the first time since Papá fell. She walked outside to the clothesline, and Rosa followed, hoping but also not hoping Eve might say more about this "adventure."

"Mamá would have loved that reading," Eve said.

"Papá wouldn't have."

Eve smiled.

"Isn't it strange how Papá calls out for Mamá now? They could scarcely stand each other when she was alive," Rosa said.

"That's not true. You can't see clear into husband-and-wife business." Eve reached for the clothes peg. "Mamá was his only friend." Eve examined Papá's undergarments, holding them to the sunlight and Rosa began to leave when Eve added, "Jeremias would like to see Papá."

"You've seen Jeremias?"

"Oui, I ran into him."

"And you spoke to him?"

"Oui, I told him to come home this afternoon."

6

Rosa awaited his arrival. She felt sure of herself when Jeremias and the boys came down off the wagon dressed in their Sunday clothes. Jeremias moved sheepishly as he climbed the steps of the verandah, the boys a few steps ahead. Eve had been with Papá much of the afternoon. He'd been giving Eve trouble with drinking the tea. He said it made him nauseated, made him piss himself, and he told Eve that no man wished to piss himself. Rosa heard Papá's voice rising in anger as she stepped out onto the verandah.

"Pépé is not feeling well." Rosa embraced the boys, then reached for Pierre's face to hold it a bit longer and examine it as she always had, as if it were the first time taking in the easy expression upon his handsome face—a face that had narrowed since she'd last seen it, that had grown faint hairs over lips that still managed to retain the blush color of a small boy's. "Go to the back and see Carlos. You haven't met him yet. And be sure to be polite to Señor Rampley."

The boys left, and Rosa was alone with Jeremias, who stood close enough that she could smell his breath. She remembered how it had soured to unbearable after his visits with Monsieur DeGannes.

"You shouldn't have come," Rosa said.

"Eve said I was welcome."

Rosa pulled the door closed. "Eve is in charge of Papá, I am in charge of this land."

"None of this is my fault, you know."

"Truly, you're saying those words? Did you forget I was there that night? Eve was not."

"Let me speak to Eve."

"She's tending to Papá."

Jeremias moved forward. His belly spread firmer now and he pushed it into her. "Let me speak to Eve," he said again.

"Or you'll push *me* down?"

"Call her or I will." Jeremias took a step back, then puffed out his chest. Rosa heard Papá inside, heard Eve's voice rising, as Jeremias shouted, "Eve!"

"You're making a scene," Rosa said. "The boys will come. And you will have to explain what you did to their Pépé." Rosa bit down on her back teeth, steadying herself, hoping Jeremias cared enough about what his sons thought of him. "Or maybe I'll explain it to them."

Jeremias peered toward the stone steps, and Rosa thought she heard François laughing. "I don't know what kinda horrible woman you've become," he said, as he left.

An hour later, Eve was searching for one more bowl, muttering to herself. Some of Mamá's dishes had cracked, some had been unsalvageable, and Eve had kept the shame of it to herself until then. "We have only five now. But Papá can eat from my bowl." Eve told Rosa that she planned to bring Papá to the table before Jeremias arrived. Papá had only recently begun again to hold his spoon, to drink from a cup. Eve wished for Jeremias to see Papá looking well. "We'll need another setting if Jeremias brings Francine."

"Jeremias came and went," Rosa said.

Eve set down the short stack of bowls. "What do you mean?" She wiped her fingertips on the rag slung over her left shoulder. "Did he bring the boys?"

Rosa nodded.

"You sent them away? Papá needed to see those boys!" Eve struck the table with the cloth. The force of it surprised Rosa. "You don't do anyt'ing without speaking to me."

Rosa felt the previous familial hierarchy mattered little now. "You couldn't manage this place without me," she said.

"Señor Rampley is here. We could manage."

"Oh, you think he's doing this alone? I am inside this house helping you and I am also outside helping him," Rosa said. "I am working as hard as three now."

"Oh yes, you're always working so hard." Eve shook her head, her eyes flitting upward. "We all work hard, Rosa."

Mamá would have said it to her in this way too.

Rosa thought to leave then, thought she would set her bowl back into the cupboard and go out with the horses, except when Rosa looked upon the table, she realized Eve had left her place un-set. "We wouldn't have to work as hard if it weren't for you."

"What does that mean?"

"Before Papá fell, you allowed Jeremias to come and go as he pleased. And you knew it upset Papá."

"Mamá would've wanted that," Eve said. "Papá enjoyed having his grandsons here."

Eve pushed back strands of hair. She tightened her bun as she stood behind Mamá's chair, looking as though nothing Rosa said would make any bit of difference. Eve seemed resigned to remain calm, resigned to state facts. But Rosa did not want Eve's calm, did not want Eve's facts. Rosa wanted someone to be guiltier than her. She had been the one to turn away from the underbelly of her father as he writhed on the floor of that stable. "Papá hasn't said a word to Jeremias in ten years. The only thing those visits did was stir the bitterness between them. And make Jeremias believe he had the right to come here and take what was ours."

"We need Jeremias back home," Eve said. "You said it yourself. You're working three times as hard. We all are." There were those facts again. Eve spoke them with impunity. "He says he's willing to help until Papá gets better."

"I will not have it. Jeremias could try to hurt Papá again."

"That's mad talk," Eve said. "If this place falls apart, it will be too hard to catch up. The horses need more attention; they mustn't get sick. The crops need tending to. You know what can happen. And Papá doesn't want you back out working the land."

"Yes, yes, and you think if you have to suffer in here, then I must too." It had been there all along—Rosa's wrong body and mind betraying what was in the best interest of them all. "Papá as we know him is never coming back," Rosa said. "If you want to be in charge, go ahead and have Jeremias come home. But when you miss me, know I am gone."

XI

Kullyspell, Oregon Country

⧑⧒

1

1830

Ma told Victor what she thought he needed to know. She seemed lightened by the telling, but Victor knew she had not told him everything. And yet, sometimes he wondered if it wasn't best to leave her to believe that he knew only what she wished him to know.

"You'll not believe that I found cured lumber in the storehouse!" Ma was almost running when she'd come to tell Victor this. "I've always wanted a bathtub!" She had only just returned from setting out Martinique. It had rained the previous few days, so her moccasins were muddied and she smelled of horse lather and manure.

"There is a lake just there," Victor said. "That isn't a big enough bathtub?"

"Aah, but it will soon grow too cold," she said. "Let's make a tub so we can sit in warm water. What do you think?"

Though Victor was not yet in perfect condition, he felt he couldn't say no. He helped Ma sort lumber, searching for cedar with the fewest knots, taking turns with Creadon's handsaw, sawing lumber into staves of three-by-threes and other boards for the floor of the tub in four-by-fours. Ma taught Victor mortise and tenon construction, told him that her Papá had taught her to build. While they worked she chatted, beginning with the story of the night she followed her brother to a neighbor's house, laughing at the audacity of that little girl who had threatened her much bigger brother.

"I vexed Jeremias so," she said.

When they finished with the tub floor, they used trench cuts to connect the staves. This required steady hands and earnest finger work, and Ma spent many nights under the lantern, turning pieces, carving and shaving to get the cuts just so. She was patient with herself, patient most especially with Victor, which became most evident when they realized that Victor had forgotten to add a drain hole.

"We could just keep the dirty water," she said.

Victor laughed. "Have you smelled yourself?"

Victor, who found the woodworking and hand sawing oddly exciting, devised a plan for adding the drain: he would carve a hole and fashion a wood plug that would certainly leak, but would do so slowly enough that one would still be able to enjoy a soak.

As Ma and Victor formed a circle with the rough-hewn staves, Ma told him about her short time at the schoolhouse. How the teacher, Señora Cecilia, had beaten her twice, leaving her with scratches and a bruised eye; how her Mamá had gone to the schoolhouse and threatened to return the favor to Señora Cecilia's face until Papá intervened on the schoolhouse steps. Then Mamá herself had had to teach Rosa to read, to do arithmetic. Ma told Victor that though she was stubborn, she had been a focused learner, and that Mamá had told her she was the hardest worker in the house, save, of course, Mamá herself.

"Only after Mamá was gone did we know how hard she worked for us," she said. "She used to say, 'You'll never know the worth of water 'til the well runs dry.'"

It was a little over two weeks when Ma declared the tub complete. They hauled water from the lake on Martinique's backside, and Ma boiled pot after pot until the tub was filled.

"Turn so I can undress," Victor said to her.

"I helped you with the chamber pot—you think I ent seen your bamsee and your lil pecker?!"

Ma turned, still chuckling, and Victor threw his clothes to the ground and climbed inside.

"How is it?" Ma said.

Victor smiled, for he had never known anything quite as wonderful as that warm wash. "I could kiss your face."

Ma laughed, returned inside, and Victor sat in the quiet of the late afternoon as the sun fell into clouds like a bee upon a bloom. He listened to trees fill their lungs with sweet air and thought that it was a captivating land, that there seemed never a more true place.

"I'm taking Martinique to the lake and will soon return." Ma began walking away then glanced back at him again. "Was that your belly making that noise? Eh-eh, no bubbles in my tub!" Victor laughed and Ma had an expression of ease as she watched the top of his head sink down.

Inside the tub, Victor examined his legs. The cuts and bruises had healed well and all that remained were the fresh scars atop old scars, marks of a boy who'd grown up in a home that stretched like the wild. Victor had not thought much about his quest since they'd arrived, but now he wondered if it would ever happen, if perhaps the girl had been correct about him—that because he did not have Apsáalooke blood, no spirit would come, no ancestor would lead him.

As Victor began to sleep, he heard the stirring of brittle fall leaves. He thought Ma had returned, and when one brazen gust of wind blew more frigid than the others, Victor wondered if Ma wouldn't be able to add more warm water to the tub.

"Ma, would you please pour more?"

Victor heard her clanging the pot and so he waited. But Ma did not come.

"Ma?"

Victor sat up, allowing his sight to set over the ridged cedar lip. He rested his chin on the edge of the tub only for it to be met by an enormous brown and furry face.

Victor bit his lip, trying to dissuade terror from overtaking him, and slid slowly down into the water. He thought his heart might tear from his chest and float up to meet the bear, who stared down at him, its face dangling, saliva heavy on its lips, its left paw gripping the edge of Ma's tub, the arc of its long claws like that of the best hunter's bow. Victor remained as still as any person ever had, remembering not to make eye contact, reminding himself that he must not concede to death, that he must fight bravely, until suddenly he found his resolve firmed and felt himself ready for whatever inevitability might come, and so he rose from the water and the bear fell to all fours, and when Victor set his chin upon the lip of the tub once more, he caught sight of the bear fleeing with his clothes!

Victor did not know when Ma had returned. When she peeked over the edge, her eyes showed relief at seeing Victor nakedly whole and shivering in a tub that had lost much of its water through Victor's patchy drain hole.

"Ha!" she laughed. "I just saw a bear wearing your robe!"

Ma laughed until Victor swore her sides would split open, and she laughed until darkness fell, and Victor would have sworn that even after she was asleep in her chair, she had stirred twice in the night, just to laugh more.

As Ma slept, Victor carried the book into the front room and, beneath the glow of the lantern, with the smell of the place now all theirs, he learned of Rampley's retreat from New Spain—the raging noon heat that was Mexico; the fat black buzzards circling churchyards. He read of Rampley's journey to the West Indies—the wretched sea baptism in a vessel that had consumed more water than Creadon; the malodorous mules eating slop above, while below, hollow and mysterious cries rang out. And in those pages, Victor eventually found what he'd been searching for: the girl named Rosa Rendón.

Victor fell asleep thinking of Trinidad, of that Rosa riding horses on a magical land that pushed and pulled brown bodies from its coral shores.

"Victor!"

Who was this Victor Rosa called out for?

"Victor!"

The walls of Victor's chest thumped and he woke with cherry-red birds and blue waters in his mind's eye. He reached for the book, but it, along with the dream, was gone.

"What is this?" Ma had snatched the diary from the table.

"I just found it."

Ma flipped through the pages, her eyes catching the English words she'd taught Victor as a little boy. Victor knew she'd always been proud of his command of languages—Apsáalooke, Spanish, English, French, the hand language of plains tribes—often telling him he could move about the world as he wished. Ma covered her mouth with her hand, perhaps glimpsing her name somewhere in the middle of Creadon Rampley's life. "How long have you had this?"

"I just found it," Victor said again.

Ma tucked the diary under her arm and slapped Victor's head. She walked to the rinse bowl, put down the book before splashing her face clean. "Walk with the spear," she said.

Victor followed her, certain she'd return later to burn the book. They walked along the dirt path, leaves twirling like chubby dancing children, and Ma spoke no words.

The cloudy sky rendered the surface of the lake's water a dull grey and the rocks Victor spied closest to shore were a beaten brown.

"Water's cold," he yelled to Ma, who watched him from atop a grey boulder. Ma had told him that the boulder and the lake had been formed by ice ten thousand years earlier. He wondered if her icy expression had been formed in the same way.

The two cutthroat and four whitefish dangled from the tip of Victor's spear. Ma walked ahead, spitefully picking up her pace, knowing well Victor could not keep up. An antelope doe and her fawn, with long hooked noses and white underbellies, waited beside the path for them to pass. Ma frightened them off when she raised her voice to tell Victor they didn't have enough wood. "You'll need to take a tree!"

The storage house had been filled only days before. Victor remembered then that the privilege of a mother was to dole out penalties whenever she wished.

Except Victor was not accepting penalties.

"He's dead!" Victor said. "That diary is all that's left of him."

Ma pointed to a young cottonwood tree farther down shore. "When you're done taking that down, you'll cook the fish," she said. "And be quick. I need to eat."

Ma began again, walking up the path.

"Why are you so angry about that foolish diary?"

Ma's shoulders slackened and she turned the upper half of her torso, causing the sun to fall in a diagonal across her face, making her appear halved, the mountain peak atop her head like a crown. "I am not angry, you are."

"I'm here waiting for something or someone you yourself are not certain will come."

"Waiting?" Ma pointed to the place where Victor had seen her clawing at the dirt. "Down there." They had walked past it that very morning, and Victor had pretended not to see how Ma had looked back at him to deflect his attention away from it. "I met Edward Rose there and that is where you and I began. We have journeyed back to the beginning, Victor. We are not waiting."

2

The whitefish was overcooked. Ma and Victor ate indoors, for it had begun to rain. Victor nibbled at what he'd plated, slumped into the crosshatch of the chair that pinched the skin on his back. He had questions. So many questions. And each time he thought to ask them, the words grew thick and fat in his mouth.

"Ma," he began.

But Ma set her finger to her mouth, and at first, Victor thought she wished not to discuss the diary until he saw the fluttering of her eyelashes. "Get down!"

Now Victor heard the approach too. He watched Ma's chest heave as he took up his bow and arrow. Ma scurried to the front, musket in hand, and closed partway the front shutter. She wedged the muzzle between a crack, while Victor waited before the door, waited for it to open.

Quiet.

The two horses slowed and Ma pried open the door. Victor put himself before her. The man and woman greeted them first in a language neither Ma nor Victor knew, then in English. The man, a Yellow-Eyes, had a pointed mouth and narrow face and appeared small next to the woman, who stood several inches wider.

"We thought Rampley came back." The woman was rugged, wide-faced, with a smashed nose, and much younger than the man. She could have been half Sioux, but Victor couldn't be certain. "He's not here?"

Ma shook her head.

"I'm Margaret." The woman smiled, then clapped her hand to her face, wincing. "Bad tooth." She pointed to her mouth. "Rampley told us all about you." Margaret took stock of Ma's clothes, her glance probing as if she'd expected something different. "Saw the smoke and thought he was around."

Ma looked up to the roof as if she had forgotten it could speak. She set the musket down after the man tipped his hat and introduced himself as Gerard. Margaret and Gerard greeted Victor with a half smile.

Ma invited them inside, and Margaret set their rifles outside the door. The lump in Victor's throat swelled. "We brought drink and meat." Gerard held up a package. "Waiting for months for Creadon to show. Don't think he'd mind if we shared it."

Victor had learned from Father that Apsáalooke were first introduced to Europeans by the writings of the first men they called "Yellow-Eyes," two French Canadian brothers who stumbled upon the tribe around 1743. The brothers believed their meeting to be the tribe's first encounter with white men, though it likely was not, and wrote in their journals that the Indians were beaux hommes, or "handsome men." It was these brothers who were responsible for the misnomer of the tribe, for they had interpreted "Children of the Large-Beaked Bird" to mean the *crow*. Father told Victor men such as those were not to be trusted for their understanding.

"This was the first fur-trading post I ever seen made into a home. Nobody's got anything like this." Gerard, who was pale like a sun-bleached bone, admired the walls, the floors, the table before them. He took in the place as if it weren't as familiar to him as he had suggested. "Me and Margaret make do. Got ourselves a little dugout, but this place is a real luxury."

Though Apsáalooke had decided not to spurn the Europeans, many Apsáalooke still considered the Yellow-Eyes wily castoffs. Yet Ma poured the Yellow-Eyes's drinks, listened to his stories, chuckled at his jests.

"We've shared a few meals with Rampley." Margaret watched Ma like she'd found something peculiar about her. Victor had seen that kind of examination before and did not like it. "Like us, sometimes he'll join a company for a few months, earn a pay, but he likes to be by himself. Not usually gone so long," Margaret said. "You must be worried."

Ma did not respond.

"Described you good, didn't he, Margaret?" Gerard added. "Told us you like to ride horses wild and hard." Gerard took a drink. "Sometimes Margaret comes to visit by herself. Creadon shares more then, doesn't he, Margaret?" Gerard looked to Margaret, and this was when Victor noticed that the two shared the same hairline, same longish ears, same pointed chin.

Gerard emptied his third cup and held it out to Margaret for more. "The lad favors Creadon, doesn't he?" he muttered.

Victor pretended not to understand. Pretended not to see Ma's face flush and her eyes dart to his, as she worked to read his expression. Victor pretended not to notice that Margaret had nudged Gerard and that the man didn't seem sorry. Victor pretended not to know what he knew now to be true.

CREADON RAMPLEY

Isle of Trinidad

❧

1814

The old man coulda stayed sick. I thought about that a lot. I aint have no claim to that hayloft. No claim to that family. I wanted to help but stayin forever wasnt somethin I ever thought bout. But I also knowed if I left his daughters when Demas was still in that sickbed or worse, after he was dead, I couldnt rightly call myself a man no more, could I?

Rainy season ended. Christmas come and went. Then the heat fell on us like a wool cape. We wasnt ready to go into a nother year without Demas. But there we was. Me and his two girls—Eve tendin to him and the house and Rosa beside me, fixin posts, pullin rotted banana trees, diggin out a well that prolly wasnt never gonna be more than a mud pit.

Some days I wanted to leave Trinidad. But on Sundays, after I visited Demas, I couldnt never get myself to do it. He would try and talk. Words dripped slow and thick and it tired me to watch him so I talked over him mostly. Told him about the shop, the crops, the horses . . . everything cept that I was scared I couldnt run that place without Rosa, that she couldnt run that place without me, scared that I got myself so tied up with them that even though the scared part of me wanted to leave that place behind I couldnt.

It was somewhere about the middle of May when I finally seent the DeGannes fella I heard so much about. He come around demandin to see Demas. He had one of them faces that could make you think he was kind. Eve told us later that when he arrived, she went into the room, propped Demas up against the wall, wiped his face and told him he aint have to speak if he was too tired to. Demas waved her away and when DeGannes went in, Eve said Monsieur DeGannes was hard whisperin like he aint want nobody to know how angry he was. When DeGannes left, Eve went in and seent her father lookin weak like he did that night he fell down. When she asked him what DeGannes said, Demas pretended to sleep.

By the first of June Demas was up every day on slow feet that didnt always listen. He aint have all his words back and that left hand of his still shook but somehow he found his get-up-and-go.

"We need to get this place into shape," he said. "We have a wedding c-coming."

Lookin back, I still aint sure how it all happened.

Not long after the DeGannes visit, an Englishman named Grayson come around. He wasnt no regular customer. When Eve greeted him, she told me she pulled in the door behind her. That he scared her that much. Grayson aint speak no Spanish. He had blue veins that looked to be ready to jump outta his skin. Said he was lookin for "Mister Runyan."

Eve brung him to the shop when Demas was only two days outta bed. Demas was sittin on his rocker tellin me where to set the sledgehammer and the anvil, how to sort the files and things. There was a pig let loose, havin his way inside a bale a hay that would be no more good. Eve called out for Demas so Demas stood to meet the man, but when Grayson spotted me, he come over and said, "Runyan" and gave me a smile big as New Spain. "DeGannes sent me."

I started to explain his mistake but not fore he added, "I was beginning to think this place had no overseers."

My face got hot and I could hear blood in my ears. Demas stood just next to me. Watchin me fight for the right words to name him.

"DeGannes tells me you have some obligations owed to him. He told me to tell you that this work will help extinguish your debts to him," Grayson said.

"Sir, you got me mixed up. Señor Rendón here owns this land." It was the first time I had to think about how we looked to the outside and it seemed it was the first time Demas thought on it too, cause all he did was stand there and wait for Grayson to grunt and take out a sketch from his breast pocket.

None of us noticed Eve still there, so when we heard her leave, Grayson stared into her hard like a nail poundin through lumber. When he turned back, he stabbed his finger into the drawin. "Can you understand this?"

Demas took a step back and it made me feel uneasy to be standin out front like that.

"The back bar must have a well-forged terminal for hair to gather," Grayson said. "The side bars must meet the back bar and there shall be rivets for fastening and a small opening for drinking."

It all sounded like Dutch to me. I turnt to Demas and confessed with my eyes that I aint knowed nothin about none a that. Demas looked tired. Like he was holdin himself up by the waist. He smashed his boot tip into the dirt fore he spoke. "Sir, I have horse bits here that might be better suited and more comfortable." Demas nodded at the wall to show where we hung them just like he said they used to be at his old shop. "We raise fine horses and I can assure—"

"It is not for horses," Grayson said.

"P-perhaps then if you tell me what animal, I c-can make the size just—"

Since Demas fell down, his words aint always come out right. Fore Grayson come that day it seemed only to frustrate him, but in front of Grayson, I could tell it embarrassed him.

"If this is too difficult, I can give you something simpler." Grayson bit down on his lower teeth. "DeGannes told me you were the best blacksmith on the island. I didnt realize you would need hand holding." Grayson took out a second drawin. Held it open. This time he set it tween me and Demas. "I need a small, circular mask that fastens in the back or through a neck collar with holes slightly larger than the head of a pin just under the nose for breathing," he explained. "There must be a firm plate to fit flat on the tongue to prevent speech and—"

"What s-sort of animal speaks, sir?"

The man looked to me then I looked to Demas, wonderin if Demas really aint understand. It seemed like he didnt cause he alla sudden started shakin and I thought he was havin a nother one of them fits til Grayson looked at him and said, "Youre having a burst of conscience now? Youve done similar work, yes? DeGannes tells me you need the money."

"Sir," Demas said, "I dont have the c-correct tools to—"

"Papá! What is the pig—" It was Rosa. Demas tried to signal to me not to let her come close, but there was no tellin Rosa nothin. She come in, tall and strong and strikin. She had on her some old work boots that climbed up them long legs of hers, and over top was her white petticoat, half tucked into old brown trousers.

"Oh." She stopped short when she seent Grayson. "Lo siento." Rosa pulled at her dress, tryna hide the trousers.

Grayson watched her til she rounded the corner back toward the house and I got the strangest feelin he wanted to do her the way that mountain lion had done the Thompson boy.

We was inside at lunch. Bout an hour after Grayson left. The wing of some dead insect was in the bowl of yellowish ñames. Rosa scooped around it. Demas aint notice it.

"What did that Englishman want?" Eve said.

Rosa looked up from her plate but Demas only shook his head. He had learnt months earlier how to pick up his cup with one hand, but that afternoon, he gripped it with both. Water dribbled down to his collar.

"He came for nutting?" Eve had gotten used to speakin for Demas. Puttin words where Demas couldnt. "If he comes again, I will tell him youve gone into town, sí?"

Demas shook his head. Didnt seem like he could explain the work he told Grayson he was gonna do or why he felt he couldnt say no to him.

"You—neither of you—should greet p-people anymore." His *sh* was more like a *th*. "We will p-post signs, make certain they dont cut tru the stable. Even if we must b-build a wall." Demas looked to me then down at his plate and wiped his eyes. "Dirty business," he muttered.

Eve covered her mouth but Rosa seemed none too surprised. "I saw them parading the new ones through town last week, like how we heard they do them in Tobago."

Eve and Rosa never once while I was there talked about livin in a slave colony. Not in front of me, no how. And I aint gonna lie. I aint really wanna think on it either. I aint wanna have to think if I thought it right or not.

Eve sat with her back straight like good posture could make somethin like slavery not stick to her. She looked embarrassed. Like she aint want me to know that this was part of her life too. That this was somethin floatin round in her lil head.

"Rosa, you said nutting of this til now?" Demas said.

"What was there to say? New ones have always come."

"Never s-so many like this."

"The Arawaks and Caribs were fighting Spanish slavers hundreds of years ago," Rosa said. "You know it has always been like this."

"It's 1814. They said it would end in 1807."

"That could mean 1907 before it is done, Papá." Rosa sounded more like Demas than Demas. She was different since Demas fell. Like she was always thinkin somethin was gonna go wrong. "You already know that labor is a problem here. The English brought the Chinese men and almost the whole lot went back on boats. And the French planters are lazy. They wont give up their slaves unless they have replacements," Rosa said. "The revolt in Chaguaramas proved this." Rosa crossed her arms. "We will just survive until they kill each other off."

Demas raised himself to almost standin. The left side of his mouth, which hadnt quite met its old place, had a deeper burrow than the right. "Surviving is not living," he said. "Your p-people, my grand-fadda, didnt fight for me only to survive. He had to p-pool his money with others for manumission fees to be p-paid to the same Spanish bastards who bring the Africans here in the first place. And then he had to p-pay an insult tax to the Crown who had blessed his enslavement," Demas said. "Them Englishmen can just—" Demas stopped himself. "You cant go there anymore."

"Go where?"

"Town."

"I mustnt go into town?"

"Nowhere. Not without Señor Rampley or me. Neither of—of you."

"That is craziness!" Rosa said.

"Rosa." Demas sat down again and whispered her name like he had failed her. Like she had failed him. "*You* are not to fight. I take care of this family."

"You just said we are to live, not only to survive."

"Sometimes you have to make them tink all you doin is survivin." Demas sliced the air with his hands. "But you ent know the world yet. You ent know that you have to fight different when they change them rules, when they de-decide I cannot own land, a home, horses, when they decide that—that I cannot work my trade or be your Papá." Demas folded his hands now like he was tryna keep the left one from shakin.

"Never," Rosa said.

His plate was still fulla yellow smashed potatoes. Demas got up, limped to the door, then stopped. The tears in his eyes looked like water trapped behind a lookin glass. Since his fall, his heart seemed tenderer somehow. "'Never' is what you say when you dont have to tink about your chil-chilren."

That evenin in the shop, me and Demas talked. He told me some things. Told me that when the transatlantic slave trade was scheduled to end it only made the intracolonial trade thrive. "They bring them in from Domenica and Grenada and they drop them all over the place, Guiana, Cuba, all up and down the coasts of the Americas. Wherever they ask for them and can pay for them, they take them, leavin a mudda here, a brudda there. And they did this same ting before, when they killed off most of them Arawaks and Caribs. And now these Englishmen wanta repurpose Trinidad into a sugar colony, which means even more slaves." Demas sighed. "The sugar in the cane in Trinidad, they say, is almost tree times that of other islands. Governor Woodford knows what is happening. The Crown knows what is happening, and nobody wants to stop it. It leaves a man like me feeling powerless."

Demas told me he wanted to protect Eve. And I said yes cause I aint have a good nough reason to say no to that man.

"If and when emancipation comes, they ent want them freed slaves believing they can own land because theyll still need them to work. A man like me will be a problem for the Crown," he said. "But the governor will let a man like you own the business. Theyll permit you the peace to run your affairs. But this is Rendón land. You understand? I need you to pr-promise you will never forget that." Demas held his stronger left hand out to shake mine then patted me on the shoulder like the agreement was all wrapped up, cept then he said, "I have debts. You understand what that means? I rob Peter to pay Paul and now Peter comin to collect." The sunken side of his face twitched. "My Peter is DeGannes. We had a business arrangement for a very, very long time, and when the governor closed my shop, I lost us both money. Plenty money. And I fell on hard times." Demas paused real long like it was the first time he ever said them words even to himself. "The governor came for the land only a short while before you came to this house and DeGannes loaned me the money to pay the taxes. I was paying him back, lil by lil til I fell."

I wanted to ask Demas why he aint tell me before, why he let his debt come due but I already knowed why.

"Without the blacksmithing work, there wasnt enough to pay him. Not without takin food from our mouths." Demas shook again, scarin me til I realized that it was just a new way he had of bein. "Once I do this work for Grayson, I will be tru paying DeGannes and I can give the land to you. This is the only way I can see to keep it."

"You gonna make them bits he wants you to make?"

Demas didnt answer so I took that to mean what I supposed it meant.

"I am trusting you. I hope you wont betray us," he said. "You must care for and protect Rosa if she doesnt m-marry before I die." He closed his eyes. He aint never done this fore the apoplexy. "I fear sh-she will wander all the days of her life, that there will be no—no one to see about her, protect her from sheself."

"Youre strong as an ox." I was scared at the thought of his leavin me to care for his property and the two people he loved most. I aint know if I could do it. "Rosa will be fine. Aint she always fine?"

"It is Eve who is always fine," he said. "Rosa needs to be understood."

Demas was right, and I was shamed that I aint know it already.

"And when men like Grayson come around, your eyes must speak of pride in my daughters."

"Can I ask a question?" Demas didnt say yes and I wondered if he meant not to. "What kinda business was it you did with DeGannes? Grayson said somethin bout your conscience."

"If you cannot do what I need, then tell me now and I will take my chances and leave my girls to fight in this world alone."

"Grayson surprised me, is all."

"I was to prepare you better. They want us never to grow accustomed to anyting good."

"Well. Too late for that." I smiled.

"But our family is not only the f-four of us," Demas said. "Everybody who looks like me and Rosa and Eve, you m-must try and see in the same way you does see us. Until they pr-prove otherwise. You understand?" He leaned toward me now and I could see the top of his lip tremble. "We does say it here in Trinidad that 'we is we.'"

Rosa was still bitin mad though I hadnt seen her much. It was a Sunday and me and Eve was just comin back from church services when Eve sat down cross from me wearin that blue dress with the round collar and shell buttons I liked. It was nice to look at her. Her face was always new. Like lookin into the bottom of a lake and seein how much life there was in it.

"I dont want you to feel as if you cannot leave," she said.

I figured Demas musta told her that he talked to me. I reached for a banana and sliced it with my skinnin knife. We shared it. "Why you aint never marry?" I said.

This aint somethin a man should ask a woman less he got intentions. So I guess I had intentions.

"Who told you I wished to marry?" Eve grinned and smoothed the ruffles on her cuffs. "You must find me quite old, is that it?"

I found her just right. But truth be told, I aint knowed how I was gonna see Eve if we ever made our way back to my world. Even though I promised Demas I would take his land, I still aint knowed if I could make nothin of myself if I stayed on that island. Up in Oregon

Country, I thought maybe I could carve out a lil patch of my own, raise livestock, grow somethin on a plot. If Eve was with me, would my eyes change there? I seent favor for a woman turn to disfavor when other men got to lookin and judgin, when a man let other men decide for him if his woman was lady enough for respect, lady enough not to bring him no trouble. Could me and Eve be the same anywhere else? Could *she* be the same anywhere else?

"Naw, youre fine," I said. "Plus you two gals dont seem to rush into nothin." I laughed and she grinned and it felt like both a us was caught somewhere soft and slippery.

"Rosa will never marry," Eve said.

"You think she dont want no family? She got a way with them nephews of yours." I seent Rosa with them boys, especially the big one, Pierre, who she wouldnt admit she favored, and I remembered thinkin she would make a fine mother someday.

Eve, memberin that she offered me tea, stood to get a cup then quick sat back down. She leaned over with her fingers pressed to her mouth. "You must swear to never mention this to anyone."

I wondered who she thought I was gonna tell.

"There were two young men I quite favored." Eve blushed and I got the feelin that that blush wasnt much real. "Their families were very much concerned that our chilren would turn out like Rosa. Of course—"

"Like Rosa how?"

"Unlovely." Eve said this like I shoulda knowed. "They were worried that my chilren would take after Papá and Rosa."

"But . . . Rosa is a beaut."

"You say that like Rosa is a mare."

"Well, I dont mean it that way."

"And this is why Papá likes you so." Eve shook loose tea leaves into my cup. "You can see the beauty in all tings. Papá said that once about you."

"Did that hurt you?"

"When those families refused me? I was angry with them, angry with Rosa, and sometimes, though Im ashamed to admit it now, I wanted to trow the truth in her face."

She aint answer the way I hoped she might. And I knowed then that my eyes could change. And maybe it wouldnt always be cause a nother man caused it. Maybe it would be me seein somethin I aint never seent in her before.

"Rosa is not displeasing to the eye, but her perception of her own homeliness stains her mind and her heart," Eve continued. "I tink this is why she will not allow herself to believe anyone can love her."

"You think she dont feel loved?"

"Of course." Eve turnt to look at the room where Demas slept and lowered her voice. "I often tink God must be very cruel to have Jeremias and I look so much like Mamá and to have lil Rosa turn out so . . . different." Eve poured water and blew at the steam that rose tween us.

I wanted to tell her that people couldnt make heads or tails of me neither. That they was always watchin, tryna see through to my blood. I figured Rosa was always bein looked at that way too, but fore I could say more, I heard Rosa poundin the steps. She throwed open the door and them eyes was wide and she shouted at me—"Come! Come!"— like that was the only English word she knew.

I ran after her to the stable. Martinique, with her flattened ears, was lappin up water but Rosa mounted her anyway then she pointed me to Espina, who was already saddled.

"The soil collapsed!" Rosa said.

I wish I could member what I seent them thirty minutes we rode. Yellow pouis, maybe. Green grasses slick like wet limes. Guavas like cannonballs. But all I can really member was hearin the wailin of that horse.

Martinique slowed and Rosa and me raced to the middle of the field. I stared into the crooked hole, a lil less than ten feet by six, the mud on its edge carved with hoof marks. Grass that used to grow above it was now inside like them blades didnt know their place no more. The young colt, Martinique's colt, Carlos, had fell in.

"I think his front right leg broke."

The colt pushed at the same corner of that pit, lost his balance then got up again, like somehow the next time was gonna be different.

"We need to get the rope around him," Rosa said.

"It wont work."

"I didnt bring you here to tell me it wont work!"

You couldnt tell Rosa nothin so I did what she said. We worked for hours, fightin against that colt with the sun bullwhippin us until finally he got tired of fightin. Then Rosa threw herself into the hole. Roped his flank and his head. Talked to him while he made a movement all over her boots. "We might need another on his hind legs," she shouted. "Throw me down the other rope."

"Naw, I cant let you get behind him."

"Damn you, Creadon Rampley!" Rosa's face was sweaty and bluish. "Im already in the hole. You dont tell me what I cannot do!"

"Imma do it," I said. "Get on outta there."

"No."

"Then I aint throwin no more rope."

"Ive just now managed to calm him!" Rosa climbed out, spittin angry, mutterin curses I aint know she knowed. "He does not know you."

"He knows me."

"He does not know you as well as me."

"He knows me good," I said, jumpin in.

I looked up into her face all shiny with sweat, then made my way over to Carlos, who clacked his teeth, tryna tell me how much he ached and how he wanted no more of it. "All right," I whispered. I tied his legs, knotted them good then worked like hell to tip him on his side. He was angry, all right. Rosa hitched the ropes to Martinique and Espina. We worked the ropes, inch by inch, easin Carlos up the incline.

The break was worse than I thought. Made worse I was sure by the towin. I wasnt gonna tell her that, though. Wasnt much we could do about it no how.

"No," Rosa said, fore I even spoke it.

I watched Rosa circle him then I watched how she stared at Martinique, how Martinique left Carlos and walked toward Rosa, head down like she was mumblin in their private language. Them

Rendóns and their languages. Rosa shook her head at the mare like she wanted Martinique to take back what she said, but Martinique didnt or wouldnt.

Rosa untied the ropes. She whispered to the colt, caressed his muzzle and his neck, told him to fight against what we knew had to be done. The colt let out a soft noise, like a purr, like it was all he had left.

"No, no, no, not you too," Rosa cried.

I watched her help that colt into the world. Rosa had been so sure of herself then. Gentle. Coaxin Martinique til she foaled the most comely creature any of us had seent. Carlos, she named him. It pained Rosa to watch him grow up with me. She snuck into the barn some nights, brushed him down, give him secret morsels. She loved him, loved all of them horses. I aint never seent tenderness like Rosa had.

"Come," I said, reachin for her. "Come." I used the word Rosa said to me when she ran inside knowin I was gonna follow her out to that field without question. I took her hand. I aint knowed I could comfort nobody til I got to that island and saw that that was what people did for each other. "You done your best."

Rosa wept into me that afternoon. Cried not just for the colt, I think, but most specially, for the shame of bein so human that she had to suffer a nother break to the heart.

October 1814

Demas wanted to throw a party. A fête, he called it.

"I cant invite Trinis to a wedding and nobody know the boy I puttin with Eve," he said.

It was supposed to be a small affair. Two of his nephews from Siparia, a handful of neighbors. But word spread.

"DeGannes not comin?" somebody yelled out from the crowd.

"We ent have nuff rum for DeGannes!" someone else replied to much laughter.

That rum was sweet and dark and flowin and I aint never had nothin like it since. The afternoon sky was pitted with swellin clouds and I remember that somebody brung a drum and a fiddle, and writin about what that music felt like inside me wont do it no justice. But it wasnt no small thing, what I felt.

When the music men broke for a nother round of rum, some of the old fellas told stories. One was about the legend of the Arena Massacre of 1699. How the Amerindians was forced into slavery and taken to other islands. How some of them rose up, killed all the priests who preached the virtues of submission, ambushed the governor and threw his body into the river before drownin themselves in the sea. "The English, when dey come and hear dat story, dey write back home to England and dey does tell how horrible life was for dat poor Spanish governor!" They laughed.

Eve warned me that same mornin not to go and fill up my belly too fast. She said Trinidadians didnt come to no place empty-handed, and she was sure right. They come with roast pork, corn pudding, ochroes, eddoes, grilled shark. The laughter was loud and reminded me of better days with Pa and the brigade. Then bout two hours in, the sky opened. Pushed guests inside and onto the verandah where they started speakin a Spanish different from how Demas spoke it to me. I missed some words. Lots. Laughed once or twice when I wasnt supposed to. Felt like a fool. Then suddenly, I felt outta place. Like I wasnt never gonna be a part a that world.

But lookin over at Eve . . . she was happy. She chatted away with the womenfolk, kissed "aunties," served "uncles" plates of food. She was wearin a dance dress. High waist, short sleeves in a cream-colored fabric. She was a real fine woman. And I was a real lucky man who couldnt quite feel all that luck just then.

Earlier, when we was all outside, I seent Rosa. She had her hair styled real neat. Had put on a simple dress to please Demas, greeted guests, smiled at the baby somebody pushed in her arms. But when I looked round again, Rosa wasnt nowhere in sight. Up in the sky, dark clouds was spinnin. That weather come up outta nowhere. It was maybe a half hour later that Demas come up to me. "Where did Rosa run off to? Go and find her, please."

I caught bursts of laughter as I passed the side window. I had on my hat but it was gettin soaked pretty good as I headed to the stable. When I got there, I seent that Martinique was missin. So I waited maybe twenty minutes and when I finally decided to go back to the house, I heard Rosa comin up.

"Your pa been lookin for you," I said.

Rosa shrugged like she aint care. She had been pretty mad since we started gettin ready for the wedding. Eve was spendin her days sewin dresses and tablecloths, and Rosa had to do even more housekeepin.

"Demas is gonna be angry you took her out." I nodded at Martinique, who was sickly, but Rosa flicked her hand in the air like she was brushin away a pesky gnat. She wrung out the rain from the hem of her dress then I seent her wipe her eyes.

"Somethin botherin you?"

"Go back inside. Youre missing your party."

"Is that why you cryin? Cause aint nobody throwin you a party?"

"Dont be absurd."

I reached for her saddle and stroked Martinique as I pulled the lead. Rosa walked beside me. Like she was holdin in her breath. She had her eyes shut in that way you do when you tryna keep tears from rollin out. Where your back teeth is set and your lips is pinched, and the worst thing you can do is talk. "It aint the party is it?"

She shook her head. Them tears stayed back but I figured they wouldnt for long.

"I wont tell nobody," I said.

Rosa loosed her bonnet strings. Her cheeks had red inside em, flushed like somebody had colored them different from the rest of her. She took the lead from me and walked ahead like she aint have no more interest in talkin. But then I heard her voice: "I went to talk to my mother. We buried her down off the south riding path—the one I led you on the first time you rode with me—over on the other side of the hills. The sun shines there most of the day and Mamá always liked the sunshine. I sat next to her grave, pulling weeds, trying to make sure I stayed long enough so everyone would be gone from the house when I returned. But then it began to rain. At first the clouds looked as if they might move another way, so I waited. When I began making my way home, it rained so hard, I could no longer see the path. I cut through to Monsieur DeGannes, thinking

I would take shelter in his stable." Rosa closed her eyes again. "No one expects a visitor to approach from behind a stable," she said. "I was such a fool." Her lashes was still wet and sparkled like ice. "I remember when Papá and Jeremias helped him build that barn. Jeremias began talking at lunch and supper about some painter. Lancelot or Lancret, I think was his name. Papá said Monsieur DeGannes had been filling his ears with too much book nonsense, he forbade Jeremias from seeing Monsieur again. But Jeremias loved Monsieur from the first days. He disobeyed Papá and began taking Francine to visit Monsieur. So there Jeremias was, inviting Francine, who he wasnt supposed to be with, to spend time with Monsieur, who he also wasnt supposed to be with." Rosa placed her hands on her hips, pressin her weight onto one leg. "Francine was with DeGannes in his stable today. They were more together than Ive ever seen . . ." Rosa smushed her palms together like that was the one way to make sensa what she seent. "At first, I thought it was a struggle—but then Francine opened her eyes and they were soft. Like how you look at someone you—" Then Rosa stared at me and I felt a strange charge. Like somebody was really seein me. "I think Jeremias has been betrayed by Francine since the beginning." Rosa dug her boot tip into the dirt like her father always did. "François may not be his child. Pierre either. My God . . ." she whispered. "DeGannes is written all over those boys. In the too-pale skin, the lumpy, long noses—none of us have that nose," she said. "How could I not have known? I was the one who told Papá that Jeremias had been with Francine. It was my word that caused my brother to be thrown from this family."

"But you seent him and her together, didnt you?"

"Did I?" she said. "I think, but I dont know anymore. If Papá had *any* doubts . . ."

Rosa told me what she seent years back—Francine up against a tree, Jeremias holdin her wrists over her head, his face at her neck, Francine wrigglin away after seein Rosa.

"You told the truth as you knowed it."

"But what about Jeremias? How long has this affair been going on?"

"Did they see you?"

She shook her head. "You dont understand." Rosa threw off her bonnet. Her hair was puffy and droopy and it looked like somebody could throw himself in and sleep in it. "If I tell Papá this truth, everything will be undone. He will take Jeremias in again and my brother will have this land. There will be no you and me and Eve sharing it. You will start with nothing and I will start with less than nothing. Jeremias hates us all too much to have any of us live here after Papá is gone."

"I aint marryin Eve for that."

"But what does it say about me that I dont wish to tell Papá the truth? That I would have my brother continue to live in a marriage of lies, raising two boys that might not even be ours."

"Course they are. Yall love all over them boys." I pulled Rosa into the stable. I think I did it cause I aint want the guests seein her like that. But maybe it was cause I wanted to be there more than I wanted to be in that house.

"So I should keep it all secret?"

"There aint nobody who can manage this property better than you." I wasnt just sayin them words. I knew them to be true. "Your father aint gonna leave this place to Jeremias."

"No, he may not. But Im not getting it either. You are. You will have it because even though you come from nowhere and my blood is in this soil, you mean more than I do to the people who decide what I can have and who I can be. My father took an oath, swore not to turn his back on this island, and yet it is this allegiance that makes him prey. And I have to look at him now, weakened, and pretend like I dont know that trying to hold on to this place has eaten him half to death. Pretend like it is bearable after what he has been through to just put it in your name, like this doesnt feel like its own kind of death."

"If Im here, aint nobody gonna make you leave," I said.

Then there was the glance and that strange charge. She looked soft. Her farhead and lips, her shoulders and course, them dark eyes. I could hear the rain purrin on the roof when she set herself against me, like she wanted a hug. I smelled lavender on her neck and inhaled it, wonderin if I could somehow keep it, when suddenly Rosa reared back.

I thought I done somethin wrong til she fell into me again, pressed her lips, soft like flour, onto mine, and I thought she wasnt herself, couldnt be herself since I aint feel like myself neither. It was the first time I ever kissed a woman. First time bein kissed by a woman. Felt like a fire was growin inside me. Like it was gonna burst through and roast my toes and fingers and hairs. I been there for almost two years tryin every day to figure out what it was about her that always made me hope she was gonna notice me. What it was about me that needed that from her.

I nudged Rosa away and she wiped her lips hard like they was stained and I left that barn. I had to tell Demas that I found her.

XII

Kullyspell, Oregon Country

1

1830

Margaret had come for a tooth key. She hoped to find the one she said Rampley possessed, but when she and Ma were unable to find it, Ma, instead, offered them the last of the overcooked whitefish.

When they were gone, Ma hummed in the front room the way one does when one does not wish to think. Victor, on the bed with the diary set upon his chest, heard Ma arranging and rearranging things as if the post were a refined Victorian home and she were expecting a cadre of gentlewomen. The tune she hummed Victor did not know, and he found himself all the more upset that Ma knew a tune she hadn't taught him. It was unreasonable, yes, but what then was reasonable on a day such as that?

"You lived here with him?"

Ma was at the threshold, watching Victor with sad eyes.

"He is my father, isn't he?"

She stood motionless.

"You took me away?"

Motionless, save for the flush across her face.

"He is dead now?"

Victor had overheard Gerard and Margaret telling Ma that there was nothing left to believe about Creadon Rampley's prolonged absence.

Victor did not know what to feel for Ma, did not know what to feel for himself.

"You're asking answers," Ma said.

"Then tell me the rest. Please."

Ma removed her moccasins and her robe, and shook out her hair. She took Creadon Rampley's diary from Victor's chest and sat in the chair with it. "Only he can tell his story and only I can tell mine. Yours isn't written yet."

"Mine isn't written because I did not know the truth," Victor said. "I've been looking into another man's face trying to understand why I didn't see myself in it. It was all untruths."

"You are not an untruth."

"No? I am a Negro boy living among Apsáalooke. I have people I didn't know until reading that book." Victor took the diary from Ma, feeling as if she did not deserve to have it. "My father isn't my father. My mother—"

"Watch me good." Ma pointed her finger. "Stop."

"You just can't say you were wrong, can you?"

That night, after Ma had fallen asleep, Victor threw open the window and looked upon her by the dim light of the moon. He wished to be angry with her, but there was so much worry in her puckered brow, in her breaths that were deep and loud, that he found himself aching on her behalf. He had unmasked his mother. And for that he felt regretful though he did not think he ought to feel this way. As he lay watching Ma sleep upright in a chair positioned to overlook him, he came to believe that perhaps mothers should not be unmasked by their children.

The next morning, Ma woke with a start, wiped her mouth with the back of her hand. "We have to go on a hunt."

They had been sustaining themselves on fish, small rabbits, deer, but Victor understood her that morning to mean buffalo. "We are staying through winter?" he said.

They'd been at Kullyspell since mid-June and it was now nearing October. Their days had been long but the months short. They had hunted and gathered, sealed the small boat Creadon had set in the storehouse, built Ma's tub, and for much of that time worked earnestly to heal Victor. They had made arrowheads, chopped wood, produced oils from fat and foraged honey for both medicine and Ma's insatiable sweet tooth. And when Ma needed herbs and roots, they'd sometimes searched for days for just the right ones. There had been nothing taken for granted, save that the sun would rise and the moon would take its place in the sky. It had been, for both Victor and Ma, a respite from worrying about an inevitable raid, yet in many ways it had been more difficult than being at camp, for they had only themselves, and every good day depended on both being healthy and firm and willing.

"The chiefs have instructed me not to return to camp. Not now," Ma said.

"In a dream?"

"Yes. I dream like my Mamá." Ma washed her face in the bowl then removed her pouch from the sack on the floor. In her damp palm, she held a clump of white flowers and leaves shaped like parsley. Bear root.

"Let us offer our prayers to God, the First Maker, before we set out."

The sky spoke through a smoke screen of wispy grey clouds. The chill in the air mentioned the coming of winter, for the hairs on Victor's bare legs felt deadened. It was an unusually windy morning when they came upon a herd grazing in a valley of short tan grasses. Ma checked the direction of the breeze, for though buffalo did not see well, their noses were keen, and thinking they'd caught wind of their approach, Ma hurried them farther north, where there seemed more still in the air. They watched the herd from afar, the buffalos' heads bowed, their great tufts of fur halos of maroon.

Ma turned to face Victor, and she must have seen something in his expression that gave it all away. Victor had been on buffalo hunts. Many. But when all the other boys had taken up their arrows, Father hadn't permitted Victor to do so. Father had told him that only when he behaved like a warrior would Father allow him to hunt like a warrior. Victor had never told Ma this.

Now Victor's throat burned and his temples warmed. He was more fearful of failure than death, for he had tasted the bitterness of failure.

Ma directed Martinique into the valley and steadied her as they drove toward the bull of Victor's choosing, a bull that had not yet noticed them moving toward it. Victor peered into the sky and saw a rough-legged hawk with a white breast, gliding fancifully from lanose clouds. He heard Ma's breaths slow, and thus he readied his lance.

Ma circled the bull, while the bull's valley mates retreated, leaving it to fend off Ma and Victor alone. The ground shook and the bull raised its head, and Victor saw its dark eyes narrowing into slender twigs. Its tail stiffened and Ma released her breath. Victor's refused to be let. He tightened his shins around Martinique's flank and watched the bull's head dip, poised for a charge. The dry in Victor's throat gave way to a dusty tickle, and he prayed for both his cough and his heart to still.

"Victor! Now!" Ma called.

They turned a sharp left, causing the bull to slip and redirect itself. Victor pressed into Ma, both hands gripping his lance. It was the correct angle. The correct moment. He plunged it into the bull's side, penetrating through its thick pad of hair and into its flesh, and there was a great deep grunt. With the top half of the lance poised upright and rigid, Victor reached into his quiver. He would finish off the bull with an arrow between its eyes.

"Good," Ma said, exhaling as the bull stumbled forward.

But then the bull rose again.

Ma pulled back. The bull grunted and charged, its eyes widening now. Victor set the arrow into his bow, but it fell to the ground in a plumy flutter. It had been his one and only. He couldn't tell Ma that he had wished to be like the great hunters who required only one blow to fell a bull, that he had brought only one arrow and one lance to prove to himself and to Ma that he could do the same as Father. Ma ran them from the bull, then turned quickly again and came up behind it. Victor felt her tensing, waiting for him to finish.

"Closer. Please closer," he said.

They were too close now. The heat from the bull was loud and vulgar. Victor tightened his shins around Martinique once more and Ma felt slack in the seat before him. Martinique inched past the bull, and Victor reached for the lance still in the bull's flank. Ma steadied him with one of her hands upon his knee and steered them around the bull with the other. Victor, with all his weight and might and hope, forced the lance down and in and under and deep. The bull groaned. Its front right knee buckled. Its head smashed into the still-dewy grasses, flattening the fur across its great brow.

When they dismounted, Ma issued another quiet prayer toward the sky. They stood at some distance and watched the bull. His runty legs fluttered, his burnished blood seeped into the glebe around him, as Ma's and Victor's flickering shadows pressed into him.

"I am sorry about Like-Wind," Ma said. "I have asked God for forgiveness, but I must seek it also from you. I brought you pain. And I have brought Like-Wind's mother and father great pain."

Ma removed her knives from the sack while Victor knelt beside her, not knowing if he had the right words. The wind streaked again, and the bull's top fur blew like reeds in a marsh, its underside, bloody and fleshy, made Victor think of the man Creadon and his father had put to death, made Victor remember Like-Wind's ruined body. Oh, how he wished to see Like-Wind as himself again, how he wished to elbow Like-Wind's ribs in laughter, to find again that oval head and see Like-Wind pull at the sheets of his hair.

Ma cut away the skin along the inside of the bull's legs and using two knives, followed the lead of the spine to split the bull in half and tear across to the rib. She handed Victor the bull's liver, warm, laced with thin ribbons of yellow fat, and Victor dug the toe of his moccasin into the grass before asking Ma to set his aside for later.

That night, Victor saw a woman in his dream. He would not be able to describe her, would not remember if she'd spoken; he would remember only that she'd tied a horsehair rope about her waist and directed him with a hand as large as any god's to pull the other end. He remembered, as he walked backward with cautious, deliberate steps, that he could see beneath him land he did not know and feel the wetness on his feet of black waters in which he'd never swum, and he was frightened, for he could not know what dangers lay behind him. Then his mother appeared with the pointed feathers of a prairie hen catching light in her hair, and she stood between him and the woman, while he continued to move away, the distance between all three growing. Ma held the rope with both hands, gripping it as if to keep him from falling, telling him that the first step had been his hardest, urging him to move faster, to an end he still could not see. An end he believed, when he woke at dawn, that he had reached.

A week or so after the hunt, Ma and Victor had finished the slicing, the salting, the drying of cuts beneath a not-always cooperative sun, and Ma told Victor they were finally going home.

It had been a fortnight since Victor had read any pages of the diary. In some ways Victor felt it had served its purpose—Ma had told him more than she would have if she'd not been competing with Creadon Rampley's telling, more than she ever thought she'd remembered.

"We were passing over one of those little rivers that came from the heart of 'Hakhwata, what the Yellow-Eyes like to call the 'Colorado River,' when we came to rest." Ma had remembered a story about her journey with Creadon Rampley, and one night as they grilled the bull's tongue she told him about the path through New Spain into Missouri Territory.

It had been a trying time through the most dangerous land Ma believed ever existed. She said it was not so much the terror of traveling that had made her feel as if she would give up so much as what she had left behind. The grief, Ma said, had felt like Papá's grindstone wheel, wearing down her dammed body, scraping and grazing and cutting, a wild rush of agonizing longing every day, every hour, a weight that made her feel she carried them all, for she could smell them on the wind—Papá, Mamá, Eve, Jeremias, François, and oh, the sweet sweaty-haired scent of Pierre. It was too heavy, this grief, this longing, and so Ma said she'd wound it up into a barely containable ball and set it way down into the pit of her belly, and when she and Creadon had come to the banks of that sublime baby river, where she was to have just a small moment of rest and fresh air, to look upon the frenzy of its gliding waters, they saw just behind them, in a cluster of broadleaf trees with their flat-faced leaves and soils littered with seeds, the bodies of five men hanging like woody cones.

"I ain't never heard of this happening this far west," Señor Rampley had said.

Rosa held her nose but did not wish to close her eyes. She wanted to remember the place she had come to, wanted to remind herself of the kind of terror she'd face in a land where men would let others wither on a rope so that a stranger should pass by and find them there as though that stranger didn't deserve better; as though that stranger had never had a name, a true place, a Papá or a Mamá, as if being "this far west" was the only impediment there should be to a stranger coming upon such a dreadful thing.

"What kinda place is this you've brought me to?" Rosa had said to Señor Rampley.

Now, Ma put her knees to her chin, leaning forward in the chair.

"Have we done what's needed?" Victor said.

"I think."

"Is it because Creadon Rampley was Apsáalooke that we had to make this journey?"

"Creadon Rampley was not—could not have been Apsáalooke."

"But—"

"He looked like part tribesman, no denying that, but what tribe I am sure his father didn't know. I'm sure his father didn't care to know," Ma said. "Creadon was writing himself into the world." Ma kneaded her fingers across her knees. "When Father first introduced me to the tribe, he told the chiefs the truth—that I left Creadon here alone." She rocked now, as if soothing herself. "He was not a man who deserved to be left alone. He was a fine man, and I believe the chiefs wished for you to know this about him. And now that you do, I expect your vision will come."

"Edward Rose knows I am not his son?"

Both Ma and Victor searched through the naked branches at the back of the post before Ma answered. The lake appeared flat, as if it were waiting for something to move it.

"Yes," Ma said.

"Everyone knew this but me?"

Ma set her mouth upon her kneecap and with her eyebrows raised, she said, "You knew."

As angry as Victor wished to be, he wasn't sure if he, in fact, was angry. And he wasn't sure if he hadn't, indeed, known all along.

2

Isle of Trinidad
December 1814

Rosa observed a spindly and uneasy draft horse hitched to a post near the stable when she overheard Papá and Grayson settling the bill.

"Damn fine work." Grayson laughed, and Rosa thought it a pleasant laugh, the laugh of a man who could be kind. "You'll bring it 'round to my cart, then. And I'll need two hundred more," Grayson said. "I'll return for them in a few weeks."

"I will not be able to make m-more by then, sir. The ironmonger is not due back to port until after Christ-Christmas."

"You can find a way."

"I do not have a way, sir."

"You'd be surprised how resourceful one can be."

"It is quite a busy time, sir. I won't—won't be able to see my way to it."

"It won't stay busy very long if you continue to refuse me service. Do—do—do I have to speak to DeGannes about this?" he said, mocking Papá.

Grayson noticed Rosa's shadow before she could make herself scarce. Papá, bent at the waist, was reaching for Grayson's crate, his brow lined as if it had on it a written recitation of all the words he would've spoken to Grayson if Papá were not what he was, where he was, if the world hadn't been as it was. Then Rosa heard Papá mutter words she'd never heard spoken:

"Chelu nu. Onye nzuzu. Uchu gba gi!" Papá said.

Grayson did not know any more than Rosa the meaning of such words, and yet they both understood the sentiment. Rosa found herself frightened by what she saw in Papá.

"Fucking Babylon." Grayson's glare, familiarly unpleasant, moved from Papá to Rosa, and Rosa found herself, in her mind's eye, scanning her own face, questioning its acceptability as she had questioned Papá's secret language.

"That," he said to Papá, nodding at Rosa, "I can have if I wish it."

Rosa turned to leave, but not before she noticed Papá looking through her, making it seem as though the man, Grayson, had been speaking of something other than his daughter.

But each of them knew.

3

January 1815

Señor Rampley leaned against the rail of the verandah, refusing to be looked upon though Rosa tried more than once. She could not stop going over in her mind what she'd done, and yet she didn't wish to take it back. Rosa thought that maybe she had acted impetuously but knew she hadn't. There had been something in the act that offered a certain kind of knowing—knowing how it felt to put her lips upon his, knowing that he'd wanted her too—and if Rosa mined her heart long enough she might have discovered that the passion had been there all along, scavenging like baby cockroaches in the dark of the night, their scurrying and harvesting barely discernible until they grew into something she felt beyond her control.

Eve had set out a bowl of roasted arvanço beans and four cups of warm soursop punch. Papá had called them together, demanding that there be after-meal teatime (without the tea, for it was too hot, he said), a tradition that had been all but lost in the year prior.

"I ran into Madame Bernadette in town a f-few days back." Papá chewed the loose strings of his sugarcane stick. Recently, the cane had begun to ache his left molar, so he had begun to set it to the right side of his mouth.

"Oh, you just ran into her? I have a feeling she ran into you." Eve laughed. "Her husband died some years ago. She's been trying to find a replacement ever since."

"Well, she can keep looking." Papá waved away Eve's nonsense, but in the light of the candle lantern, Rosa noticed a slight blush of color beneath his cheeks. "She said that boy, her nephew, Lamec, got m-married and lost his wife less than a year later. A shame." Papá sat himself straight, set down his cup. "A big fancy wedding they had. She tell me we sh-should keep your wedding small, Eve. We ent want no bad eye."

"Oh, these people and their chupidness!" Eve removed her shawl, the presence of which rang absurd in such a noxious heat. "People don't want me to have a big wedding because they frightened I'll show them up!"

Papá smiled. Eve had somehow become more like Mamá since she and Señor Rampley had become engaged. Theatrical. Impudent. Papá appeared to enjoy it, as though it said something more certain about her happiness and about him as her father.

"Lamec asked about you, Rosa." Papá scanned Rosa for a reaction. "He told his aunt he'd like to c-come and see you again."

"His mouth's not still burnin'?!" Eve threw her head back. "He better not bring that uncle of his or the old man will surely kick the bucket this time."

"Hush, Eve." Rosa took in the slight smirk upon Papá's face. They'd had fun with that story over the years. Laughing had been Papá's way of forgiving her. But it seemed the debt was still to be paid.

"I told her to have him come next Sunday for lunch," Papá said.

"Next Sunday?" Eve steadied the rocker beneath her. "That's a fortnight before our wedding. We can't entertain then."

"And I don't want him to come again," Rosa added.

"He'll be my guest and allyuh will make somet'ing for lunch that day." Papá said this to both of them as though neither had spoken.

"Papá, I said I have no interest." Rosa glanced at Señor Rampley, who hadn't looked up from his muddied boots. Papá caught the glance but pretended as if he hadn't.

"He'll bring the lil ch-chile and—"

"What chile? He have a baby?" Eve clapped her hands, then said to Rosa, "He's lookin' for a caretaker. Ooh, guess who'll be the evil stepmudda?"

"I will not be any child's mother."

The air that early evening was thickset and gouty. Rosa felt strong, certain of herself. She drank the remaining punch, and only when finished did she notice that Eve hadn't placed a sliver of sugarcane inside her cup.

"Why don't I have cane?" Rosa said.

Eve set the shawl back upon her shoulders as if she were playing dress-up. "You don't?"

Papá tossed the husk of his cane out into the yard. It landed a few feet beyond the lip of the verandah. Flies attacked it as if they'd been lying in wait. "What does it m-matter, Rosa? Go and cut cane if you want c-cane." Papá said this as if Rosa complained often.

Rosa knew she shouldn't, knew Señor Rampley had advised her against it, so Rosa set her jaw, wondering if it might keep. But it did not. "The afternoon we had the party here, I was caught in the storm." Rosa began as if this would be a story like any other. Half listening, Papá took the bowl of beans from Eve and set it upon his lap. He ate the charred ones first, guaranteed to upset his belly and thus guaranteed to keep Rosa and Eve awake much of the night. The arvanço bucked around in Papá's mouth.

"I've been meanin' to tell you how very rude it was of you to run off like that." Eve aired herself with a green silk hand fan, purportedly made in the East Indies. She'd bought it in town when she and Señor Rampley had gone to sell Fat-Gyal-Hen's eggs. Rosa noticed now that despite all the housework, Eve's long fingers had remained so very delicate, like waxen finger puppets, the skin barely rippling, the nail beds a healthy blush.

"I had to take shelter at Monsieur DeGannes's," Rosa continued.

"I heard from someone that he's been quite under the weather," Eve interrupted.

"No, I think not," Rosa said. "Or if he has been, Francine must be his private nursemaid."

Papá stopped crunching. Half-gnawed beans sat like pottage on his back teeth. He moved forward, off the seat of the rocker, toes roosting, straining to hear her. "What is this you saying? You only now m-mentioning this?"

"But you're only now telling me about the lunch next Sunday," Rosa shot back.

"That's not the same," Eve said.

"And what would you have done, Papá?" Rosa continued. "You said many times that Jeremias is no longer your son."

Eve shook her head the way Mamá would have done. *Rosa is not good enough. Rosa has never been good enough.* "How long has this been going on?" she said.

"Perhaps since forever." Something about this thought amused Rosa. The idea that they all had pretended to be guided by the mores of integrity and decency and high moral rectitude, and still they'd suffered the shame of whores. It was as if nothing had ever been perfect and Rosa felt she could no longer trust that the earth beneath her would not open its big, ugly mouth and swallow her.

Arvanço balls, little purveyors of belly wind, were scattered across the verandah. They had fallen during Papá's harried departure, and now, Eve was on her knees collecting them, muttering loud enough for Rosa to hear. "You can t'ink of no one but yourself?"

Candles flickered at Eve's bare feet. Always, Eve washed them before bed, massaged them with coconut oil. Those soft feet were the marks of a woman who held her place in the annals of womanhood.

"This will ruin our wedding day. You only mentioned this now so Papá would forget about Lamec. But he won't forget."

There were tears in Eve's eyes. Eve, who had stood tall and emotionless the day they buried Mamá, gripping the family's Bible. She'd read Mamá's favorite psalm in the certain way she'd read it every night that Mamá had lain in her sickbed: "Surely, he will save you from the fowler's snare." And continued reading even as they lowered Mamá's casket into the ground, her voice unwavering. The undertaker hadn't told Papá until just before the burial that they'd set Mamá into a casket made for another woman, average-sized, who'd died clearing bush for a new coffee plantation. That they'd had to break Mamá's ankles and set her chin upon her shoulder to fit her inside. "He will cover you with his feathers, and under his wings you will find refuge."

"I'm getting married," Eve said now. "And Papá's got his eyes set on Madame Bernadette. Nobody wants to tend to you any longer."

4

Jeremias turned Papá away. Papá returned to Tío Byron's the next morning and the next. In the evenings, he reported all the happenings to Eve:

"They does have my boy in a lil lean-to that they put up in the yard, tellin' him it's best if he and his wife have some time apart. There Jeremias is, livin' in this six-by-six room like he ent have a home." Papá told Eve how he wanted to snatch up Jeremias from the place, but Jeremias wouldn't budge. How he was sure some root had been put upon his boy. "You shoulda seen Philippe and Byron c-carryin' on at the door, callin' me every unholy name there is, and oh! how them chil'ren bawled seein' this com-commotion between their abuelos!" Papá told Eve that Francine had not been home the first night he'd gone there, but she'd been ready for him the second day. "She wearin' that white lace t'ingy on she head, some charlatan's idea of a nun's habit, and she c-climb my back like the snake she is, p-poundin' me with both fists, like I ever done anyt'ing to she! At least Jeremias had the decency to p-pull the woman off me, but eh-eh—what kinda woman is this they raisin' up there?" Papá adjusted his hat. "I shoulda beat her. But me promised Myra when we married that I ent never ever beat a gyal and never would, and I wasn't lettin' that Jezebel push me to b-break my word to my woman."

It was the third day. Papá's face was still webbed with fine pink scratches when he left in the early morning for Tío Byron's. Before leaving, he told Eve that that would be his last attempt, that Jeremias might very well wish to stay with those people.

That same morning, Rosa set out the horses slightly west of the usual riding path. The earth was crisp and unwelcoming, as there'd been no rain since the afternoon of the party, the same afternoon she kissed a man for the first time and he'd run away. When Rosa steered the horses back onto the usual path, Monsieur DeGannes was at the bend.

It's a funny thing about sunlight. Like odors and sounds, sunrays falling in just a certain way can bring back memories too. The light that day fell striated and hungry, like the first morning she'd set out the horses with Señor Rampley. She'd been angry then, confused about Señor Rampley's place there, and now she thought how so little had changed.

The horses strained against their tethering, eager to begin their grazing. They pulled the line, hoping to inch past Monsieur as he dismounted. Purple bags of flesh puckered beneath Monsieur's eyes. He seemed unsteady on his feet as he tied his horse to a crown-shaped saman tree, among many like it, which he and Papá used as markers between their lands.

"Are you in need of help, Monsieur?"

"My wife cannot know." Monsieur walked a crooked line toward Rosa. At first, she wondered if he'd been drinking, then thought better of it, thought Francine must have spoken to him, must've told him that Rosa had seen them.

"Come with me." When Monsieur reached for Rosa, Martinique reared back and Monsieur, disgusted, swiped Martinique's snout. Rosa wished to strike Monsieur, but instead she set her hand gently upon Martinique so that she wouldn't forget herself.

"She's there." Monsieur pointed into the thorny sunrays as though he'd lost his sense of direction. "Francine is there. She has done a thing, a most terrible thing." Monsieur pressed his palms together, as if to plead for a trust he had not earned. "My wife cannot know."

By the time Rosa arrived to Monsieur DeGannes's stable, Pierre had bled out. Monsieur had left him to die in a ravine of blood, fearing that if he sought help for the boy, his wife would leave him. And take with her the money.

This he did not say, but he did not have to.

Rosa knelt beside Pierre and lay her hand upon his chest, staring down at his blood, sticky and rich and horrible, soaked through to his skin, his bones beneath the sodden shirt, delicate like a robin's breast.

She felt, even as she touched him, his absence. Felt the guilt cutting and splitting away at her for ever questioning his belonging to the Rendóns. Pierre had always belonged to them. Rosa had long believed she would never have a child of her own, so Pierre had become her Quite a Bit of Fun. Her Quite a Bit of Fun who would never again smile for her.

Monsieur told Rosa the story in fragments. Francine had brought the boys with her. It had been early morning. The house was still. Francine knew he liked to get away before the wailing of his colicky baby began. He'd complained to Francine about his new life. He'd told her it was an arrangement about which he was not happy. He knew it was what Francine had wished to hear. When Monsieur arrived at the stable, the boys were petting the horses. Francine had never before brought them with her. They were handsome boys. Pierre, not even eighteen, had the maturity of an older man. Was most articulate. Reminded Monsieur of Jeremias. Monsieur said those words to Francine. *He reminds me of Jeremias.* And it was then that Francine became visibly angered. Said she needed to speak to him alone. They walked deeper into the stable. Pierre kept François entertained, seeming to pretend he couldn't hear his mother telling Monsieur that she wished for Monsieur to commit to a future with her. That he was obligated to do so. When Monsieur laughed and said he could not, that he would not, Francine turned for a cutlass that Monsieur had stored behind two wooden pails and she ran toward the boys. Pierre had protected François. He'd taken the slashes in his little brother's stead, and Monsieur had run after Francine intending to snatch the blade, he said, but was unable to stop her from taking it to her own neck. Afterward, he placed the hysterical François into the wagon Francine had driven and steered it several hundred yards behind the stable and bound the wagon and the boy to a tamarind tree. "Because my wife cannot know," Monsieur said again.

Pierre's face was frozen in a grave sneer. He appeared nothing like the smiling boy who'd devoured Mémé's crème and begged "Rotha" to take him to sit upon the big horse. That smiling boy was who Rosa wished to remember, even as she and Monsieur set that smiling boy's body onto the wagon bed beside his mother, even as Rosa lifted

François, covered in that smiling boy's blood, to sit on the sundrenched seat beside her.

"Her neck . . ." François turned toward Rosa and begged with his confused expression for Rosa to peer again at the two bodies behind them. "Her neck is smiling," François said of his mother. "She doesn't like to smile."

Rosa turned to observe Francine, the white of her dress barely discernible beneath the bright red, and the new scar stretching as if to bury the old.

"Will Pierre wake up on the third day like Jesus, Tante Rosa?"

Rosa pulled François close. She did not wish to tell him that Rendón soil did not seem to yield miracles any longer.

5

They set Pierre to rest into the ground early Sunday morning. He lay next to his Mémé. Papá would have it no other way. Padre José could not or would not offer rites for Francine. She was lain to rest on Robespierre property.

The same guests who'd been there to celebrate Eve and Señor Rampley's upcoming nuptials had returned. Someone had given the Rendóns 'bad eye,' it was said. Too much happiness with that Yankee coming to marry the older spinster. The house needed a cleansing. Madame Bernadette told Papá that she and the other women from church would take care of it before the wedding day.

By late morning, the house was empty and Jeremias took to Papá's bed. In the coming nights, he and Papá would sleep (or barely sleep, as it was) with François between them. Papá would pat François's head, Jeremias, his back. The father, the son, the jumpy ghost of a child.

It was early afternoon when François sat beside Eve at the table. His thin lips seemed to have broadened from the black molasses Eve let him lick from the spoon and the two spoke not of the funeral but of the wedding. Of the dessert crème he would eat, of the new trousers Eve would make for him, of the bougainvillea she'd put in her hair before she danced. And when François found himself swelling with the future, he went upon the verandah, pulled at his braces, and told Eve he still hoped for Pierre to come.

The man arrived inside a striking wagon of cherrywood that bore a curved bed and a supple leather seat. He wore a topcoat and a tall hat that looked to be from a catalogue. He had an impressive physique, and the smell of bastille soap folded itself in a breeze that blew past Mamá's lace curtains, as he approached the portal holding a white orchid. He touched François gently on the head and greeted Rosa with a slight bow at the waist, offering her the flower.

"Oh Lord, bon dieu! I—" Rosa began.

François walked down the verandah stairs to peer into the wagon bed. Eve arrived at the door then, gathering Mamá's apron in hand. "My God," she said. "Please, please, come in."

After finding the wagon empty, François returned to the verandah and asked the man, "Mon frère is not coming, is he?"

The man smiled. "I'm sorry, lil one, I don't know. I comin' only for lunch."

Papá apologized and told Lamec what a time it'd been for them, but that they were pleased to have him. After Lamec offered his condolences, Papá set him on the verandah with a cup of tea while Eve dished out the funeral food the guests had left behind: stewed fish, fried cabbage, boiled cassava.

"Rosa, c-come lemme speak to you for a moment." Papá beckoned her in a throaty whisper. Between seeing guests out and keeping François company, Rosa had not had an opportunity to change out of her service clothes. She was in unusual form, wearing Eve's low-waist indigo-blue dress with her hair coiled like a boa resting easily on a sturdy branch. Eve had told her more than once that she looked nice. Apparently, grief became her. As Rosa followed Papá to the back of the house, she thought what a thing for grief to be one's most lovely state.

"Papá, I don't want—"

"You t'ink I bringin' you back here so *you* can talk?" Papá dug his boot tip into Fat-Gyal-Hen's dirt. He formed letters but not words

in the earth. He had said almost nothing since Rosa had driven that
wagon with Pierre knocking into Francine like rotted melons. Rosa
didn't know how he'd managed to stay on his feet during Padre José's
reading from the Book of Wisdom. "The souls of the righteous are
in the hands of God." But now, Papá looked stronger, bitter like tea
steeped for too many hours.

"You're spoiled, Rosa. And this is my fault," he continued. "But it's
ending right here."

"Spoiled" is what men called girls whose disobediences they secretly
enjoyed.

"The man is here and I does need you to behave."

"Behave" is what men said to girls whose "spoiled" begins to embarrass them.

"I'm not—"

"You t'ink I ent know you does have feelings for Señor Rampley?"

They were so ugly, those words. Like a pus-filled boil, unsightly,
festering, and Rosa felt angry with Papá for pelting her with them,
especially now that every good memory seemed to be overshadowed
by a cutting grief.

"You must get out from between he and Eve, and this is the only
way." Papá sighed, believing, it seemed, that his coming words would
hurt him more than Rosa: "Señor Rampley will never have you. You
cannot win against Eve."

Rosa now knew this to be true. For Papá had been the window
through which she had seen herself. "I never thought I could," she
whispered, though when she'd kissed Señor Rampley there had been
a moment when she believed she could make him love her.

Papá drew a circle in the dirt. Fat-Gyal-Hen came to inspect it for
supper crumbs. "The man s-sitting on that verandah is decent and he's
willing to take a chance on you. You'd be foolish not to accept his offer."

Papá reached for her hand, and she remembered how Mamá had
tended to that very hand after his shop and thumb had been snatched
away. Rosa took her hand from his. She did not wish to feel pity for
Papá when she wished to feel it only for herself.

*   *   *

Papá called Jeremias from the back room to join them for lunch. Jeremias appeared uneven now. Shoulders narrower than his belly, hair wider than his face. When Jeremias sat, he pulled François next to him. It seemed none of them would ever again consider the boy's face without questioning the paternity of its features.

"We are so woefully unprepared, Mr. Benoit." Eve took her seat next to Papá and across from Señor Rampley. She looked to Señor Rampley and smiled, and Rosa was surprised by the warmth between them.

Lamec and Papá took up their spoons first. Lamec winked at Rosa before taking his first bite, and as lunch became supper, it seemed Lamec had always been there.

"The English ent bargain for our kind," Lamec told Papá.

Lamec told them of the special tax levied against free Negroes and coloreds for dances and public entertainment and how the coloreds were beginning to demand better. "The French can have their masquerade parties until the middle of the next morning, but not us? The English are used to controlling their coloreds. That's the problem. We does have to be off the streets by nine t'irty, and they insult us with that bell they does ring, t'reatening to t'row us into their new prison on Frederick Street if we ent disperse quickly enough."

Lamec was bold with his words in the way Jeremias had been before life had carved the insides out of him.

"And they findin' new ways to take our land," Lamec added. "Lies and trickery, so they can plant more cane and send the money to their bruddas and faddas in England." Lamec wiped his face with a handkerchief. "But with each day, I plantin' more of my own rows. And makin' a decent living, whippin' me own back and nobody else's. We have to compete. And maybe eventually we will get them to leave this island."

Señor Rampley cleared his throat. Rosa was surprised to see him eager to join the conversation. "The Chippewas got a way of makin' sugar from maple trees. Finer and sweeter than your cane. Strange to me that the English would come all the way down here when all the Indians prolly want is buyers," he said.

Lamec cocked his head. He could have been more polite, but no one could insist upon it. "So you sayin' that if the English would simply buy sugar from the same Indians being run off their land by Englishmen posing as Americans, that they would just up and leave the West Indies? Is that what you t'ink?" Lamec pointed at Señor Rampley, then looked to Papá and said, "I see your guest is a real court jester."

Papá looked embarrassed for Señor Rampley, then said something about Señor Rampley not yet understanding the ways of Englishmen, not yet understanding the critical importance of West Indian cane to Europe's thriving economy. Rosa wondered, if she'd married Lamec long ago, if things might've been better for the Rendón family. If a marriage to Lamec might have saved them all from the grief stuck in their bellies like slick, hard zaboca pits.

"I grow what I need here," Papá said proudly. "But I have more land I could farm."

Lamec had energized Papá in a way Rosa hadn't seen in some time, and she now understood that Papá had long ago seen himself in the young man.

"Yes, but you must be careful, eh. It's all the land around St. Joseph they lookin' to have first. And this is a choice piece a property. They'll triple your taxes and tell you you does have only days to pay it. This is what they doin' to us now."

Papá said nothing to this.

"Well, this is why Papá will sign over everyt'ing to Señor Rampley after we are married," Eve said.

Jeremias looked up from his plate then. He told François to go outside. When the boy said he'd rather not, Jeremias told him that Jesus would reward him if he did. The six of them watched the boy walk onto the verandah to look out at the road, as if hope had business there.

"Since when?" Jeremias said. "No one told me about this."

Jeremias turned to Señor Rampley, but Lamec, not at all interested in the family rift, spoke then to Rosa. "I hear you're quite good with horses."

Rosa caught sight of Papá, who nodded, encouraging her to say more. "Yes, other than cooking, it is my favorite thing to do," she said.

They laughed. And it was as if the bottled sorrow had been let out for a brief whiff of air.

"What kinda horses you does have?" Lamec said.

Rosa remembered what Papá had said. She had to make do. That there were no families without small sufferings. "My favorite is Martinique. She has Andalusian blood, round hips, good bones. She's lovely."

"You'll take me to see her?"

Señor Rampley stood, his napkin still wedged between his thighs. "I'm going out now. I'm happy to show you."

"No, you sit here with us, Señor Rampley," Papá said. "I'd like you to c-catch up Jeremias on some t'ings."

CREADON RAMPLEY

Isle of Trinidad

1815

"Are you well?" Eve looked me over like I was gonna topple.

"Just got up too quick." I sat back down but what I really wanted was to run. Run, cause I could feel the beginnin of the end and I aint knowed if the end in that place was gonna be as cruel as all the other ends I come to.

The mornin they set her nephew into the ground, Rosa wasnt Rosa no more. If you coulda seent her face when she told Demas and her brother that she found em out in the fields. She told em she thought Pierre had prolly tried to stop his mother from hurtin herself and that Francine musta killed him first then tied the lil one to a tree so he wouldnt run off and die alone. The boy François told a different story, but Rosa told everyone that the shock of losin his brother and mother had confused him. If you coulda seent how that brother of hers ran to the wagon to find his wife and boy dead. How he tried to strangle the life outta Rosa. Them big hands on her skinny neck. How she just stood there, takin it til me and Demas pulled him off.

Somethin changed in Rosa. Whatever that somethin was chewed all her goddamn flesh from the inside. Demas knew she was different and still he sent that new Rosa out to the stable with that Lamec fella. But I guess I couldnt expect no different since Demas wasnt right no more neither. You see, the man I knowed Demas to be wouldnt have just gone to get his boy after learnin what went on between Francine and DeGannes. He woulda marched next door and had a word or two with DeGannes. A word about what DeGannes had done to his boy. But instead, Demas sat chewin on his back teeth, and when I asked him why, he took me out to the cacao field, kicked some loose soil around, and pulled out a pair of iron manacles, puttin em to my face, angry like I asked to see his soul.

"I made thousands of these over the years," he said. "DeGannes told me they were for p-prisoners, that they were building prisons all across the Americas, that criminals needed to be restrained. And Monsieur DeGannes made arrangements for the shippin and he got me buyers for all kindsa tings I was makin." Demas throwed down the manacles. "All I had to do was heat and hammer. I never asked why a ting so simple wasnt gettin made in a big big shop in Liverpool, why it had to be so so secret, why it was me, in the m-middle of nowhere, supplying manacles. It was easy work. Too easy. It put me on all this land, built me a fine fine house, kept me a good good woman, and my ch-chilren were all right. And then Grayson come here questionin my conscience? My conscience? What reason, I wonderin, does he have to question my conscience til I come to see that maybe them blasted chains wasnt for no prisoners. Maybe all along they was for Africans," he said. "Africans just like me."

Demas didnt have to say much more. I knowed the truth was somewhere tween what he knew was wrong and what he said was right. And as I watched that Lamec fella walk round the side of the house with Rosa alongside him, I knew he wouldnt know the truth of her either, cause she couldnt—none of us could—be quite who we was no more.

XIII

Isle of Trinidad

⁓⁓

1

1815

The morning after Lamec's visit, Rosa stashed dry goods inside the well hole that Señor Rampley and Papá had begun digging before Papá fell ill. In Port of Spain, Rosa inquired about the charge for one passenger on seaworthy ships, as well as their routes and capacity. She learned that in the coming two weeks ships would be sailing to Martinique, Guadeloupe, and even Campeche, Mexico, where supporters of King Fernando intended to send supplies and horses to fight against the guerrillas. In the late afternoon, when the sun sat high and virile, Rosa went to the cacao fields where Papá hid the family's money to see if there would be enough, and she uncovered enough for her passage, just enough for her to begin again.

Before Rosa had made it back to the house, Jeremias came up behind her, quiet and amber-eyed. She remembered then the night she'd followed him. How she'd waited, lying beneath a pudgy-faced moon, wondering what he was doing with Monsieur. Remembered how he'd erupted from the trees and she'd looked up to see his face backlit with the lantern. And he was smiling. Happy. As if there'd been something pleasurable beyond Papá's home, beyond the schoolhouse and working in the fields and tea on the verandah. And when he'd wrapped her bonnet ribbons around her throat and pulled until she felt the air fill up in her jaws, Rosa remembered thinking that she had wanted to ensure that her brother was safe.

"What are you planning?" he said.

"What makes you think I'm doing anything?" Rosa knew Jeremias could not be trusted, but as she spoke those words, she also felt shame for having planned to leave her home.

"I heard you were in town asking questions," he said. "You think you can be in that black-black skin of yours and go anywhere you want?"

"You heard incorrectly."

"You planning on leaving Trinidad? Isn't there enough here to fill you up?"

"Enough to fill me up?" Rosa said. "What's left, Jeremias?"

What's left? Those words could not have been spoken without both of them thinking of all Jeremias's losses. Rosa, for the first time since she brought home Pierre and Francine, wondered what it'd been like for Jeremias, mourning a woman and a child, both of whom he loved but neither of whom belonged to him. She spied her brother now, his gaze resting on the dark timber of the drying house where Papá went at nights to inspect and rake the cacao beans, where Papá covered them if the rain clouds hovered or uncovered them if the sun promised to shine the next morning. Rosa watched as Jeremias looked upon the chalky trunks of the cacao trees, their earthen pots dense with dried thick-faced leaves, nests for their bright fruits, alongside the wooden handles of their enemies, the cacao knives, upright like flagpoles.

"I need you to help me," he said. "I need to claim this land. Monsieur says—"

"You've seen Monsieur DeGannes?"

"Of course. He is my closest ally. I could not—"

"He is no friend of yours." Rosa tried to remember why she had felt the need to protect DeGannes, but now all the reasons that had then been so clear were muddled. "And this land is not yours. You only want to ensure no one else has it."

"I'll have it, you can work it, and you will never have to marry that illiterate farmer."

"Eve and Creadon Rampley should have it. That is what Papá wishes."

"Papá is not the man you think he is." Jeremias picked up a cacao knife, turning the long handle over, its blade shaped like a spade's, kept sharp by Papá's grindstone. Rosa was certain Jeremias had never before wielded a spade, certain that he didn't know how much it took for Papá to keep that land, how much it took for Papá to keep that crop, keep that house, keep that family. Rosa was certain Jeremias did not know how the soil they stood upon had Papá's blood deep deep inside its veins.

"Nothing he's done is bad enough to deserve what you're planning."

"You don't think so?" Jeremias glared at Rosa as if she were a foolish girl. "You think Papá could have acquired this house and this land by making only nails and axes?"

Jeremias seemed to have always known. Always known what he then told Rosa about their father. Of Papá's dealings with DeGannes, of supporting the institution Papá professed to hate; how Papá's innocence was not plausible, had never been plausible.

"This is not true." Rosa said these words because she felt they were necessary to say, for herself and for her Papá, but she was certain Jeremias, who'd relayed it all with particulars and fine subtleties, had not spoken an untrue word. "Papá is not that kinda man."

And to this, Jeremias said nothing. Which pained Rosa more than she expected, for it felt as if Jeremias knew to let her stew in her doubts, knew she would question everything she'd ever known of Papá; she would contemplate each word Papá had spoken, reconsider every decision he'd made, disbelieve a man whose words were once certain for Rosa.

"You mean to take his land?" Rosa said, still stunned by the arrogance of the endeavor.

"With your help."

"Because you think he's not deserving of better? Who are you to judge Papá, Jeremias?"

"I am not judging him. He did what was best for his family at the time. And now this is what is best for his family. He cannot see this as yet, but he will." Jeremias spoke as if he'd never been more certain of anything.

"You only wish for my help so you'll have someone to blame if things go wrong."

"Yes, it's true. Because we all know Papá would never dare turn on his darling Rosa."

Papá came then, with his shirt opened a bit past his neck. Rosa noted the skin on his chest, striped with age and wear, the curly hairs a bright silver. "You have no work to do?" Papá looked toward Rosa as if worried for her, then offered her the smile he'd once saved only for her.

Jeremias smiled too at Papá, then said to him, "We were just now planning what work to do next."

CREADON RAMPLEY

Isle of Trinidad

⌒⌒

1815

The man rode in from the back of the stable but Demas had me
set down my weapon. The Cordoza man, built small, made his way
toward us like he had cannons for balls. His skin was rough like
prunes, and his eyes was fiery when he spoke to Demas, askin him if
his daughter and son was close by.

"Would you like for me to call them here, Señor?"

"No, quite the opposite," Cordoza said.

The Cordoza man looked at me like to ask Demas if it was all right
to speak open with me there, then started speakin in English thinkin I
aint understood it. He told Demas that Jeremias had come to see him
and said that both he and the black-black daughter believed Demas
was now simple. "Your children say youve not been well since your
fit, and that in order to do what is best for you, they want to strike a
deal with me."

"A deal?"

Demas had been makin a set of bells for the new church. Padre José
asked this favor of Demas for havin turned a blind eye to his wife and
grandson not bein laid to rest in a proper cemetery like English laws
demanded. Demas had worked on the molds each night since the
funeral. Now, the Cordoza man rested his hands on em, lookin like he
was tryna figure out what kinda money them bells was bringin Demas.

"Your son wished for me to accompany him down to George Street
and Marine Square, into the office of the contador. He said he could

have his sister there to attest to your ill health. They wished for me to support them in their efforts to have the land transferred into the name of your boy, your rightful heir, then to have the governor transfer ownership from Jeremias to me. They said they trusted me to sign it back over . . ." Cordoza paused nice and long, and I swear I seent a lil grin on his face fore he said, ". . . after you are dead."

Demas didnt give him much to delight in. He said, "I will come and visit soon, Señor." They shook hands then Demas added, "And will be sure to bring someting that shows my appreciation for your friendship."

Cordoza smiled big, mounted his horse, and set back out cross the fields.

Demas pointed at the bubblin crucible, the fire ragin in it and said to me, "Take care you dont get hurt."

The pit fire was lit for two days. Hens plucked, split, marinated. Breadfruit was salted. Carrots, onions, garlic, tomatoes, and peppers diced. Coconuts cracked, emptied, shredded, pulped, juiced, chopped. Butter churned. Corn kettled. Peas soaked. The mornin fore my wedding, we aint sit for breakfast. Eve holed herself up in the back room to finish her dress. A dress that always needed more this, more that. We was gonna have to fend for ourselves at breakfast, she said.

Rosa set a few broke-neck sardines and hard-boiled plantains in the middle of the table. Wasnt so much havin a meal as sufferin enough to get us through to lunch. Demas was actin like nothin was different. Like he was always expectin to get stabbed in the back by his children. He smiled in Rosa's face, still slept one space over from Jeremias, laughed when François tossed his head and pretended to be Eve in front of the lookin glass.

Made me wonder if I knowed him at all.

It was near high noon when I seent a wagon kickin up dirt. Demas was still workin on the bells when he sent me to the house to tell Rosa to start puttin out lunch. It was all but empty inside since Jeremias had took the boy to see his other grandparents.

Sun wasnt out that day. Wasnt no wind in the air either. I member cause it was the breeze that always got me through them days workin with them bellows. And that day, I couldnt hardly breathe. I was so tired that I aint notice that the wagon wasnt on the road no more. That it cut through the fields and the driver was walkin up to the stable.

"Ive come about my order," Grayson said, with his lip real tight and angry.

Demas aint tell me this but I knowed he aint make that first set a bits right. I knowed the second they was fitted in some African mouth and that African man walked a mile, that that metal that was supposed to hold his tongue in place was gonna come flyin out. So I was at the ready. Tryna get Demas to hear me while he banged the third bell into shape. He had told Padre José he never made no bells. That he was nervous they might not ring like they should. Padre told him he didnt much mind how they sounded so long as people come to Mass when they heard em.

"Ive come to pick up my order," Grayson said to Demas.

I was damn relieved. At least I was til I seent Demas look up, wipe his brow, streakin his farhead black and squintin like he aint knowed the fella.

"I have come to collect my order," Grayson said once more.

Demas dropped his head back toward the bell, and the mare, Martinique, let out a lil air that sounded deep like a growl. "Sir, I told you I would not be able to—to take that order."

Grayson looked to me, like to ask if Demas had lost his damn mind. And Imma tell you that I wasnt so sure he hadnt. I guess I knowed all along that Demas was that kinda big-in-the-chest man, that he had to bottle up all them lil undignities that I swore sometimes would choke him. But that day when I seent him speak like a man who aint care no more, I got scared for him. I knowed the world wasnt tryna make no room for no Demas kinda man.

"Pardon?" Grayson said. "I was clear I needed two hundred more, was I not?"

"Sir, I said when you were here last that I c-could not take the order." Demas glared at the bells like to tell Grayson they was the good Christian reason he couldnt finish his order.

"You used my metal for church bells?"

"The church supplied its own metal, sir."

"You shouldve used what they provided for my order. First in, first out."

Demas had this look on his face. Like a big dog told he couldnt bite a lil dog.

"I have a buyer expecting those fasteners," Grayson said.

"Sir, we can have them ready by next week. The supply ship was a month late, but we have the materials now," I told him.

Grayson wasnt lookin at me though. "I need them by the morrow."

"My daughter is marrying tomorrow, sir. I need at least tree days."

"And Imma bring them to your place so you aint gotta pick up," I added, tryin like hell to get Grayson to focus in on me and not on Demas and his aint-care-no-more face.

"Tomorrow," Grayson said.

"I cannot agree to that, sir."

"'I cannot agree to that' is akin to saying no, isnt it, you bloody boon?"

"I cannot say," Demas said to him.

"I cannot say, *sir*."

"I cannot say *sir*."

Grayson was like a geyser. You ever seent one of em? Water shootin straight into the sky like the earth aint want it no more. You could think it lovely, but it could scare the dickens outta you if you aint know what was comin. And we, for sure, aint knowed it was comin.

When Grayson turnt to leave, I thought that Demas had gotten mighty lucky. I made a note to ask Demas later why he just didnt say yes and put us to work through the night. Lookin back now, I think Demas mighta fooled himself into believin that him and Grayson was the same kinda man. Mighta fooled himself into believin Grayson was a man at all. That was how it always happens. Thinkin men is men when sometimes its just evil lookin like a man.

Did I tell you that there wasnt no sun that day? That it was the first time we didnt all meet in the house for a cup a somethin or a lil morsel of bread to start off the day? That I was supposed to be gettin married the next day to a real good woman and that me and Rosa had come to a place where we just set down all them feelins that was between that kiss, and we was all gonna make do and make a life there, together? And that it was all undone that day?

Eve screamed first.

When me and Demas rounded the corner, Grayson had Rosa by the hair. He was draggin her down them porch steps and both Eve and Rosa was givin him a fight. A helluva one. Nails, fists, feet, pummelin him til he got real real mad and stomped Rosa on the head with his boot. She fell still. And Eve threw herself over her sister. And the next stomp was more vicious than the first. Landed on Eve. At the side of her face. Her cry was so loud it liked to funnel the blood right outta me. I was almost to them when I seent Demas, who come through the house, set himself on the bottom step aimin that rifle. I ran and took it from him, knowin well what could happen to me if I used it, and knowin even better what could happen to Demas if he did. I ran up behind Grayson who started in again on Rosa. I beat his head with the end of that musket. I membered once askin Demas how he made that rifle. Strips of iron hammered round a rod, "heatin and beatin," he said, laughin. Then his face fell and he told me that the Governor had took his special lathe and his fingers wasnt so easy with the rods no more.

Grayson fell down clutchin his head. I smashed his hands til they turnt tongue pink. The lusty fingertips of that girl, Violence, had returned, and it felt goddamn bloody delicious. Like hot meat and gravy. I wasnt that lad with his Pa no more. I aint have to pretend to like the way it felt when I heard the crack of fine bones. Now I had to pretend that I aint like it.

Demas musta seent the delight I was takin in the beatin. "Let him go," he said. "Let him get on his feet."

I stepped back from Grayson and let him stumble his arse back onto his wagon seat and after he drove off, I turned to Demas, feelin the heat of my own breath on the tip of my nose. "There aint no goin back, is there?" I said.

Demas shook his head. "He will come again soon. And he wont be alone."

XIV

Isle of Trinidad

❧

1

1815

It was past suppertime. Behind the house the Northern Range loomed and wound, tinged in a bile-colored light, making shadows of the only land Rosa had ever known. Sheets that had been hung with the same wooden pegs that once pulled Rosa's nostrils into a narrow line now lay against the stiff air, as Rosa, seated on the ground beneath them, waited.

Papá had wiped the blood from her brow, but still Rosa's head throbbed and her vision remained smoke white. She could not stop the tremors that made her jaw sputter, could not stop worrying about what might happen next. Fat-Gyal-Hen, in her cage, watched Rosa with watery black-roe eyes, pecking the grille as Rosa crawled toward her. The hen smelled of musk, salt, mildewy fur, and her speckled feathers were like white potato mash hiding droppings. That man with his red face and the way he threw her to the ground so hard, and Eve pouncing him and Papá not coming quickly enough—Rosa ran it over again and again in her thoughts. Fat-Gyal-Hen looked to Rosa as if expecting her to speak, so Rosa told the hen what Papá had said in the house while he bandaged her head and reset Eve's jaw: "You will have to go away."

She did not think he meant the sort of go-away Rosa had had in mind. Not the kind where she pretended she was leaving only to have

Papá beg her to stay, not the kind where she went on an adventure of her own making. It was the sort of go-away that terror, in its no-ripples-in-the-water, no-footprints-on-the-shore, brought to bear on wrong-bodied, wrong-minded women.

What had Rosa done to bring such rage? The man, Grayson, had had no restraint, no hesitation, before running onto the verandah to attack her. His hands had landed with such force across her face and back and neck that she'd seen him rise off his feet after each blow. She remembered screaming out for Eve and hearing Eve running toward her, the sucking sound of Eve losing her breath as the man unchained a violence that she and Eve both knew to be reserved for men; a man's violence that made Rosa feel like a weak and vulnerable, pitiful and disgusting woman. A violence that made Rosa hate the body that had accepted it, hate the body that had wailed beneath it, the body that ripped and bled and bruised and pained and ached; a violence that made Rosa resent everyone who could not stop it all from happening.

The dirt where Rosa lay next to Fat-Gyal-Hen's cage felt cool against her sweaty torso. She thought of Eve, only a half hour before, taking Papá by his scarred hands, begging him to allow the family to remain together. "It is too much of a risk," he'd said. The plan was for Jeremias to take Eve and François away, north along the coast to someplace safe. A place from whence Eve might one day return home.

Not everyone would be as fortunate.

Eve's wailing had sent Rosa into the backyard. Rosa could still hear Eve through the side window, shuffling about, setting her things into Mamá's Martinique valise. Fat-Gyal-Hen pecked at the grille again, ready for her post-supper scraps, and Rosa wondered what would become of the hen after she left. Scrawny-Gyal-Hen. Dead-Gyal-Hen. Rosa would not think of what would become of Papá until she turned to see the mass of land that she would always call home wither into a thin line of green on a sea of blue.

CREADON RAMPLEY

Isle of Trinidad

1815

I aint never birth my own dream. I dont know if anybody ever had a dream of his own. I think we go about livin life lookin forward with other people's eyes. Like maybe shared dreams is what makes us human.

I think I wanted to share a dream with Eve and Demas and Rosa in Trinidad for as long as I could stand to. I think I wanted quiet Sunday lunches, evenins on the porch, cacao nibs, coconut trees, and a stable of virile horses. I think I wanted to learn how to be a proper man. A brave man. A man scared men dreamt of becomin. I think I had took the dreams of every person I ever knowed and set out a life to reach for. And I almost had it too.

I told Demas that the only hope he had of gettin outta trouble was to say he aint knowed me good. That I was a drifter who beat Grayson without any promptin. It wasnt much of a plan but Grayson was comin back and I had to give Demas a fightin chance.

Demas looked the way he did that night his wife's brother come to take the horses. Big strong body, frail egg eyes. His hair was white like meltin snowflakes on a massif and thin like a cobweb. I could prolly tell you that life was harder for men like Pa than it was for Demas. Pa aint have no verandah and hot teas, no daughters cookin him meals. I could prolly tell you that life was harder for men like Meleanos too. He had scalpin Indians to deal with and thievin missions thinkin a ways to get rid of him. But I cant pretend to know the kinda toll that

Trinidad life took on Demas. You see, me and Pa and Meleanos, we could all just pick up and go when we wanted, where we wanted, how we wanted, but Demas, Demas aint have that kinda choice. He had to make good where he was and make good the first time he set out to do so cause Negroes aint get more than one go. Demas knowed that, and I come to know it as I listened to him tell me what he wanted me to do, how he was passin his "go" on to me.

"Where to?" I said.

"Set her in a place where she—she wont have to run." Demas pushed his palm into his chin, his lips thinnin as he frowned. He had to know no place like that existed. Not for Rosa.

"I only know one place. Where I been. And you aint never gonna see your girl again if I take her there."

Demas already knowed this. It was in them frail egg eyes. It was *why* he had them frail egg eyes. He was choppin off his own legs and hopin to make em go.

"Rosa needs a land. All people must have a land," he said. "Help her find her f-footing. She can make her way. I know she will."

Demas aint knowed what he was askin cause he aint knowed what kinda place I left behind. How hard life was there. How hard it was gonna be for Rosa lookin the way she did, bein the way she was, to live a life worth livin.

Goddamn impossible.

I told him no. He give me his family Bible, told me his wife woulda wanted Rosa to have it. I told him no again. "I never asked anyting of you," he said. I didnt like how it felt, him pleadin with me. He aint owed me nothin. I owed him everything.

"You aint got to ask me no more," I said. "I put you in this place. And Im real sorry bout that. Imma take Rosa anywhere you want me to if she wants to go."

XV

Isle of Trinidad

∽∽

1

1815

Rosa helped François onto the wagon to sit beside his father as they waited for Eve. The boy had been crying. Rosa supposed it was the first cry of many to come, as she returned to the house and brought back bread with fresh sweet butter for him to take on the ride. When François opened the cheesecloth, he smiled down at Rosa, and she was certain the next time they met that François would not remember her face. But Rosa believed she would remember his, though later his features, in her mind, would become Victor's.

"Be good." It was all she knew to say, though later she'd realize it hadn't been enough.

Papá had wound Eve's bandage from the crown of her head to beneath her chin, so when Eve stood before Rosa, her tears fell in a stiff straight line as though free-falling from a cliff. Eve reached for Rosa's face, examined Rosa's swollen cheek and the eye that flickered from the strain of opening in sunlight. Eve set Rosa's hand in her own and brought it to her mouth to kiss it. Rosa remembered then her big sister's kisses. She remembered how Eve had oiled her hair, wiped her face clean, scrubbed her neck of dirt all the many days Mamá could not. And so when Eve tried to speak, tried to say something that could embody all that sisters were, all that sisters could never be to each other, Rosa, with the tips of her kissed fingers, traced the lines of her sister's mouth, willing her not to. Instead, Rosa pondered her sister's face, her beautiful mouth so much like Mamá's, and Rosa realized she could not remember a day when she had not resented Eve's prettiness, her face so much like Mamá's, and as she stood trying to piece together a tapestry of memories, she now wished to see Eve's face whole and unspoiled so she might remember it until they saw each other again.

Rosa helped Eve up onto the wagon bench. Eve was unsteady on her feet, still trembling from the scourge that had come upon them so suddenly. Rosa looked to Jeremias, hoping to remind him that Eve needed extra care and that he must play the role of brother and father and mother and sister, but Jeremias did not look down to see her. Rosa thought that perhaps Jeremias understood that anything that rang like affection between the two of them might have rendered everything that had come before as inconsequential; that a goodbye might have made them regret the resentments, all the lost time. And perhaps to Jeremias it was not worth the risk for either of them to contemplate wrongdoing. At least not then.

As they drove off, Rosa was certain Eve would not stop searching for the house in the cloud of wagon dust they left behind, but Rosa could not bear to wait for the wagon to disappear from sight. She returned inside and there, on the floor where Jeremias once slept, Rosa found Papá, on his knees with his head pressed into the tabletop. He wept just loud enough for God to hear him. And prayed for Mamá to watch over them. Rosa did not know if seeing Papá on his knees in this act of supplication made Papá seem more broken or more whole, did not know if it made *her* feel more broken or more whole.

Rosa went outside and drew herself again into a ball next to Fat-Gyal-Hen's pen. The sound of Papá's footsteps made Rosa's stomach curdle.

"Come, Rosa." Papá reached for her hand.

"No, please leave me." She told Papá that all she wished was to lie back down in his dirt. When she looked up to see his damp face, his eyes swollen, Rosa felt that her heart might never unbreak. She wished to hate Papá. She wished to hate him for Lamec, for Creadon, for Grayson, for DeGannes, for making her love that place so damn much. But there before her stood her Papá, the anguish like a too-thick rouge upon his face, and she felt for him the same wretchedness she felt for herself.

"You're sending Eve to Blanchisseuse, but I have to leave Trinidad?" The bandage had loosed from Rosa's head, the corner of it dangled across her left eye, and when she looked up again at Papá, his expression was one of pity. As though she were both hopeless and helpless. "Why didn't you send Eve away with Señor Rampley? She is his fiancée," Rosa said. "Grayson won't be looking for me. He will come for Eve."

"You don't know this." Papá set his hands under her arms and pulled her to her feet. He tucked the end of her bandage into the fold at her forehead, performing the task as if it were a duty, pressing hard against her skin.

"I am sorry, but I won't go," Rosa said. "Who will I be away from here? What will I do with that man?"

"He will make sure you're on your feet and you can be anybody you wish."

Until then Rosa had not thought Papá serious. But she now knew what he and Señor Rampley had been planning.

"Anybody I wish? I will be the same Rosa. Except I will be lost."

"You were lost here, Rosa."

Papá almost made her feel useless. But Rosa told herself that she'd had a purpose. And even if she hadn't, Trinidad was still her home. "I won't go," Rosa said again.

Rosa wished to tell Papá that she understood all that had happened to make things as they were. That the English had come and disrupted their lives, with their perfect mismanagement and indecision and inconsistency, with their slow unraveling terror, with their chaos that prevented sure footing, and caused Papá never to be certain of what would be his. And so the Rendóns had become stuck. Eighteen years in a state of arrest. But Rosa was certain the English would soon leave. She felt deep inside that their experiment on the island would prove a failure, that the Rendóns need only be patient.

"I don't want you here," Papá said.

"Grayson won't hurt me. I won't let him this time." It was imperfect, this reasoning. But it was all Rosa had.

"It is not for that." Papá closed his eyes as if again in prayer. "This has all c-come at the right time." Papá's nose flared now, and he dug the tip of his boot into the dirt, looking down and away from Rosa. "After Eve's wedding, I was plannin' on tellin' you. I wanted to wait 'til Eve was settled b-before makin' you go."

"Go where?"

"Go from my house and off my hands." Papá drew Xs in the dirt next to Fat-Gyal-Hen. Xs that might have been tilted crucifixes, but Rosa could not be certain. "You t'ink I wouldn't find out? Señor C-Cordoza come straight here, tellin' me what you and Jeremias tried to do," he said. "You hung your hat higher than you c-could reach."

Papá set his sight on Rosa now, letting his eyes drag across and around her face, a face everyone said was so much like his. There was nothing in Papá's expression that Rosa had seen before. It was as if a wick had blown, and Rosa felt herself on the outside of this man who had been the only one ever to let her inside.

"I told Jeremias no. No hice nada." Rosa felt the tears burning her throat.

"If you did nutting, this was the same as doing somet'ing, Rosa." Papá dusted his hands onto his trouser legs. "If you ent agree with what Jeremias was doing, why not come to me?"

Rosa did not believe Jeremias would have gone through with it. This was what she wished to tell Papá, but instead Rosa struck back. "We all have dirty hands, Papá."

Papá's face did not register any surprise, though Rosa had surprised herself. She wanted to take them back—her words. This was her Papá.

"This is what your brudda tell you? Well, I guess it's really best we part ways."

"Papá, you cannot—"

"I have one daughter now. She is the one I will have stay here on the island, close to me."

Papá scratched out the Xs with the heel of his boot, looking down into the dirt, hoping, it seemed to Rosa, to keep her from seeing his eyes now brimming with tears. Rosa thought he would give her the smile, the one he saved only for her; thought he would tell her that it would be only for a short while—this exile—and as she watched him shake his head as if to fend off something, Rosa did not know what to make of him, make of them, and so Rosa could not have foreseen what Papá said next.

"You've never been worth the tr-trouble you caused me," Papá said. "Never."

XVI

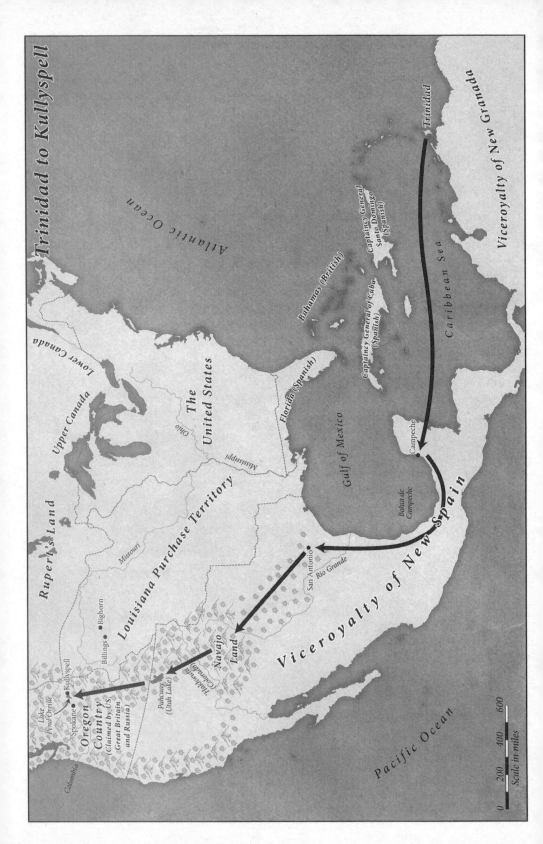

Kullyspell, Oregon Country

✺

1

Spring 1819

Rosa woke early to bathe. Her monthly bleeding had been both unexpected and unpredictable since delivering the baby. It was a maddening flow, too often leading with a spidery, irritating bubbling of blood, only then to quickly leak down the insides of her thighs until loosing clots in thick bursts. At home, women caught monthlies with scraps of cloth that they would boil and hang to dry at night, but Rosa and Creadon had no cloth. During those months on the ship, Rosa had had to wash herself with salt water, saving fresh water for drinking, and by mid-journey, she had collected floriated clumps of an itchy, milky-colored discharge in her privates, relieved only after the one other woman on the boat had shared her stash of a most bitter red berry juice.

Their first winter had been merciless. Creadon had taught Rosa how to make warm clothing and bedding from skins, and Rosa learned in the most distressing manner that hot water was not a summons for frozen fingers. Food had been so scarce that Rosa thought her head might never stop its spin, and an itchy rash had overtaken the folds of skin on her arms like tangled ivy. By midwinter, Creadon had grown so ill that Rosa feared he wouldn't recover, and though he could barely speak, she made him map out a plan for her survival. When he began to recover, the roof of their small cabin, or "post," as Creadon called it, buckled under the weight of a great white curse from the skies, burying their tools, forcing them to dig and pray for sun.

That whole first year, Rosa longed, hungrily, for her island. For the warmth of a monogamous, unwavering sun, the displays of fruit it produced, the waters bristling with fish atop easy currents. But now, in that place Creadon called Kullyspell, the longing had receded a bit, especially when the sun began to re-warm the world. "Spring," Creadon had called it, as if it were a wildling ready to pounce; fish drew closer to the surface, trees took on new skins like mistresses, and leaf buds, like millions of eyes, seemed to wonder if it was safe to enter.

It was just before dawn when Rosa found herself awake before Creadon. She had fed the baby and set the boy down nose to nose with Creadon on the bed they had built together. She hurried to the lake hoping to make it before the child awakened, before the night blood insisted on its great exodus.

Rosa dipped to beneath her chin. The lake water was frigid, like a rapacious fire singeing her flesh, and she thought then that there could be no way for comfort to find her in that place, for every single thing there existed in the cold shadows of her old life. To Rosa, comfort was Jeremias's trousers, a well-built stable, a verandah, forged pots. Rosa's life now was a life undressed. Lonely and stark and shriveled. It was a life that with all its colorlessness had drawn her and Creadon to each other, for in each other they had found memories, the parsing of which made for a certain sort of intimacy—a hunting and gathering sort of intimacy.

Rosa had thought of Eve the first time Señor Rampley touched her. Eve was a thought intruder, a meddler of bliss, an invidious interloper. When they made love, Rosa thought of how Eve might have liked his lips, might have liked the way the pads of Señor Rampley's fingers felt like the mild march of a ladybug on the soft skin between her legs. Rosa wondered if Eve would ever feel as she felt, as though she wished to break a man open, climb inside, close up the top.

Rosa shook off the water from her skin and climbed onto a crag next to the shoreline. The warmth of the sunlight soothed the cramping in her woman parts. She thought of the talks she and Creadon had had since they'd arrived at Lake Pend d'Oreille. He would stay, he told her. And they would build a life together. Rosa had held firm with Creadon on obtaining boat passage for Martinique, and now in Kullyspell their hope was to breed horses and perhaps raise livestock.

They had made it. Through Comanche and Mexican territories, inside the long range of arrows and metal balls, after two wretched bouts of illness and a mangy wild dog they'd been forced to smother to death, she and Señor Rampley had made it.

But it was never easy between them. Would never be easy, though she could not know that then. Theirs was a reluctant alliance. Papá had told Rosa that Señor Rampley would get her settled, then get on with his life. That Señor Rampley would find a place free of war, where a woman like Rosa could make of her life what she wished. And after almost a year, across seas and oceans and rivers, he had. He'd brought her to Kullyspell and taught Rosa what she needed, and each day she'd dreaded waking and each night she'd dreaded sleeping, for though she knew she could probably make it alone, she also knew she wanted him there.

Then one morning, under an ugly dust-colored sky, Creadon Rampley kissed her. Or maybe she'd kissed him. Again. And the Eve between them became the Victor. And though Rosa should've known that this meant he'd stay, still she feared waking and sleeping, not so much any longer because she would miss him if he left, but rather because she was unsure a future was possible without him.

The baby would soon wake. This is what she was thinking when she saw the men. Two tribesmen and one she could not easily make out. They were rinsing their bare feet in the lake water, splashing like naughty, unwatched children. Rosa moved slowly, rolling off the stone onto her knees, slipping back into her dress. She was scared. She had seen evidence enough in Mexico of the fight over land. The violence on that continent was a far cry from the feeble Spanish in Trinidad throwing up their hands at a minor English aggression. Her stomach tightened and a clot of blood pushed its way to the bottom of her woman part. Her breasts were tingling with milk, like baby chicks pushing out their beaks. Rosa gathered her frock up near her chin, her bottom exposed, for she was determined not to ruin her last dress, and crawled uphill, her head low, wondering if Creadon had awakened and if the baby was crying to be fed. When Rosa felt sufficiently masked by the thicket of woods, she stood, desperate to get back to the post, until a man who had hair puffed like a cloud and a scarred face that looked to have been carved from stone stood on the path before her.

"Are you a runaway?" The man reached out his hand, speaking the words first in French, then following with English. He had a knife on his belt with a blade half as long as her baby. "You don't have to be afraid." His voice was like the call from an old bell chamber, the tone deep and hypnotically melodic.

Rosa's heartbeat quickened, for she had no idea how he could have been so far down the shoreline then suddenly standing before her. She wondered if she weren't dreaming him and quickly searched for the other two men to assess both reality and danger.

"I left them down aways," the man said, as if reading her mind. "Do you live here?"

Rosa shook her head no, then nodded, then shook for no again. She didn't know what to make of this man with the flinty eyes and soft mouth. She felt the wetness of the milk prickling beneath her dress top and wished to be home. Not with the boy and Creadon, but that faraway home where fright didn't feel quite the same, for the safest place, still, was home.

"My name is Edward. Edward Rose." The man spoke slowly, taking her elbow, for her hands were filled with the hem of her dress. It was an awkward gesture and he grinned slightly as he did so. "And you?"

Rosa swallowed hard, watching his eyes as they followed the lump in her neck. "Rosa Rendón," she whispered, rolling her Rs as Mamá had required she do no matter the rules of French or English.

"Rose and Rosa." He took care to roll his Rs for both her name and his. "You're not from here."

"No," she said. "I am from a place in the sea."

Edward Rose's face brightened and his neck upreared as if she were some unbridled creature he now wished to examine. "How do you mean? You've been to the sea?"

"You've not?"

"I want to." He smiled with his eyes, as if absorbing and delighting in her. Recognizing it as such pleased her. Pleased Rosa in a way she thought she should not have been pleased.

"Do you live with someone here?" He glanced up at the post as if he knew where it stood, hidden between rickety grand firs.

"With my . . . my child and husband," she said, though she had never before thought about what to call Creadon Rampley.

Rosa brought Edward Rose and the two tribesmen home with her. Creadon had armed himself, had hidden the baby and the Bible that Demas had given them behind the curtain on the floor of the cupboard, precisely as they had planned.

It took more than a few moments to talk Creadon down. When finally Rosa was able to make formal introductions, she excused herself and hurried to the back of the post to tear a piece of cloth from the hem of her dress to pad her flow. When she returned she fed the baby, then served the men: corn, berries, cold kokanee salmon. Rosa remembered how much she had once resented serving visitors, but now she delighted in receiving any visitors at all.

That midmorning, Rosa and Creadon ate under the watchful eye of Edward Rose. Edward Rose told them he was the first Negro to be welcomed into the Apsáalooke tribe. A place of honor, he said. He described himself as the most able guide and interpreter anywhere west of the Mississippi River. Said that rumor had it he'd been with Lewis and Clark for part of their first journey, but that he needn't claim their expedition to establish his bona fides, for there were stories of him dating back to 1807 in the journals of many men. Edward Rose told stories of being captured as a slave in Arkansaw Territory, then of his escape and adventures in the Canadas and Indiana Territory. With the exception maybe of her father, Edward Rose was like no man Rosa had ever met. He had a dry humor beneath a grim, self-assured exterior. A solidness that seemed unshakable. He seemed capable, hearty, wild as untraversed land.

"You're not bashful, are you, Mr. Rose?" she said.

"There is no place in this land for humility."

Creadon shared with him his own story of growing up within a Hudson's Bay company, of his own father's knowledge of the Canadas and of Rupert's Land.

"And after your father fell, you led your men?" Edward Rose said.

"Only when I moved to North West Company."

"You were with one company your whole life and then you abandoned them?"

Creadon looked to Rosa. He'd never explained to her any of this. "I needed a fresh start, Mr. Rose."

Edward Rose picked at the berries on the plate before him. He set them into his mouth one at a time. He had striking white teeth. Like Papá's. "I remember a story of a Hudson's Bay brigade up near the Missinipi. Some were butchered, others gunned down with their own flintlocks, all of them found hanging from ropes after a helluva windstorm. It was said that they were some of Hudson's Bay's best men. All the trappers up there swore it was the Cree, but there was nothing about that crime that made me believe it'd been Cree," he said. "You remember that story?"

Creadon looked as if deciding whether to tell what he knew of the story, surprising Rosa, who began to take note of the way he knotted his hands. "Was prolly workin' for Thompson by then," he said.

Edward Rose had been watching Rosa but now turned to Creadon and slammed his cup upon the table. "David Thompson? I know of the man. Good mapmaker. The men I guide carry them. He is a careful fellow."

Rosa grinned, remembering when Creadon first came to Trinidad and told them of the Thompson man. Creadon had described Thompson as arrogant and careless. Now Creadon only nodded. "This was his post. Kullyspell, he called it."

"Yes." Edward Rose said this as if suddenly remembering. "It has been almost five years since anyone's been here. I used to come across here quite a bit." Still speaking to Creadon, he looked to Rosa now. "You came here because your woman says she wished to be alone, do I have that correct?" Edward Rose beamed at Rosa. It was in that very same way that had pleased her before. "She is like the little shadow which runs across the grass and loses itself in the sunset."

The two tribesmen laughed, and Creadon shifted in his seat, searching Rosa for a reaction.

"No, I brung her here 'cause I helped build this place," Creadon said, hoping maybe to dampen a joke that still had embers.

"I guess you didn't know better." Edward Rose shook his head, explaining to his friends in a hand language Rosa had never before seen, something about her and Creadon's home, for the three men looked up into the ceiling beams, then at the stone fireplace.

"Didn't know better? I ain't done nothin' wrong," Creadon said.

Edward Rose rubbed the burn of Creadon's mash into his chest. Creadon had been saving that drink for a special occasion. Later, he would regret thinking of Edward Rose's visit as special. He would be angry with Rosa for bringing those men into their home with their child. Bringing all that talk and all that chest thumping. He would tell her that Kullyspell was not Demas Rendón's home. That strange men couldn't come and go as they pleased in *his* home.

"Harm was done here. Harm will continue to be done until men like you stop pushing west," Edward Rose said.

"And what 'bout men like you?"

"If you hadn't noticed, I am black-skinned, sir. Men who look as I look are brought here by men who look as you look," Edward Rose said.

"My mother was Crow."

"Perhaps." Edward Rose seemed skeptical of this claim. "But what do you know of Apsáalooke? Have you lived among them? I have. And I have built forts too. Built Fort Manuel at the mouth of the Bighorns. But I didn't go away and hide in it."

Rosa hadn't expected them to be at odds. She had invited Edward Rose into their home because she'd found him compelling. "Monsieur Rose, you are an interpreter, isn't that so?" she said now.

Edward Rose turned to her, surprised, it seemed, that she'd interjected. She wouldn't know until much later how Creadon would replay in his mind each successive moment at that table. How he would see this interjection as proof of her lack of faith in him.

"Yes, I help to maintain peace," Edward Rose said.

"You maintain peace between those who've been here and those who wish to settle here?" Rosa patted the baby, trying to lull him to sleep, despite the unfamiliar voices and the charge between the men.

"No, not who wish to settle," he corrected her, "but with those who would do harm if they are not restrained with rules and order."

Rosa knew fearmongering when she saw it. "If you'd come from where I come from, you'd understand treaties to be death warrants, not meant for peace but intended to be broken so war will be necessary. Bait." Rosa set the baby across her lap, burying the child's face in her stomach, tapping her foot on the floor to steady him. "But I don't blame you for not being able to see the role you are playing in the dismal future of your people. A small piece of bread can make a hungry one feel very full."

Edward Rose sucked a berry seed with his big white teeth, and there at the edges of his mouth, Rosa saw a little compressed smile.

"So you were saying, Monsieur Rose," she continued, "that you take issue with us claiming this post?"

"No, I don't, but others will," he said, before looking over at the two of them again, as if remembering something more. "Rampley, did you say your name was?"

"For as long as I knowed."

"I think I came across your father once. Good guide. Yes, I remember. Reddish hair, skin showing a bit at the crown?"

Creadon cocked his head like a wild dog. "In Rupert's Land?"

"Couldn't be." Edward Rose seemed earnest in his effort to remember. "I've never been that far north. He must've traveled south."

"No, I don't member ever comin south. No need to do it. We had plenty." Creadon sat still as iced snow, waiting to hear more. "About what year?"

"Not much more than . . ." Edward Rose looked then to Rosa. She must have appeared terrified of what he'd say next. "I'm sure I'm mistaken. Too many Englishmen on this land now. Easy to confuse them," he said. "So tell me, is the sea quite nice?"

"The most beautiful thing any man has ever seent," Creadon said, his tone surly still.

"Then why would one leave?"

Rosa gathered the baby, hoping the boy would be able to nap in the room beyond. From there, she heard Creadon deflect Edward Rose's question by asking the men to teach him how to pronounce Crow words: kaheé for "hello" and ahó for "thank you." Then Creadon must have risen to remove from the mantel a deck of cards they'd brought with them from Mexico, for Rosa heard him next explaining the rules of poker.

After some time, the four men began to laugh, and it was well into the afternoon when Rosa began to find it painful to be in the comforting presence of others who would soon leave.

In the early evening, the baby began to whine. Rosa gave him to Creadon, who took him out beneath a setting sun. The men gathered their belongings.

"Can't say I've seen that before," Edward Rose remarked.

"It is what they both wish." Rosa did not feel she should have to explain why it was all right to give her baby over to his father. She was sour now and knew it was because she wished for Edward Rose to stay. She walked alongside him, down the plank Creadon had built for easy access to the door. The other two Apsáalooke unhitched their now rested horses, and she heard the baby on the backside of the post, purring in Creadon's arms.

"Maybe one day you will tell me why you're here." Edward Rose handed his lead to one of his mates, pulling Rosa away from the horse, as if she might be hurt by it. "You miss your home. I see it everywhere on you. In the way your shoulders bend, in the way you search for things with your eyes. Do you ever say it? That you miss home?"

"Yes." She thought it all so very peculiar—this man, this sort of talk with this man. But the peculiarity did not inhibit her as much as she would've expected. "Where a horse is tied is where it must graze. My child is of here. Anyplace he can lay his head, I will learn to love."

"Your boy will need others. He will need men, other mothers; he will need to know women, a woman. That man will never be able to give your son those things. Look around."

Rosa searched the land past where they stood. It seemed there that clouds didn't move away with the winds so much as stay to dip and rise. There were pines and dry brush she couldn't yet name, soil she didn't yet understand.

"He will not be able to protect your son or you. He has a good heart, but that is all." Edward Rose glanced up to see if Creadon might be coming back around. He seemed to wish for Creadon to watch him as he placed Rosa's wrist into his hand; he seemed to wish for Creadon to see Rosa open a slit of herself and allow Edward Rose's words to wedge themselves into that small, vulnerable place that'd been open since leaving home. "Your nose flares when you worry. It's beautiful. So much is in your face." He drew his pointer finger along her wrist. "I will return soon and then you will come with me, yes? I will take care of you, protect your boy, raise him as mine."

His words were so terribly absurd that Rosa smiled, for it was all she could do. Yet there was no humor in Edward Rose's eyes, nothing that betrayed the sincerity of his petition.

"Your husband ran away from these parts once before. He said it himself. He needed a 'fresh start.'"

2

Kullyspell, Oregon Country

1830

Now Victor knew. More than what any boy should have known of his mother. He understood that Ma's storytelling had been a distraction, that she'd wanted his attention away from that diary. Ma did not yet know that Victor had finished reading it.

"You didn't have a musket?" Victor said. "Your Papá taught you how to use one, but you didn't carry it down to the lake the day you met Father." Victor was on the floor before the fireplace, seated between her legs on a mat of bulrush they'd stripped and sewn together. Ma parted his hair, rubbed his scalp with oil.

"I wasn't accustomed to needing it. I thought of the lake as part of our land," she said. "I learned better later."

Victor turned to study Ma's face. She was beautiful, more beautiful now that he knew how much it took for the creases of pain to be smoothed from her brow. He was ashamed that he'd ever been ashamed of her. He wished he'd not read to the end of Creadon's story. Tears pooled in his eyes.

"I'm fine now," she whispered. "You can live in grief or you can push grief outside of you. Papá used to say what don't kill does fatten. "

Victor faced forward again, finding it too hard to look upon his own mother. "I want to go back to not knowing."

Ma laughed, though it was not a funny laugh. "I've been telling you this all along. Ignorance is wasted on fools and children."

She took up clumps of his hair and hummed another tune he'd never heard. It was again the sort of humming one did to quiet the mind. He had never before noticed this about her.

"I disliked when my mother sat me down like this between her legs," she said.

"I like it." Victor did not wish to tell her that he had sometimes hated his hair, that it was only when he sat between her legs and felt her fingers love his wiry strands that he remembered to love them too.

"Aah, you're a strange child," Ma said.

Silence again fell between them until Ma began to tell him the story of meeting Father and deciding to leave Creadon. When she was done, she turned his shoulders so he could again see her face. "Did you think I didn't know you would find it?" Ma tapped her foot on Creadon Rampley's diary, and Victor felt a sort of relief.

"You knew he was dead?"

"No, but this was all he had to give you. He would leave it here if he thought there was any chance he wouldn't return."

"He wrote that he didn't think he would survive after you left."

"But he did." Ma said the words with such sharpness that it seemed to Victor that she might have argued the point with herself many times over. "We would not have survived together."

"Because he couldn't protect you?"

"Because I knew joy before. And it was not fair to raise you without it." Ma reached for Victor's hand and held it against his chest. Her breath was heavy and cool. "Edward Rose became my anchor. Creadon Rampley was only a bridge."

CREADON RAMPLEY

Kullyspell, Oregon Country

$\backsim\!\!\sim$

Memberings from July 1819 to about 1820

"Ignorance is wasted on fools and children." It was the first thing Rosa said after it happened.

Some days she would sit and stare at nothin. Wouldnt answer the boy when he cried, wouldnt nurse him, wouldnt cook or eat or talk. Other days she was wild like nettle. Couldnt sleep or sit or clear her head. One time she left on the boat for half a day and come back with fish. So much goddamn fish. She sliced them thin and long like reeds, then cooked them piece by piece. At the end of the day when the baby was hungry I took him outside and set him beside her. She aint even look at him. She was so focused on them fish, but he stopped cryin so I walked back inside and fell asleep in a chair. I woke to Rosa standin over me with my skinnin knife pitched deep under the skin of my neck. Her eyes was dead and her face like stone and I whispered to her to think about what she was doin and she twisted that knife and the pain was like a burn and I punched the knife down and away, and when she saw it clatter to the floor she went to grab it and I thought what a helluva thing it was gonna be to die by her hands like that. So I slapped her. And she stopped. And course I was sure it wasnt Rosa behind them dead eyes, but it was. And I knowed then we was too long gone.

By the time that happened, I had only just finished hatin myself and figured it was better to hate her. At first, I aint wanna be in the same

room with her. Then I just started hatin that she was still livin. That
I was still livin. That that boy had kept us both livin.

The mornin it happened, I was makin ready for a hunt. Weather
was kind, ground had enough wet for easy trackin. Told Rosa I was
gonna be gone only for the mornin. Nothin different than any other
day. I always come home fore sundown. Always.

Cept they come for her while the sun was bright and hot and sober.

The sky that mornin was the bluest I ever seent. It wasnt regular ole simple blue. Like how you say "blue" and people just think
a blue. No. This blue was a Trinidad blue. A layered kinda blue.
Stacked like you could peel it away and find more blue behind it,
inside it, under it.

I took the boy out to sit in the grass while I prepped the runty stallion that me and her had come cross a few months earlier. Rosa come
out to see me off. "I need a goat," she said. I reached to kiss her, but
she gimme her cheek. Always the cheek. Like she wanted to punish
me for pushin her away the first time.

"Be back soon," I whispered to the boy, and handed him over to her.

There wasnt no signs of what was comin. No dark sky, no bad
dreams or ugly birds, no hesitation in my bones. I heard Demas talk
about signs once, but there was nothin. I swear it. And, believe me,
I woulda membered, cause in my mind, I went over and over that
mornin, wonderin if I missed it, wonderin if I woulda done somethin
different if I caught a whiff of it, wonderin if deep inside there wasnt
a power I hadnt tapped that shoulda made me know.

The post was empty when I got back in the late afternoon. Door
was closed, windows open. Rosa always did wash on Saturdays. That
was what her Mamá and Eve did. What she would do, she said. So I
dont know why panic set in straightaway. I guess cause I knowed the
dangers that was out there. Had talked them all through with her. I
started searchin. For bear tracks, wolf tracks, man tracks, but I picked
up no tracks but mine and hers. Her gun was still mounted. The boy's
favorite sealskin blanket was on the floor.

"He doesnt need that," she had said when I asked why she wouldnt
let him carry the blanket around.

"But he likes it."

"He likes you and me too, but he must learn to live without us. It is not good to be so attached to anything."

Rosa was a different Rosa from the younger woman I first met in Trinidad, but she still had a way of makin sensa my world. A world that only had her and that boy in it.

"Rosa!" I was angry with her now for makin me so scared. I couldnt hear nothin but my own ragged breaths while I searched for her. In them seconds, thinkin about where she was, I got old. My legs wasnt movin fast enough, my voice wasnt screamin loud enough. "Rosa!"

I ran down to the lake. I promised her, months earlier, that I was gonna dig a well. *Gonna start it tomorrow*, I thought. I wouldnt be angry that she was ignorin my calls and that there wasnt no supper. "Imma dig you a well," I was gonna say. And she would offer me a lil of that fish broth she liked to make and gimme that half grin of hers and we would go bout our night.

I made my way through the copse, down the incline, along the path me and her marked when we decided to stay at Kullyspell. I took her there cause Demas told me to take his child someplace safe, someplace I loved. From the moment I seent that place alongside Thompson, I loved it. And when she come close to lovin it, I knowed that if me and her could find somethin to love in the same two lands, we was gonna be all right. Funny thing is that I knowed she thought I was gonna leave her. That I was gonna drop her there and take off. But I aint never planned to leave. What she aint know was that every day after I moved into that hayloft, I needed to see her. I aint know what that feelin was but I knowed it to be true. And I knowed I was never gonna choose a life without Rosa in it.

Now through birches and firs and aspens that I shoulda knowed from memory, none of it looked familiar. It was a foreign land without her.

"Rosa!"

The sun was dimmin. I cursed it, cursed all them damn mountains that hid away the sun, everything workin against me. Me, there, without a lantern or candlestick, me who couldnt member what moon was in the sky. I couldnt go back without her.

"Rosa!"

She is fine, I told myself. *Fine.* Then I membered that I thought the same when I got back to camp and couldnt find Pa. He was a real mountain man. Had once chopped through a foot-thick ice block to free himself. Had to reset bones in his arms, legs, hands and had almost bled out twice. And still he wasnt fine. I was charged with his care and there he was hidden away on a mountain sill that looked to be made just for catchin and smashin his drunken body.

"Rosa!"

The boy gasped loud enough for me to hear. His voice aint sound right. I found him off in a parched pool of leaves round that tight north bend steps from the shore. He looked up at me, nose wide, legs swolled from scrapes. Mud he ate was caked on his tongue and round his chin and onto his chubby neck. I reached for him. Glass eyes. Like he aint knowed what my hand wanted with his lil body. I lifted him but he wouldnt rest his head til I pressed it into my shoulder. "You tired, aint you? So, so tired."

I knowed somethin was really wrong then. That kinda mother dont up and leave her baby in the wild. I wanted to take the boy back to the post but I also needed to track her, needed answers for what was happenin to my life.

"Rosa?"

I carried the cryin boy as I walked the shore of that lake, wishin for his words but knowin that even if he could speak, I wouldnt like what he would say. The water was loud. Like it was angry that I couldnt see her layin right there in front of me.

"Rosa."

She was on her stomach. Her dress ripped and bloodied. Her open legs had swirls of blood from the thighs to the backs of her knees. Her backside, her matted hair, her fingers, was covered in a thick dried skim. So much skim that I knowed it come from more than one. I aint wanna touch her. Im ashamed I aint wanna touch her. But it felt like if I touched her, it was gonna all be real.

But it wasnt no dream.

She was warm. But everything else spoke of death. And I knowed this cause death language was my first tongue.

"Rosa, Imma move you now, all right?" I rolled her to me. Her breasts was sliced like them fish she liked to cut up for us to eat. The rock they used to break the skin on her face, to split open her head, to smash her neck, lay beside her, like innocence. But wasnt nothin innocent there. Not that stone, not that God who watched it happen, not that boy, not me, not even Rosa.

It was that last thought that she read in my eyes in the days after. She told me this later. That I blamed her for bein there. For doin what she did every day. For not stayin at the post. For not fetchin water fore I left. For not fightin harder and for fightin too hard. That I blamed her for lurin me into that life with her. For lettin that man Grayson see her. For being both too much a woman and too lil of one.

"What man would not hunt them down?" Rosa said this once when the headaches didnt stop and when she couldnt walk straight cause her eyes aint work right. "You want to blame everyone but the men responsible for this."

She was right. I was afraid to go after em, afraid when I found em and exacted the sorta revenge I done three times already in my life, that it wouldnt work no way. I knowed vengeance and it wasnt no healer. Them memories dont just up and go just cause you make pain for a nother. But you could know this only if you done it. So I hid the passin of time behind her not gettin better, tellin myself that when her headaches stopped, when her eyes seent right again, when her chest closed up, I was gonna set out to find that man, Wallace.

"He was watching us," she told me.

Rosa wanted to say that he come for her cause he knowed I was weak. He told her that she aint had no right to put her hands on his wife and child, pretendin she knowed what she couldnt know, pretendin we was in too much a hurry to help him bury Beverly and his boy. Then she told me that he had watched the men he brung with him take her like . . .

like she was a . . .

like she aint have no . . .

like I wasnt . . .

I wished she hadnt told me none of it.

We stayed there, both of us not knowin whose side to take, bringin up a boy who wouldnt know whose side to take either.

Now, writin all this down, I wish I coulda made her trust me to take care of her again. I wish I could take back all them careful sentences I spoke that aint never have the right words in em. But I left too much unsaid, too much to undo.

Course, I could lie and tell you that I aint knowed she was gonna leave. That I aint seent the packhorses when they come a year after his first visit. That I aint recognize them two Crows who rode up with him. But I did. I knowed that Negro would come back for her. What I aint knowed was that I was gonna feel her gone-ness so bad I was sure if I peeled away every piece a my flesh that I wouldnt suffer more pain than I suffered in them years after. What I aint knowed was that I would fight and live through all them days only cause I believed that one day she and my boy was gonna come back to me.

XVII

Kullyspell, Oregon Country

~~

1

1830

The first snow came the day before they were to leave. They had already made preserves and prepared pemmican with leftover fall berries. The clouds were lace thin and stretched, as though they had been asked to perform too big a task. It was a sawdust snow, covering only the base of trees and branch tips, but it left a dazzling rime over the landscape.

"That's one helluva story he put down in that lil book." Gerard and Margaret had come through again on their way to their homestead. Ma didn't think it right that Victor shared with them so much of Creadon's story. Ma had told Victor that if Creadon had wanted to share all his story with Margaret, he would have done so. But for Victor, the telling made Creadon Rampley more real.

"Wish I could read it." Margaret sipped Ma's elk stew. They'd run out of fat a few weeks earlier, so Margaret drank it like a bitter tea, face pruned, showing three less teeth than when they'd passed through before. "Are you certain you don't wanna see winter through? It's dangerous to ride now. Storm's coming," Margaret said.

"The old gal might not make it to spring."

Ma had had a dream that a Yellow-Eyes who ruled all the territories had demanded that horses have ownership papers. She said that in the dream she and Victor were headed southeast toward home, and when they arrived at the place in the woodlands where they had left Like-Wind's and the Frenchmen's corpses, they were stopped by a short and muscular Englishman. Ma said she was afraid the Englishman would chain them and take them away, but the man didn't want them, he wanted Ma's horse, and when Ma couldn't produce the proper ownership papers, Martinique fell into the earth and died.

A few hours after, Ma and Victor sent Gerard and Margaret off with as much as they could carry. They said they didn't need much, that the kind of life they had couldn't hold things. Before leaving, Margaret told Ma that Creadon was as good a man as she'd ever known, and she held Ma in an embrace that lasted longer than it should have.

Victor didn't sleep well that night, thinking of what his life might be upon his return, wondering how they would explain Like-Wind to Bluegrass, wondering what life at camp would be without him.

The next morning Ma woke Victor while the sky still shone black. The wind blew snow in a blinding northwest swell. Martinique whinnied as they mounted. Their pace was swift, and though they'd made layered clothing for the harsh weather, it remained bitter cold. Ten miles outside the perimeter of the post, Martinique, who had begun stumbling along the old buffalo trail, braked. Ma dismounted, whispered in her ear, and the two remained like that for some time while Victor girded the packs. As the sun lightened the sky enough to make the three of them different from shadows, Ma examined Martinique. She stroked her flank, inspected her hooves, her muzzle, her legs; then Ma offered her a breakfast Martinique refused.

"We'll return to the post, eat a bit, wait until tomorrow morning," Ma said.

When they arrived back at the post, the door sat ajar. Ma gathered the musket. The re-boarded windows offered no point of vision inside.

"Did we leave that portal open?" Ma whispered.

Victor moved forward, ready with his bow and arrow.

"You see?" Ma smiled. "They came back and took everything we offered them yesterday."

Anything that wasn't affixed to the post had been taken. Ma didn't much care. Said she expected as much. But Victor did. He'd told those people—Margaret and Gerard—Creadon Rampley's story. One does not give up one's father's story to thieves.

"Go and rest," Ma said. "I can't have you and this horse dragging behind me."

Victor must have appeared as tired as he felt. Gerard and Margaret had taken the blankets, so Victor remained in his coat and folded into himself for extra warmth. When Ma came in, she laughed at the sight of him. Ma may have nodded or said something about being lucky that Margaret and Gerard had left the floors, but Victor did not hear. When he woke, Ma was at the front door, her hand gripping the jamb.

"Ay, Ma." Victor was certain that Ma's dream had come true. As he moved toward her, he wished to the First Maker that they weren't a people who believed in dreams. What use was it knowing what's to come when you could do nothing to stop it? He had imagined, many times, the day Martinique would no longer be with them and what that would do to his mother. He reached for Ma's hand, sidling up beside her. "It'll be all right." He said this as if there were any words to comfort her after the twenty-seven years she and Martinique had shared. Victor looked out now toward Martinique, expecting that she had fallen just like in Ma's dream. Down on her belly, into the snow-covered dirt. But there she stood.

"She made us come back because a big storm just turned this way," Ma said. "I'll bring her in."

Victor gathered firewood from the storehouse. Later, the post's roof began to bow under the weight of a snow that fell in such heavy thuds that it sounded like a thousand bucks overhead. Victor had become spoiled living indoors, his skin and blood now thinner, more susceptible to misery. Victor fed the fire, but it behaved like a new baby, taking only enough to return to sleep, while Martinique, pressed against the door, remained pitifully wide-eyed, still refusing Ma's treats.

In the morning light, Ma noticed that Martinique's lower lip hung lower and that a foamy drool had begun collecting along the corners of her mouth. Ma determined the cause was ulcers and said it would be a few days before Martinique's mouth healed.

That night as they slept, the ice on the lake rended and rumbled, and the corner of the roof caved atop the bed. Victor had slept there every night since their arrival, save that night. That night, he and Ma had slept on the floor next to Martinique.

"We would have been crushed," Victor said.

"*You* would've been crushed." Ma smiled. "You haven't shared that bed since we got here!"

By the third night, Martinique was improved enough to sleep outside, and Ma told Victor they would leave in the morning.

At dawn, the snow was brutish with its luster. Victor had overslept and woke feeling guilty that he had not packed the travois.

"Is Martinique better?" Victor retied the moose-deer boots that now pinched his toes. Ma stood in the doorway and Victor was certain she was angry with him. "I'm ready."

He looked past her to Martinique who was outside, bright-eyed, her tail aflutter. And past Martinique, between shaky limbs, Victor made out a rider, back straight on the topside of a fine black Arabian.

Ma stutter-stepped onto the snowy plank to get a better look. The wind blew soft as if it wished to be humane. Victor stood a few steps behind her, bow in hand, watching the man pull his reins for a prompt halt. The man stared at them as though he thought he'd taken a wrong turn. His face was lined and hard, with black and silver stubble along its lower half. He loosed a knot in his scarf, then removed his hat, showcasing thick white-flecked hair, and dismounted. He never once removed his eyes from their faces, even as he steadied his stallion. Ma stood for a moment longer, until finally she set down her musket and inched her way carefully along the plank covered in a churlish snow. She paused at the end of it, then sprinted toward the man as though she were a small child, throwing herself into him, gripping his face, as if she needed to feel what her eyes could not assure her existed.

Ma sobbed into the man's neck, then pushed him away and beat his chest until he kissed the top of her head. His lips disappeared into Ma's hair, and when it resurfaced, the man's face was flushed, as if all of him had been stuffed inside that big lacy ball.

2

They stayed the winter—the three of them together—staring out onto snow drifts that rivaled the height of the post. Between storms, they repaired the roof and made a sturdier bed where Ma and Victor slept. Sometimes when Ma thought Victor asleep, she'd leave the room and she and Creadon Rampley would trade stories of their years apart. They had a way together—careful, kind to each other—like two people who only wanted to be their best selves.

On his travels, Creadon Rampley, whom Victor had begun to call Da, had been given a fiddle that he sometimes played at night before they slept. Ma laughed when he first tucked it under his chin, for it was too small and the bow too short, but Da said he had grown accustomed to the misfit, and indeed he had, for the notes were stirring and long and the trills so perfect Victor believed at times Ma had been brought to tears.

"Would you like to play it?" Da said to her one night. Ma's eyes softened as she reached for it. Da positioned her feet apart, taught her how to tilt her face into it, how to make her fingers appear as if they were suspended on the side of a magnificent sloping ridge. Ma winced when the spiraling note rang wrong, set the bow down quickly as if hoping the sound had not offended them.

"Try again," Da said.

"My Mamá didn't want me to play," she said. "It reminds me too much of her now."

Da nodded as if he knew the story. "Do you ever think of going back home?" he said.

Ma turned the logs, then poured herself another mug of water. "Each day. But I couldn't risk my children's lives." It was the first Victor heard Ma mention her other children—the twins—to Da. Victor could see in the way Da flitted his eyes that he did not like hearing of them. "When I left home, I had to believe I couldn't go back."

It was a night that Ma called "New Year" when Da came into the room and lay upon the bed beside her. "Member when we built that first bed?" he whispered. "I wanted to just lay down in it with you forever."

"You wanted to hide me away in it forever."

Victor felt Da turn toward Ma. The bed sunk deeper in the middle. "Hide? I wasn't hidin' you away. I was tryna give you what you had."

"You couldn't make this place Trinidad."

"I was givin you a beautiful, quiet land. A lake like an ocean right outside your door."

"This was not your land to give."

"But that's what Demas asked me to do."

"What is this?" Ma said. "What did my father ask of you?"

"You knew your father asked me to take you away."

"Yes, because he was angry." Ma sat up, and Victor could no longer pretend he was asleep.

"He was protectin' you. He knew you was only gonna stay away if you thought he ain't want you. He knew you was gonna fight to the death for that land. He wanted you to live."

"And only now you're telling me this? Do you know how long I believed otherwise?"

"You left here, Rosa. You left me," he said. "I thought we'd have time. A whole lifetime."

Ma said nothing for a while. "I couldn't stay here," she finally said. "We both know all that I had before. This piece of land couldn't replace all of that. I know you tried your best, but—"

"But he did it better?"

"You mean Edward?" Ma said Father's name, Edward, with such tenderness that Victor felt she must have been speaking of a stranger. "Edward didn't know what I had before, who I was before, so I could forget with him."

Victor thought Da would leave then, for Victor imagined that Ma's words had hurt Da very much. And there was a quiet, long and full, between them. "I wrote 'em a letter every year after you left," Da whispered. "I hoped just one would make it, but I ain't never heard back."

"No, I'm sure you wouldn't have."

"You think they got it but just ain't write?"

"If they're gone, they wouldn't have seen it."

"Is that how you do it? Make yourself believe everybody's gone?" Da paused, then said, "I think Demas got the letter and wrote back," he said. "I think he was happy we had a son."

"And he'd tell me how my mother would expect the child to be christened. That I should find a good priest to do it."

Da laughed. "François is a big boy now, and Eve married Lamec."

"Lamec? What? Never! That man?"

"Yes, and I think they got three lovely lil girls. Martinique, Myra, and Rosa."

"Eve wouldn't name any child after me." Ma paused, as if deciding whether to play, then she added to the story. "And the land is still Rendón land because Papá led a revolution to overthrow the English and won Trinidad's independence."

They sat with that thought for a while.

"And your Papá wants you to know that when he looks into the lookin glass, he don't see an old man with grey hair," Da said. "He sees only your beautiful face."

3

1831

When the snow began to melt, Da and Victor set out on their first hunt. Victor expected it would feel strange, but, in fact, it felt stranger.

They rode to the edge of a snow-covered field. The sky was washed white, and branches had been wind-shaken so they alone stood as narrow tunnels of color against the blanched landscape. Victor hadn't spoken since leaving the post and couldn't determine if this was due to having too much or too little to say.

"I'm one of the best hunters in our clan," he decided to say.

Da looked over at him with believing eyes. "Your Ma told me that anything you put your mind to, you do good at."

Victor was certain Ma never told Da that, certain that Da said it only because he thought Victor was doltish enough to believe it. But

Victor wasn't the doltish one. When Victor looked at Da, he didn't
see an Apsáalooke warrior, he saw a Yellow-Eyed loner who'd done
nothing save make a son he let be taken away by another man. "You'll
believe anything, won't you? You think Ma would've returned here
if she hadn't been told to do so?"

Da looked hurt.

"Did you ever look for us?" Victor said.

"No."

Victor was always surprised by Da's frankness. "And you're pretending you've been here waiting for us all along?"

"You're sore," Da said. "You got every right to wonder why I wasn't
with you."

"I never wondered that. I didn't know you existed until we arrived
here."

Da hadn't known this.

"I always knew where I could find you. I coulda took you away from
your mother," he said. "I coulda brung you here to live with me. But if
I had, we was gonna be right here, right now, and you was gonna still
be angry." Da looked down at the tracks he'd lost beneath the shade
of a hemlock. "A father's got to earn his love. I learnt that from your
grandpa," he continued. "You wear your feelins on the outside just
like him. Men like y'all choose to be a man in a different way. And
ain't nothin' wrong with being that kinda man."

Victor felt they had nothing between them but words. But perhaps
that's all there ever was between people—good words, hurtful words,
silent words. Da had given Victor his words. Now Victor had to choose
whether to give his words to Da.

So, Victor began: "Before you came, Ma and I went on a hunt."
Victor moved Martinique next to Da's horse, Caleb. "I took a bull
that day. It was my first." Victor looked over at Da to see if he could
find a reaction. "Ma carved out the liver and handed it to me to eat."

"That musta been a fine day," Da said, as if he wished to pat Victor on the back.

"No. It wasn't. It was bloody awful. Slimy and horrible and . . . Ma
probably wouldn't tell you, but I had to ask her to cook it for me
before I ate it."

"I guess you do take after me. Never could eat raw meat." Da laughed, then Victor laughed, and both seemed to understand that now there were newer words between them.

4

"The most I heard of is twenty-five years, but nothin' more," Da said to Ma, as they watched the two horses from the back of the post.

Before the heaviest snow of the winter arrived, Ma and Da had built a double stall for Martinique to rest beside Caleb. Martinique was an old gal, but Da and Victor knew that Ma had done this before.

"By this time next year," Ma whispered.

She said it as if they had forever there.

Winter was nearly ended, but Ma had said nothing more of their return to camp. And Victor was beginning to prefer their life with Da. Sometimes he pretended Da had always been with him, that those Yellow-Eyes had never come and hurt Ma, that Edward Rose had not been her anchor, that Da had not been only her bridge. When he watched them together, he wanted their good memories to be his.

"He's a fine boy," Da said to Ma one night. "Better than I coulda dreamt."

"I want him to grow up slowly. To be a boy as long as he can," she whispered.

"I want him to be at peace with his life. Not like me," Da said.

"I think he is now. There are times when different things are needed, different people are needed to find your place in the world."

There was a long pause, as if Da were thinking on this. "I knew you'd bring him."

"I knew too."

It was a few weeks after the land turned green and the grasses grew tall and thick that Martinique refused to graze next to Caleb. Ma looked pleased, for this was the surest sign yet of gestation, and the next morning, still buoyant, Ma suggested that they make their way across the lake, where beneath the butterfly mountain, Victor watched Da grip trouts, slippery and squirmy, the hair on his arms flattening and glistening, while Ma gathered berries. By midafternoon, Ma had kindled their lunch fire, but Victor still had no catch, so Da called Victor to stand next to him, urging him to focus, to bend his knees, to still himself in the chilly lake water, showing Victor the heart-shaped formation he would need to clamp them. Victor waited with Da beside him, the whiff of Da's breath on his ear, and watched as a trout neared, swimming cautiously about his legs. Victor lifted the fish out of the water. Ma said its color reminded her of Da's hair. Then Victor threw the fish back into the lake and Da's eyes alighted upon Victor oddly, but he said nothing until Ma called them to shore.

"It was a fine day," Da said.

Victor nodded and turned to watch Da whose eyes were focused on a hawk, a locust hawk, its wings tipping back and forth as if it were off balance. Da grimaced and Victor noticed for the first time that Da had not been wearing his hat and that the color of his skin now matched Victor's. "Was everything in your diary true?"

Da turned to Victor now with this look of concern or perhaps it was compassion, upon his face. "I didn't write in it to tell you lies."

But indeed, when Victor woke the next morning and found Ma gone, he felt everything had led to a lie.

"No note? She simply left?" Victor ran down to the lake, back into the woods, then climbed up onto the hills to the east and to the north and to the west. When he returned, Da was there at the post's door, his hands buried in his pockets, his face sallow, looking at him as if Victor should have known better than to expect a woman like Ma to stay.

Victor thought of the days before, tried to remember if there was anything different in her eyes. He remembered only that Ma had reminded him of what she said on their way to Da's post: "The job of the child is to fight—to always fight for Breath. She is your mother."

But Victor didn't want another mother.

Victor ran to saddle Caleb. He would find Ma and bring her back. She could not have gotten far. He would convince her that his sisters would be well taken care of by the women of the clan, that Edward Rose and so many others loved them, that he—Victor—was the one who needed her most. But when Victor rounded the corner, Caleb was missing. And only Martinique was there.

"This is the note she left for you," Da said.

5

1832

Martinique foaled toward the end of winter. And by spring, her filly was strong and lean and lovely. Victor had been angry he could not follow Ma the morning she left, but the risk to old Martinique seemed too great.

But now, Victor had the filly.

He broke the girl early and the two were inseparable—Victor and the pony he named Trinidad. He took her for long rides, practiced for their arduous journey back to Bighorn, and during their days alone, Victor thought often of how life would be when he returned to camp. What would it feel to live there again, to live among people who had known him as a boy, who had made offerings for him to grow into a brave man? What would they think of him now? Victor felt he knew the answers to such questions, felt that he would still be loved, for he knew now that home was something that couldn't be denied him; home was not one place but rather it was one experience after another, one memory after another that left one feeling as if one had become more of who one was to become. And Victor understood he had been a fortunate young man after all. He'd been a young man of many homes.

Of course, Victor hadn't come to such thoughts in one day, but rather he'd come to them over the nearly two years he'd been at Kully-spell, most especially after Ma left, when he began seeing her in his dreams, when he realized that Ma's love showed in her leaving Victor to care for the things she cherished most—Da, Martinique, himself. And that in her absence, Ma had given Victor the chance to become the man he was to be.

Then one afternoon, after running Trinidad up into dry bluffs and down toward Pack River, Victor returned home to the post to see the backside of a packhorse being ridden by a hunched man. A man he was certain was Apsáalooke. Victor thought to go after him, for surely it must have been someone he knew, but Da was seated at the table with the door ajar, a cup of his mash next to him, with this look, this woundedness upon his face, as he upheld a sheet of onionskin. He held it up for Victor to see, saying something about the chiefs having sent it for him.

"Why would they write?" Victor said. "Tell me what he said to you, not what's written."

Da paused as though he wasn't sure he should, as if perhaps he was uncertain what would become of Victor after the telling, and Victor felt then that something was terribly wrong, for he and Da had had too many words between them for this sort of silence now.

"Edward Rose was returnin' home," Da started. "He took some men cross the Rockies and traded with a small band of Sahnish. Under the cover of night, two Dutchmen in Rose's expedition doubled back to the Sahnish camp and took a young girl's innocence. Weeks passed and Edward aint knowed nothin' about this. He'd collected his pay and had sent the men off, down toward Osage. Rose was three days from home when him and his men, includin' a man named Glass, who was ill with fever, noticed some Sahnish advancin'. They hid themselves. Found a ledge of rocks, piled up more stones and some branches, givin' themselves a real advantage, 'til them Sahnish tried to attack from the top of the ridge.

"With their water dwindlin', one of Rose's men escaped. When he got back to camp he told Rosa that it'd been Edward Rose who'd fell ill, and your Ma told the chiefs that she couldn't let Edward die alone."

Victor felt his breaths heavy now and to calm himself, began drawing circles with the tip of his boot into the wizened floor boles.

"She rode off with a hundred Crow, and by the time they got to the junction of the Milk and Missouri rivers, it was late mornin'. They found the Sahnish still levelin' fire at the ridge, and so the Crow attacked while your Ma, intendin' to rescue Edward Rose, rode 'cross the top of that ridge."

Victor pressed himself forward, over Da, as if to make his presence known, as if that would keep Da from saying what Victor did not wish him to say.

"She didn't understand that Edward Rose and Glass had taken days of fire from that exact spot. She was low, so as not to be a target for the Sahnish, but when she called out to Edward Rose, him and Glass ain't hear her. But they seent somethin' and leveled fire. And she fell from her spooked mare like a great tree."

Victor heard the grunt beneath his own breath but didn't know it'd come from him. He told himself that many had taken shots to their bodies, many had lived well past their injuries, and he looked again to Da, hoping there was more for him to tell, relieved when Da continued.

"When Edward realized what they done, he scrambled up, lifted your Ma into his arms . . ." Da cleared his throat, and Victor pictured Father with all his bigness, all his valor, carrying Ma. She would be safe with Father, he thought. Ma had told him so. She had told Victor that Father had been her anchor, that he had given her a place to hope again, given her a home again. "Edward Rose took seven Sahnish arrows to the back and tumbled down with Rosa onto the earth."

This time Victor knew the grunt was from somewhere inside him, in some dark place where it had lived, waiting for the terror to be enough to take away Breath. Victor wished to ask Da to finish the story, but there were only grunts, with barely a lungful between them. And so the silence caused Da to look away, caused Da to consider the fireplace, dead and cold; consider the three plates, the three cups, the three chairs.

I should have been with her is what Victor thought but could not say. He didn't know he'd never see his Ma again. Of course. If he had known, he might have done something simple and childish like smell her sweet-scented skin or stroke her face or watch her full lips move with each word. Victor wondered if his friends—if Lone-bull, if Fire-Bear, if the other boys—had been part of the fight to save her. And if so, he wondered if they had thought of the bighorn sheep, if they remembered the day they'd tempted fate. Victor knew that even if they had, his friends would've fought with honor and Victor wished for little else but that he'd been there, beside them, fighting fate, fighting for Father and Ma.

"Some of the men say your Ma wasn't dead when they pulled her from Edward Rose's grip. That they brung her back to camp with life still in her and that when she got there she spoke to her girls. But only them girls and the other women in the lodge know this for sure. And they won't tell, saying that Rosa Rendón was a woman who wished to speak her own story. That she would not want them to put an end to it."

Da dropped his face to hide his tears, and Victor took the paper from him.

Cut Nose felled by Sahnish near River Missouri. Rosa traveled with warriors to retrieve him. Died before she returned home.

"'Died before she returned home.'" Victor found the words there atop the grunts and the barely there breaths. Yet, as he read them aloud, he felt nothing more profound in the letter than in the anguish that had already darkened his heart.

Twenty words. Meaningless. For Ma and Da had already given Victor her story. Ma had already given Victor herself. He'd had her. All his years. And yet, as he stood next to Da, staring out the open door at pinkish clouds, Victor couldn't help but feel as if all the hours with Ma had made no difference at all, for her absence felt as large as the biggest Bighorn sky and the emptiness seemed to have aged him years for each second since he learned that he'd never again feel her fingers working strands of his hair, never again sleep beside her, feel her warmth, and glimpse her as she watched him, watched him as though she'd harnessed all that love from that home she'd left behind and set it right there inside of him, wishing only to look at it, wishing only to look upon him.

"'Died before she returned home,'" Da whispered. "Home."

Victor sat down, for his big toe tingled, and he placed his head on the table, remembering the first time Ma fed him there. Fish broth from an Ocean Woman. An Ocean Woman from a faraway land.

"She had to change so many times. Maybe even death is only a change for her." Victor mumbled this inside the crook of his arm, as he hoped to make sense of it before the grief began to eat. "Sepanee."

What else was there to believe of this woman? A woman like Ma fights on, yes?

"We gotta go," Da whispered.

Victor saw Da's sights set on the door where his saddlebag rested. Victor noticed now new lines in Da's damp face, deep shadows beneath his eyes, a more silvery silver in his hair.

"Where to?" Victor wiped his eyes.

Da put his hand to Victor's chest so Victor could feel the words. "If they are yours, if they are Crow, if they are Edward Rose's, them girls is still hers, and so they're mine too," he said. "We is we."

Creadon Rampley would have written those three words on the final page of his diary if they had not left just then.

Acknowledgments

Only a divine being could have given me this novel when I felt so in need of it. The day it arrived, I was very low and beginning to think I might never write a story worth reading again. And so I thank God for the gift of this fully formed story, for the gift of renewals, of which I have had many.

I'd like to give special thanks to those who make this writing life possible. To my mother, Jen, who by all accounts was my first love and to my Dad who always knows exactly the words to say to keep me writing, even when I don't feel I can. To my children, Sage and Ava—you are each uniquely magnificent and I can't tell you how much I look forward to every day with you two, despite the chaos. To Anand, for a deep and restorative love. Sometimes I marvel at us. To my sister, Halcyon, who knows how to evoke the most perfect giggles when I need them most. Thank you to my in-laws, Anita and Khem Sharma, for your support and nourishment, and to my trio of sitters, Johanna Lopez, Nia Smith, Taylor Forbes, for being the big sisters and aunties my girls needed. Thank you to my friends, Tanisha Brown, Tricia Bent-Goodley, Tebogo Skwambane, Raqiba Bourne, Cathy Goldwyn, and Amanda Bastien for your love and encouragement. Real friendship seems a dying art but you all make me still believe. Thank you to Elizabeth Nunez for giving me some new tools to put in a toolbox I almost forgot I had. Thank you to Bernice McFadden for taking my calls and offering your story as a reminder of purpose. Thank you to Dolen Perkins-Valdez and Tiphanie Yanique for offering me a seat at the table. Thank you to those who gave their time to make this story the best it could be, including Andrea Perry Webber, fellow carpool mom whose phenomenal researching talents brought this book to life; Scott Bear Don't Walk, who held my virtual hand through the scariest parts of writing about a community that I hoped to honor in my depiction; Jade and Chaz Bends for those extraordinary and magnificent hours on your mountain; Tim McCleary and the library staff at Little Big Horn College; Margaret Ball, for slapping my wrists for the love of horses; Renata and Antonio David for your command of languages; Mat Johnson, Renee Sims, and Peter Ho Davies for your time and assurances. Any and all errors in this book are mine alone. Thank you also to my beautiful and bad-ass agent, Victoria Sanders, for your love and support, and to all the women in her agency, most especially Diane Dickenshied, Bernadette Baker-Baughman, and Jessica Spivey. Also to Benee Knauer and Gilda Squire, both of whom I was happy to have with me on another journey. To my editor, Amy Hundley—thank you for loving this story and for all your hard questions and careful attention. And to all those at Grove Atlantic who've been behind the scenes championing this book, with a special shout to Deb Seager, Kaitlin Astrella, and Savannah Johnston. I wrote much of the first draft of this novel at MacDowell Colony—I can't thank them enough for making the kind of space that allows for deep extended artistic dives. Thank you to Jen Grotz, "Queen of Bread Loaf," for being a wonderful mentor and friend whom I get to work alongside while we do work that I believe is crucial to our art. And thank you to all my readers who sent encouraging emails and messages, reminding me that you were patiently waiting. I hope you enjoy.